RETURNING OFFICER

Historical Novel

By

GORDON AIKEN

- 1982 -

R.O. Publication

RETURNING OFFICER

Printed in Canada by
Thomson Seyffer Graphics Ltd.
Orillia, Ontario

Illustrations and Design
Paul Miller

Published by
RO Publishing,
an author registration,
Gravenhurst, Ontario

ISBN O - 9691059-0-8

The characters in this story were real persons;
the dates given are accurate;
the main events are part of Canadian History.
The personality of most of the characters
was developed from available material,
but personal attributes were occasionally assumed.

CHAPTERS

CHAPTER 1
THE WAYFARER

It began the day I first saw the green waters at Washago Mills churning under the paddles of the steamer "Emily May". The curious tint of the water and the dark mystery of the forest beyond set something afire inside me. Until that moment I had simply been a traveller, making my way from one part of Upper Canada to another. Suddenly it became an adventure, the call of the undiscovered. The ominous silence of the distant hills dared me to come and explore, and my spirit responded.

As we approached land, the engine went hard in reverse. Green water eddied and whirled around the wheels as they changed direction. Captain May watched anxiously from the bridge, and we passengers hung nervously over the rail. With a heavy bump, she struck forward. A deck hand jumped over the bow, snagged a line through the wharf ring, and hung on. The stern swung out. Captain May signalled slow forward and turned the wheel hard over. With the bow secure, the stern inched inward to the wharf, and a second line was thrown. The engine stopped and the deck hands heaved on the line. Shortly the whistle blasted journey's end, and the gang plank went down. It was a routine landing for Captain May in those uncertain currents. He had to drive right in and then heave to smartly. But for the passengers it was a jolt into a new world.

The little ship rolled gently at her moorings, her task completed, her passengers delivered to the frontiers of civilization. Washago Mills, northern terminus of Lake Couchiching, was on the edge of the wilderness. Beyond this point the traveller went at his peril.

"Good luck," the captain called out as we went ashore. He didn't add, "you'll need it," but it was in his voice.

It was a sweltering hot day in August, 1864. The air was deathly still; the woods strangely silent. No birds were singing, no sound came from the forest ahead. There was a slight smell of smoke in the air, from where it came I couldn't tell. But as the half dozen new settlers moved off from ship-side, I had a strange feeling of loneliness. Near the wharf was a rickety saw mill, surrounded by piles of lumber. Close by were a couple of weather-beaten warehouse buildings and a few frame shanties. There was little else; except rattlesnakes. Someone had posted warning signs, and a few snakes were displayed in cages. It was an ominous welcome.

The ship, the sawmill and the other signs of human presence only made the loneliness of the forest more striking. Northward, two wheel tracks wound their way through an opening in the bush and then suddenly disappeared at a sharp turn. Charred stumps, lying distorted as if in agony, crowded to the very edge of the tracks. Half-dried mudholes with abandoned poles sticking out, left deep pits in the roadway. Uprooted trees leaned precariously overhead, seemingly ready to come crashing down on some hapless traveller. And beyond, nothing but dark forest. It was that wild mystery that made it all so intense.

At wharfside three of the passengers looked around helplessly. A timid little woman with a small child hung on to her husband's arm. There was no stage nearby, as there should have been, so they sat down by their belongings and waited.

I lifted my heavy bedroll and threw it across my shoulders. Then I picked up my canvass bag containing tools and provisions and started up the road. An axe in my right hand gave me balance and protection. Two other passengers, waiting uncertainly, watched me load up. They hesitated only a moment after I went into action.

"We'll be on our way too," said the man to the woman with him.

They picked up their belongings and followed me.

Striding along I felt the vigour of manhood, and was glad I had acted so quickly. I plunged onward into the wilderness without looking back. It was comforting, nonetheless, to have the other two close behind. The road was every bit as bad as it looked. It twisted and turned through the heavy bush. But each turn opened to view another length of the fragile life-line to the north. Within an hour we reached the Severn River, and I went up the steep wooden bridge that connected us with the precambrian shield. There the terrain changed completely into rugged hills and deep valleys. The view from the bridge was spectacular. Directly ahead was a great mountain of rock, tufted with pine and spruce, stunted oak and sumac. The road swung sharply around the base of the rock, and above it rocky pine-clad hills blocked out the horizon. And at the first bend in the road stood the few scattered buildings called Severn Bridge.

I didn't stop there. The pair behind me were a challenge. I pushed on into the bush, anxious to use every hour of daylight. I was half conscious of danger signs, the smell of smoke became heavier and the forest silence deeper. A dark haze hung almost to the tree tops. But it was new to me and my head was filled with other thoughts. I walked on blindly.

The people following were strangers. I had seen them a couple of times on board and fleetingly at the wharf. The man was well built and rugged and had a massive greying beard. He spoke with an Irish accent. I had not observed the woman clearly. She wore a long black dress and a dark bonnet that concealed most of her face. She carried a heavy bundle on her back. They stayed close together as if for protection.

As for me, I was on my way to Draper Township in the new Muskoka settlement, to claim my land. My brother and I had bought it, sight unseen, the year before. I only knew that it was lot 26 in the fifth concession, located on the Peterson Road just east of a settlement known as Uffington. I had to go up the Muskoka Road to the South Falls, also called the Great Falls, then east on the Peterson Road eight or nine miles until I found it. If I came to a lake I had gone too far. These were my only directions, plus a rough map. A couple of days should get me there. I would have to sleep out overnight, unless I was lucky enough to find shelter. When I arrived, nothing but a vacant lot would greet me.

I struggled along under my heavy burden with my eyes constantly to the road, avoiding the countless snags that could send me heavily to the ground. My speed began to slow down and I felt darkness pressing in. Suddenly a shout from behind startled me.

"Hello," I called back.

"Look yonder," the man replied, pointing to my right. I looked and saw a heavy pall of smoke.

"It's well off course," I shouted.

"Look ahead."

Smoke billowed over the hills ahead. I noticed that the dead calm had ended and a breeze had come up. I stopped and waited for the other two.

"These fires are quite common," I said confidently, "sometimes they're started by lightning, sometimes by careless lumbermen."

"We must watch closely, nonetheless," he said firmly. It pleased me that he accepted my statement, which was much more confident than I felt. We walked on, closer together now, watching the hills around. We were, I guessed, three or four miles out of Severn Bridge, and I had no intention of turning back. But the pall of smoke became heavier and the wind rose.

"Look, there is more smoke on our left," the woman said. Her voice was pleasant and had a feminine quality that seemed almost out of place in that wilderness. It made the place less desolate; brought me the sound of hearth and home. But what she said caused us to stop again.

"It's no bonfire," the man declared, looking around, "we had better take stock. There is a steep hill just ahead."

Among those giant hills and in the thick forest, vision was limited. We hastened up the long hill, stumbling over roots and stones as we lifted our eyes from the road. In twenty minutes we were at the top, and the view alarmed us. Now we could see the flames of burning leaves and underbrush, forming a rim of approaching fire. Here and there the flame swept upwards into the pine branches, bursting into orange balls of sizzling destruction. The wind was gusting fitfully, but growing steadily stronger.

"We have to go back," I decided reluctantly, "we can never get through." Without a word, they turned and went back down the hill, and I followed, feeling some triumph with my regrets. They were accepting my decisions. Down the hill, across the valley, up the other side we trudged, then stopped in horror. The fire had

4

moved in behind us in a heavy wall. I looked at the Irishman in despair, but the woman spoke up again.

"We must go back where we were," she declared, "I am sure I saw a river ahead, and that could be our safety."

"Back into the fire?" I asked sceptically.

"Yes," she answered, and she was so certain that we discussed it no further. We turned once more, hurrying now, gripping our belongings and stumbling as we went. The air was hot, and cinders floated around us in great chunks, streaking our faces with black smudges. I began to feel the presence of this woman. She was calm and sure, worried but not numbed with fear, positive yet pleasant. I saw her face for a moment and it was attractive through the cinders and sweat. Feelings of admiration and even attraction passed through me, but there was no time to give them thought.

"Look," she said as we returned to the summit once more, "there is a bridge up ahead, and I can see water."

We plunged into the fire zone and the heat became intense. The road was our only salvation and the hope of water kept us going. Ahead, behind, on both sides, the underbrush was aflame. The big trees were burning and sheets of flame scudded above us, carried by an ever-increasing wind. Head down, hands over our faces, we pushed through the inferno. It was like a tunnel of fire, but a tunnel to safety. Suddenly, our hopes ended. With a mighty reach, the flames shot across the river before we reached it, and began to burn towards us. We were cut off.

Hell, we are taught, is fire. I began to understand why. The noise was terrifying, with shrieks and groans from twisting timbers, like demons swept up from everlasting damnation. The wind howled through the flames. The heat seared our flesh, and the smoke left us choking. As we stood there, not knowing where to turn, a wrenching noise burst out behind me.

"Look out," yelled the Irishman, and I spun around. The trunk of a dead tree, 20 feet high, its roots burned free by the fire, was teetering on its base. I jumped out of the way as the wind gave it a final push, and sent it thudding down across the road a few feet from me. I felt ill. Smoke and my scorching clothes cut off my

5

breathing and turned my stomach. I felt buried, swallowed up, as in a giant furnace. I expected to die. And as I watched helplessly, the woman was sick at her stomach and brought up.

The man's voice reached me from up the road.

"This way, quick" he called, "the river runs beside the road." We struggled towards him, then stumbled down the slope to the river bank.

"Jump," he commanded, and I twisted to remove the load from my back.

"No, take it all," he said, "better wet than burned."

Still determined to take the lead, I took everything under my arms and jumped, feet first. Down, down, I went, sinking like a stone with the load. The water was ice cold after the scorching air. When I was up to my neck my feet miraculously touched bottom. The moving stream tugged at me, but I held steady. I let my tool kit sink to the riverbed, but couldn't get free of the load on my back. I looked around for the others and saw them close by; two heads bobbing on the water like corks. We were safe.

The flames were all around us, burning the grass to the very edge of the river. Small trees crashed into the water; the big ones stood, seared of their foliage. I ducked my head under water to cool my face and to keep my hair from burning. Again and again I sought the cooling and protecting stream.

How strange it was, paddling there in the cold waters of the Canadian forest, with flames all around, struggling to stay alive. How could I, Richard James Bell, recent immigrant from England, fortune seeker in the new Muskoka territory, end up near death so quickly? And how had this woman stirred me deeply, as I now thought of it? What was happening to me, only a few hours into a new life? If I die here, I thought, Decimus will be to blame. Yes, Decimus, my brother. He drove me into this mess, with his superior attitude and bullying ways. Smug man; he always made me feel useless. I keep trying to do something great, something he has never done, just to show him. But always I come out looking stupid. Even in death. I can just hear him now, talking to his friends. "Poor Richard fell into a creek up North and drowned himself."

6

I tried to think of something pleasant, but nothing came. I watched constantly for falling branches; I struggled to keep my balance in the flowing waters. Now and then I waved to my companions, to show that I was still in good spirits.

It seemed like hours, but eventually the heavy fire passed, and the river bank was a mass of black branches and scorched earth. Little flames burned here and there, but it was mainly over. My companions went ashore, so I fished around for my tool kit and finally waded in. I saw them clearing a patch of ground beating out the embers with sticks. They waved me over, and I dragged myself along the bank, dripping and miserable.

The woman turned toward me, and I caught my breath. She seemed to have taken off her underthings and her wet garment was pasted tight against her body. Her full breasts stood out clearly, as if she were undressed. The skirt clung around her waist and thighs, extending down the smooth curve between her legs. It was so clear I could see where her thighs came together, and the gentle bulge of her private place. I stood gaping.

She saw me looking and she knew what I saw. For an instant our eyes met. Her face was unashamed, almost roguish. It was as if - as if she wanted me to see her. As if she were glad it happened that way. After a moment she calmly turned away.

When she faced me next, the fabric had been pulled away from her body and hung loosely from her shoulders. Her neck and shoulders were bare, and her long hair hung down her back. Her face was clean now - and lovely. I had hardly noticed her before, struggling along under her load, her hair hanging in wisps and her face streaked and perspiring, half concealed by her bonnet. I saw a different person now, a woman hidden under all those clothes, a female set apart from strangers. It gave me a feeling of intimacy, as if admitted to her private world. And she was the most desirable woman I had ever seen. Inside me somewhere a vague, long-suppressed yearning suddenly burst out and filled my heart and head. Could it be love, at this impossible time and place?

But as she affectionately touched the man beside her, and they laughed together about some private joke, my heart sank. It was too late for me. She belonged to someone else.

"It's full time for introductions," the man said as we stood warming by a burning log.

"It certainly is," I agreed, "my name is Richard Bell."

"I am Nathaniel Mills," he replied, holding out his hand, "and this is my daughter Anne Mills."

"Your daughter!" I almost shouted as I took his hand. I pumped it so hard they both laughed, and then I was laughing too.

"Have you no family?" he asked curiously.

"Just my brother."

"And where are you going?"

"To Draper Township, on the Peterson Road."

"Is your brother coming too?"'

"No," I answered briefly, "he wouldn't lower himself to grub in the ground."

They both looked at me curiously, hearing the resentment in my voice.

"My brother's name is Decimus," I explained.

"I see."

"He's an architect's assistant, has all the brains in the family, and knows it."

"I begin to understand," nodded Mr. Mills, "and what about you?"

"I'm 32 years old, a simple man and a bachelor."

Then looking at Anne, I added, "And today I'm glad of it."

She turned her head away suddenly, but not before I saw her blush. I had my answer.

Shortly after, we struggled out of that burning desolation, travelling along the river's edge until it crossed the Muskoka Road. Then we worked our way north along the Road, around fallen trees and across hot rock, until we passed the fire belt. Once in the clear we stopped for the night. I opened my blanket roll and spread things out to dry. Then we lay down in a pine grove, exhausted, and slept.

Soft daylight on my eyelids woke me. I had a deep feeling of contentment, and suddenly I remembered why. A soft breeze in the pine trees above brought me to time and place; the joy was

8

Anne sleeping nearby.

I got up quietly, but the rustle of my movements woke the others. What a mess we were! Blankets, tools, clothing, lay all around us. A residue of cinders still floated in the air, and our faces were streaked with it. Our clothes were dirty and wrinkled and damp. Anne disappeared at once to put herself in order. Her father gathered up some soggy biscuits he had put out to dry, and when she came back we ate them. Then we packed and set out northward along Muskoka Road.

The way ahead took on new meaning for me. I no longer cursed the mudholes, the hills, the swamps, rocks, snags and stumps. I wanted them to go on forever, for soon would come the parting of the ways. At the Great Falls I would turn off to the east; they would continue north to settle somewhere in the new township of Watt. We walked together now, talking happily in our new-found friendship.

"Why did you come away up here?" I asked Anne.

"Because my father needs me." She smiled at him and I cherished her for that. Some day, perhaps, she would give such loyalty to me.

"And your mother?"

"She died on the way over."

We walked quietly for a while after that, and then I began to sing some of my favourite songs. I have a good voice and I wanted her to hear it; but I was happy too.

"You sing well," she said pleasantly, seeming to enjoy it.

I hoped she could see that I was more than an ordinary sod-buster.

In a few miles the land levelled out and the going was easier. Near noon we came to a clearing and found the "Freemason's Arms", a tavern at McCabe's Landing, just that month renamed "Gravenhurst". The place was just a log shanty in the bush, but we got a wonderful reception. The place was neat and tidy, with white curtains on the windows, and a shiny big buffet against the wall. After we ate, Mrs. McCabe found a bed for Anne to rest on, while Mr. Mills and I lay down outside and listened to the

9

breeze pass through the big pines. I was anxious to talk to him. "I find your daughter very attractive," I said directly, feeling the pressure of time.

"So I noticed." He smiled, and I was encouraged to go on.

"She is very calm and confident."

"She has a mind of her own," he corrected me, "and she can not abide a man who takes her for granted. Consider yourself warned."

It sounded almost like advice he would give a prospective son-in-law and the thought thrilled me. He too must know that time was short. I hardly considered what he said; I only thought of the intimacy it brought. I was satisfied, and we both lapsed into silence. We took off soon after that, refreshed and ready for the remainder of the journey.

Half a mile along we passed the Gravenhurst cross-roads; a store, a few houses and a road leading west to Muskoka Lake. Now it was only a few miles to that inevitable parting. My feet dragged. We were separating so soon; such a short time left to say what I wanted, and I couldn't find the words.

"I have really enjoyed your company," I said, and it sounded awfully weak, considering what I felt inside.

"I'm glad," she answered, and I felt she was also struggling for words. Damn it, why didn't I say what I felt? Why couldn't I come right out and say I loved her? But I didn't want her to think I was just a fast talker. What I felt was deep and very new. To throw it all away with some loose words might lose her forever. Besides, I didn't know how she felt about me. Aside from that fleeting glance by the river, and her warm friendliness, I couldn't tell. How could she have any feelings for me in one day? Yet we had been through so much together.

As we walked I had a strong impulse to abandon the Draper lot and go with them to Watt Township. I could find good land near them and clear it. I could leave the Draper lot for Decimus. Yes, let him come up and work it. Then I thought: what are you, a man or a puppy dog? Does anyone have respect for someone who just follows along? No, I had to be my own man. Already my leadership and strength had been established with them. I would build my own place, and bring her to it.

As these thoughts were passing through my mind, she suddenly stopped and looked directly at me. I noticed that her eyes were clear blue.

"And what do you think, Mr. Bell?" she asked, "are women the equal of men?"

I was so shocked I didn't know what to say.

"I have often heard it discussed."

"That is no answer. What do you think?"

I considered the matter for for a few seconds. "I think *you* are."

"I'll remember that," she declared, but pressed no further.

I had no idea whether I answered well or badly. And the faint smile on her father's face gave no indication. We walked on in silence.

When we reached Muskoka Falls I said the piece I had been preparing.

"I hope after I have my place ready," I said, choosing my words carefully, "I can come and talk to you."

"Certainly," she answered immediately.

Her father nodded in agreement. I hoped she understood my real message.

As we parted I stood by the Peterson Road turn-off, the roar of the falls in my ears, silently watching them struggle up the narrow trail that was Muskoka Road. Just before they passed out of sight Anne turned and waved. I was thrilled; I knew it was her answer. She had heard my words and understood.

I picked up my gear and started east along the Peterson Road. At first I dragged along feeling empty. But soon I thought of the future stretched out before me. I would find my lot, build my house and clear my land. Then I would go for the woman of my life. My steps quickened. I could hardly wait to get at it.

CHAPTER 2
THE SETTLER

I had just hit my stride when a clearing appeared on my left. I stopped and stared in amazement at the beauty of the place. It wasn't big, and the house was built only of logs, but there was a touch of perfection about it. The logs were long and straight, fitting snugly together and gripping squarely at the corners. The front yard was level and clear of stumps, with a neatly trimmed lawn of real grass. A fence, sitting square and even, completely surrounded the place and a sidewalk led in through a swinging gate. I never expected to see anything like that away up here in the wilderness. Yet I saw no unusual materials, and I was sure I could do it too.

A man was pumping water by the house and he saw me staring.

"Well, young man," he called out, "where are you off to?"

"Out past Uffington," I answered, "I'm taking up my land."

"And what do you expect to find out there?" he asked.

He seemed like a jovial type, so I answered lightly.

"My fortune, I hope."

He considered that a moment.

"Well," he concluded, "you'll probably find it."

He asked me to come in for a drink of cold water, and I gladly accepted. We sat under a big pine tree and talked a while. I learned that he was Thomas McMurray, first settler in Draper.

"Why go away out to Uffington?" he asked, "we have a good community starting right here."

I was impressed with his place, all right, but it only made me more eager to get at my own.

"I want to go where others haven't been," I told him, "I want to share in the riches of Muskoka; the fertile land, the timber limits, the minerals. They say there is even gold here. Those who come early and search diligently will find them." I stopped, thinking my romantic little speech would amuse him. But he thought about it seriously.

"It's a game of chance," he declared, "there are prizes hidden all over the district."

"Out beyond Uffington?"

"Everywhere," he nodded, "the Muskoka Road is just the spine. You have come to South Falls, but this is only the beginning. Three miles farther on are the North Falls. Beyond them, more falls, more rivers, great expanses of new territory. This Peterson Road opens new land all the way to the Ottawa valley. You are right. There are riches here."

Now we had both made speeches. We sat quiet for a while. "Now let me tell you something practical," he said finally, "you have to survive until your fortune comes."

He showed me how to corner the logs in my building. He told me what materials to use and where to look for them. He warned me of the dangers in new country. I was grateful.

I took a liking to Mr. McMurray right away. His eyes made me feel comfortable. He looked me squarely in the face when he spoke, and there was a faint twist of humour about his lips. He seemed amused at my ignorance of the backwoods, but he wasn't vain about his own knowledge; just confident. He was big, with a full face, smooth forehead and a long black beard that descended neatly to a point in the middle of his chest. His clothes were of good quality, but well suited for outdoors. He seemed like a country gentleman ready to help out with the chores.

Time was passing, so I thanked him for his help and advice, and turned to go.

"Glad I saw you," he said, "I've seen quite a few settlers plodding past here. They hardly raise their eyes from the road. You're different."

"I'll build a good place," I declared, feeling flattered.

"Well, don't try to chop down the whole forest at once."

I thought he was joking.

"I'll do my best," I declared.

"No, don't," he warned, "if you cut too much, you can't look after it. That's the biggest mistake people make. They chop out ten or fifteen acres right away and half of it lies idle. The place looks sloppy, stumpy and neglected. Start off with five acres, and look after it well."

"You've certainly given me your secrets," I said as we reached the gate, "and I'm grateful."

"They're not secrets; people simply don't ask."

"I'll be back to see you if I need help," I promised, "but it does seem such a long way."

"There are good people in Uffington," he pointed out, "if you need help, they will give it."

Then I was on my way, eager to feel my axe bite into the long straight timber for my cabin, curious about the lay of my unknown land. I travelled two miles along the South Branch of the Muskoka River, marvelling at its deep beauty; then a mile south and four miles east to the 20th sideroad of Draper. The obstacles in the road were more familiar now; I took them in my stride. Darkness was approaching as I came to a group of shanties at Uffington. But I didn't stop; it was so close now.

I looked at my map and there was a mile and a quarter to go. But the road seemed to take a long curve off the concession line, that would make it farther. I took a rough guess at 2500 paces and started counting as I walked. Down the hill, 200; around the swamp and up another hill, 850; then another swamp, another hill and a long turn to the left. I felt lost. My sense of direction was gone. Thank goodness I had counted; 2100. The isolation of the place was complete; no clearing, no sign of life, and darkness had fallen. The road narrowed to a trail, vanishing into the gloom ahead; 2499, 2500. I must be there.

A patch of flat rock lay just off the road. I strode onto it and took possession. I set down my bedroll, my bag of provisions and my axe. I could see nothing but the surrounding trees, hear nothing but the lonely rustle of leaves. I opened out my bedroll and climbed in. I was dead tired, but couldn't sleep. The night was still and silent; the great canopy of heaven spread out above me. A feeling of intense loneliness and emptiness came over me, as if I were the only person in creation, like Adam on the first day. A chill struck me suddenly and I tucked my blanket in closer. I tried to recover my warm thoughts of Anne in our new home, and how envious that would make Decimus. But nothing happened; I was just a lump of clay cast down on deserted rock. Mercifully I finally fell asleep.

In the morning when I woke, there was a glimmer of light in the eastern sky. The jagged edges of white pine and spikes of tall spruce stood out dimly against the horizon. Away in the distance I heard a dog barking, and knew there were people around somewhere. I got up and went exploring.

Five days later the first tree came crashing down. Lot lines marked, terrain explored, I knew my property. There was high ground near the road, that's where I would build; lower land at the side was for root crops, and a broad level space at the back was for grain. A creek ran through the back fifty, winding into a big lake nearby. Along the creek was a broad band of fertile soil. The place wasn't everything I had hoped for; the land sloped sharply in spots and there were ridges of rock. But it was good enough. My buildings would be high and dry, my crops well nourished.

By mid-September I was sleeping within the four walls of a partly completed shanty. I was very pleased with it. The logs sat square and level. I had six logs up all around, twenty feet along the front, sixteen feet on the sides. It was a slow business, but I was doing it right, and I had a young neighbour, Jimmy Patterson, to help me.

The top logs were causing problems. I needed some kind of hoist to put them up. Two men simply couldn't handle them. I asked Jimmy one day if he knew how it was done.

"There's a way we do it around here," he said, "maybe we can manage it tomorrow."

"Is it some kind of hoist?" I asked curiously as he left for home.

"Sort of," he answered, "I'll show you."

I did some thinking that night. The logs were cut to length and ready to place. I had to rig up a lifting device, and remembered seeing a picture of a log derrick somewhere. There were three long poles fastened together above the building like an Indian tepee. A rope hung from the junction of the poles like a pulley.

I needed a piece of metal to hold the poles together and to secure the rope. Maybe that's what Jimmy had. Next morning I looked around the horizon and saw a clump of tall spruce. They made perfect poles and I went toward the building to get my axe.

At that moment I heard voices by the road, and went out to look. There were six big men coming in, all carrying axes. It gave me a start, for they looked rough. Then I recognized my neighbour Matt Patterson, and Jimmy was with him.

"We've come to give you a hand," said Matt.

"This is our hoist," added Jimmy

I only knew three of the men. The others were strangers, but not for long. They took off their jackets and went to work. They trimmed and notched the logs and we lifted them into place. It was so easy with all that manpower. When the walls were twelve logs high they cut a doorway. Then we started on the roof. Out into the woods they went, bringing back long straight lengths of pine and cedar which some of them split into boards. One of the men was an expert with his broadaxe. He could get long wide boards from a pine log. Others split roof slats. The ground was littered with chips and splinters.

At noon we had a good pile of slats for the roof and boards for framing. They were rough, but thick and solid. When we stopped for lunch the men brought out their own lunch boxes. I tried to do something for them, like heating water and making them comfortable. But they would have none of it.

"Sit down and eat, for goodness sake," Matt snapped, "there's plenty of work yet."

They ate in silence, as they had worked. Then they brushed off the crumbs and relaxed in the shade.

"Things is sure in a mess," said Matt.

I looked around the clearing and it was true. But I soon learned he wasn't talking about my clearing, it was politics. There was a lot of excitement then about a Grit named George Brown, joining up with his arch-enemy, John A. Macdonald, to give the province of Canada a stable government. I followed things in the newspapers when I could get one.

16

"No doubt about it," agreed one they called Fred, "but I never thought Brown would join up with John A."

"He had no choice," declared Matt, "he's no politician by himself."

"What the hell do you mean?" Fred demanded, "Macdonald needed him. The country needs him."

"Like a hole in the head," said Matt.

When they started talking politics I hung on every word. Back home in England it was the business of the rich and noble; an ordinary man like me had no place in it. But here in the new world things were different. Any man had the chance, if he had the will. And I wanted to learn.

"I don't know too much about Canadian politics," I admitted, "I've only recently arrived."

They complied immediately.

"Very simple," Matt explained, "John A. Macdonald is the greatest statesman in these provinces. He's Attorney General and Premier most of the time. Every now and then the people go soft in the head and elect some Grit like George Brown. He's the worst of them. But in spite of the interference, John A. is bringing the provinces together; he's trying to make us into one country. They're talking about a Confederation now."

"He's got it all wrong, as usual," corrected Fred, "Macdonald is bringing us all to ruin. He bribes the voters and steals Brown's best men with lies. Ever since we joined up with Lower Canada twenty some years ago the Frenchmen and the Catholics have been grabbing everything for themselves. And now Macdonald is giving them the country to stay in power."

"John A. is simply trying to be fair to Lower Canada," Matt argued reasonably, "there has to be some give and take."

"Don't try to deny it," Fred challenged him, "John A. is a tool of the priesthood."

Matt got right up off the ground and I thought there would be violence.

"That's dirty damn Grit talk," he said, angry now, "you've been reading that misbegotten writing of George Brown."

"Well, Macdonald's always surrounded by a bunch of

17

Frenchmen; you can't deny that.''

Matt didn't try.

"Why not?" he asked, "they're part of our province. Anyway, the people don't know what they want. In the last three years we've had four governments. They threw out Sandfield Macdonald in March and John A. came back in. Now the Members have voted against John A. in the Assembly. It's hopeless, a mess; like I already said.''

"It's Brown that's saving the country," Fred declared, "he joined Macdonald against his personal feelings. He's preventing anarchy. George Brown is a big man.''

"Big turd," Matt declared, "big fat turd.''

Well that started it. They were all on their feet, shouting, arguing, waving their arms. Did I call them silent?

"Time to get to work," someone said finally, and the argument stopped. They picked up their axes and went back to splitting roof slats in silence.

I took it all in eagerly. Politics, I could see, was the most important thing around here. In politics, a man could be a champion. I saw right away how my stock could rise in this community, and I determined to get into public life. I would read, and talk, and know more than anyone else around here. It was a strong sensation, a desire to step out beyond the others, to be one of the decision-makers. I took no part in the discussions then, though I felt like a John A. man. These men were all my benefactors; another time I could talk politics.

They went to work on the roof. At each end of the shanty heavy poles were run up from the corners, coming together some eight feet above the walls in the form of an inverted "V". They fastened a solid pole between the end pieces and several more supports were put in along the length of the building to hold it solid. Then they began fastening on the roof boards and slats they had split.

As we worked, I could see the shape of my future. This community was going ahead; I was lucky to arrive early. I would be among the leaders when our town grew. Clustered around the corner of the fifth concession and the 20th sideroad half a

18

dozen clearings had already been chopped from the forest. All along the Peterson Road settlers were moving in, and now I was starting the Bell settlement. I planned to buy more lots and expand into a large holding. I could imagine this little shanty turning into a big frame house; the barn, the drive shed, fields of waving grain and herds of grazing cattle flashed across my vision. A broad road would lead to the house for our fine carriages and prancing horses.

And Anne would be there. I remembered her waving goodbye as she disappeared up the Muskoka Road. I saw her standing by the riverbank, her clothes clinging to her body, and her eyes drawing me invitingly to her. She will be the mistress of this manor house I am building. She will be firm in the affairs of the household. I remembered her piercing blue eyes, her direct gaze and lips compressed at times with determination. She will be no shrinking violet in the community. Richard Bell's wife will be well regarded.

I thought of Decimus, cooped up all day in his office, living in some ordinary house in the city. How envious he will be of his young brother - local squire and political figure! I almost felt sorry for him.

"We'll just frame up your door, and I guess that's it." Matt's voice broke in on my thoughts.

"I don't know how to thank you."

"Don't," he said, "it isn't done. We're just being neighbourly."

When they were finished, they picked up their coats and lunch boxes and headed off.

"Be sure and invite us to the wedding," Matt demanded.

"What wedding?"

"Well, you're not building this place for one person, are you?"

They all laughed. I guess I must have blushed.

"If there's a wedding," I promised, "you'll hear about it."

I stood watching as they went up the road. Then I looked around at my shanty and couldn't believe it. That pile of logs was now a building; roof, door and slatted gables.

"Thanks," I shouted up the road. But they were gone.

A shanty is not enough though. It would do for some of the desperate settlers who came to the wilderness to escape their creditors, or to shelter them from the cold. But my place would have fields for grain, a garden for vegetables, a shed for chickens and animals. I could not ask my wife to shut herself in a shanty, cleaning and cooking. She should be able to watch a garden grow, gather eggs for food and pin money, feel the benefits of success. So I began clearing my land.

I started chopping as the maple saplings in the swamp turned a flaming red. Each day I saw their colour spread into the big maples. Soon the rubbery leaves of the scrub oak turned to bronze; the birch and poplar matured to yellow, and the sumac leaves and candles ripened into rich reds. There was a briskness in the air I had never felt before. I went to my task exhilarated.

I was chopping when the leaves had fallen and formed a crisp blanket on the forest floor. I worked first on the under-brush, the small trees and scrub growth. Within the five acres I was clearing, I laid out the small stuff in windrows, ready to burn. I was still cutting it as the wild geese passed overhead, honking their way in V formation to the south. Soon I felt the chill of approaching winter. I wore a coat to the bush and back again, glad of some extra warmth.

In my spare moments I read the newspapers Jimmy Patterson brought over, and occasionally I visited my neighbours and discussed affairs of the day. I did my thinking while I worked, and seldom stopped except for the Sabbath.

As light snow fell and ice formed on the puddles, I was into the heavy timber. I felt strong as the great trees swayed and fell, crashing to the ground through everything around them. Then I would tramp over to the fallen peak, trim off the branches and limbs until it lay bare, one more enemy defeated. The light branches went into the brush piles for burning; the heavy limbs I left for later. Every week Jimmy Patterson came over for a day and we laid our backs into the cross-cut saw. Big limbs and giant trunks were cut into lengths and piled. One day I would burn it all.

Then one morning Jimmy Patterson didn't arrive when he should have. It was snowing heavily and I realized his father had kept him home. He must have expected bad weather, for soon the wind came howling through the barren forest, cold, relentless, bringing squalls of snow. Little gusts of frigid air came seeping into the cabin, around the door and windows, up from the floor and down from the eaves. Frantically I stuffed bits of paper, wood and moss into cracks I never realized were there. Still the cold crept in. I fired up my tin stove till it was almost red hot. I put on all the clothes I could wear, but still I was cold. When I went out for wood the wind cut my face and chilled me to the bone. I stacked enough wood inside the building to last the day.

Toward nightfall the wind went down and I breathed a sigh of relief. I stoked up the stove and dampered it down for the night. Then I went to bed with all my clothes on.

Sometime during the night I woke as a gigantic chill shook my body. I lay motionless a while, trying not to create a draft; but I knew something fearful was happening. I had never felt cold on my face like that. I got up shivering and went to the stove. It was warm, but it might as well have been out. My hands were stiff, my feet cold lumps. I fired up the stove, but a foot away from it you couldn't feel a thing. I sat down in my chair and got colder and colder. I became numb, my thoughts were slow and incoherent. Time passed.

Cold, cold.

The whole world was an iceberg.

Trees were cracking like rifle shots.

I never heard them so loud. The walls shook with the sound.

Feeling numb.

Stay awake! Stay awake!

I knew I would die if I fell asleep, and it didn't alarm me. Yet something inside me still functioned. I had to stand up. Stand up, Stand up, a voice seemed to say. I got to my feet and walked around; I swung my arms; I stamped my feet. I swallowed warm water and ate from my scanty stores. All night I kept moving. My wood was gone before morning, but I didn't dare go outside. When daylight came, it seemed to renew my strength. The world was still there; I had survived the night.

But I chopped no more in the bush that winter. I just worked on my building. First I closed up the chinks where the cold came through. Then I went to work on the stove. I put it on a solid base, and piled stones in a circle around it to absorb and hold the heat. My furniture was rough; a chair carved from a tree stump, a block of wood for a table, straw shoved into sacking for a bed. It was no place for a woman. So I brought in big chunks of pine and maple. From the pine I made a clothes chest, a cupboard and bunk beds. From the maple I fashioned a table and two chairs. They were no cabinet maker's delight, but I put them together with loving care, knowing she would use them. The winter dragged on.

Then Spring arrived; and as if to make up for her crude effort to kill me, Nature smiled. The sounds and smells of Spring raised my spirits high. One morning I came out my door, smelled the fresh, clean air and shouted:
"I'm alive."

It wasn't just that I was un-dead; I felt wonderful. The frogs were singing in the swamp, with the odd croak from the bullfrogs. The loons called on the lake, the robins began to chirp. There was a smell of sweet grass in the air, and balm-of-gilead gave off its fragrant aroma. The warm sun drew out the familiar scent of cedar. I went back to chopping, and my hands toughened up again on the axe handle. There were sunny days in April, more in May. The winter wood was drying.

Now and then I went to Uffington for a social event. I had to maintain my standing and courtesy. But my real interest was to get my home ready, and generally I was tired. Around the first of July I was ready for the burn.

One morning Matt Patterson and Jimmy arrived at my place early. Matt had sensed that the day was right for a burn; dry and clear with a stiff breeze. He looked around the clearing carefully.

My five acre patch, roughly 450 feet by 500, was one big field of brushwood. It was all systematically piled. The big logs formed the base of hollow squares. In each square was easy-burning softwood; pine and hemlock with pitch oozing from the ends; a bit of cedar, winter-dried and ready to spit out its burning embers. On top of each square were piled dry boughs and branches.

Between the squares of heavy wood were windrows of slash; underbrush, tree tops and light boughs. It was a mixture; evergreen for a quick start; hardwood to burn hot and hard. It was all piled loosely and crosswise to let the wind blow through. The whole clearing was a network of connected piles and rows.

"Looks all right," said Matt, and I was glad he approved.

"Shall we start now?" I asked.

"The sooner the better."

I took a handful of pine slivers and plunged them into a bucket of coals I had brought from the house. As they caught fire I passed them out to Matt and Jimmy, and we fanned out through the clearing. We set fire to each of the little piles of birch bark and pine branches, which were set among the rows and under the log piles as kindling. In half an hour the clearing was alight with hundreds of fires. We moved back to the cabin to watch.

A burn, Matt had told me, is more than setting fire to piles of brush. It's like glazing a pot or firing a blast furnace; a certain peak must be reached. Otherwise your burn is a failure. I watched him anxiously for reaction, but he stood there stolidly watching the flames dart into the sky, saying nothing. In less than an hour the whole field was ablaze, fanned by a strong wind.

"Have we got a burn?" I asked anxiously.

"Not yet," Matt answered, shaking his head.

"How can you tell?"

"Well," he said, "it's like being in love I guess. You'll know when it happens."

The heat was fierce. I had brought a barrel of water from the creek, and had it near the shanty. The walls were getting hot, and I was about to douse them. But Matt held up his hand. As the fire grew hotter, we backed right to the road. Still Matt stood impassively, watching the flames. The piles of timber were now alight, and some of the stumps started to smoke. An hour passed; and I began to worry. Nothing had happened that I could feel.

Then suddenly the whole five acres exploded into one roaring, blasting inferno. It became a single fire. Flames went skyward a hundred feet, carrying smoke, embers and burning needles. The shanty started to smoke, and Matt nodded his head. We doused the logs with water, braving the heat and smoke. As I passed between the fire and the shanty, I could feel my hair singe, and my clothes smelled of burning wool. Stumps in the field began to burn from the surrounding heat. The big logs at the bottom of the piles threw off flame.

Matt looked at me and smiled. He didn't have to say anything. I knew we had a burn.

All day long the fire roared in the clearing. Each hour moved me closer to clear ground and green fields. By nightfall it was almost over. The great heaps of logs and the charred stumps smouldered on. We raked the unburned chips and branches into new fire piles. When darkness came, the ground was still covered with burning coals, like the firepot of a giant furnace.

When I went to bed, singed, seared and saturated with smoke, I was an established settler. I had taken my homestead from the forest.

CHAPTER 3
THE SEARCH

The shanty was spotless, floor washed, furniture arranged and entrance raked. I took a last look around and pulled the door shut. I threw my bedroll over my shoulder and started up the road. I was going for Anne.

All the fires in the clearing were out. Charred stumps still cluttered the field; half-burned logs lay starkly where they had fallen. There was a lot to be done yet. But I knew all along I would go after the burn, and the time had come. I could wait no longer.

I was eager now to see the mysterious land to the north, to walk the roads that Anne had walked, to find my love and bring her home. In my grim determination to prepare our home properly, I had hardly left it. The year that had passed was gone like a shadow, and I emerged once more into the light of day. I hadn't even been to Bracebridge. But now I was ready; I could ask Anne to marry me. And this time my voice would be clear.

I hiked gaily up the road, waving at friends as I passed, but no-one knew my destination. I stopped to see Mr. McMurray at Muskoka Falls, and he was home.

"Where are you off to now?" he asked as if I was always travelling.

"Up to see Bracebridge," I answered, "and perhaps I'll go on to the country beyond."

"Found your fortune yet?" he asked.

"It's growing," I·said cheerfully.

"Well, come in and have a bite to eat."

I accepted at once for there were things I wanted to know and table talk can ramble on easily. Mr. McMurray travelled a lot. We talked about the north townships, Macaulay, Monck and Watt.

"Where do most people settle in Watt?" I asked casually.

"Well now there's two or three places," he answered, "exactly who are you looking for?"

That was a bit too direct for me and I told him a half truth. "A man named Mills," said I.

"Don't recall hearing the name," he said thoughtfully, "but call at the Shea settlement, Three Mile Lake. They know everybody."

The man was a ferret. I only asked one question and already he figured I was looking for somebody. I decided to ask him no more or he'd have me spilling the whole thing. We talked generalities from then on, and I took off when we had eaten.

I came to the Muskoka Road, the place where I last saw Anne. The roar of the Great Falls brought back those memories sharply. I walked to the spindly bridge that crossed the deep chasm of the Muskoka River. The view filled me with a sense of awe and power.

As I looked up-river two steep falls, splashing and spraying toward me, made me grip the rail for safety. And beneath me, passing under the bridge and down stream, was an immense cataract which deafened me by its thunder and made me dizzy from its movement. Tumbling in two perpendicular leaps to depths of a hundred feet, the white water crashed down. I went to the other side of the bridge, looking down-stream where the chasm narrowed between vertical walls of rock, squeezing the rushing water in violent sprays of white foam. At the first level young maples and birches grew luxuriously in front of a screen of pine. Along the lowest basin was unbroken pine forest.

The Great Falls! So close to where I live; part of my township. I felt a pride of ownership in this wonder of nature. "Yes," I could say to newcomers, "this is our Falls. The Great Falls, they call it." Then I would stand back modestly as they went into ecstasies. I will stand here with Anne when we come back, and hold her hand tight as she peers over the bridge.

After an hour's walk I heard the sound of North Falls, around which the community of Bracebridge had grown. I felt a bit jealous of this place; it was a rival. Some said it had taken over; that Draper and Uffington were being outgrown. Now I would see for myself.

At the top of the hill above the falls I came to the Victoria

26

Inn. There was nothing there to make me jealous; a grubby little post office and a tavern - the stopping place for the stage. But over the crest of the hill, perched at the very edge of the falls, I found the Royal. That was something else again.

Here was an inn, clean and comfortable, with rooms for the travelling public, a store attached, and a magnificent view of the River. Mr. H.J. McDonald, the proprietor, was on hand himself to make me welcome.

"Yes sir," he said after I had introduced myself and sat down at the bar, "I was the first person to live here at North Falls. Came up as storekeeper with the surveyor Dennis when he laid out the Muskoka Road in the summer of '60."

"The very first?" I asked, partly a question, but more an exclamation.

"The first. Now him that runs the Victoria up there claims to be the first, but his place was away down the river. Not at North Falls at all. And the Beels up the road, they claim to be the first. Well they were the first settlers all right, but I was here in the survey camp to welcome them when they arrived."

His words excited me. What a person to know! He wasn't just a resident of Bracebridge; he was Bracebridge.

"What did you say your name was?" he asked.

"Bell. Richard James Bell."

"And you live in Uffington?"

"Been there a year."

"Well that makes you a Muskokan, I guess. Welcome to your capital."

Suddenly my jealousy was gone. I had a sense of belonging here, a feeling of ownership. This was my village too. I was beginning to spread out; to become known across the district. And I could bring Anne here on my way back; introduce her to my important friends. A thought struck me; we can spend our wedding night at the Royal Hotel in Bracebridge. Yes, that's what I'll do.

"And what do you think of our Falls?" McDonald asked, after pouring me another drink.

"I haven't seen them yet."

"Well come and I'll show you," he said, and we went out the front door and down the road to the bridge. These falls didn't have the magnificence of the Great Falls nor the awesome depths. They had a different character, softer and friendlier, and I felt more comfortable on the bridge above them. Beneath us the water swirled as it rushed into the first cataract and then down the rapids leading to a second descent. Wide and sturdy, the main falls were roaring their strength and power as they fell into a deep basin below.

"The Indians claim there's a spirit in these falls," McDonald said, "and the longer I'm here the more I believe it."

"Are there Indians hereabouts?" I asked in surprise for I had seen none.

"They pass through here on their way to hunt," he explained, "it was old chief Musquokky himself who told me about the spirit."

"You actually know him?" I exclaimed.

"Knew him well. A fine Christian gentleman," said McDonald, "he died last year well over a hundred. He well deserved to have this district named for him. His real name was William Yellowhead." These bits of history, this aura of eminence, filled me with excitement. I was becoming part of it. We went back into the hotel and talked a while before I got up to leave.

"I'll see you again soon," I said, "perhaps I'll stay overnight next time."

"My pleasure," he replied, and I set out through the village.

Now I was ready to inspect Bracebridge; to see, almost, what I had inherited when I settled here. As I crossed the bridge over Muskoka river I heard the high-pitched ring of a saw-mill down river; that was the sound of progress. Then there was a carpentry shop just across the bridge, and the fresh pine shavings filled the air with a pleasant odour. A little farther up, on the right, was a log shanty, and right next door was a frame house, something I hadn't seen north of Orillia.

On the other side of the street I passed a log house and then came to a steep hill. Part way up on the left was a general store

28

and across the road a blacksmith shop. Near the top Browning's new frame store had just opened. This village was really going ahead. Mr. Browning told me there was only one more building. "It's about a quarter mile north," he said, "belongs to a man named Beel. First settler here, you know." I was impressed. The first settlers would be important people to know. I decided to stop and see them.

I was attracted immediately to Mrs. Beel, for she looked a lot like Anne, and her name was Anna. What a story they had to tell; a hard trip through the forest in October, 1860, with only a survey line to follow and two small children, one in arms and the other hardly walking. Then the long lonely winter with no neighbours and no help. The husband was lost in the bush for two days, his feet badly frozen, and he only survived by a miracle.

I had to tell them about the forest fire I came through on the way up; and how Anne and her father and I survived by jumping into the river. And how I nearly froze to death my first winter. They hung on every word, and I felt a comradeship in the perils of pioneering. Suddenly I had to tell them about Anne.

"I'm going for her now," I blurted out, "they're living up in Watt township."

"Call in on the way back," he urged, "we'll be very happy to meet her."

I took to the road completely refreshed, ready now to bring Anne back. The way was prepared; a triumphant return among important friends was certain. I drank in the fresh air as I strode along, and from time to time burst into song as the joy of it all came over me. The world was a beautiful place.

I turned west onto the Parry Sound Road after two miles, and there my real journey began. The track was clear enough, better in fact than the Muskoka Road, which continued northward. I decided to make no stops along the way and headed straight for the Shea settlement at Three Mile Lake. That was where Mr. McMurray had directed me so I followed his advice. I promptly put four miles of road behind me and came to a turnoff to the left. I stopped at a settler's cabin.

"How far to the Shea settlement?" I asked the man there.

"A couple of miles," he replied.

"Do you know a man named Mills?"

"Can't recall the name." he said, "but I'm new here. The Sheas will know."

I found the settlement easily. There was a well built cabin just off the road to the right, but no one answered when I knocked. I looked around outside and heard a clang of wood on metal from behind the building. There, amid steam and vapours billowing from an iron kettle, a well-built woman was stirring away vigorously with a heavy stick. The kettle was fed with liquid dripping from a piece of hollow wood, and was heated by a brisk fire. I introduced myself, and asked curiously: "What are you doing?"

"Making soap," she said, stirring away, "what did you think?"

"Never saw it done before. How is it done?"

She took a moment to tell me that you had to use hardwood ashes, and household fats, and how you mixed and boiled.

"Do you know a man named Mills," I asked.

"Not around here," she declared.

"I guess I'll have to go on."

"Not up this road. I know everybody that's up there."

I stood there uncertainly and she asked where I came from.

"Uffington, down in Draper township," I replied.

"You'll be hungry, then," she said, "wait a bit and I'll get you something to eat."

We went into the house shortly and she sat me down at the table. She brought out ham, fresh bread, blackberry preserves and tea. I knew I should eat sparingly for none of the settlers are well supplied. But she insisted, so I dug in.

"And did he not say where he was going?" she asked as I ate.

"He's not a man to accept crumbs from a land agent," I said of Mr. Mills with pride of family, "he wanted the best land, wherever he finds it."

30

"Go back to the Parry Sound road then," she said, "and turn west. Suffern's settlement is a few miles along the way, and there are clearings everywhere. You will find them along there sooner or later."

I set off again late in the day, prepared to spend some time in my search. When I got to the main road I turned west as she had directed, and began enquiring at the shanties. But nobody recognized the name Mills. Time and again they shook their heads, anxious to help, but helpless.

I had almost given up for the day when I saw a well-used path leading into the bush. My pulse quickened; something inside urged me to follow it. There's a shanty in there, it seemed to say, go and see that I'm right. Almost afraid to believe it, I turned in and followed the path. Sure enough there was a shanty, small, neat and tidy, nestling in a clearing. There were lacy curtains on the window, sure sign of a woman's touch. But something else made me certain - flowers in front of the building. My mind flashed back to another place. "I hope the flower seeds don't spoil," Anne had said to her father as we dried our things on the Muskoka Road. The inner voice that urged me onto this path now told me I had found them. Go on, go on, just knock on the door and Anne will open it. I was trembling with excitement as I walked to the door and knocked.

I heard a chair scrape inside and I knew she was there. The latch moved and the door swung in. My heart was in my mouth. It was dim inside and I couldn't see her at first. I stepped forward, ready to take her in my arms, and found myself smiling into the face of a stranger. The world collapsed on me then. I stood stupidly.

"Yes?" she asked in a startled voice.

"I'm sorry," I mumbled, "I was expecting someone else. Is this the Mills place?"

"Never heard of them," she said, and I turned and stumbled back to the road. That took the wind from my sails completely. It was late and I should never have started out from that settlement without making enquiries. But I wasn't thinking and moped along the road in a dark brown mood. I walked with no idea of the time, hardly seeing that it was dark and that I passed no clearings.

I never saw the caved-in pit of stinking swamp water until I was in it; sprawled full length and soaked to the skin. I came out of my trance abruptly, but a little late. I crawled out of the puddle and found a dry rock ahead. One by one I wrung out my wet garments and flapped them in the night air to dry. But it was a waste of time. I could only crawl naked into my blankets which were fairly dry, and hope my clothes could be worn in the morning. Exhausted by the long day, I fell promptly to sleep.

The snap of a twig startled me to wakefulness during the night. I looked carefully around and saw two eyes staring at me from close range. I lay still, considering what to do. Then I jumped up suddenly, shouting like a wild man, and throwing a rock. Whatever it was, it scuttled off into the forest. I climbed back into my blankets and lay there, shivering from the cold and fear. But fatigue overcame me finally and I dozed off again.

As I lay there a voice came to me from far beyond. I dreamed that the end had come and my Maker was calling me Home. The voice came closer, louder, and I felt in my muddled half-sleep that if it reached me sleeping, I would die. With a great effort I woke myself. I was still on this earth, chilled, tired, but alive.

"Hello. Hello. Is anybody there?"

The voice was real. I could hear footsteps nearby as someone came along the road.

"Over here," I called, and the footsteps ceased.

"Where?"

"Off the roadway to your right."

Heavy boots crashed through the underbrush and I hastily crawled from my blanket and pulled on my wet underwear.

"Are you all right, man?" he asked anxiously.

"Cold, wet and scared," I answered truthfully, "but otherwise all right."

"Follow me home."

That was the beginning of a warm friendship with Anthony Suffern. He had heard me shouting and got up from his bed to seek the lost traveller. He gave me a warm place to sleep and hung up my clothes to dry. In the morning his wife served me a hot breakfast. I told them where I came from and why I was travelling. They couldn't help me in my quest, but didn't discourage me either. They didn't know everybody farther west; but they gave me the names of some friends to call on.

The Sufferns were so kind and wonderful that I felt embarrassed.

"I'm not a wandering vagrant as it might appear," I explained, "I have my own homestead in Draper."

"I would have brought you here anyway," he said.

"I'm sure you would. But I am, in fact, a person of some standing in my community."

"You give that impression," he agreed and that encouraged me to go on.

"Public affairs is one of my main interests. There's more to life than eating and sleeping."

"I agree", he said, "but many people around here are just interested in staying alive."

That started us into a discussion of politics and philosophy. We talked about the Quebec and Charlottetown conferences on Confederation last Fall; the voyage John A. Macdonald and George Brown made to England in May and June. I related the funny story of them going to the Derby together and shooting peas at passersby from their carriage. London was all agog at these colonials.

I don't know why I laid it on so thick. I guess I was making up for the disreputable way I arrived there. And of course, I had read it all in the papers, though I gave it a personal touch as if I had inside information. In any case, Mr. Suffern was impressed.

"It's a pleasure to talk to you, Mr. Bell," he said, "gets away from the everyday things of life. I wish you well."

"I am beholden to you," I acknowledged, "some day I will show my gratitude."

"That's not necessary," he protested, "just to help a fellow man in distress is a privilege.''

How well things turned out! As I waved them good-bye I felt elated. I was making friends with important people all along the way. Mrs. Shea had mentioned Suffern's Settlement, and this was Mr. Suffern himself. When I come into my own, I'll remember Anthony Suffern.

But now the task at hand was to find Anne and her father. I had no doubt I would do it; it would just take time. I travelled west, stopping at every homestead and clearing. The settlers were pleasant, happy to talk to a stranger. But everywhere the answer was the same; no, never heard the name Mills; don't remember a man and daughter; try farther on, there are new settlers farther west. By nightfall I had passed through the township of Watt and found it hard to stay cheerful. Late at night I knocked at the door of an empty cabin and decided to sleep there. I didn't rest well and started off again before daylight. The trail was getting narrower and rougher. It left the woods in places and when it crossed an open area, there were no marks whatever. Then I would have to find where it re-entered the bush. Finally the trail disappeared completely and I thought the road had ended.

I sat down to rest and consider my next move, and shortly heard the sound of an axe biting into wood up ahead. Then came the short, sharp chop of someone splitting kindling. I got up and walked toward the sound, knowing I would find a shanty. Much to my surprise I found a whole village; the village of Rosseau on the edge of the big lake. In the safety of the settlement, I lay down in a dry place and had a good sleep.

When I got up I started once more the dreary round of questions. My hopes faded again, for nobody knew the Mills. "If they came this far," someone said, "they would likely go on to Parry Sound."

But good news waits until the last hope has faded. At the final shanty in the village I was describing Anne and her father when a flash of recognition crossed the old man's face.

"I remember them well," he declared, "they went through here last fall. She was a lot younger than him."

34

"Spring and Fall," added the lady rocking by his side, "that's what I said to my man at the time."

"They are father and daughter," I explained.

"That would be them all right."

The spring came back once more into my step, and I went on with new hope. The road was now only a thread through the wilderness, a path along the surveyor's line. I steeled myself for a long rough walk, but shortly I heard chopping ahead. It was not an isolated sound but a multitude of axes thudding, trees crashing and voices shouting. Suddenly I was out of the bush onto a wide, open roadway. Workmen were clearing, stumping and burning their way in a broad swath towards Rosseau.

"We're Beatty's crew from Parry Sound," one of the workmen told me, "they have the road contract."

"How far is Parry Sound?" I asked him.

"Twelve good miles, right into the village," he claimed.

No human habitation appeared on the new road for several miles; then the shanties began. I stopped at each one, asked my questions and got the same answer; no, don't know them. I went on into Parry Sound village and stumped it door by door.

After that I scoured the surrounding settlements for days; up the Great North Road to the isolated clearings and lost shanties of McKellar and Hagerman townships. Everywhere the response was the same; a puzzled frown, a shake of the head.

"No, I don't recall the name."

"No, I haven't seen them"

"No, sorry."

It finally got me down. I almost went to pieces. My God, can they say nothing but "no". I began shouting it in the silent forest. No, no, no. Some people heard me and thought I was demented. Perhaps I was. I no longer waited for words. The expression on their face was enough; a vague look, a puzzled forehead and I would turn away, an icicle in my heart. I only looked at their faces now, eager for a smile of recognition, a nod of the head, lips broadening into a "yes."

"Yes, I know them."

"Yes, I saw them."

But it never happened. The hope that a door would open and Anne would be standing there never left me. And it only made me hurt the more.

"Go on," they said, "go on a little farther."

But eventually I came to the end. There were no more shanties, and the road stopped abruptly.

I came back down the Great North Road and went up the tracks and trails along the Georgian Bay; trails that led nowhere, ending in abandoned lumber camps, or melting away into the forest. Roads that led to the water, leaving me to stare blindly at pine-studded islands on the bay.

For two weeks I searched. I slept in clearings close to a protective building. I slept in deserted shacks; in the open bush. I no longer shaved and a grimy stubble covered my face. My clothes became dirty; torn in places from the sharp edges of splintered stumps, and grimy from the damp ground.

I came back to Rosseau and questioned the helpful old couple who had seen Anne and her father. They weren't so sure now. The descriptions didn't fit. It could have been someone else. I retraced my steps through Watt township. I knew every shanty I had called at; now I did the others. But it was hopeless. Anne and her father had disappeared into the wilderness. I came back to where I started; the Muskoka Road.

I sat down there and gave way to tears. Oh Anne, Anne. Why did I let you go? Where else can I look for you? Were you caught in a forest fire; crushed by a falling tree; drowned in the Spring floods? I should have gone with you. My impulse had been right, but my pride led me astray. Perhaps if I had come sooner I would have found you. But it's no use.

Finally I got up and started home; back to my lonely shanty at the far end of nowhere. I didn't stop at the first settler's, didn't even look in for fear they would see me. I crossed the North Falls bridge and went up the hill, hurrying past the Royal Hotel where I would have no wedding night. Back down the Peterson Road to Uffington in hopeless despair.

I slept nowhere. I walked until my legs ached and my back

felt broken and I could think of nothing but the pain. Late at night I was home. I took off my pack, my worn-out boots and my soggy clothes. I put on a clean suit of underwear and climbed into dry blankets.

A whole year had passed, but I felt as empty and alone as the night I arrived.

THE MUSKOKAS
~1871~

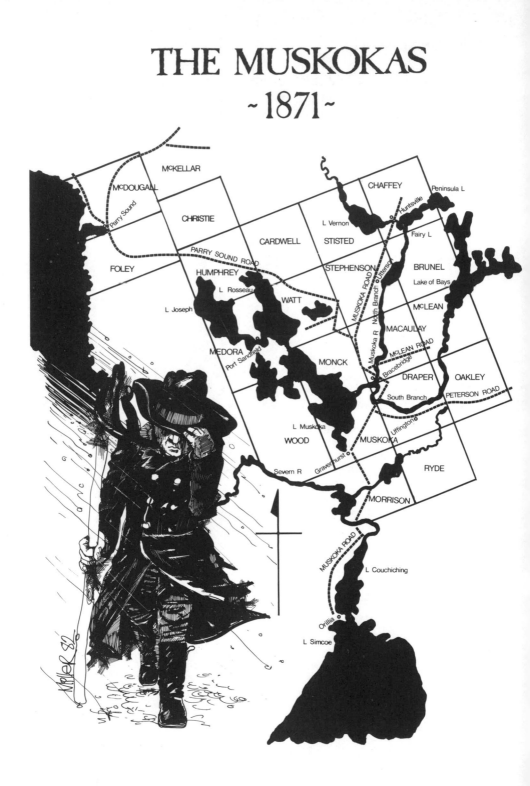

CHAPTER 4
ALEXANDER P. COCKBURN

Nobody in Uffington knew the real reason for my long journey, and for that I was thankful. I couldn't stand the embarrassment and the expressions of sympathy. I preferred to suffer in silence. Soon after my return, the Matt Pattersons invited me over for supper. They were very interested in my travels. At first I thought they suspected something, but it wasn't that at all. They were curious about the "country beyond".

"You must have travelled a goodly distance," Matt remarked, "I have never been beyond Bracebridge myself."

"Yes indeed," I began, warming to the subject, "I went all the way up the Parry Sound Road to the Georgian Bay and the village of Parry Sound; then up the Great North Road as far as it goes."

"The Great North Road!" Matt repeated, savouring the mystery of it.

"I stopped in all the settlements along the way too. Had tea with Mrs. Shea at their colony in Watt; talked politics with Anthony Suffern at the Suffern settlement. I even had a few words with Mr. William Beatty in Parry Sound. He's the king pin up there, you know. Runs the saw mill and does road contracting. I ran across one of his crews building part of the Rosseau Road."

They looked at each other in amazement.

"By George," exclaimed Matt, "you certainly are an adventurer."

"It's all part of our district, of course," I explained, "somebody should know what's going on."

It dawned on me suddenly that the disaster of my long trek could turn into a triumph. The Pattersons were eager to hear about the far reaches of Muskoka. They assumed that I had simply taken out to see the world. I waxed eloquent. They laughed when I told them about falling into the water hole; they were relieved when I described my rescue by Mr. Suffern.

Mrs. Patterson wanted to know more about the soap-making at Sheas; and Matt asked about those last lonely settlers on the Great North Road. I stayed quite late, and went home with a rosy glow of satisfaction.

After that I became a popular guest around the township. Once the Pattersons asked me to speak to eight or ten friends they had invited over. I discussed almost any subject; travel, lumbering, road-building, politics. I had seen it all. I became intoxicated with my own eloquence. Then, as it must, the axe fell. And the event was a disaster.

I looked up from my work one morning and there, like a spectre, stood my brother Decimus. He was immaculate, as if he had just stepped across the street in Toronto. I recalled the letter I wrote him about my own trip up; caught in a forest fire; nearly drowned; choked on smoke and dust; dirty, exhausted and heroic. I felt like a fool seeing him arrive so casually. I am positive he had stopped nearby to wash and shave, clean his boots and brush off his suit and bowler hat, just to embarrass me. And he succeeded.

There he was; tall and slim, his face clean shaven, his long sneering nose hooked above thin, slightly disgusted lips. I could almost smell the odour of antiseptic shaving lotion and carbolic soap that always surrounded him. His pasted-down hair, parted neatly in the middle, was exactly in place as he took off his hat to fan himself; as if the whole thing were slightly boring.

"Well, Richard," he greeted me, his nasal twang gritting on my nerves, "I see you've managed to cut a few trees and throw a shack together. Not bad for a year's work."

"Hello, Decimus," I said, determined to be friendly, "it was good of you to come."

"Nothing at all, brother, just a short jaunt."

"Would you come in?"

"I suppose so," he answered, looking at my place doubtfully, and picking his way towards the door.

"We don't often get to have architects around here."

"Obviously."

40

I didn't much enjoy the next two days he was with me. If he had any brotherly feelings he concealed them well. We walked around the clearing, down the creek to the lake and along the shore to my favourite point with tall pine trees and spreading maples. It was my showplace.

"What do they call it?" he asked with an effort to show interest.

"Poverty Lake."

"Well named."

I took him over to see the Pattersons. They praised me up as a good neighbour and hardy adventurer. If Decimus was impressed he didn't show it. I decided to take him up to Bracebridge. We stopped in to see Mr. McMurray on the way and my brother showed some interest.

"Fine place - for this part of the country," he decided after we left.

"Yes, Mr. McMurray sets a good example for the neighbourhood."

"Too bad you didn't follow it."

When we reached Bracebridge I went straight to the Royal. There were several people sitting in the lounge, one of them a stranger to me. Mr. McDonald gave me the greeting I hoped for.

"Well Mr. Bell," he exclaimed, "and how did your journey go?"

"Quite well."

"That's what I hear. Quite an adventure."

"This is my brother Decimus. He's visiting me from Toronto."

"Glad to meet you. Make yourselves comfortable, and let's hear all about it."

The stranger didn't say anything, but looked us over coolly. He seemed a bit younger than me. His long, well formed face was partly concealed by a huge moustache, and his visage seemed stern for a man his age. His hands were big and his complexion ruddy, like a woodsman. But he was no labourer; his clothes were too good. He wore a grey flannel shirt with tie,

41

store-bought trousers and a woodsman's wool jacket. On his head was a grey slouch hat; no black derby like the others but it looked expensive. I took him to be a well-established farmer or maybe a lumber scaler.

After Mr. McDonald's effusive greeting I knew what was expected of me. And I gladly obliged. I had been waiting two days to do or say something without Decimus cutting me down. The presence of a newcomer brought out all the story-teller in me. I described my journey west and north; the settlements, the people, my adventures, my discussions; the whole series. I could feel the room tense with interest.

"Well, you've made a start," the stranger acknowledged when I paused, "there are certainly opportunities in the North."

"How do you know?"

I hadn't intended to be abrupt, but it came out that way. He flushed.

"Well, sir," he said, "I will tell you."

He looked at me coldly and began to talk.

"I came up this way three weeks ago from my home in Eldon township and started across Lake of Bays from Cedar Rapids. I don't suppose any of you have been up that way."

Nobody claimed to have been.

"Only Indians have been there; and a few explorers. We started at the east end of the lake and paddled west. The shores are dense with timber, pine and spruce, maple and oak. My companion, who is a timber man, spotted timber inland like I have never seen before. The straight smooth trunks of virgin pine stretched up at least ninety feet. They grew close together and the tops made cover so dense that no sunlight came through. The timbers were three and four feet across and no underbrush or small trees survived near them. There was nothing in the grove but a carpet of moss and pine needles. Our voices echoed as in a cathedral. ' Original pine forest, ' my companion said, almost reverently, ' I used to see it in the Ottawa Valley, but it's almost all gone now.' What a sight it was."

Our visitor paused to recover his breath.

"Then we paddled on through bays, peninsulas and islands;

42

we portaged into Peninsula Lake and then Fairy Lake and finally ended up at Lake Vernon. From there we set off north into really wild country, small lakes and rivers, Doe Lake and the river system of the Magnetawan. We travelled by canoe and portage over 75 miles and never saw a living soul. When we came back to Lake Vernon we found the trail leading south and finally reached Bracebridge on foot.''

''And here you are,'' I commented as he paused, feeling a bit foolish now.

''No. That was a week ago. We went on down to Gravenhurst and stayed at McCabe's. The lady there insisted that we take a trip on Muskoka Lake. I didn't really want to at the time; I was in a hurry to get home. But she insisted, and I'm glad of it now. We travelled right up the Lake in a row boat. It was beautiful, but terrible. The rowing nearly killed me.'' He then stopped, apparently finished his narrative.

''That's quite a story,'' Decimus finally spoke, ''makes my brother's trip through the settled parts like an afternoon breeze.''

It was cruel. I could feel them laughing at me now, especially this fellow and Decimus. I detested them both. But I didn't have sense enough to shut up.

''Why just travel around?'' I asked sarcastically, ''have you nothing else to do?''

''Looking for timber,'' he answered, ''I manage our family lumber business.''

I was drowning, down for the second time. I knew I was heading for self-destruction, but I couldn't stop. There was still one subject on which I was well informed, and this young smart-alec was fair game.

''Are you interested in politics?'' I asked, innocently enough, but really challenging him onto my own ground.

''In a small way,'' he answered, ''I'm presently reeve of Eldon township.''

''But in the broader field,'' I pushed on, ignoring the sinking feeling his answer gave me, ''in the provincial field for example.''

"Well, I managed the campaign for Samuel Ault in Stormont in '61, and before that I worked for Mr. Mattice in '57."

"You don't look old enough."

"I was 20; good age to get started. But Mr. Mattice suggested I try municipal politics when I came up to Victoria County. The people there are pretty conservative."

"You'll be a John A. man then."

"I'm afraid you don't know your Members, Mr. . . . ah. . ."

"Bell," chipped in Decimus.

"Mr. Bell. Both Mattice and Ault were elected as Liberals. I got to be Reeve in spite of my politics."

At that moment I only wanted to get out of there. There was nothing I could do or say. McDonald came to my rescue.

"Well gentlemen," he announced, "I'm afraid I must interrupt this interesting discussion. I have to clear up the lounge before dinner."

I got up and stumbled out, totally defeated. I hardly spoke to Decimus again before he decided to go back to Toronto. And the other man - I never wanted to see him in these parts again.

After Decimus left I found things to do around my place. Winter was approaching and this time it would find me prepared. I put in wood, banked up my foundation to prevent drafts and closed up all the new cracks left by drying logs. Then I built a shelter for the chickens which had been running loose since I got them. I didn't particularly want to talk to anyone; I felt done in and discouraged. I was curious about the man I had clashed with in Bracebridge, but I didn't want to ask anyone.

In a couple of weeks, though, I went to see the Pattersons. I knew they would always be my friends, no matter how I disgraced myself.

"Haven't seen you recently," said Matt casually when I showed up.

"I've been busy, getting ready for winter."

"And I suppose your brother has gone."

"Thank goodness."

"I'd never have guessed you were brothers. He's tall, thin and sort of - reserved. You're . . . well more short, fat and friendly. Well, you're not really short and fat, either, but you incline that way."

There was a friendly twinkle in his eye, and it warmed up my disposition right away. If he wasn't a real friend, he wouldn't have said it.

"I guess I do."

"I hear you had quite a discussion with Cockburn."

"Who?"

"A.P. Cockburn; you know, from Cockburn's Lumber. They say you were trying to outdo each other with tall tales at the Royal in Bracebridge."

"What are people saying?" I asked, trying to appear casual.

"Not too much. You're certainly moving in high circles."

"I'll tell you honestly, Matt, that fellow made a fool of me."

"There's a little of the fool in all of us."

"What's he doing up here?"

"You'd better ask McDonald. Cockburn stayed there overnight."

I felt a little better after that. At least I was over the hurdle of talking about it. Now I could go and talk to H.J. McDonald; he was a friend too. I went up to Bracebridge the next day. McDonald was alone, reading the paper.

"Things have been quiet since you were last here," he said, to open the conversation.

"I've wanted to thank you for ending that awful affair."

"I guess you didn't know what you were into."

"I was just a fish out of water," I admitted, "what's that man doing up here."

"That's a good question. The day after you were here he had someone take him up to the head of the Lake. Puttered around the rapids up there between Lakes Muskoka and Rosseau. It looked as if he wants to put a boat through. He's interested in more than lumbering. There was talk about a boat on Muskoka Lake."

"Any ideas?"

"Well he was writing out a request of some kind to the government."

"I can't see John A. doing much for a Liberal like him."

"You never know in politics," McDonald declared, "the ministry's a coalition now, and George Brown is part of it. D'Arcy McGee is in charge of development and agriculture and he was a Reformer once. Cockburn says the ministers are so busy with this Confederation thing, and all the big conferences, that nobody's thinking about the backwoods at all. If somebody comes along with an idea, they will fall for it."

"That Cockburn's too smart by far," I said resentfully, "I hope someone puts him in his place."

"Maybe you will."

"I've a long way to go," I admitted, "but the day may come."

But nobody put Alexander P. Cockburn in his place that year. In November D'Arcy McGee, on behalf of the government, made a deal with Cockburn. In return for his promise to put a steamboat on Muskoka Lake to assist in settlement, the government gave him a monopoly to carry settlers into the new territory. It also promised him help in improving navigation, and roads to meet the boat. And I was the fool who tried to lecture him on politics and travel.

Considering my lack of success in other fields that fall, I should have known enough to stay away from the ladies. But winter was the time for socializing, and I was lonesome. The church socials, the house parties, the dances, all brought out the young ladies in their finery, and stirred up my aching heart. Anne was always in my thoughts, but she was gone. My success as a narrator, traveller and letter-writer brought me to the attention of the matchmakers. I was inexperienced, but that winter I learned a lesson or two about women.

There was one young lady who seemed to find me attractive. I saw her looking at me several times at affairs, and when I looked back she blushed. Others saw it too, and one evening I was invited to her place for dinner. Afterwards I sat in the living room with the man of the house. He was a person of few words, and as he sat rocking and smoking his pipe, we heard voices in the kitchen. His wife and another woman were giving the young lady a lecture on the facts of life. We couldn't help overhearing some of it.

"Don't let them touch or look, even after you're married," the mother cautioned, "it just makes them silly."

"Very true," agreed the other woman, "a woman's body is an altar."

"But mother," protested the girl, "I want to have babies."

"That can be managed," her mother replied, "when the need arises."

"Absolutely true," the other woman agreed, "I've had six children and my husband has never seen above my knees."

"I guess you know best," the girl admitted.

That scared me off completely. They already practically had me married, and that wasn't my immediate intention. And they had my love life all laid out. It reminded me so warmly of Anne. She would never be so cold and distant as these bleak women. I remembered her standing by the river; her body exposed by the wet garments, and looking at me so unashamed. Wherever she is, she is mine. And I am hers.

But Satan gives a man no peace. He tempts the lonely with an easy cure for loneliness, and the faithful he leads from the paths of righteousness. Just before Christmas two young men told me they were going to Orillia and asked me to go along. I wanted some new fowl for my flock, so I went. We walked to Gravenhurst, hoping to catch a ride from there. When we got to the village the people were all excited.

"They're building a steamboat right here in Gravenhurst," a man told us, "it's down on the Bay."

We checked on stage times; then went to have a look.

Half a mile west of the Muskoka Road, along the shore of Muskoka Lake, a giant keel was laid. Up and down its 80 foot length men were setting in posts to form the framework. Cutting, hauling and hammering they swarmed around like bees at a hive. We were astonished to see this great ship coming to life right in the Muskoka backwoods, on our own lakeshore.

"How long will it take to build?" I asked one of the workmen.

"She'll sail in the Spring," he answered confidently.

"Who's the builder?"

"Why, Mr. A.P. Cockburn," he replied, seemingly surprised that I had to ask.

I lost another shred of my self-respect.

"And that's not all, he added, "he's also building a new store on the main street, and a lumber mill around the Bay. Gravenhurst is coming into its own."

The man's pride showed through, and I felt once more the lack of worth that Decimus had built in me. This Cockburn was too smart; but I had to admit to myself that he got action.

It was time for Harvie's stage to leave for Orillia, and we had to go. But all the way to Orillia they talked about Cockburn and the steamboat. We arrived late in the day and took a hotel room. Next day we went about the business we had come for. I found a very fine rooster and three hens to improve my flock. I got a sack of feed grain to supplement the pickings around my yard. I bought some newspapers and a few trinkets for Christmas gifts for neighbour children. It was exciting to see Orillia; all the stores, hotels, blacksmith shops and feed mills. It was the commercial centre of the North. I felt elated when the day was over. My friends were pleased too; their business had gone well.

After dinner we sat at the bar a while.

"It's dull here," one of them complained, "let's go and look for some women."

"Where?" I asked curiously.

"We know a place. Want to come?"

Right then I should have said no. I should simply have gone to bed. But I was keyed up and curious, and the way he put it sounded interesting.

"Sure," I said, and we took off into the night.

I had no idea where we were going, so I just followed along in the darkness. They finally came to a house and knocked on the door. Someone half opened it, and when they saw my friends we all went in. There was a sort of waiting room with a sofa, a couple of chairs and a coal oil lamp.

"You wait here," said my friends and they went into another room.

I took off my overcoat and sat down on the sofa. There was laughter coming from inside and I felt annoyed at my friends for leaving me alone. But in a couple of minutes the door opened and someone came out. The perfume of violets crossed the room. A woman came toward me and I stood up. She took my hands in a very friendly way, and I felt a thrill pass through me. Her hands were warm and soft.

"Why don't you sit down," she said, "it's much more comfortable."

"That's very kind."

"Do you mind if I sit beside you?" she asked. I didn't mind at all. She was still holding my hand. It was something new to meet such a friendly woman. All my life females had played coy with me; gasping, frowning, turning away if I came too close. This one was different.

A shadow of doubt flitted across my mind. "Too easy; too easy," it whispered. But I cast the doubt aside. It occurred to me that my friends had told her about me, and she was impressed. Yes, she wants to be better acquainted with such a well-travelled person. She wants to hear about the far reaches. Anyway, a woman so gentle and friendly couldn't be one of . . . those. I relaxed.

"And do you live alone?" she asked.

"Yes, I'm sorry to say."

"And do you come to Orillia often?"

"Not often, I'm afraid. Much of my travelling is in the hinterland."

"Tell me about it."

As I started talking she snuggled up close to me. It was wonderful to have someone who really cared. I had been so lonely for so long. I put my arm around her shoulder, and she came closer. I noticed that she was wearing no heavy undergarments and her warm body was pressed close against me. The touch of her bosom against my chest aroused my desires. I suddenly remembered Anne, standing by the river bank, as I had seen her on that oft-remembered day. It was easy to think that Anne was in my arms. I stopped talking and we held each other close.

"Come with me," she said finally, taking me by the hand.

The warning bell rang sharply inside me, but I refused to listen. I got up to go with her. At that moment the front door opened and a man lurched in.

"Hey," he yelled when he saw us, "get away from my girl."

"I'm not your girl," she answered, holding onto my arm.

"I'll show you whose girl she is," he shouted, coming at me. Sixteen months I had wielded an axe in the forest. My body was strong and my hands hard. I had never before struck a man in anger. But then I did. I hit him on the chin with all my might, and he collapsed on the floor without another sound.

I stood there a moment in shock. Brawling over a woman! What a terrible way to lose the respect I had built up. Decimus would disown me, and rightly. My friends in Draper would be shocked. But it was done, and I couldn't undo it. So I picked up my coat, opened the door and went out without a word.

When my friends got back to the hotel they were ecstatic. "Man, what a blow! The fellow was out for five minutes. Everybody wanted to know who you were."

"And did you tell them?"

"We never saw you before in our lives."

"Let's keep it that way."

"Right. We'll never breathe a word."

All the same, I was nervous for the next couple of weeks. When nobody came looking for me, and I heard no rumours, I felt easier. But I was all churned up inside. What with my public appearances, and my contact with A.P. Cockburn, I had emerged into the limelight. But it had brought no glow of satisfaction, just humiliation. And my efforts with women had been a disaster. Right then I thought seriously of retreating to the safety of my homestead in the forest and staying there. But that was not to be.

CHAPTER 5
CONFEDERATION

I might have gone along serenely in life; I would never have got into the mess I did, had it not been for George F. Gow. He arrived in Bracebridge some time in the early winter of 1866, and we soon knew he was there.

Gow was a tall, lean, hard-looking man who seemed older than his 32 years. He had a quick tongue, was sarcastic and intolerant of those he did not agree with. Where he came from, nobody knew; why he came up here was never explained. He claimed to be a Scotsman born in England and he went to the English church. There were rumours that he had been chased out of the place from whence he came, but these may have been malicious invention. He made no effort to please anyone, either by care with his words or concern for the feelings of others. He spoke his mind freely and went at his business directly. He opened a little store on the main street.

While no bundle of geniality, Gow was no recluse either. The first time I saw him was in the post office. He came right over while I was still wondering who he was. "My name's Gow," he said, holding out his hand, "George F. Gow."
"R.J. Bell," I replied, "I live out Uffington way."
"Glad to meet you Bell," he said, looking me up and down, "what are you doing out there?"

It struck me at first as a silly question. What else would a man be doing in Uffington besides farming? But then, perhaps he didn't see any ordinary root-stumper, and that made me feel good. "I've got a shanty out there," I answered, "and I do some farming and gardening. I'm pretty good at writing and figures too. Help out the local people with their problems."
"Quill driver, eh?" Gow cackled scornfully, and when he saw me wince, he added, "damn useful type to have around though."
His directness left me without an answer. That didn't bother him.
"Do you belong to the Lodge?" he asked, hardly pausing.

"Certainly do."

"Well we've just got organized here," he explained, "come in some Wednesday night."

"Thanks, I will."

"And how do you think John A will make out in the next election?" he went on, innocently enough. I knew what he was driving at. He could have asked my politics right out, but that was too much even for Gow.

"Oh, he'll win, never fear," I assured him.

Gow was enthusiastic; everything was falling into place. He reached out and pumped my arm vigorously.

"You should do well around here, Bell," he exclaimed, "I like the cut of your jib."

It was damned presumptuous for a man who had no more than arrived.

"Good of you to say so," was all I could think of.

"Consider me a friend," he went on, "I have quite a bit of influence around here. Call on me if you need anything."

And then he was gone. I realized he had learned all he wanted to know about me and told me nothing about himself.

But I heard more about Gow in the days that followed. He was an enthusiastic supporter of John A. Macdonald, and was an excellent campaign organizer. He had worked, they said, in several elections. This interested me. In spite of my experience with Cockburn, in fact because of it, I craved political insight. And there was a man who could give it to me. Within a week I met him again, this time in the Royal, and decided to plumb the depths of his knowledge.

"John A. has certainly changed the face of the Tory party," I began earnestly, anxious to impress him, "I'm told that when he was first elected in 1844 the party was the sole preserve of the Family Compact, the English clergy and the well-to-do. But he has taken in people of moderate views, Frenchmen and even Reformers. The change of name to Liberal-Conservative shows it is a party open to all."

"Well!" Gow grunted, without so much as a comment.

"The Tories condemn him for taking in moderates, and the

Orangemen for catering to the Catholics." I was wavering a bit in the face of his silence. "Don't you think that's a fair statement."

Gow looked disgusted.

"You figurin' on taking over the party?" he demanded.

"Of course not."

"Then leave them things to the leaders."

"Shouldn't a man know the policies of his party?"

"Why?"

"Well, he just should."

"Can you figure them out?"

"No," I admitted, "that's why I'm asking you."

"Don't ask me, I'm just interested in politics."

I was puzzled, and probably looked it. He let me think about it for a while. Then he asked me:

"You want to know about politics?"

I nodded my head.

"You win elections," he said.

"That's all?"

"That's all. And after one election is over, you get ready for the next one."

"And how do you win elections?" I asked curiously.

"Now you're askin' the right questions," he replied, coming to life. "You twist arms, spread rumours, threaten voters who scare easy and bribe the ones who don't. At the polls you get the right people for D.R.O.s and poll clerks, pack the poll that nobody's watching and start fights to scare away the other side. That's for starters. Then there's some finer points it takes a while to learn. I'll show you some day if you're interested."

I sat there stunned. He watched me with grim satisfaction as it churned around in my mind. The man was unscrupulous!

"Do those things win elections?"

"Every time. Especially the rumours. Dirty rumours," he repeated, settling down in his chair, "you tell a man something straight and he won't believe it. But let it come to him as a rumour and he swallows it hook, line and sinker. Take George Brown, for example. He sits down there in his Globe office in

Toronto and writes all that high-minded stuff about policies. Where did it ever get him? John A. beats him every time. It only works when he prints dirt. When he writes things about John A. giving in to the Catholics, it even gets me mad. Last December Brown quit the coalition, because he was jealous of John A. Now he's starting a campaign to get all Liberals out of the coalition. It won't be long till the Globe gets back to the dirt again. You can tell when he's desperate; he fills the paper with rumours."

"So you do read the papers?"

Gow looked at me sort of funny.

"Listen, Bell, I may talk like a clod, and look like a clod, but I'm not. Don't forget that, because I may never admit it again."

He got up from his chair abruptly and walked out the door. Our discussion of politics was over.

That winter and spring Cockburn's boat was the talk of the district. The hull was closed in, the decks were laid and the big engine and paddle-wheels arrived by six-horse teams from the South. She was ready for her maiden voyage the third week in June. I struggled the whole time against the resentment that filled me. The man had made a fool of me and I couldn't forget it. But I kept my feelings to myself because everyone else was praising him to the skies. When the big day came I went down to Gravenhurst to watch the proceedings. Perhaps I should forgive and forget; after all I had brought it on myself. And when I saw that boat I was glad I had come.

There she sat in the waters of Muskoka Bay, a giant among the rowboats and sailboats that surrounded her. There was a hissing of steam from the engine room as they fired up her boilers. The lower deck, at dock level, housed engine, freight and crew. The upper deck was open, with chairs laid out aft; the wheelhouse was up front. Amidship the giant paddles were enclosed in a circular frame the entire height of the vessel, and across the centre of the frame was painted her name, "Wenonah." They passed out posters on the dock claiming that she grossed 83 tons, travelled ten miles an hour and car-

ried passengers free today. Other times it cost fifty cents for a
settler to journey up the lake.

They finally took the chain off the gangplank and people
started to go aboard. I decided I might as well go along. At the
top of the gangplank the purser asked my name.

"Bell," I said, "Richard J. Bell."

"I don't have you down here," he said, looking at his list.

"I just came to look around."

"Only certain people were invited," he explained, not moving
out of the way.

People were looking at me, so I turned around and went
ashore. I was seething. All my resentment flooded back. I
couldn't even get on Cockburn's boat.

I didn't have long to wait for satisfaction. Three weeks later
the Wenonah piled up on the rocks at the Muskoka River entrance. Right then I decided to test Gow's theories.

"I guess that fellow was right," I mentioned to H.J.
McDonald, "if she won't pay one way, she can pay another.'

"I don't get your drift," he declared.

"I don't know exactly," I explained, "but I heard a fellow
saying that. He also said the Wenonah was well insured."

"I see," said McDonald, suddenly getting the point.

By nightfall the news was all over. Cockburn had run the
Wenonah aground for her insurance. I was astounded that
anybody would believe it. Gow was right. Spreading rumours
brings results.

I didn't rely on Gow alone for my education. He obviously
worked in a narrow field, and though I found his ideas useful,
they didn't entirely appeal to me. Gow didn't care what people
thought about him; I did. So I discussed things with Matt
Patterson; he had been in Canada quite a while, and had a lot
of common sense.

It was then November of 1866, and John A. Macdonald was
in England, along with Cartier from Lower Canada, Tilley
from New Brunswick and Tupper from Nova Scotia. They
were making a final effort to tie up a Confederation of the provinces. Not many people thought they would succeed; it had

been dragging on for so long. John A. was Chairman of the conference, and Matt was sure he would bring things off. "He persuades people to his way of thinking where nobody else can," Matt assured me, "he gives each man due attention, but still presses on to his goal."

"Don't his weaknesses let him down?" I asked, and we both knew I referred to John A's drinking. "His weakness is his strength," declared Matt, "people don't resent him. He has his faults and admits them. No man feels that John A. is superior. He's not like George Brown and that tight-lipped Grit Mackenzie, who think they can do no wrong. He's human."

"But doesn't that lower respect for him?"

"No. It's hard to explain," he answered, thinking hard, "he's also strong and determined. In fact, nobody has succeeded in putting him down. Even when he seems defeated, he always comes back. That's the combination of things that make him great."

"So you believe he'll pull the provinces together?"

"Absolutely; he has the Governor General over there to buck up the faint-hearted, and even our enemies are helping things along. These raids across the border by the Fenians have everybody worried. England would rather unite us for defence than send troops to defend us."

I had read a lot of this in the papers, but Matt could boil it down into a few words. I decided to ask him about something else. George Gow's election tactics didn't seem right for a man like John A. Macdonald.

"Does John A. know what goes on at elections?" I asked curiously.

"Does he ever!" exclaimed Matt, "he jumps into them with both feet."

"But there's a lot of dirty work goes on."

"That there is; they all do it, Tories, Grits, the lot. But John A. is the best."

"I don't remember things like that in England," I said regretfully, "but then, an ordinary man has little part in it there." It seemed wrong that great men like John A. Macdonald allowed the kind of thing that Gow had described.

"He's got to win elections," Matt explained, seeing that I was disappointed, "otherwise he wouldn't be in power. Then we'd have some foolish Grit like Brown running the place. He did it once and fouled things up for years."

Matt always spoke sense, so I accepted his word. I found it strange that he agreed with Gow on this. My political education was definitely expanding.

The following February the conference in England reached an agreement, and then the papers were full of news: a Kingdom called Canada; a House of Commons in Ottawa, just like in England; Assemblies in each province. Upper Canada would be Ontario, Lower Canada Quebec. Elections were being called for the Commons and the Assemblies. We would now have two Members, one in Ottawa and one in Toronto.

We became enveloped in politics then. Candidates began to move for position and to declare themselves. With my new knowledge of politics, I watched things eagerly. Perhaps there was a place for me in all this.

Things were happening locally too. We had no municipal status in Draper or Macaulay townships, and a move to incorporate them began to take shape. When a meeting was called in Bracebridge early in 1867 I saw an opportunity to push myself forward. I went to the meeting early, and made the rounds. I was excited to find that people greeted me warmly, and I knew almost everyone there. Just as I began to feel the acceptance of the people, in walked A.P. Cockburn. It sure spoiled things.

When I got over the initial shock, I wondered why he was there. He had no interest in Draper or Macaulay. His docks were at Gravenhurst; his store and sawmill were in Gravenhurst, and his home was there too. But George Gow was at the meeting, and he smelled things right away.

"Do you know that man Cockburn?" he asked me.

"Not too well," I admitted, "I met him once, to my sorrow."

"What's his party?"

"He sounded like a Grit to me. But he should be a Tory. John A's government has given him a lot."

"That's true. And now they've given him something else. Muskoka was added to North Victoria provincial riding under the Confederation bill. He's the only man with connections over there and here too. They've practically handed him the riding."

"Would he want it?"

"Would he? He'd just love to get his fingers into all the pies; government contracts, patronage, influence."

"Can we stop him?" I asked hopefully.

"Not likely, if he wants to. But maybe we can squeeze him in the right direction."

Aside from Cockburn's presence, the meeting was a success. Everybody was in agreement; we needed to incorporate. Cockburn was up and down, making suggestions, giving opinions. He mentioned his municipal experience in Eldon Township and offered it to Muskoka. We passed a resolution asking that the Townships of Draper, Macaulay, Ryde and Oakley be formed into a municipality with its own council.

When the meeting was over, Gow walked up to Cockburn. "My name's Gow," he began, "and this is Richard J. Bell. I believe you have met."

Cockburn looked at me without any expression.

"How do you do," he said.

"We think you would make an excellent candidate for the Assembly," Gow went on, "would you be interested in running?"

I was astounded at the man's nerve. Cockburn appeared surprised too.

"It's an honour to be asked," he admitted, "who do you represent?"

"No formal group," replied Gow, "we aren't really organized here. But we favour Confederation and support the union government."

That was clear enough.

"I support Confederation too," Cockburn agreed, "your proposition is very interesting."

He turned to talk to someone at his elbow.

"Why on earth did you do that?" I asked Gow, "you don't have any authority."

"He's going to run anyway," replied Gow, "that's why he's here. We might as well get to him first."

I saw my own chances dashed before they were even raised. And sure enough, before he left Cockburn came back to us.

"I've been thinking about your suggestion," he said to Gow, "I trust I can count on your support if I run."

"I asked you, didn't I?" Gow assured him, giving Cockburn a hearty whack on the back.

Cockburn winced, either from the blow or from the contact. He turned and left the meeting.

Now if Cockburn thought he could avoid George Gow that easily, he was mistaken. Gow kept up the pressure for a commitment to John A. Macdonald's unionist cause. And Cockburn kept dodging. Even after the Confederation bill went to the Imperial Parliament on February 12th, 1867, Cockburn hadn't declared himself. He should have, because there was a lot of satisfaction over Confederation, and John A. Macdonald was a national hero. In our part of the country his candidate would be a sure winner.

Cockburn dropped comments that he might consider running for the new Riding of North Victoria.

"We're right behind him," Gow stated when he heard it, "I have a deal with him."

That statement got right back to Cockburn, who didn't let it pass. He made another statement.

"It's true the Conservatives have asked me to be their candidate," he declared, "and so have the Liberals. I seem to be the unanimous choice."

But he chose no party.

I really wanted to understand the issues, so I went and talked to McMurray.

"Brown is put out at his own Members," McMurray told me, "he considers those who are staying in the coalition with Macdonald are traitors."

"Why would that be?" I asked, "he started it all himself. He was the first coalitionist. It happened when I first came up here."

"That's true, but now that confederation is achieved, he thinks it time to go back to the party system. Otherwise Reform will die, swallowed up by John A. Macdonald. He only wants one party - his."

I could see the point, and nodded my agreement. McMurray seemed pleased, and asked if I was interested in Reform. "Not exactly," I said, "but I like to know both sides." He seemed satisfied, and I congratulated myself for keeping in with everybody.

Where Cockburn stood, however, remained a mystery. He had certainly worked for the Grits; he told me so himself at that memorable meeting at the Royal. He had also managed to wheedle a shipping monopoly from Macdonald. Could he run against him now?

On March 4th, 1867 the Imperial Parliament gave second reading to the British North America Act. On April 29th, Queen Victoria gave Royal Assent. And in May Her Majesty appointed John A. Macdonald to be First Minister of Canada, effective on July 1st. He would form a cabinet in Ottawa, set up provincial governments and then hold general elections. Still Cockburn avoided George Gow, made no party decision and lost the opportunity to join with the jubilant Macdonald forces. The campaign linking Brown with opposition to Confederation was successful, and Brown's candidate would get mighty few votes in Muskoka.

Early in June, John A. Macdonald announced he would continue the coalition and form a "no party" government. He offered ministries in his new cabinet to several Reformers, and they accepted. Brown called them traitors, and he was joined by Alexander Mackenzie, a Grit Member in the Assembly. Together they called a Reform Party convention in Toronto for the 27th day of June, a last ditch stand to get the Reformers out of the government. They were particularly after Howland and McDougall, men of high virtue and standing, who had accepted Macdonald's offer. They were put on the platform, ridiculed, pressured and finally kicked out of the Reform Party. But they stood firm, and the Brown forces were in turmoil, split down the middle and with no policy except opposition to the men who created our country.

And the most amazing thing of all was that A.P. Cockburn still sat the fence.

The antics of the Reformers put no damper on Dominion Day. There were celebrations everywhere. In Muskoka the day broke bright and clear and the settlers from our townships all headed for Bracebridge. The village had become the hub of the surrounding townships without any formality. The Wenonah landed daily at the wharf. People came in to do their business and shopping. The storekeepers were an energetic lot, and for this occasion they organized a big Dominion Day program.

I came in with a group from Uffington. We watched as they ran off the races in front of Willson's store. We cheered as the children ran in the hundred yard dash, stumbled through the sack race and scraped their chins in the wheelbarrow race. It was a real family day, and I felt a little bit lonely. When the races were over they blew up the anvil. It went flying into the air as a charge of gunpowder was set off under it. When the smoke cleared they did it again. Lemonade, made from ice cold spring water and real lemons, was served free. The sun shone; people strolled around and chatted or relaxed under the trees.

At three o'clock they had the speeches. My friend, H.J. McDonald "just about the first man here" was made the Chairman. He called on several local celebrities, and they made fine patriotic addresses.

"Three Cheers for the Queen," McDonald called when the speeches were over. We all gave three loud cheers and a tiger. "Three cheers for the new Dominion," he shouted again, and the forest echoed with the sound.

Then everyone packed up and went home to do the chores.

George Gow looked around for Cockburn during the celebrations. He wanted to put him on the spot publicly about his party affiliations. But Cockburn didn't show up, and Gow had to content himself with asking loudly where Cockburn was and why he avoided Bracebridge.

It couldn't have been that great a time for Cockburn. We didn't know then about the letter he had written to George Brown on March 7th of that year. It was ingratiating, high in its praise of Brown, the Globe newspaper and the Reform movement. He asked for Brown's support in his bid for election in North Victoria. When it became public later, you could see the spot Cockburn had put himself in.

"Dear Sir: I had the honour and pleasure of an introduction to you last July in Ottawa . . . I may be a candidate for the North Riding of Victoria in the local parliament. I have always been a staunch Reformer and a warm admirer of yourself and the Globe newspaper . . . I became very interested in the prospects for Muskoka, and induced my father to join me in constructing a steamer and a saw mill . . . I am thoroughly acquainted with the riding, of which I fancy I have a greater knowledge than any other well known man. I have been universally popular . . . I request your influence on my behalf should I be the candidate chosen by the Liberals. Yours very sincerely, A.P. Cockburn."

All along Cockburn had been secretly committed to George Brown and the Reformers, Liberals, Grits, or whatever else they called themselves. As Brown lost ground and the party split up, he must have been sick. He could never run on an anti-Confederation ticket in Muskoka. And he could hardly run for Macdonald after that letter. But he wanted to run for somebody.

Perhaps Cockburn thought that things would improve; that before the election the winds would change and blow more in Brown's direction. Then he could declare himself. But he was in for a shock.

CHAPTER 6
ACCEPTANCE

The light was fading through the single dingy window of a shanty on the concession road. The place was damp in spite of the summer warmth outside. It smelled of the soil; musty, earthy. Rotting wood, damp moss from the logs, earthen floor, stale human odours and no ventilation combined to make the place stifling. It was a familiar smell in settlers' shanties, but here it was specially oppressive. I was anxious to leave.

"Now you just sign there, Mr. Sheppard," I said as I pointed with my finger, "I don't think they'll come on your land again."

"It's wonderful to have an educated man around here," he declared as he wrote his name in a childish scrawl, "I wouldn't know how to write this letter at all."

"I'm always ready to help out," I answered.

"That's what we all like about you, Mr. Bell," he said, "you're still willing to help out an ordinary man. You certainly understand business and politics, and you travel a lot. I wouldn't be surprised to see you in politics."

"I'm very interested in those things," I agreed.

"Well, we're all behind you around here."

His words raised my spirits above the depression of the place. It was worth while after all to do these neighbourly acts. Stone upon stone, I was building the foundation for my career. One by one, I was adding to my stock of friends and admirers. When the time came, all this would be remembered. The man opened his creaky, handmade door and stood aside for me to leave.

"You really shouldn't do all this, Mr. Bell," he said gratefully, "you have your own place to look after."

His words were well meant, but they cut me like a knife. My own place, yes, I should be thinking of that. The truth was that my crops that year were a failure. What could I do about the cucumbers, the tomato plants, and the corn, all destroyed by a late frost? Why hadn't somebody warned me about that? And my tiny potato patch, with one piece of potato in each hill. How could I complain when I had eaten into my seed potatoes in late winter? And the acres I had so strenuously won from the forest - they were covered with scrub and fireweed. Mr. McMurray had warned me about that; but even five acres was too much.

Of course, I wasn't the only one; it was happening to my neighbours too. We struggled mightily, but nature was always in motion, winning from us even as we slept. I wanted so badly to have some money for Decimus this year, to pay back something of what he had lent me. But there wasn't much chance now; I'd be lucky to get through next winter. My farming was a losing battle. Yes, I had my own place to look after, but I wasn't doing it very well. I came back to the present with a start and realized the poor man was still standing there, waiting for me to go.

"My own place," I said aloud, "yes, I have to think of that."

"It's been bad for everybody," he consoled me, "but you have your education and a great future."

"That puts no food on the table."

"Not today," he said, "but I'll be proud to know you tomorrow. If you can't farm, you can do something else."

He meant it kindly, but when I thought about it later, it wasn't much of a compliment. Unconsciously he had spoken the truth, though. I was half way between farming and something else. I went home depressed.

But the world took another turn, and the news from Toronto stirred me up again. A Premier for Ontario had been appointed and the elections were called. I slipped away from my struggling acres with no regrets and took off for Bracebridge. The time had come for "something else".

"I can't believe it," Gow cried out the minute I saw him, "Sandfield Macdonald is Premier, the last person on earth I expected."

"Isn't he a Catholic?" I asked.

"Not only that; he's a Reformer and an old crony of George

Brown," Gow exploded, "he fought against Confederation right to the wire. Can you beat that for Ontario's first Premier? I don't know what John A. - I mean Sir John - was thinking about."

"Does that mean Sandfield is supporting Sir John?"

"Must."

"I guess he knows what he's doing."

"Maybe he does," Gow declared, "but what about me? How can I go out and ask Tories to vote for Sandfield? They always voted against him."

"Maybe you could ask Grits to vote for Sandfield," I suggested, more as a joke than anything, "and tell Tories they're really voting for Sir John."

His mouth fell open, then closed again.

"By God, that's it," he shouted, "I can see it all now. We've got both sides with us."

As the whole thing fell together, Gow became more and more excited. Nothing delighted him more than an underhanded scheme to trap voters. Now he recognized the hand of a master. "Cockburn!" he exclaimed suddenly, "he's got to come with us now. He hasn't anyone else."

"He's got Brown."

"Brown! Brown! Who would go with Brown? The man's dead. John A. has mangled him."

And it certainly looked that way. The Macdonalds formed a working partnership for the elections. Their candidates in Ontario could be either Conservative or Liberal, so long as they supported the coalition. They made deals with local political parties; the federal seat for a Conservative, the provincial seat for a Liberal, or vice versa. Everybody jumped to get on the bandwagon. Party lines went down the drain. George Brown's declared candidates could only get support among the die-hards, for Brown had nothing to offer. His nightmare became reality.

But in Muskoka, Cockburn made no move to the unionists. He said only that he was his own man, and ran on his record as Muskoka's benefactor and Victoria's favourite son. His

Reform views, he added, were well known.

As soon as Gow learned that Cockburn was running as a Liberal of some kind, he jumped in behind a Conservative named Joseph Staples. Gow went right to the nomination meeting and proposed Staples' name. I went along with him to second the motion, but somebody else from Victoria county did it. Of course Cockburn was there and when it was over, they had words.

"You played me false," Cockburn accused Gow, "you promised me your support."

"I never said I'd support no damn Grit," Gow answered angrily, "you're the one who did the double-crossing."

"You put no limit on it," said Cockburn, "your words were quite clear. If I ran, you would support me."

There were a lot of people around, and Gow began to get in his licks right away.

"Well I never thought you'd work against Confederation," he declared.

"I'm not against Confederation," Cockburn shouted angrily, "stop twisting facts."

"Then why aren't you backing Sandfield Macdonald?"

Cockburn opened his mouth to answer, but thought better of it. The issues were too complicated to put into a word or two.

"You can't see beyond your noses, any of you," he declared, and swept away indignantly.

I suppose he was right in avoiding explanations. Gow went out and worked his head off for Staples, but it did no good. Cockburn was well known and Staples wasn't. Cockburn had jobs to offer in mill and boat, and he used all the influence that gave him. But even more, he played both sides of the fence. His election address, for example, which he published in all the local papers, left him firmly on all sides. "In politics I am independent," he wrote, "I have no other desire than to serve you impartially and faithfully." He did not run for the union government or the Macdonalds, but he declared:

"I consider Confederation is a great boon, particularly in the

66

local legislature.''

While the Grits, led by George Brown, were calling for dissolution of the coalition, and crying havoc, Cockburn denied them.

''I will exercise my utmost efforts to make our new constitution work.''

But Cockburn didn't limit himself to the national issues. He put up a good program for the riding too. He wanted a better homestead law, more free grants to bring in settlers, mining development and better transportation. These were things we all wanted.

He had to do something to satisfy the Grits in the Riding, so he took a little knock at John A.'s former ministry. ''I am opposed to the system adopted lately in the management of our Crown lands, and immigration.'' But that was as far as he went. During the whole election campaign of August, '67, Cockburn straddled the fence. He said nothing to annoy the Conservatives but let the Liberals know he was a Liberal. He acted as if there were no issues, no parties, no differences; just Alexander Peter Cockburn, the man who did so much for Muskoka.

''Lily-livered bastard,'' Gow exclaimed, ''why doesn't he come out and fight.''

''Maybe he doesn't have to,'' I said, knowing the local feelings. Gow glowered at me indignantly, but made no reply. He'd never admit defeat till the last vote was counted. And when it was, Cockburn won easily, 676 votes to 407 for Staples.

It was a hollow victory for Cockburn, because Sir John won the House of Commons easily and Sandfield took Ontario in a walk. The Macdonald team was in full control. George Brown was out completely. I couldn't see Cockburn lasting long on the outside of things, and that's where he was. I hoped he would soon tire of it and give somebody else a chance.

Well, sir, I wasn't much for Reformers, but that Sandfield Macdonald, with Sir John's backing, made things move in Ontario. He had majority support in the Assembly and a determination to change things. Luckily for us, he believed that the way of progress was development of the north, and Muskoka soon began to reap the harvest. His program included a campaign at home and abroad to settle Muskoka, provision of government facilities, passage of a new homestead law and much more. They opened up a Crown Lands office on Dominion Street in Bracebridge shortly after the election and I went in to look around. As I opened the office door I heard a voice booming out from the dimness. "Charlie, he says to me, I'm going to send you up among the Indians and the bears to open up the country."

It was a rough voice, with the hoarseness of a throat burned too often with raw spirits. I stopped in the doorway, feeling I had interrupted a private conversation. I could see a pair of boots propped on a rickety table, their owner leaning back in his chair. There was a glass in his hand and a cigar hanging from his lips. He looked at me without stirring.

"Well, what do you want?" he asked abruptly.

"I'm looking for the Crown Lands office."

"You're in it. Shut the door."

He went on with his conversation.

"So that's what Sandfield said to me, sitting there in his office in the Parliament Buildings. I couldn't let an old friend down, so here I am; all my legal education thrown out the window."

The front legs of his chair suddenly slammed to the floor and he got to his feet.

"Well, I got business," he said. His visitor took the hint and left. I asked to see the list of available Crown lands. He threw a book on the table.

"That'll be a quarter," he said.

I was surprised.

"I thought the Crown lists were free," I objected.

"You never heard that from me," he declared, "and I'm the only authority around here."

He went back and picked up a newspaper.

"You live around here?" he demanded.

"I live in Draper township," I answered, "name's Bell."

68

"Well, I'm Charles W. Lount," he announced, "and if you have any government business around here, I'm the man to see. As I was telling that man who was just in here . . . but I suppose you heard, eh?"

"Yes I did. I guess you're Crown Lands Agent."

"Crown Lands Agent, Justice of the Peace, Issuer of Provincial Licenses and Commissioner for Oaths," he declared, "and if you can think of anything else, I'm it."

The man was gruff, belligerent and high-handed. I knew he'd make enemies fast, but he was the government man and I had no desire to cross him. I was glad of that later. For now, at least, he represented law and order.

But before I made any judgment of Charles W. Lount, I had a question for him.

"Are you acquainted with our local Member, Mr. Cockburn?"

"You mean the Grit who sat on his ass while Sandfield struggled?"

"The very one," I agreed gleefully.

"No, I'm not, and I really don't care. I do my business with the Premier."

"Very pleased to meet you," I exclaimed, reaching for his hand, "very pleased indeed."

He seemed surprised for a moment, then took my hand and shook it warmly.

"What did you say your name was?" he asked.

"Bell."

"Glad to meet you, Bell. Drop in any time."

So it was established. Now I had two fighting fools for friends.

It didn't take long for Lount to get in trouble with the local Grits. But a few things kept them silent. Premier Sandfield Macdonald, only a month in office, had recognized the worth of Muskoka and sent up a government man. You couldn't complain about that. And sending him to Bracebridge made it the capital of Muskoka. That was a victory. Things were moving along nicely, and nobody wanted to halt progress.

Just a week later Decimus landed. I knew why he came, he wanted money. Not to borrow, but on account. For about two minutes I was glad to see my brother again. We shook hands and he came into the shanty.

"Haven't done much," he commented right away, "I suppose you've been saving your pennies for a payment."

"It's been a bad year," I began, but he cut me off.

"Never mind the sad stories. How much have you got for me?"

"Nothing."

His sallow face flushed, and he half rose from his chair. I knew he was very angry.

"Listen," he commanded, "I've bought two more lots, right on the lake. This could be made into a good ranch if you got off your butt and did something."

"It takes time."

"Why didn't you grow some oats? They bring a good price."

"I tried oats," I explained, "but the soil isn't suitable."

"You've got all sorts of chickens clucking around. Don't you sell eggs, or do you eat them all yourself?"

"The poultry looks real promising," I exclaimed brightly, "next year I should have eggs to sell."

"Next year, next year. What about now?"

"Right now, nothing's paying."

"My God," he exclaimed dolefully, shaking his head, "I never saw such incompetence."

"We're not all as smart as you."

"Don't flatter me. It won't work."

We quarrelled for four days, bitter, angry words followed by long periods of silence. It was all so familiar that our childhood came flooding back. Decimus, the smart one, always doing and saying the right thing; Richard, the awkward one, fumbling and making excuses. I had almost grown to maturity before I realized that Decimus was the cause of my problems. He did little tricks to me, and then complained to our parents. Now he was belittling me in another way. He worried at me like a dog at sheep. He remarked on everything; the

70

condition of the shanty, wormy vegetables, the way I dressed. The fact that I owed him money on the lot seemed to give him the right to run me down. Eventually I could take it no more.

"Decimus, why don't you go home?"

"I like it here."

"You what?"

"I like it here. Why should I leave? It's really my place."

"So it is, and you can have it," I said, "work here a while and burn off your hate."

"Hate? I don't hate you. I'm just speaking for your own good."

"I don't need your advice."

"You need it from somebody."

When he had taken his money's worth in fault-finding, my brother decided to go back to Toronto. In spite of everything, I felt some remorse.

"I'm sorry I didn't have any money for you," I said as he left.

"I really didn't expect any," he replied, and I suddenly realized that was true. Money would have taken away his right to run me down; and he needed that for his own vain pride. I vowed that next time he came he'd have nothing to complain about.

But after he was gone, and I was alone again, I started thinking about Anne. Two years had passed without a whisper of her or her father in Muskoka. I had asked people as they came in from the far townships, but nobody knew them. My questions finally stirred up rumours, and people began to wonder about my strange concern for Mr. Mills and his daughter. Decimus, for all his hatefulness, at least kept my mind from her. When he had gone, the deep loneliness returned. I went miserably to bed.

And then I found her. She seemed to float towards me along that rough, stumpy road that led to my lonely cabin. She stretched out her arms to me and we melted together. I could feel the warm swell of her bosom against my chest; the smooth curve of her body against mine. I called her name in ecstacy; and the sound of my voice woke me from one of those night-

71

time dreams that lonely men encounter.

Oh God, I cried, why am I tortured like this? I am still alone. Anne is still lost. There were tears in my eyes as I fell back to sleep again.

A week later, still feeling my loneliness, still smarting from my brother's ridicule, I gained my first public position. In late October, when the crops were all in and the days were shortening towards winter, there was a gathering of the clans of Muskoka. Up from Severn Bridge came James H. Jackson its founder, and Moses David along with him; down from Humphrey township came George Milne; Richard Lance came in from Watt and David Hogabaum from Stephenson. Matthias Moore came down from Falkenburg and all the pioneers of Monck, Muskoka and Draper tramped in to Bracebridge. Provincial Member A.P. Cockburn came up from Gravenhurst. They were resolved to establish for our time a Settlers' Association.

"We should have someone keep the minutes," said H.J. McDonald, the Chairman, as the meeting began.

I got up right away.

"I will gladly help out," I offered, and they made me Secretary.

I wrote down what was said, and read it back when required. I worded resolutions so that they read sensibly. I undertook to write letters and receive replies. I summarized, when the Chairman requested it, the consensus of opinions on any subject. I felt that the meeting relied on my judgment.

After that, things began to happen in Muskoka and I took my rightful place in the community. The drive for local government, which I had pushed for months, was finally successful and the townships of Draper, Macaulay, Stephenson and Ryde were formed into one municipality. In December we had our first elections and Thomas McMurray was elected Reeve.

On New Year's day, 1868, I walked up to South Falls. At McMurray's place a welcoming gust of smoke swirled up from the chimney. The wind was cold and the snow was piled high in front of his house. But there was a path freshly shovelled out, and I knew he was home. When I knocked on the door he called out "come in, come in" and in I went. He was sitting comfortably by the stove, the fire crackling and the kettle steaming.

"What brings you out on a day like this?" he asked.

"I came up to wish you a Happy New Year, Mr. McMurray," I replied, "and to congratulate you on your election."

"That's very good of you," he said.

I stamped the snow off my boots and sat down by the kitchen table.

"The kettle's hot," he said, "I'll make some tea. I never take spirits, you know."

"I know, Mr. McMurray," I replied, "that's very commendable. I seldom touch them myself."

We chatted a while, and he seemed amused about something. Perhaps he guessed that I didn't walk eight miles for a cup of tea. Anyway he gave me the opening.

"We'll be having our first council meeting in a couple of weeks," he said.

"It's a great occasion for our people," I answered, "have the officers been chosen yet?"

"Strange that you showed up today," he mused, "I have just been thinking about a township clerk."

"And you thought of me?" I asked hopefully.

"Exactly," he answered, "you have been here for a while, and seem well qualified."

"It would be an honour to be the first clerk," I said.

He poured the tea and sat down. There was a long silence. I certainly didn't want to over do it, and I guess he didn't want to commit himself.

"It's up to the council, of course," he finally said, "but I will certainly suggest your name."

That was good enough for me. We chatted a while about various things, but I was ready to go. So I got up.

"Well I must be going," I said, "I'm sure you have a lot of things on your mind."

"Come to the council meeting and we'll see what happens," he suggested, "you might as well bring along a pen and some paper and at least you can take the minutes."
I thanked him for the opportunity and left.

In the end, my three years of friendship with Mr. McMurray paid off. When the council met, I was asked to take the minutes. I read out the agenda which Mr. McMurray had prepared. The first item was appointment of a Clerk.

"Are there any proposals?" the Reeve enquired.

"That should really be your choice," suggested councillor Matthias Moore.

"I asked Mr. Bell to take the minutes," McMurray said, "perhaps he would do a good job as Clerk."

"Carried," echoed the council; and I became the first Clerk of the united townships.

"Thank you, gentlemen," I said, "you can rely upon me to do the job."

I was elated. If only my smart-ass brother could see me now, sitting there at the council table, administering the affairs of the union. And A.P. Cockburn, he who knows everything, he'll have to deal with me now.

How I enjoyed those first months as Clerk. I wrote to the provincial government in Toronto about township affairs, signing my name in large bold letters, "R.J. Bell, Township Clerk". I received replies from departments of government in their formal script, and I could imagine the writers sitting in their offices in the big two-storey brick building on Front Street. I had been there once, in the days when the Assembly met in Quebec City and in Ottawa, and the building was just a backwater. But now the Ontario Assembly was held there, with all the authority of the Queen; and life had returned.

Our council began to put some order into township affairs. The only school was at Bracebridge so we set up boards for new school sections. That very year we had two new schools going, and one of them at Uffington. The local people saw my hand in that. We appointed pathmasters to keep our wretched roads passable, and fence viewers to settle boundary disputes among the settlers. We licensed taverns and dogs, and I became issuer of licenses as well.

When the Ontario Assembly met in Toronto early in the new year Premier Sandfield Macdonald's interest in the north became more apparent. The Free Grants and Homesteads Act was immediately placed before the Assembly and was passed in February of 1868. It was just what Cockburn had asked for. A settler who located a lot, cleared 15 acres, built a shanty and occupied it for five years, got his hundred acres free. He could buy another hundred for fifty cents an acre. He received a Patent from the Crown; his own land free and clear. It was something few settlers had ever possessed.

That was nothing A.P. Cockburn could complain about. Oh how he must have wished he could take credit for it! But it wasn't his Premier who brought it about. All Cockburn could do was strut around saying that was exactly what he had asked for; all the time sitting in the Opposition.

Sandfield stepped up his campaign to settle Muskoka. Throughout the province and beyond the seas the Province published advertisements telling the world about the free lands in Muskoka. People started to pour in.

We petitioned the province for a Division Court for our district, to settle disputes between settlers. A.P. Cockburn presented it. We got a Court and it was set up in April. Charles W. Lount, naturally, was appointed judge, and that must have torn a strip from Cockburn's vanity. But he managed to take credit for it anyway; not for the judge but for the Court. And even better, a great new provincial government square was planned for Bracebridge, Court House, Registry Office, Crown Lands Office and Gaol. Charles W. Lount was appointed Registrar of Deeds.

Things were moving and the people were satisfied. We were satisfied with our Premier; we were satisfied with our progress. Our local Member, A.P. Cockburn was reaping the benefits of Sandfield's leadership, running along like a little dog yapping, "me too, me too." There was little he could complain about and though he sat in the opposition he voted time and again with the ministry.

And me? Well our township grew in wealth and population, and I accepted my share of the credit.

"R.J." Matt Patterson said to me one Spring day, "we're mighty proud to have the Clerk of all the townships living here among us."

His words were music to my ears. I had arrived and the solid people of the community were behind me. There was no telling where it all might lead. But then, no man can read the future; and perhaps that's as well.

CHAPTER 7
ANNE

It happened so suddenly it left me weak. One day in March I was casually chatting with a neighbour when he remembered something.

"Oh, by the way," he said, "I met a friend of yours in Toronto a couple of weeks ago."

"Is that so?" I answered vaguely, "who was that?"

"I don't just remember her name. It was a young lady. Very nice."

I suddenly became curious. I didn't know that many young ladies.

"Where did you meet her?"

"Well, I was waiting for my wife in a Yonge Street dry goods store, and got talking to this salesgirl. When I said I was from Muskoka she asked if I knew you. I told her I most certainly did, you were our township clerk."

"And you don't remember her name?"

"No, it was a short name like Miles or Miller; you know, something like that," he recalled.

I went numb for a moment, my heart in my throat. I was almost afraid to ask.

"Was it Mills?"

"Mills. Yes, that's it," he exclaimed, brightening up, "Miss Mills. She was very interested. Asked a lot of questions."

My heart was pounding like a trip-hammer, and I felt a lump in my throat. He looked at me strangely, and I can imagine why. I felt like crying and shouting for joy at the same time. I wanted to shake his hand till it hurt, but I was also vexed at his carelessness. He had known about Anne for two whole weeks and hadn't even come to tell me. What if we hadn't happened to meet? How long would he have waited to tell me, if ever?

"Yes, she's a friend of mine," I said after a moment, getting hold of myself, " a very good friend. Where did you see her?"

He was quite vague about that.

"I don't know, exactly," he admitted, "my wife came along in a few minutes and we left. She might know the name of the place but I doubt it. She didn't talk to the girl; thought I was just flirting. We were into every damn store on Yonge Street."

I went through the rest of the day in a haze. Home at my cabin I lay down on the bed to savour the wonderful news, and to make plans.

"She was very interested." That made me feel warm all over. Anne still thought about me.

"Miss Mills." So she isn't married. Maybe she is waiting for me. But why has she never written? She knew where I was, even though she was lost to me. Surely she could guess what I had gone through in the past four years; how I had searched for her; longed for her. But then, how could she know? We were only together for 24 hours and I told her so little. Perhaps she thought I had forgotten her. I'd said so many things to myself over the years, things I should have told her. Now I couldn't remember exactly what I had said and what I had thought.

"Very interested. Asked a lot of questions."

I could remember every word he told me and it came back phrase by phrase. I forgot to ask him what her questions were. What did she want to know about me? What did he tell her?

"A dry goods shop on Yonge Street."

That's all he knew.

But Yonge Street isn't that long. It doesn't run for fifty miles like the Parry Sound Road. I'm good at searching; I can find her in Toronto. I decided right then to go.

Two days later, at the foot of Yonge Street I began my search. Working my way north, I went into every clothing and dry goods store, millinery and hat shop on the street. At each place I looked around carefully to see if Anne was there. Sales people came to wait on me, and I just looked at them, mumbled something about looking for a friend, and went out again. After a while I began to wonder if I would recognize her; it had been so long and my dreams had been dreams. Could that be her? or that? She would certainly have changed in four years. She would look much different in a store than in a fire on the Muskoka Road. So I started to ask for her by name.

"Does Miss Mills work here?"

Then I worried about walking up to Anne and asking, "does a Miss Mills work here?" as if I had never met her. But I put down my fears and kept going, determined not to be put off by such silly doubts.

But as people shook their heads and gave me that silly vacant stare I had met on my long trip to Parry Sound, all the hopelessness of that experience flooded back.

"No, I'm sorry, nobody by that name."

I began to regret my haste. Maybe I had missed her in those first shops when I only looked for her, and didn't ask. Perhaps I should start over again. Once more I put down my hestitations. No, I'd keep going, even if I had to do it all over again tomorrow. One thing I had learned and that was to push ahead.

Suddenly I saw her. It was no dream, I had no doubt. I walked into a shop and there she was by a counter near the door. The face so dear to me was clear in my memory after all. Everything flooded back as if we had parted just yesterday at the South Falls crossroads. She looked different, yet the same.

"I'm Richard Bell," I said walking toward her.

Her face lit up and she came to meet me with her hands out.

"I'm so glad to see you," she said, and I could tell she meant it.

"I must talk to you," my words spilled out, "I have so much to say to you."

She hesitated, then saw the panic in my face.

"Oh, I want to talk to you," she said hastily, "but it's terribly public here, and I have to work until six. They are very strict."

"I'll come back at six," I declared, and then blurted out recklessly, "anyway, maybe you won't need to work here any more."

She looked startled for a moment and then understood what I was saying. She didn't blush or act coy; just looked at me thoughtfully. I stayed no longer for she saw what was in my heart.

We met at six, had dinner together and talked and talked. Maybe it was foolish, I didn't care any more. I told her all about my thoughts, my dreams and hopes. I told her how I had looked for her, and tears came to her eyes. I went on without ceasing, a great torrent of words. Nothing was left out; I would not go back to my cabin and wish I had said something more.

She told me what had happened. The very next day after we parted, her father took ill. It was on the Muskoka Road, near the Parry Sound turnoff. A kind settler who lived a mile up the Muskoka Road had taken them in. They stayed a week and her father was still bad, pains in his chest, weakness and dizziness. They went back to Toronto and she nursed him for two years. And one day he died.

I couldn't reproach her, but I had to know.

"Did you ever think of me?" I asked.

"Many, many times," she answered "but I didn't know you cared."

"Did you ever think of writing?"

"I could see no point in it," she said, "my duty was to father."

"If you only knew how much I loved you."

"Did you love me?" she asked, "in one day? I was just a very bedraggled little girl. How could I guess? Maybe you loved a dream."

"No, no, I loved you then. I love you now."

She looked at me in that open, wonderful way I had seen before.

"I remember you kindly," she said, "I like you now. Perhaps our friendship can continue."

"That would please me very much" I replied, and the words sounded so very weak.

It was late as we walked to her door. We met again several times before I returned to Draper, and our friendship grew to affection. When I left, true love was ours.

As soon as I got home, I started building an addition to my cabin.

80

"Adding on an office?" the neighbours asked, and I said that could be. No one suspected the real reason and I decided not to tell them. If they thought I had nothing but my work, let them keep on thinking so. They were no longer teasing me about a blushing bride for they knew it hurt. But I was soon to give them a real surprise. One day, around the first of May, I went up to see my neighbour, Mrs. Patterson.

"I'm going away again for a while," I said "would you watch things for me."

"Certainly," she answered, "are you going to . . . "

She stopped right there, the joke was stale. And then I sprung my surprise.

"Yes," I said, "I'm getting married."

The surprise and pleasure in her face brought tears to my eyes. She reached out and embraced me; and then I was on my way.

We were married, Anne and I, on the 5th day of May, 1868 at Bond Street Congregational Church in Toronto. Even now I can remember every detail. A goodly number of people came, considering I was almost a stranger. It pleased me that Anne had so many friends. My brother Decimus was living in Toronto then, and his family was there to swell the ranks; his wife Janie, his son Richard 5, my namesake and little Anna Maria 3 who carried flowers. Decimus was well known in Toronto where he worked with the architects Gundy and Langley on Victoria Street. Quite a few of his friends came, and I was very grateful. Rev. Marling, minister of the church, performed the ceremony and then we signed the register:

Richard James Bell, age 35, Draper, Ontario

Anne Bumford Mills, age 25, Toronto, Ontario.

Witnesses: Decimus Bell; George T. Davis

I was surprised at my brother. He wasn't the same person at all when others were around. A bit odd-looking, as always, prim and proper, but some of the people there thought him droll. It turned out that Decimus had been boasting about me. Several people asked what it was like to hold such an important position in the newest and most northerly township in the whole province. Others asked me how well I knew the

Premier, who took such a special interest in our progress. I told them it was all very exciting. In a fleeting moment I realized that my position as clerk made Decimus a little more brotherly. It had been that way even as children. If I had a piece of candy or some extra pennies, his jealousy turned to fawning friendship. Nevertheless, I appreciated his kindness on my wedding day.

Anne was solemn and calm, and I thought her beautiful. Several times I found her looking at me with those bright, direct eyes of hers, as if seeing me for the first time. Then a quiver of excitement would run down my spine and into my stomach, ending, I am sure, in a blushing face. My wife! And as I went to stand beside her, I realized that I hardly knew her.

That came home to me in our downtown hotel room that night. When we were in bed, I realized that my long wait to hold her in my arms was over. This was Anne, my Anne. I reached over to put my arms around her.

"Don't," she said.

I lay quietly, confused.

"I won't be taken for granted," her voice came from the darkness.

Still I lay silent, not knowing what to say or do.

"We should have an understanding," she went on, "that I consider myself a person, not a chattel. My mind is my own, as well as my body."

"So your father told me," I said, finding my voice.

"My father told you?" she asked, and there was doubt in her voice, "when did he talk to you?"

"At McCabe's, while you rested inside."

"What else did he tell you?"

"He warned me that you were a jealous person."

"Why would he tell you those things about me?"

"He seemed to think we might marry."

She was silent a while, then reached for my hand.

"I'm glad of that," she said softly, "my father knew me well. Now we have a long day tomorrow and we should rest."

I was in turmoil. Part of it was anger. This was my wife,

turning me down on our wedding night. That was wrong. Part of it was disappointment. All those lonely nights were past and my dream had come true; but I never dreamed it would be like this. I had made some mistake, but it was too late. I had to insist on my rights or I would lose them forever. Yes, this is the time a man has to be a man. Even if she has her foolish ideas, I have to make the decisions. I had decided to assert myself when she spoke again.

"Richard?"

"Yes."

"You won't always find me so difficult, but I'm tired tonight. I'll be a good wife to you. But please don't take me for granted, and don't ever be disloyal to me. I once had a bad experience that I can't easily forget."

"I understand," I replied, forgiving, but not entirely forgetting.

She shifted closer to me in the bed and I could feel her warm body beside me. My anger and disappointment dissolved in anticipation of better things to come. I've often wondered if that was a mistake.

Next morning when I woke her arm was thrown lightly across my chest, and a thrill of excitement passed through me. She truly loved me after all.

We dressed and went to the railway station. I decided to take Anne by way of Bracebridge and then on into the country. The coach of the Northern Railway, sitting at the City Hall Station, was crowded. Anne went down the coach looking for a seat while I tended to the baggage. When I finally walked down the aisle, who should I see sitting with Anne but H. James McDonald from Bracebridge. They were chatting away as if they were old friends. Jim looked up in surprise when I stopped.

"This is my husband," Anne said rather proudly.

"Your husband!" exclaimed Jim, "he sure has kept it quiet."

"We were just married yesterday," Anne explained.

"Do you two know each other?" I asked, wondering where they had met.

"We do now," Jim answered, "I was half asleep when this beautiful Irish voice asked if the seat was taken. I had my feet on it."

"He jumped up so quick, his hat fell on the floor," added Anne, "and I stepped on it. We both laughed."

"And then we were friends," said Jim, "what a surprise this will be in Bracebridge."

"It's a little late in life for me," I admitted, "but it's never too late for a good thing."

Nothing could have pleased me more than their friendship.

I sat there glowing with pride. Anne was beautiful. She wore a stylish grey travelling suit, with long full skirt, slim at the waist and full above. The lace of a fancy blouse showed at her wrists and throat. Her hair was piled neatly, and her hat was a large flowery thing that looked magnificent. Her hands were neat and firm, and she proudly displayed the wedding band on her finger. I could see Jim McDonald look at her from time to time, and his admiration showed in his face.

We chatted as the engine puffed into action and the train moved out of the station yard. The little houses behind the board fences began to thin out, and soon we were in the country. Anne was delighted to meet a man from Bracebridge, one of the pioneers, too. He told her all about the village and its beginnings. We stopped at the little stations along the line. The bustle of the early morning kept us peering out the windows. In no time at all, we reached Bell Ewart on Lake Simcoe.

"End of the line," I said, "now we take the Emily May."

"The Emily May!" Anne exclaimed, "how well I remember."

"Have you been here before?" asked Jim in surprise.

"A long, long time ago," she said, and it seemed that way to me too. The Emily May took us to Orillia, and we changed to the Cariella for Washago. Anne was a little seasick from rough water and excitement. But as we approached the wharf at Washago I reassured her.

"We will go by stage coach this time," I said, "it meets the boats regularly now."

84

She looked around as we got off.

"Well the stage is late today," she said.

"No, it's here," Jim declared.

"Where?"

"Over there."

She looked to where he was pointing, and there was an open wagon drawn by a team of heavy horses.

"The roads aren't too bad right now," explained Jim "one team can handle it."

It wasn't the kind of stage coach she had imagined, but it was better than walking. Our boxes and bags were heaved into the back of the wagon, and tied with rope. We were helped onto the seats, rigid pieces of board held in place by heavy diamond-shaped springs. The driver slapped the reins over the horses' backs, and Harvie's stage took off for Gravenhurst. Almost immediately the left front wheel dropped into a hole. Anne grabbed my arm and held tight. I was gripping the seat with both hands.

"It's a little steadier when we get to the road," said Jim, "the dock area is pretty rough."

He was optimistic. The Muskoka Road was still a mess. "Used to be a big mudhole right here" said the driver, pointing with his whip, "we needed two teams to get through."

I could see that Anne was feeling miserable. We crossed the Severn and stopped at the hotel. She got down to walk around. Some children were coming out of the hotel stable with books in their hands.

"What on earth are they doing in there?" she asked.

"Oh, the school room is above the stable," said the driver, "they'll be getting out for the day."

"I hope my children don't go to school in a stable," she said, and then blushed in spite of her pallor. I could see where her mind was, and it suited me well enough.

We started out again, lurching across the rocky ledges, bumping over planked sections and small bridges. The wagon slowly made its way through the rough bushland. We passed the place where the Kahshe River crosses the road, the place we remembered so well, and we told Jim what it meant to us. Here and there a stumpy clearing and a settler's log shanty showed that settlement was under way. But for the most part, it was still empty wasteland. Anne was in agony all the way. We stopped at McCabe's tavern and Mrs. McCabe remembered us well; then on through the village of Gravenhurst, past Cockburn's store, Dugald Brown's Steamboat and Stage House and down the road to the wharf. There the Wenonah was waiting.

As we started out on the last lap of our journey to Bracebridge, Anne quietly went to the rear of the ship and was sick. Then she came back and sat with us. "I'm sorry, Mr. McDonald," she said, "you started to tell me about the lake but I wasn't feeling at all well."

'So I noticed, Mrs. Bell," he said, and it thrilled me to hear her called Mrs. Bell, "you are a brave woman."

The Wenonah shortly turned from the lake into the Muskoka River towards her destination.

"You will like the falls, Mrs. Bell," said Jim "they have attracted me ever since the day I arrived. There is something special about them."

It was dark when we landed. We went up the steep path to the road, across the bridge and in to the Royal Hotel. We had decided to stay for the night. Nobody else knew that I had chosen this place once before, and I said nothing now, for Anne was fatigued and out of sorts. She went right to bed, and fell asleep.

In the middle of the night she woke and sat up. She seemed listening for the noise that wakened her.

"Are you all right?" I asked anxiously.

"Much better," she answered "I feel very peaceful."

Finally she sensed the deep vibrations of the falls, and it made her feel comfortable. She understood what McDonald had meant. She snuggled down beside me and went to sleep again.

In the morning we were both awake early. "I have some things to do in town," I said, "would you like to come along?"

"No, I'll just look around."

I liked that. Business was my affair, and she would have it that way. She went walking, and when I came back she told me about her exploration. She had crossed the bridge and looked at the rapids. She loved the sound and sight of them. She went into Mr. Cheney's grocery just on the other side, and bought a few things. Then she walked past the Orange Hall, the Dominion Hotel, Kennedy's shoe shop and Cooper's carpentry, which were all new to her. She went through the village and up the hill to Mr. Browning's frame store. She came back, and looked in the little Presbyterian church across the road from the Victoria. The fresh clean air, the bright sun and the silent forest gave her a good feeling.

We went for a walk beside the falls. There was a path along the steep rock, and we went down hand in hand. At a rock near the bottom, we sat down and looked around. It was good to be alone together. The rush of the waters seemed to cut us off from the rest of the world. I took her in my arms and we held each other close. Then we came back up to the outside world.

I had hired a buggy to take us in style to Uffington. We stopped at Mr. McMurray's, and he came out to wish us well. But Uffington was a great disappointment; the place was deserted. When we finally got home I found out why. The whole village was waiting for us there. Such cheering and embracing and handshaking you never saw. They had set up a table outside, and had lunch all spread out. Once more my quiet neighbours had shown their loyalty. And when lunch was over, they gracefully cleaned up and departed.

Anne was pleased with the cabin; it was neat and roomy with the new addition. She was delighted with her new neighbours. That night she was in her own home, at peace with the world. The soft rustle of the wind through the pines and the frogs singing a welcoming chorus, relieved all her tensions. It was then we became husband and wife. Our union was thrilling and unrestrained. All our pent-up feelings were released. I lay there contented.

All my lonely nights and empty dreams were behind me. Anne was here, really here; the one I had always wanted, the woman I had searched so long for. My life was complete.

CHAPTER 8
THE HERO

Willson's store was the gathering place for farmers who came to Bracebridge. An old iron stove, a couple of chairs, a spittoon and a tobacco can for butts made up the trappings. The customers sat around talking till closing time and then did business. Many an argument was settled there, and many a new one started.

One August day, three months after my wedding, I was shooting the breeze there with a couple of locals when A.J. Alport walked in. He was one of those prosperous farmers with a big farm and good stock in Muskoka township; and he was proud of it.

"Just got some new cattle," he announced, "without a doubt the finest north of Orillia."

"Now I wouldn't say that," argued Mr. Willson, "there's some pretty fine stock in Macaulay township. In fact, I would say that my son-in-law has just about the best Holstein around."

"That may be," replied Alport, "but mine are well-bred Durham and Devon."

"There's plenty of well-bred stock around."

"Not Durham," declared Alport, "that makes the difference. You can't compare oranges and apples."

I couldn't let Draper down.

"My neighbour Patterson has some of the best cattle I ever saw," I declared, "I don't know if they're well-bred, but they are sure fat and heavy."

"What do you know about it?" Alport demanded, "you're not a cattle man. Just stick to your books."

He shot a wad into the spittoon and turned to go. "I'll tell you this much," he declared, "I'll put up my cattle against anything around these parts."

He stomped out, annoyed at being challenged.

"I'd like to take him up on that," said Willson, feeling irritated, "there are good herds around here besides his."

"There sure are," agreed one of the settlers, "I'd like to show the beggar up."

"How about a cattle show?" I wondered aloud.

"Good idea," the others agreed, and I was surprised at the response.

"We could get a judge up from Orillia," I went on, the notion taking root, "that would end the argument."

After that we toyed around with it for a while, and finally decided to form a committee to hold a cattle show. We settled on a day in September, built some hitching rails in the flats by the river, and put up posters. We got hold of a cattle man to do the judging, and then we were ready. It was all very informal; nobody's name went on the posters, and the judge agreed to come on speculation.

I put the squeeze on Matt Patterson. "Get those beasts of yours fattened up," I demanded, "and have them there clean, brushed and shining. Our honour is at stake."

At the last minute we decided to include farm produce in the show. For the produce we got the upstairs of a carpentry shop near the flats. On fair day Anne and I went up the rickety stairs with my best potatoes and a jar of her raspberry jam. We ducked into kind of a loft where the owner had set out a few planks along the wall. There were already two other potato displays, though mine looked the best. There were also some turnips, a few samples of wheat in the straw and some oats in a sack. The household display was Anne's jar of raspberries, some butter in a small wooden bucket, a couple of aprons and a quilt. I set out my potatoes, and as there was nobody else around we went on down to the livestock show.

Outside it was a pleasant fall day. We walked down the Macaulay Road towards the river, with the breeze in our faces and a warm sun beating down. Just off the road we could hear the bawl of calves and the sound of people talking. When we turned in to the field I was pleasantly surprised at the good showing. Tied side by side along the rail was a long line of cattle, their fat rumps facing the crowd, their tails switching flies and their manure spattered out behind them. It's not really a

90

bad smell, cow manure, sort of dairy-like, as long as it's fresh. The new-cut hay had a fragrance of clover and the crisp odour of falling leaves was in the air. At the edge of the clearing, red maples and yellow poplar stood out against the green background of spruce and pine. The surrounding forest gave a feeling of endless time and the falls in the distance were nature's soft drums. We stood by the entrance for a moment, absorbing the rustic beauty of it all. I looked at Anne and she was smiling with pleasure. Some friends waved and we went in among the crowd.

It was just like old home week. People were there from miles around, some old friends, some strangers. Anne met Mrs. McDonald who introduced her to several Bracebridge ladies, and they all started gabbing. I wandered off to see who was there, and ran across Matt Patterson. As we stood talking something took my attention.

"Who on earth are they?" I asked, pointing at a clump of people I had noticed when I came in. You couldn't miss them. They were almost like a dark blob floating around in the crowd. They seemed to be a family of about a dozen, father carrying a baby, mother a smaller body, two or three toddlers holding onto mother's skirt and others ranging to a boy as tall as his father. They stayed together as if tied by string. Their clothes were tattered, washed-out, grey sacking, torn at the sleeves, held together with pins and buttons. The father wore a stained mis-shaped hat and a ragged jacket, out at the elbows and with only one button. He was unshaved and grimy. The mother wore a single piece of the same grey material, which covered her from neck to the ground. The older ones had worn-out boots and laces trailing and the younger were barefoot. Their faces were round and blank, except for the one bright-looking child who seemed out of place.

"You wouldn't believe it," said Matt, "but that family spent the winter on the next concession south of me, and I ever knew they were there until Spring."

"How did they live?"

"I'll never know. They were packed together in a little shanty about ten feet square. It was thrown together with crooked logs and packed with earth; the roof was made of poles and branches. They must have lived on wintergreen and spruce buds, and perhaps the odd rabbit or bird. There was nothing in the shanty.''

"That's the worst I've heard!'' I exclaimed.

"Nobody tells these people what to expect. Some families survive on their wits, but this outfit doesn't seem to have many.''

"What have they got for this winter?''

"Damn little. A few vegetables which they'll have eaten before Christmas. But now we know they're there, and I guess the neighbours will look after them.''

"How did they get up here today?''

"I told them about the fair, and the whole kaboodle of them walked up. It's the only time I've seen them out of the woods this year. I suppose they'll walk the whole twelve miles back again tonight, unless somebody takes them in. And I don't know who would.''

"I'll put them on the township roll,'' I said, "but I can never keep track of people like them. My records are away behind.''

Just then the cattle judge arrived from Orillia. He took one look at the cattle and started to sputter. "You can't put all those beasts in one class,'' he said, waving his cane at them, "you've got the damndest collection of animals here I ever saw.''

"That's what I told you,'' Alport gloated, to nobody in particular. So they sat down and made up several classes for cattle, and one for calves. Then they switched the animals around and he started judging.

While the judging went on people gathered around in groups to watch. Matt went off to see that his entries stayed clean and behaved themselves for the contest. The Reeve, Tom McMurray, came over to talk to me, and we formed the centre of attention. People approached, passed a word or two, then moved on. Innkeeper Jim McDonald had closed up the Royal until after the fair was over, and he joined us. "I don't know where they all come from," said McMurray, shaking his head, "I thought I knew everybody in the four townships."

"I see them coming through," McDonald declared, "they all pass my door, dragging along with their pathetic oxen and skimpy belongings. They're off to somewhere in the wilderness; God knows where, but nobody else does. They hardly look human sometimes, from the heat or the cold or the fatigue. Sometimes they come back, months later, to recall their terrible trip in. Some are better off, some worse. But they're in there, somewhere, and one of these days we'll be surprised how many there are. There's more stores around, and blacksmiths and carpenters. It takes a day like this to bring them out."

"They're not all poor, either," said McMurray, pointing at our Judge, Charles W. Lount, who was just arriving, "there are some who manage to grab everything for themselves while others starve."

"He's a friend of the Premier's," I pointed out.

"And what does that make him, God Almighty?" asked the Reeve, "certainly that's what he thinks he is."

"I gather you don't like him."

"No I don't. Look at him; striped pants, fancy waistcoat, big cigar; coming down from his new Court House and Registry Office to mingle with the masses."

"I find him a bit rough in the tongue," I agreed, trying to please my boss.

"Rough in the tongue!" echoed McMurray, "he's uncouth for a man who's supposed to judge the people and represent the province. It makes me doubt Sandfield Macdonald's sanity." I didn't want to get into a political argument right then, so I made no comment. McMurray's Liberal leanings and his friendship with Cockburn strained things between us at times. But this was too nice a day to spoil.

"Ladies and gentlemen," a voice called out from the stock rail, "we will now have the result of the judging."

The people gathered round the judge, who stood with a paper in his hand.

"For Durham and Devon, first prize goes to A.J. Alport."
There was some clapping, and Alport smiled politely. "For Holstein, first prize goes to William Holditch." Holditch was Willson's son-in-law from Macaulay, and there was a round of applause from his friends and neighbours.
"For other breeds, first prize goes to Matthew Patterson." All the Draper people cheered, and Matt took a bow.
"Now, ladies and gentlemen," the judge went on, "I can judge best in show if you wish."
He looked around enquiringly, because there was really nobody in charge. I could see the dangers in that. We had three winners, now, why cut it to one? I felt I had enough authority to speak up.
"Let's leave that until next year," I suggested, "then we can set up proper classes and awards."
"Well said," remarked the Reeve, and there was applause all round. It was gratifying. I could feel the approval of my judgment.
"Very well," said the judge, accepting my suggestion, "my duties are completed. Thank you for your attention."
That ended our first show.

But it was really the beginning of the Fall Fair. A couple of weeks later we had an open meeting and set up a Fair Board. Alport, Holditch and Patterson all showed up to give it a boost. For the next year we decided to have prize lists and an awards night.

And I was elected Secretary.

My hunger for position and influence was being satisfied. The more I got, the more I wanted. And things were going well at home too; mostly. My little shanty and stumpy clearing had grown into a small farm. I had added a kitchen at the back of my house, and raised the roof six logs to put in sleeping quarters. As my public duties grew I bought a horse and built a stable. Around the buildings I had a rail fence, which gave it all a neat appearance. The example of Mr. McMurray's place was always there. We had poultry, venison, fish and partridge for meat, and vegetables stored for winter.

Unfortunately Anne wasn't as pleased as I was. She complained about my continual trips to Bracebridge. She harped about being taken for granted. The frustrations of our first night together in Toronto occurred more often. And as she became more critical, I paid less attention. But then one day I learned the reason for Anne's restlessness. I rushed out and bought a cow.

There was good reason for the cow. Anne was going to have a baby. When she told me, I hugged her for joy. Then I rushed out and bought everything she would possibly need.

My other responsibilities kept growing as well. The Orange Lodge had been meeting in Bracebridge for some time informally, and in December we got our charter. I took on a recording job. The Settler's Association and the Ratepayers' group appointed me their secretary. At special meetings of ratepayers and citizens I was asked to take the minutes. I practically became secretary-in-chief of the district, and had the records for everything.

The Church of England had no building, but once a month Rev. Wray came up from Orillia and we had services in the Orange Hall. I went every time, and assisted in the service. If anything needed doing, they could count on me. I went to everything for miles around, and knew most everyone in central Muskoka. I was working for the day when my talents would be recognized and my services required for the public good.

It wasn't all clear sailing, though, far from it. Tragedy and terror were with us too, always lurking in the wings. One night in November, when we were asleep, a neighbour boy came to the door.

"Come quick," he cried, "mother is sick, and father has gone to South Falls for help."

"I'll come right away," I answered.

"I'll go too," said Anne, "she probably needs a woman's help."

It was over a mile, so I hitched up the horse and we drove. The woman was in labour, and her husband had gone for a midwife. She was in great pain, but there was little Anne could do except bathe her face and encourage her.

"There's something wrong," the woman said, "it was never like this before."

"Everything will be all right," Anne assured her, "when the midwife comes she will know what to do."

The pain was continuous, not like normal birth pains at all. When the midwife arrived, she hurried into the tiny bedroom, and Anne with her. All through the night and into early morning, they came and went. There were long periods of silence, then the woman would cry out with pain. Every sound was magnified in that small shanty, and the children sat shivering with fear and cold around the fire in the kitchen. The husband and I waited around helplessly, stoking the fire and calming the children. As the cries became more frequent and tortured, I took the children to our place and left them there. Early in the morning, as daylight was breaking, we heard a piercing scream and then silence. I waited for the baby's cry, but everything was still. Anne and the midwife came out after a while, pale and shaken.

"She's dead," said the midwife, "she couldn't deliver the child."

For Anne, already several months into pregnancy, it was a terrifying experience. She woke up nights after that, crying out from nightmares. Her own time was close and that terrible memory haunted her.

"You know," she said thoughtfully one day as we were talking about it, "We just sat and watched that woman die."

"But what could anyone do?" I asked, for these were things they seldom discussed with men.

"I'm not sure," she answered shaking her head, "maybe a doctor could have saved her life, and the baby too."

"But there's no doctor for forty miles," I said, "there isn't even time to go for one. It would take a whole day, assuming he would come at all."

"Maybe she could have gone to Orillia,"

"In her condition . . . " I began, but Anne broke in.

"What's her condition now?" she demanded.

There were times when our fears and doubts subsided. Just before Christmas Anne came in to Bracebridge to do some shopping, and her condition was very obvious. How proud I was to walk beside her as friends greeted us with delight! It was vain and selfish on my part, but it made me feel very manful. I never realized how much my lonely bachelorhood had bothered me until it was past. Even George Gow with his vulgar tongue couldn't spoil things. He was slouching towards us on the slushy street, eyes on the ground as if looking for a penny, pretending not to see us. Then he stopped in mock horror as we came close.

"My God, Bell," he said in a loud voice anybody within a block could hear, "you sure nailed the old girl promptly. Now let's see, when was it you were married? Last summer eh?"

"It was May the fifth, Mr. Gow," said Anne coldly, "and if you were able to add you wouldn't make such a fuss."

Gow was seldom taken aback, but Anne had him. He mumbled some good wishes and brushed past. We both went grinning up the street. Her pregnancy seemed so normal and joyful to everyone that we started back home completely at ease.

"I guess we had bush fever," I decided. Anne nodded, and her eyes were bright above the wollen scarf pulled tight around her face against the winter wind.

There were other things that made life hard for her. Sometimes I had to stay in Bracebridge after a late meeting, and Anne was alone. One night a lynx passed near our cabin and let loose its terrifying scream. Anne had never heard one before and she lay tense and quiet for an hour before dropping off again.

Early in December the stove pipes caught fire. Anne was alone, with a hot fire going. There was a whoosh of smoke and flame down the pipes and out the stove lids. The green wood had built up a tar deposit which caught fire. In her panic she somehow knocked the pipes down, and they lay smoking and flaming on the floor. She doused them with water, but there was a lot of damage, and she was badly shaken up. I feared for the baby she was carrying. In January I cut my foot with the axe one morning and lay on the bed in pain for several days. My foot and leg swelled up, but I recovered with only a limp. It was just as hard on her as it was on me. She had no way of going for help, and was in no shape to walk. Fate seemed to demand its payment for the joy we had been given.

We talked secretly about Anne going back to Toronto to have the baby. She would have help there if she needed it. But our pride was at stake. Did she not have the courage to face an ordinary childbirth? And how would it look if the township clerk packed his wife off to Toronto at the first sign of danger? We decided against it.

It was at supper time one night in the middle of February, 1869, that Anne began to have her pains. I hitched up the horse right away and went to get our neighbour Mrs. Patterson. Then I headed out for Muskoka Falls to get the midwife. It must have been midnight when we got back, and I thought the baby might have arrived. But nothing had happened. I put the horse in the stable to rest, and took off its harness.

When I went back into the house, everything was quiet. I stoked up the fire, brought in some wood and water, and cleaned up the supper dishes. I could hear voices from the bedroom. After a while I heard Anne groaning in pain, and the two women seemed to be giving instructions. Her pain got worse and eventually I couldn't stand it.

"I'll be out in the stable," I called at the bedroom door.

"Don't go too far," Mrs. Patterson answered, and the tone of her voice frightened me. I had reason, too, for in about half an hour she called out from the back door and I went in.

"I'm afraid there is trouble," she said seriously, "nothing is going right. Anne wants to see you."

When I went into the bedroom, Anne was lying there pale and tired, her hair matted, her eyes dull and her face swollen. She spoke in a far-away voice.

"We have to go to Orillia," she said, "I need a doctor."

"But it's impossible," protested the midwife, "in this weather? in her condition?"

I remembered Anne's comment about condition some time before, and I knew the burden was now on me.

"Is it really serious?" I asked, looking from one to the other.

"I'm afraid it is," answered the midwife, "she seems to be having the same trouble that other woman had. I can't understand it."

That was all I needed.

"We'll go," I said, and turned to leave.

"But nobody ever did such a thing before," objected the midwife as if to relieve herself of responsibility, "it's insane."

"Well, we're doing it now," said I firmly.

As I ran to the driving shed, I realized that my mind had been preparing for this moment and I knew what to do. I pulled the cutter out into the pale glow of the snowy night, took my heavy timber axe and smashed the back completely off the seat. Then I went to the shed and wrenched a small door off its hinges, and took it out to the cutter. I lashed the door at the dashboard and the seat, and had a firm surface for Anne to lie on. I harnessed the horse, grabbed all the horse blankets I had and pulled up to the door for my passenger.

The women in the meantime had wrapped Anne in every warm garment she had, and filled a hot water bottle. We carried her out to the cutter, laying her on the blankets and then wrapping her up in them completely.

"What if she has the baby while we're going?" I asked anxiously.

"That would be lucky," said the midwife, "just take her in to the first shanty you see."

I laid the lines across my horse's back and she jumped forward. Lumps of packed snow bulleted against the front of the cutter from her hooves, and the runners squeaked in the road. The night was clear and cold. From under the blankets all was silent. I knew that Anne was not asleep, but she would make no sound until she could hold the pain no longer.

The miles crept slowly by as I travelled the Muskoka Falls road for the third time that night. The chill began to penetrate my clothes and the perspiration turned me into a damp cold lump. After a while Anne began to groan under her pile of blankets. I leaned down to ask if she was all right.

"Go on, go on," she said, and I turned and whipped the mare into a run. She heaved and groaned and snorted as she raced along, billowing clouds of snow around the cutter.

As we turned down the Muskoka Road towards Gravenhurst the horse began to tire. I got out and walked up the hills, both for the animal's sake and my own. Anne cried out more often now, from the cold and pain.

"Oh, God," she said between cries, "Oh, my God."

Tears came to my eyes, but all I could do was run beside the cutter, taking great gulps of cold air.

When we got to Gravenhurst in the early morning, before the light of day, the horse was staggering along, fully spent, and Anne was silent. We carried her into Brown's hotel, and when they lifted the covers I expected to find her dead. But her lips moved, and her eyes followed me as I hovered around her. They gave her some soup, set her near the fire and warmed up a hot water bottle. I changed horses and we took off again in half an hour. Daylight came soon after, and the travelling was easier. I whipped the fresh horse along, and we made good time to Severn Bridge. But it was cold in that early morning, and I could hear Anne shuddering beneath the blankets. When I asked how she was, she just urged me on.

I changed horses again at Severn, and set off on the last lap of the journey. By then I was so cold and tired I moved like a machine, numb and unthinking; just a big lump of flesh moving along to keep from freezing solid. Sometimes I got off and walked. Anne cried out from time to time, but I was even more alarmed when she was quiet. I could only think that she had not survived. Near noon, and just a few miles from Orillia, she began to struggle in her blankets, and she screamed.

"I can't go any farther," she cried, "I'm bursting apart. I'm going to die."

100

"We're nearly there," I called, jumping out and whipping the horse, "hold on, we'll soon be safe."

"No, I can't," she screamed, "stop, stop. Turn in somewhere."

There was no use doing that. It was all or nothing now. We had come so far I wouldn't stop. She became hysterical, and I had to jump back on the cutter to hold her down. The horse kept trotting along. After a while the hysteria passed and inside the blankets everything went limp. I couldn't see her face, and I was glad I couldn't. I feared she had died. I felt as if I would collapse myself, but I had to go on. I saw a man at the edge of town, and the directed me to the doctor's. It was like a dream then. I felt as if I had completely frozen up, except for my eyes which were guiding my movements. My brain, my hands, my feet, were simply responding to my vision. But I made it, finally stopping the horse in front of the doctor's with my silent burden.

They carried her quickly inside, past several waiting patients, and placed her on a table in the inner room. I sat down in the waiting room, and the floor suddenly came up and hit me as I passed right out. They left me there as they worked with Anne. The next think I remember was a baby's cry.

We came home in triumph two weeks later. The whole community knew of our desperate journey and they turned out to welcome us, Anne, myself and our daughter, Margaret Hannah. Such rejoicing that they were both well! Such praise for Anne's courage and my strength! The affair seemed to raise the spirits of the community. It was possible to go to a doctor; women didn't need to die in childbirth.

It seemed to me then that I had gained a permanent place in Anne's love and devotion. I had saved her life, and that of our child. And people told me that no matter what happened I would always be a hero in Muskoka. My devoted service in keeping their records, in organizing the Fall Fair, and now setting an example of physical strength, would keep me permanently in their affection.

TORONTO. THURSDAY. JAN. 28. 1869

MR. COCKBURN AND THE *GLOBE*.

AFTER a week's delay the *Globe* yesterday ventured upon publishing the letter
of Mr. A. P. COCKBURN, M. P. P. Our
contemporary no doubt thought that by
the time it gave the letter and the ac-
companying comments to the public, Mr.
be so far from the city
ake any reply to it,
however, in town,
es to the labor-
ie *Globe* makes of

s in a becoming
of our unscrupulous
ain matters of a
ch have no bearing
tions to the minis-
nts. He tells the
t " those who live
hould not throw
piece of advice
exion, a very strik-
that pass. The
had
own
Department
nature
N
to

CHAPTER 9
THE NINE MARTYRS

The Toronto newspapers in those days were more than publishers of the news. They were the means of assault on any one who displeased the editor. This was particularly so with the Globe, which was George Brown's personal property. He used it to attack his enemies, defend his friends and push his own ideas. He was a Grit, but he sometimes went off on his own crusades, and not always with the other Liberals behind him. It happened early in 1869 that he took offense at some of the Reform Members of the Ontario Assembly, and told them off. They threw his words right back in his teeth, and that set the stage for one terrific political wrangle. It was called the affair of the Nine Martyrs. And that affair put A.P. Cockburn right into our hands.

Cockburn's position was typical of the "moderate" Reformers. They ran for the Assembly as Liberals, but stayed well clear of Brown's violent denunciation of the Macdonalds and the coalition party of Confederation. Brown himself was defeated in 1867, but he kept up his personal attacks on Sandfield Macdonald. Quite a few opposition Members couldn't do that, and they had good reason. A.P. Cockburn was one of these, and I got wise to him by degrees.

Quite by accident I came across an item in the Toronto Leader, a Conservative paper, late in 1868.
"The owner of the 'Dean' has sold her to Mr. A.P. Cockburn, M.P.P., for inter-lake trade. No delivery date was announced."

That casual note, published in the commercial section, raised my curiosity. There was nowhere in Muskoka, that I knew of, where you could travel between lakes. I waited for an announcement of some kind by Cockburn, but nothing appeared. It made me wonder, because Cockburn wasn't normally backward about his big deals. So I sounded out Thomas McMurray about it.
"I hear Mr. Cockburn is buying a new boat," I said to him one

day after a special council meeting.

"That's news to me," he replied, "where did you hear that?"

"Oh, just a rumour."

"I don't believe it. He claims the Wenonah is losing money. What would he do with another boat?"

"Put it on inter-lake trade," I guessed, using the words I had read.

"What inter-lake trade?" McMurray demanded, "there's no inter-lake trade around here."

I didn't know either, and that's what made it all so strange. If McMurray didn't know, nobody did. He kept pretty close track of events around the district, especially with Cockburn. But in a couple of weeks, he met me on the street.

"By the way," he added, after some other discussion, "I happened to meet Mr. Cockburn the other day and asked him about the rumour you heard."

"And is it true?"

"In a way. He told me privately the government has promised him $35,000 for a lock between Lakes Muskoka and Rosseau. He bought the boat to run on the upper lakes. But he wasn't saying anything until the estimates for the lock passed the Assembly. Doesn't know how on earth it got out."

"I have friends," I boasted.

"Well, he'd like to keep the matter confidential for now," McMurray went on, "he said I could give you the information on a personal basis."

By sheer accident I had smoked Cockburn out. He was making inside deals with Sandfield Macdonald's government while still sitting in the opposition. I wondered what else he was into; timber licenses, mail contracts, patronage. He was really on the wrong side of the fence, but trying to climb back over. I spelled it out to McMurray without thinking.

"Looks like your friend Mr. Cockburn is playing both ends against the middle."

"No, he's an independant," he replied defensively.

"In politics, there's no such animal."

"You're getting awfully smart," he spat out, "you'd better just look after the township books like you're supposed to."

104

"I'm hoping for a better fate than that."

"That's just what I suspected," he declared, "but remember this too. There's no such animal as a political Clerk."

We hadn't had such a sharp exchange before, because I generally deferred to McMurray. But discussion of A.P. Cockburn easily stirred me up.

It bothered me to think that Sandfield Macdonald would play along with a man like Cockburn. But then, the northern development policy was directed mainly at us, and it wasn't Sandfield's fault we sent a Grit to the Assembly. Timber, roads, navigation and settlement were all government affairs, though they put money into Cockburn pockets too. I thought how galling it must be to Cockburn, having to vote time and again with the other side. What a queer business! Right then the nasty editorials Brown had been writing in the Globe started to make sense. He had attacked Liberal Members for backsliding; railed at them for voting with Sandfield's government; called them disloyal, self-serving and traitors. And one of his targets had been A.P. Cockburn.

The government spending estimates for 1869 brought it all to a head. Brown practically ordered the opposition to vote against them, though he was not even a Member. He did it through the columns of the Globe. He considered Sandfield shamefully extravagant, and demanded that the opposition act together to show some unity. There was a stormy Liberal caucus meeting and the discussion leaked out. A.P. Cockburn was mentioned.

"I can't vote against the estimates," he was quoted, "I have a number of things to get through the departments first." And sure enough, when the vote came, Cockburn voted with the government in favour of their proposed spending, and so did a number of his colleagues. Brown was furious and raked them over fiercely in the columns of the Globe. They were traitors, corrupt, dishonest, stupid, and had better straighten up or else.

I had to gloat a bit over their problems, so buttonholed McMurray.

"I see Mr. Cockburn voted for the estimates," I remarked,

105

shoving the needle, "Mr. Brown didn't like that."

"What else could he do?" McMurray asked, "he's got a bill before the Assembly to incorporate our township of Monck. Would you have that thrown out? And there's another one for Watt and Cardwell. For the good of Muskoka, he can hardly antagonize the ministry right now."

"I guess the money for the lock is in there too," I ventured, "he certainly wouldn't want to lose that."

"Certainly not," McMurray declared, flushing, "that's for the good of the riding too. When the government gives Muskoka something, how can our Member vote against it?"

"George Brown thought he could," I mentioned, "who do you think is right, Cockburn or Brown?"

I thought I had him, but he had an answer.

"Brown's not the leader any more," he pointed out, "and don't try to make out I'm a George Brown Grit, because I'm not. I think Cockburn is doing a good job for us, he believes in Reform, as I do, and I support him."

"I can't argue with that," I allowed.

He knew I was needling him, but I couldn't be totally obnoxious.

There was a lot of local discussion in Muskoka. Some thought Cockburn right, some thought him wrong. A few days later they had more fat to chew on.

The issue of the Toronto Leader of January 18th, 1869, brought the heady stuff. It printed a letter written to the Globe by nine Reform Members of the opposition. The Leader had received a copy to make sure it was printed. The nine Members told off the Globe in no uncertain terms. They were sick and tired of being denounced for their actions. George Brown had no warrant to criticize honest Reformers who voted with the government, and he didn't speak for the party. "The Globe has caused infinite mischief in the past by assuming to be the organ of the Reform party," they wrote.

Then they made it clear they were not the kind of Members to be trifled with.

"At the last election we were returned by large majorities in

106

our respective constituencies as open and avowed reformers, proposing to give the government under the new order of things a fair trial."

They didn't stop at defending themselves. They took a hearty slap at George Brown and the Globe. Brown had no right to criticize Reformers who supported a coalition. He had started it off himself.

"We refrain," they declared with mock delicacy, "from discussing the subject of coalitions. You justify your support of the 1864 coalition on the ground of the specific object of Confederation. We support the present order to give Ontario a pure and efficient government."

They flayed the Globe for its black political record.

"It has always badly treated political opponents, or even members of our own party who have dared to differ ... it has held up to scorn and derision the honest actions and purest motives of the people's most trusted servants."

Their main message was delivered in words of ridicule.

"We do not acknowledge your right to dictate. Your criticisms are no more than breath-blown grains of dust."

It was signed by Members Greely, Eyre, Lauder, Craig, H.D. Smith, Barber, Swinarton, McGill and lastly, A.P. Cockburn.

The Globe didn't print the letter the Monday it appeared in the Leader. It wasn't even mentioned. Tuesday passed, and it looked as if Brown was going to ignore them. Not by a long shot. He had his staff at work rounding up all the dirt they could find on the nine complainers. On Wednesday the Globe exploded with their findings. In his most sarcastic style, Brown wrote his headline, coining a phrase for the poor lambs:

"Nine Martyrs"

He tore them apart one by one, smearing their characters with all he could imagine. Craig and Swinarton had erred, which was nothing new; Sandfield Macdonald had taken the measure of Greely's foot; Eyre was a deserter to the enemy; H.D. Smith had sworn allegiance to Reform at the big convention, and broke his oath; the other four were worst of all.

"They were gradually bought up by Sandfield Mcdonald," he

charged, "and their price is known to every Member of the Assembly."

But for A.P. Cockburn he reserved his special venom. Brown must have kept that letter Cockburn wrote in March of '67, that letter so full of praise and loyalty. For Cockburn now to be attacking Brown was heresy, and there could only be one reason; Cockburn had sold himself to Sandfield for timber licenses.

"Mr. Cockburn is a lumberer and had a number of things to get through the department. What his number of things were we can readily imagine. He admitted his corruption to the caucus." After delivering his blast, Brown concluded by affirming that he was no longer in public life, and the Reform party was in no way responsible for his utterances.

Every copy of the Globe and the Leader was grabbed by eager Muskoka hands and passed around. Was Cockburn really selling his vote for timber licenses? That's what Brown said, and there were those who believed it. Tories like George Gow, who never believed a word George Brown ever wrote, suddenly found him reliable. Grits who always read the Globe and quoted it word for word now couldn't find their copy. I managed to bump into Tom McMurray.

"I thought you'd show up," he growled, "you enjoy seeing Mr. Cockburn in trouble."

"No, I don't, I replied, "and I'm very sorry, but . . . "

"But nothing," McMurray snapped, "go and talk with someone else. I don't believe a word against him."

On Thursday the reply from the Nine was printed in the Leader. They accepted as total victory the admission that the Globe did not speak for the Reform party.

"We forebear to remark on the style and tone of your comments, bristling as they are in every line with perversions of truth and with unfounded and reckless assertions. By your admission in your closing paragraph our whole object is attained. You say that the Reform party can now in no shape be held responsible for your utterances."

They then asserted their success.

108

"You have been driven by our simple letter from your assumed position as dictator."

Having thus won their victory, the Nine were ready to call it quits.

All, that is, except A.P. Cockburn. Special attention from Brown deserved a special reply and he gave it. In a separate letter printed under the main one, Cockburn gave back to Brown all he had received, and then some.

"I merely wish to draw your attention to a gross misrepresentation you made today in reference to myself, in your onslaught on the nine M.P.P.s," he began.

"You are so palpably incorrect in ascribing to me certain corrupt influences that you have not so far an inch of tenable ground whereon to stand."

Then he went on to call Brown a liar in clear words.

"Now sir . . . your accusations are manufactured out of whole cloth. I am not a lumberer, and do not deal in timber licenses. Your statement about me having a number of things to get through the department is equally untruthful. I challenge you or any of your friends (which are getting fewer every day) to elicit knowledge of any transaction for my own purposes, directly or indirectly.

Yours truly,
A.P. Cockburn"

Legislative Assembly,
Jan. 20, 1869

For a few days there was silence. Nothing appeared in the Globe or the Leader. But on January 27th George Brown was back on the attack. This time he had only one target, A.P. Cockburn. He repeated his charges of corruption.

"He is a lumberer and as such had improper dealings with the Crown lands department."

He came back to the caucus statement, which Cockburn had already denied making.

"Mr. Cockburn told the caucus that as he had a number of

things to get through the department, he could not go with the opposition then, but when the number of things were once disposed of, he would go thoroughly with the opposition."

Cockburn now had a champion. No cause could have pleased the editor of the Leader more than to run down the Globe and its editor George Brown. The Leader praised Cockburn in an editorial for his dignified conduct.

"Mr. Cockburn has treated our unscrupulous contemporary in a becoming manner," he wrote, "he refuses to surrender his political freedom at the dictation of a man who has ruined his party. Such manliness as Mr. Cockburn shows is deserving of commendation."

The Leader gave Cockburn full access to its editorial page, and he used it. The Globe had spent a week looking for wrong-doing, declared Cockburn, and all it could do was repeat falsehoods.

"I am not a lumberer or dealer in timber limits," he repeated, "I ceased all connection of this kind two and a half years ago. I have no axes to grind in the Crown land department."

Cockburn denied that he had admitted any wrongdoing in the caucus. He denied saying that after he got a number of things through the department he would vote with the opposition. He called on his colleagues to prove that Brown was lying.

George Brown did not go on calling Cockburn a liar. He had his satisfaction in the publication of a description of Cockburn asking Sandfield Macdonald for favours.

"We can imagine him, with fox-like face and eye seeking the ground, asking for things and offering his vote."

And he summarized his opinion of his former admirer, A.P Cockburn, in one sentence.

"It's the most astonishing example of open and unblushing corruption of which we have knowledge."

The debate over the Nine Martyrs went on for a long while, even after the angry exchange of letters in the papers had ended. I admitted to Gow that I felt just a tiny bit sorry for Cockburn, and he surprised me.

"I've been thinking about him myself," he said, and for a moment I thought the man had some feelings. Then he straightened me out.

"But save your tears," he went on, "the man's no fool. Maybe he'll play ball now."

"You think maybe he'll come over?" I asked.

"Where else can he go?" Gow demanded, "he's through with the Grits, the Nine Martyrs have split from the opposition, and Brown will never forgive him."

"Do you really think he would become a Conservative?"

"We'll see," said Gow with a determined edge in his voice, "now let's get down to business."

"What business?"

"The man needs help," he declared, "don't you want to help him? I thought I saw tears in your eyes a minute ago."

I doubted that Cockburn would appreciate the help Gow had in mind, but I was more than willing to listen. The thing about Gow was his surprise value. You never knew what he might do or say. And now he was right back to our first discussion with Cockburn.

"I still think he should be one of us," he declared.

After all Gow had tried to do to Cockburn, it seemed impossible that he now wanted to be buddies.

"What we have to do is make it easy for him," Gow went on, "you can help by giving him the club-house treatment, one of the family and that sort of thing. If he doesn't get the idea we'll have to be a little more direct."

Right then the campaign to make A.P. Cockburn into a conservative had its beginning.

Gow and I had become friendly in the way opposites attract one another. For me it was the fascination of the unexpected; you never knew what he would do next. I don't think he ever had any close friends for he was prickly as a porcupine. He charged around, constantly on the offensive, aggressive, accusing, looking for an argument. He carried a home-made cane as if it were a weapon, using it to make his point. I was often a bit nervous around him, wondering what dirty job he was about to drop on me. The only time he was anyways pleasant was when he needed you for something. He looked the part, too, with several days' whiskers on his face, his hair wild and carrying that stick. But he was more than a talker; he always had something going, and pushed right ahead with it. He kept store on the main street, owned the Dominion Hotel and contracted for anything. He had a surprising interest in music and organized a band when he arrived in town. When they started a County Orange Lodge that February of '69 he became County Master. He was a family man too, with a seldom-seen wife and four children.

But when it came time to cajole A.P. Cockburn he knew his limitations and shoved it onto me.

Cockburn was a willing victim right then. He spent more and more time in the Riding, attended council meetings, Settlers' Association and social events. I started off sending him copies of the council minutes, and he acknowledged them very graciously. After that I sent him copies of all the minutes I kept, Settlers' Association, ratepayers' meetings and even meetings of our Conservative Association. He surprised me pleasantly by a letter acknowledging the latter.

"It is most helpful to have the views of those interested in public affairs," he wrote, "your party is the only one which keeps me informed."

Even his best friends seemed to help along our cause. His ardent supporter, Mr. McMurray left us and went to Parry Sound in September to publish the Northern Advocate.

But it was the move for county status that really brought us close. In fact, it moved us to Cockburn rather than the other way around. At one of our Settlers' Association meetings we got up a petition to make Muskoka a junior county. Everybody was excited about it; recognition of our importance and self-government. It was practically agreed that I would be County Clerk.

Cockburn presented our petition to the Legislature on November 23rd, and it was then we got our eyes opened. The

112

main opposition was stirred up by none other than William Lount, Conservative Member for North Simcoe and brother of Charles W. Lount. It was just selfish family interest. Charlie Lount held all the positions of senior government and he would lose some of them under county status. It was as simple as that. They pulled out all the stops, talked against it, lobbied against it and succeeded in defeating it. The legislature turned down our bill.

Things came to a boil in Muskoka then and it left us Conservatives in a funny position. A.P. Cockburn was on our side; the unionist government, urged on by a Conservative Member, had rejected us. A lot of people were really angry. It wasn't all civic pride; those public positions that seemed within grasp suddenly dissolved. We held a public protest meeting after the municipal nominations on December 20th. Mr. Teviotdale, the Reeve-elect was Chairman and I was Secretary. George Gow, newly elected as a councillor, had a few blunt things to say. Everyone was furious with the government of Ontario and the Lounts. We were grateful to A.P. Cockburn who was working for us. We expressed our feelings in a series of resolutions. For A.P. Cockburn we had praise and we resolved:
"That the thanks of this meeting are tendered to A.P. Cockburn Esq. M.P.P. for his indefatigable efforts on behalf of Muskoka District."
For the legislature we had condemnation.
"This meeting expresses its regret and indignation at the steps taken in the Legislative Assembly of Ontario to throw out the District bill."
And for the Lounts we showed our resentment.
"This assembly hails with great dissatisfaction the intermeddling of any one Member from personal or family interest."

Cockburn was not at that meeting so I made up a copy of the resolutions, certified it as secretary and delivered it personally to him at Gravenhurst. He was pleased, very pleased, and invited me in for tea. We sat and talked for a while. He became quite confidential.

"I'm in a difficult position right now," he admitted, "but that happens to anyone who takes an independent stand."

"We all appreciate that, Mr. Cockburn," I said, "the speeches at our meeting were all high in your praise."

"I am now supporting the Premier," he pointed out, "because he is giving support to Muskoka."

"That brings us all very close," I commented, feeling sentimental.

"Indeed it does," he agreed, "it's too bad they let us down this time."

I came away with a pleasant feeling, the sensation of being on the inside, of sharing his problems and thoughts. Certainly he knew me better now and the plan to improve relations with him had gone right ahead. And really, he wasn't such a bad fellow at all, once you got to know him.

The New Year, the beginning of the seventies, found us discouraged about the failure of county status, and much closer to our Member. Personally, I was gratified by my own activities.

"I think things are going well with Cockburn," I said to George Gow cheerfully after the January council meeting.

"That's just where you're wrong," he answered roughly, spoiling my pleasure as usual, "we've walked right into his hands. If we're not careful we'll all end up in his camp instead of ours."

"That's not very likely," I laughed, trying to imagine Gow going over to Cockburn.

"No?" he asked sharply, "we're the ones who are out with our party. We're the ones who have strayed away. That's when John A. picks them off."

"So what do we do about it?"

"I think we should have a testimonial dinner for our Member," he decided, "and then he can come to us."

He carried it through with his usual vigour, and the dinner was held in March, 1870.

When our honoured guest arrived at the Dominion House in Bracebridge for the big event a welcoming committee was waiting at the door.

114

"Welcome to Bracebridge," said councillor Gow, as if he owned the place.

For just a fraction of a second I saw a look of pain cross Cockburn's face. He didn't like George Gow, but he did his best to conceal it for this occasion. The shadow passed and he managed a nod and a smile.

"Yes, we're glad to have you here," added Reeve Teviotdale, annoyed himself at Gow's presumption.

"Always happy to be in Bracebridge," responded Cockburn, adding after a pause, "and it's an honour to be met by the Reeve and council."

It wasn't exactly a council dinner, and Cockburn knew it. But he preferred to pretend it was. He wasn't entirely sure who his hosts were. The invitations went out from the "friends and supporters of Mr. A.P. Cockburn", and he couldn't think of refusing. But some of these people had their finger in every pie; council, Orange Lodge, church, provincial and federal politics. The council was practically all Tories, and they were practically all there. You could see the uncertainty in Cockburn's face as the group gathered round him to escort him to the dining room.

The manager of the Dominion House took Cockburn in charge. We went in through the lobby with its familiar stale odour of cigars, beer and coal oil. A few people were standing around there, and Cockburn stopped to shake hands. But they led him on through the lobby into the adjoining room, which was really another building added on to the first. You could hear the clink of glasses at the end of the corridor and the sound of voices. Once again the manager steered his guest off to the left, into the dining room. It was bright and cheerful there, tables spread with white, and laid with shining silver. The room was filled with men in their Sunday best, who immediately gathered round to greet their Member warmly.

"Glad to see you, Captain."

Some called him that because of the boats, now two in number.

"Good of you to come, Mr. Cockburn."

"A real honour."

115

You could see him begin to relax and smile. He seemed to be enjoying it, once the uncertainties were over. They took him up to the head table, and an oyster supper was served. As we ate, I could see him looking around at his "friends and supporters", trying to put a tag on them: John Teviotdale, George Gow, Jim McDonald, Browning (Andrew the Tory, not J.B.), Byers, Cooper, Cornforth, Ennis, Foster. All Conservatives. But he went on eating calmly, and next time he looked around he spotted Tom Myers, who leaned to Liberal. I could see him stare at Myers for a moment, probably wondering if he was simply a decoy, or if he had switched politics. A minute later I looked up from my plate, and Cockburn was staring at me. You couldn't tell what he was thinking.

When dinner was over, they came to the toasts: The Queen, The Dominion, The Province. Then the Chairman, John Teviotdale, toasted our honoured guest. He was high in his praise of Mr. A.P. Cockburn, M.P.P.

"He understands and meets the wants and wishes of our people," he declared, and got great applause. He went on in this vein for a while, and then concluded:

"We are all happy that he is now one of us."

This was greeted with cheers and a standing ovation. Cockburn smiled and responded graciously. But when he sat down you could see the doubt in his face.

"Now one of us."

The words sounded as if he had just joined something. He most certainly knew it was not council. The only other position Teviotdale held was president of the Muskoka Conservatives.

If Cockburn had any doubt, it disappeared before the meeting ended. The Chairman made another little speech, praising Sandfield Macdonald as Premier and Cockburn as his supporter. He then moved, seconded by George Gow, "that we have the fullest confidence in Mr. Cockburn as our representative."

Everyone agreed by standing and applauding. I started them off on "Auld Lang Syne" and then we broke up.

116

When A.P. Cockburn closed the door on the Dominion Hotel that night he had been accepted, like it or not, into the ranks of the local Tories. It looked as if we had him.

A. P. Cockburn, Esq., M. P. P., was entertained by his friends and supporters on the 22nd ult. at the Dominion House, Bracebridge, a grand "oyster supper" was prepared by Mr. Ross, in his usual first class style; after the piscine removal, and the Queen, and other customary loyal toasts were given, next came the one of the evening "Our Guest"—by John Tevoitdale, Esq., Reeve, who made a very handsome comment on Mr. Cockburn's assiduity in meeting the wants and ___hes of our people.

Mr. Cockburn re___d ___rief speech, and after ___ ___ ___nds for their kind hosp___ ___ ___d to matters of greate___ ___ ted as he intende___ meetings th___ ___of ___ tha___ sub___ isfa___ W___

CHAPTER 10
RURAL JUSTICE

On the evening of September 15th, 1870 an excited crowd milled around the Gravenhurst wharf, waiting for the arrival of John Sandfield Macdonald, Premier of Ontario and his offical party. It was the first visit ever by a Premier of Ontario to Muskoka.

Here and there bursts of laughter broke through the dusk, and a grizzled face would shine and fade in the sudden flare of a rekindled pipe. The steamer Wenonah rode gently at the dockside. On the upper deck a steward quietly shuffled chairs; by the gangplank the purser stood brushing at a spot on his uniform. Everything was in readiness.

I stood slightly apart from the others, ready to assume my duties as township clerk and official greeter. This event was the rebirth of interest in political affairs. For eighteen months nothing much had happened in our outpost Muskoka; there was balance in the struggle for power. My duties as clerk were routine; A.P. Cockburn, having burned his fingers in politics, busied himself in his shipping interests. Thomas McMurray had gone to Parry Sound, and George Gow was all tied up as County Master of the Orange Lodge. Judge Lount found plenty of time from his duties to go fishing and trapping. No election was in the offing, and we had been like roosters in the barnyard, scratching away for food and ignoring all rivals.

The Premier's visit changed all that. All the local officials brushed off their seniority and stepped into public view. A.P. Cockburn became the local M.P.P. once more, modestly making his "fleet" available to the Premier. The Reeves of the Townships got out their good suits, trimmed their beards and bought their wives some new clothes. I was invited, as Clerk of the United Townships, to plan the trip and accompany the Premier on his tour. Those with no duties turned out to watch.

A procession of carriages clattering down Bay Street brought the crowd to life. With great fanfare the Premier stepped down, shook hands and then went aboard the

119

Wenonah for the trip to Bracebridge. He walked the deck a while to shake out the dust of his long ride, and then settled comfortably in a deck chair. A.P. Cockburn went up to the wheelhouse to assume his authority as owner. I stood near the Premier and introduced the local people to him as they approached.

The Wenonah chugged off into the night, edging her way carefully up Muskoka Lake and into the Muskoka River towards Bracebridge. The river was black and silent, save for the echo of the labouring engine. Deckhands stood forward to watch for logs and loose stumps, and fended them off when they appeared. Captain Scott paced the wheelhouse nervously, peering first forward and then to the sides to check his clearance. Behind him on the upper deck rode the most illustrious group of passengers that ever came aboard.

Suddenly, as we rounded the final bend in the river, huge bonfires flooded the shore ahead with blazing light, and the air was filled with shouting. The passengers rushed forward to look up the river.

"Bracebridge welcomes you, Mr. Premier," I called out, relieved that everything was ready.

"Brilliant," he exclaimed, "what a welcome!"

The Wenonah came to a grinding halt at the Bracebridge dock, and the passengers lined up behind the Premier to go ashore. They were met by a group of burly citizens who shook Sandfield's hand and applauded. Then the Honourable John Carling, Commissioner of Public Works for Ontario descended, followed by the Honourable Stephen Richards, Commissioner of Crown Lands, some distinguished English visitors and several M.P.P.'s When they were all on shore we gathered round them in the glare of the fires and raised three cheers that echoed around the dark forest. Then the whole crowd streamed up the hill to the Dominion Hotel. There we gave our distinguished guests a banquet, showered them with compliments, and finally let them go to bed at two o'clock in the morning.

The official party was eager to hear and see. For Sandfield

Macdonald it was a triumphal tour. He had backed development of the north as a major policy. Now he had come to reap the harvest. Carling and Richards were eager to see this unknown public property of which they had charge. The English visitors came to see what kind of place they were recommending to emigrants. And A.P. Cockburn desperately wanted to shine. He was the opposition Member who risked his career by backing Sandfield; now he was with the Premier in his glory. He was the Reformer dragged into Tory circles in Bracebridge; now he could be condescending. He was the Muskoka man returned from the city, bringing with him the great men of the province. But most of all, two of his personal projects were at stake. He wanted government support for them.

The new day found everyone up early, in spite of the late wining and dining. When the Premier came down, I took him in to breakfast. I ate briefly, then excused myself to look after the arrangements for the day. When the Premier learned that I had organized the tour, reception and dinner of the previous day he was loud in his praise.

"Very well done, Bell," he exclaimed, "don't you think so, gentlemen? Wish there were more like you around."

Everyone applauded and I was thrilled to be complimented by the Premier of the province.

About ten o'clock we sailed to the head of Muskoka Lake and into the Indian River which connects with the vast, unknown waters of the Upper Lakes. When we got there, Carling was delighted to see the place that had been named for him. He must have decided on the spot that his namesake, Port Carling, could hardly remain a flowing stream in the wilderness. A major construction of locks was certainly worth the cost here, he declared. Cockburn could hardly conceal his pleasure, hearing his first project assured.

Then we moved on to the waters between Lakes Rosseau and Joseph. Excavation had already begun on a ship passage, Cockburn's other dream. If any doubt remained about pushing ahead here, one of the English visitors settled that.

121

Taking up a piece of plank near the site, he nailed it to a pine tree and engraved the words "Port Sandfield" on it in large letters.

"I name this place Port Sandfield," he announced with the importance of his clerical office, "in honour of the great Premier of this province."

The crinkles around the corners of Sandfield Macdonald's eyes opened wide as we all gave three cheers. He walked around shaking hands with everyone, and his grave face came close to smiling. Could Port Sandfield be abandoned by the government and allowed to sink into oblivion? Cockburn knew it could not.

We came back to Bracebridge after that and sent the visitors on their way in great spirits. They were enthusiastic about the prospects for settlement, and for the projects under way. Cockburn was so pleased he shook my hand as they left. He knew he had won a victory. These projects of his, once completed, would make his hope of navigating the big three lakes a reality, and his ships would prosper.

Of course, I was pleased too. I had become personally acquainted with the Premier, my preparations had been successful and everything came off without a hitch. It was a feather in my cap.

No sooner had they left than I plunged into another big affair. Our Fall Fair at Bracebridge had grown into quite an event, and for the year 1870, the new decade, we decided to have a banquet after the show. We invited a lot of important people, and to our delight, they all accepted. What an occasion it was! John Morrison, our M.P. from North Victoria had never been to Bracebridge, so he took the opportunity to visit us. A.P. Cockburn, of course, accepted immediately. Then we had H.H. Cook of the Barrie lumbering firm; the Reeves of the Townships, the fair judges and the officers of our Society. It took some diplomacy to get everyone seated in the right order, but I managed.

After dinner we had the toasts and speeches. The members of our local Society were sitting on the edge of their seats as the

122

important people spoke. First there was Mr. Morrison.

"I sincerely apologize," he began, "for not having visited your beautiful village before. Your hospitality is unexcelled. I shall certainly come again as soon as I can."

It was quite an admission after being our Federal Member for three years.

Then A.P. Cockburn spoke; and the judges, and someone on behalf of the ladies. H.H. Cook got a lot of attention. The Cooks had been lumbering in Muskoka for years, but we seldom saw the big men of the family. Perhaps they had begun to realize they would have to work with us. In any case, here was Hermon H. Cook himself, telling us about it.

"I have travelled Muskoka for 14 years getting out square timber," he began, "but I have seldom seen such a large gathering of the important people of the district."

This started him out on the right foot, and then he proceeded to tell a whole string of stories about the early days. It was a thrill for everyone there.

J.B. Browning, our local lawyer, then got up and proposed a toast to me, for the work I had done as Secretary. There was loud applause, and I thanked them for the opportunity of serving.

Finally there was a toast to Mr. and Mrs. Ross, our hosts at the Dominion Hotel. Mr. Ross replied suitably, and just before he sat down, he had an afterthought.

"Our Secretary," he announced, "in addition to his other accomplishments, is a very talented musician. I think it would be appropriate to close the meeting with a song."

I was taken by surprise, but didn't let them down. It seemed like the occasion for a good patriotic song, so I delivered my favourite, with its ringing chorus:

"Three cheers for the Red, White and Blue,
Three cheers for the Red, White and Blue,
The army and Navy forever,
Three Cheers for the Red, White and Blue."

As the guests were leaving Mr. Cockburn came over to where I was gathering up my papers.

"You are a very accomplished person, Mr. Bell," he said, and I could see that he meant it, "I am happy to be associated with you on these pleasant occasions."

I felt good about that. In his distant way he was finally admitting some friendliness.

"Thank you," I replied, "we are always glad to have you among us." He looked at me strangely, as if the words reminded him of something. As he turned to leave I saw his lips move. He was not speaking to me, but I heard him say very distinctly:

"One of us?"

I wondered briefly if he blamed that Tory dinner on me, but I didn't really care. Tonight he had come to me, and I had won a victory. He had finally acknowledged that I was someone worth knowing.

It was from this plateau of well-being that I got sucked into the inevitable battle between Thomas McMurray and George Gow. McMurray arrived back in Bracebridge that fall, and brought his paper "The Northern Advocate" with him. It gave a big boost to the community to have its own newspaper, and McMurray threw himself immediately into political life. He followed the Reform line and knocked hard against the Conservatives. He took some sort of peeve at Charles W. Lount and made nasty remarks about him in the editorials. He hired James Boyer as editor, which left him free to go into real estate development, conveyancing, and several commercial enterprises. He built himself a big house in town and put on such a show that some people resented it.

I had always stayed on good terms with McMurray. He felt some paternal interest in me, I suppose, right from the day I arrived. He and George Gow disliked each other thoroughly, but I managed to keep my friendship with both of them. But that winter . . . well, it was the beginning of my troubles.

The township of Macaulay, which included Bracebridge, separated from the other townships late in 1870, and elections were called for a Reeve and Council. George Gow, who was a councillor in the united townships, pulled me aside during a

124

break in our November meeting of council.

"I'm running for Reeve of Macaulay," he informed me.

"That's great," I said, "you'll make a good Reeve."

I didn't say it just to please him. He was a hard man, but he got things done.

"McMurray's going to run against me," he added casually, "anything you can do will be appreciated."

It made me sick at my stomach. I couldn't work against McMurray. Gow must know that.

"That makes it tough for me," I said gently, "you are both good friends. McMurray made me Clerk."

"Politics is always tough," he reminded me.

"As Clerk I have to be independent," I pointed out, grasping at straws.

"You're Clerk, but not in Macaulay," he came back, "however, you could be Clerk of Macaulay if we win."

I couldn't think of anything to say, but the prospect thrilled me.

"McMurray's a real Grit," Gow went on, "and he's got his editor, Boyer, all lined up as Clerk. That leaves you out in the sticks in Draper."

He was beginning to dint my armour.

"Anyway," he said, "you just now agreed to support me."

"I don't have a vote in Macaulay," I protested, as my resistance faded, "so I can't help much that way."

"Don't worry, I'll think of something."

Nothing more was said then, but I knew I had lost.

I had to make my peace with McMurray, so I told him Gow had asked for my support. He was blunt.

"You don't live in Macaulay," he said, "so I've asked Mr. Boyer to be my Clerk. I'd get no votes backing a Draper man."

"I expect to move into town shortly," I explained, knowing it was pretty weak.

"Well it's too late. We're on opposite sides this time."

"Anyway, I do appreciate all you've done for me," I said, "nothing can change that."

He softened a bit, and forced a weak smile.

"You did a good job," he admitted, "even though you are a Tory."

We shook hands on that and parted.

I heard nothing for a couple of weeks, but one day Gow cornered me in Willson's store.

"Well, are you coming out canvassing with me?" he demanded.

"I'd rather not. I wouldn't feel right."

"McMurray's abandoned you. He's got someone else for Clerk."

"I know that," I said, "but I still don't want to go on the stump against him. Maybe I can help some other way."

"As a matter of fact, you can," he replied immediately, and I knew I'd been trapped.

"It's real easy," he said, "you just have to do nothing,"

I waited for him to lay it out.

"Yes, do nothing about the taxes till the election's over. There's some cheap friends of McMurray's that haven't paid their taxes. When they go to vote, they'll be challenged."

"But maybe they'll remember, and pay up."

"That's just the point," he said, leaning towards me with his eyes gleaming, "you keep the roll out of sight. The collector won't accept any taxes unless he has the roll. And he says you have it right now. Just keep it out of sight."

"That won't work" I said, "any man can vote as long as he's assessed."

"Those idiots don't know that," he declared, "as soon as a man is challenged, I'll have him thrown out of the poll."

I was trapped; but I had made my choice. I was through with McMurray, and if I fooled around with Gow much longer, I'd be out with him too.

"I'll keep out of sight," I promised, and that seemed to satisfy him.

The contest between Gow and McMurray started off at full tilt, and it was one of the dirtiest local elections ever fought in our parts. They both had money and spent it. They used every trick in the trade that could get a vote. Anyone who owed either of them money, or a favour, was squeezed for a declaration of support, to include his family and relatives too. And there was no escape in anonymity either. Votes were cast aloud at the polls in those days, and the poll clerk wrote it down in the poll book. The agents at the polls and everybody else knew what way you went.

Charles W. Lount jumped right in behind Gow. And he was no pussyfooter, judge or not. He talked against McMurray during the whole election, even taking obvious cracks at him from the bench. McMurray used his advantage as a printer to get out posters, something never done before in a local election. Gow went off to Orillia and got posters of his own. Then, of course, the rumour mill got running, and the mud-slinging started.

But McMurray was no match for Gow when it came to dirty tricks. Everything he tried, Gow went one better. And in the end it paid off. George Gow won the election.

I didn't go to the first council meeting, expecting that Gow would look after me. I waited for a call to take over as Clerk, but the call never came. Then I learned that Gow had missed the meeting. Mr. James Boyer was there with paper and pencil while I lolled at home. The council appointed him Clerk. Gow was furious.

"I was sick, damn it," he exploded when I asked him, "why didn't you go and tell the council I'd appointed you Clerk."

"I didn't know . . ." I began.

"It serves you right," he shouted, "when your side wins, grab the rewards. Don't wait for somebody to hand them out. It never happens."

"I found that out," I admitted sadly.

"Well you've nobody to blame but yourself. After all that work I end up with McMurray's Clerk. What a mess!"

One thing pleased me about the election, though; I didn't lose McMurray's friendship. The fact that I went to him and put my cards on the table seemed to increase his respect for me. He may have suspected my involvement in the tax roll

127

scheme, but he never mentioned it. I was glad I'd been frank with him. Gow would never have done it, and I began to realize that George Gow was his own kind of politician, not mine. You catch more flies with honey than vinegar.

There was one unpleasant aftermath, though. McMurray did not forgive Charles W. Lount; he blamed him for his defeat. So McMurray set out to even the score and used his newspaper, The Northern Advocate, to accomplish it. First he ran a nasty story running down the way Lount ran his court. He printed a satirical headline, "Court Day in Bracebridge; the Reign of Despotism." That article went over well so he wrote another one, stepping up the abuse: A PEEP INTO OUR COURT HOUSE. It was written to make Lount look ridiculous.

"There seated upon the Orange platform sits Mr. Lount with the Clerk of the Court on his right and a barrister on his left. One hundred men or more with half a dozen females and a few dogs make up the audience. Considerable din and clamour is observable and C.W. calls out 'Silence gentlemen, we can't hear a word'. Then comes a lull when all at once the Stipendiary calls out 'who's that man smoking? put that man out'. Presently the dogs begin to fight, and the judge with much dignity (?) cries, 'kick that dog out, throw it over the rail'."

Another week McMurray described Lount at his duties as land commissioner:

"If you go and knock on the door of this petty tyrant, you may hear the well-known voice belching forth 'go to H--'. If you enter his office to transact business you are in danger of being thrown down the stairs."

Lount retaliated by removing all court notices and time tables from the Advocate and placing them in the Northern Light of Orillia. This not only deprived McMurray of the revenue, but people had to buy the opposition paper to find out when their case came up. The debate then moved to the Northern Light, which delightedly reported that McMurray had preyed on local people in his early days by peddling pigs cheeks at huge prices. In return, Lount was accused of buying them to keep from starving.

Then the inevitable happened. Someone sued McMurray in Lount's court and McMurray lost. When he discovered there was no appeal he was furious. Lount wasn't fit to be a judge, McMurray claimed.

"He is good at trapping muskrat," he wrote of Lount in the Advocate, "but as a lawyer he is far below mediocrity."

After this appeared, the Advocate claimed that a "bully boy" was sent by Lount to assault McMurray. As the fury rose, the village divided into two camps.

Then one day I was approached by a group of "concerned citizens" most of them merchants.

"This feud has to stop," Mr. Willson said, "it's bringing the whole district into disrepute. You know them both, Bell, do something."

It made me feel like Solomon, so I undertook the task. I went to Judge Lount first, asking him to end the quarrel.

"When that rag stops libelling me," he declared, "I may give them back their advertising. But if they don't stop, I'll sue them in the High Court for everything they have. Go tell that to your printers devil friends."

"They're not my friends."

"Then mind your own business."

I should have taken his advice, but the thought of playing Solomon to our own little court overwhelmed me. So I went to the Advocate office and saw McMurray.

"Don't try to interfere," he warned, "with the freedom of the press. As long as we have a drunken, biased judge it's our duty to expose him."

"He may sue you for libel."

"So-o-o," McMurray exclaimed, as though seeing a great light, "you have been sent to threaten us."

"No, no," I protested, "I just heard Lount mention it when I saw him."

They didn't believe me.

"You can't frighten us," Boyer chipped in, "go back to your master and tell him to sue. We know our duty."

Well I didn't go back to Lount, and I quit playing peace-maker. Everybody was mad at me; Lount, McMurray and the citizens. Worst of all, McMurray never really forgave me.

George Gow let me off quite easily in the circumstances. He never believed in peace-making.

"You silly bastard," he said, "you shouldn't be out alone."

I put it all down to another lesson in the school of hard knocks. And as time went by I realized that my stock was still high. At least the important people of the district came to me in time of trouble. And they all contined to talk to me. I would be wiser next time. I determined to rise above all these petty people, my older brother, my critical friends, yes, even a demanding wife. Soon they would see my star rising, and come to me again for help. And I wouldn't let them down.

130

CHAPTER 11
THE SINKHOLE

On the road between Uffington and Bracebridge, right in the middle of a swamp, there was a sinkhole. According to local legend an early settler and his team of oxen dropped into it and were never seen again. True or not, enough logs, rocks, brush and gravel were poured into that hole to fill a good sized barn. And still the surface shook when anything passed over it. Passage was worst in the Spring when the swamp was wet, and water covered the surface of the road. Then you had to steer your way through the water, trying to stay in the middle where the road bed was solid. Quicksand deep under the surface kept the sides continually shifting.

The trick in crossing the swamp was to stay in the middle of the road and keep going. To stop, even in the centre of the road, was foolhardy. Every now and then a plunging team with a heavy load would get off into the soft spot and down they would go. There's a load of logs somewhere in that hole, still sitting on the sleigh they went down on. The team was cut loose and the horses thrashed their way to safety.

One day, late in December of 1870, I left Bracebridge to drive back to Uffington near dusk. I hated to start out; it was snowing and dark and I could hardly see the road ahead. But I had to go, for Anne had been alone two days. The first few miles weren't bad, and my mare Nelly trotted along easily. But when we turned off the Muskoka Road there was no other track, and she slowed down to pick her way more carefully. We drove along steadily, encouraged by the faint glow of light through the settlers' cabin windows.

A couple of miles before we reached the swamp, the weather closed in. Hard-driving snow blew at us from the North, and I turned my coat collar against the wind. I loosened the reins, for Nelly could find her way better without direction. When we came to the big hill, I slapped the reins over her back to remind her to move along. Up the hill we went, into the thick forest, guided only by the border of trees on each side. She heaved and snorted as she pulled, and I got out once to ease the load. But the snow was so deep that I climbed back in again. Half way up she stopped to rest, and I turned my back to the wind. Going again, the left runner climbed onto a big rock and the cutter turned on its side, throwing me out, and twisting the shafts and harness against the poor mare's legs. She whinnied nervously and kicked to release the pressure. I turned the cutter upright, but she wouldn't move. I let her rest, adjusted the harness and shafts, and then pulled her up by the bit. We reached the top of the hill and rested again.

The swamp was just ahead of us, down the hill, and around a sharp bend. It was a dark dismal place, no houses, no fences, no lights; the rattle of dead branches, the smell of rotten vegetation and the dampness of the air made it fearful for man and beast. My mare hated the quivering surface at the sinkhole, and she knew we were coming to it. Nervous from the upset, she picked her way down the hill, into the swamp and right to the edge of the sinkhole. There she stopped. I let her stand for a few minutes; the force of the wind was broken there and the snow was blowing less fiercely. Then I picked up the reins and slapped them gently on her back. Nothing happened. We had to cross, there was no alternative. We'd done it a hundred times before, but this time she baulked.

I got out of the cutter and grabbed her by the bit strap, pulling her forward. She started to move gingerly across the spongy ground. The sharp crack of a falling limb startled her and she reared up. The strap was pulled from my hand, and as I sprang for it, the mare backed away, breaking one of the shafts on the cutter. She reared again and plunged into the soft ground of the sinkhole. I let her go and crawled out. Then I went to get some planks stacked on the roadside for emergencies like this. I shoved one of them under her belly and another by her front feet. She soon crawled out, dragging the broken cutter behind. The water in the sinkhole never froze up, and my feet and legs were soaked. We were both caked with mud as I led her home.

Well, that did it. I'd been thinking for some time of getting out of the wilderness. I spent half my time on that road between Bracebridge and Uffington; twelve long miles of primitive horse-track, dusty and stifling in the summer, snow-clogged in the winter. The few days of statute labour that was spent on it each year did little more than keep the underbrush from closing in completely. I'd had enough of it.

Living in Uffington had always worked against me anyway. It was inconvenient, of course, but there was also the snob factor. When I first came up, Uffington and Bracebridge were about even. But now Bracebridge was the county town; Bracebridge was the commercial centre; Bracebridge was a lake port. The rest of us lived in the sticks. People never said it in so many words, but it came through clear enough. "Out there in Uffington" they would say, as if it were in the slums. It wasn't that an Uffington man was inferior; he had just shown bad judgement.

I knew that I would eventually have to move if I wanted to get ahead. From Bracebridge I could step up my public image, improve my social standing and enlarge my circle of friends. I would keep in closer touch with current affairs and be on hand when things happened. Most of my interests were in Bracebridge anyway; Agricultural Society, Council, Orange Lodge and the Church. In fact, I had a lot to do with starting them up. But I knew that a farmer had little chance of getting a political nomination. It always seemed to go to business or professional men. I had the knowledge of a professional man now, what with my council experience, assistance to settlers in business affairs, and practice in land registry, crown land applications, and so forth. I could fill out forms and complete affidavits. I was a professional man in fact, if not in name. My apprenticeship should be over, and I could easily qualify as a land and general agent. I just needed a push to get me moving, and that sinkhole did it. When I got home that night, I told Anne we must move.

It was a hard decision. It sounded exciting to be where things were happening, to live near the stores and churches, the mills and carpenters. But Anne was a home body, and her home and

133

friends were in Uffington. I was the one, though, who travelled the long miles, and she knew it was hard. One final event tipped the scales; Anne was with child again. There were two new doctors in Bracebridge. Dr. Byers had opened a professional drug store, and Dr. Bridgland had a small hospital in his house. More than anything else, Anne wanted to be near a doctor.

"I'll never go through that again," she stated flatly, thinking of our terrible ordeal when Margaret Hannah was born. I took her words as approval.

The preparations to move began at once. I already had a lot on River Street in Bracebridge, and a building site was partly cleared. Now I bought lumber and supplies, and hauled them to the lot. I stayed overnight in Bracebridge more often. I applied for a position that was advertised, and miraculously got a prompt acceptance. I broke the news to Anne as soon as I got back home.

"I got my appointment today," I told her, "it arrived in the mail."

"What appointment?" she asked, for I had said nothing to her.

"I am now the sole Muskoka agent of Traveler's Insurance Company of Hartford, Connecticut."

"And do they pay a salary?" she asked at once.

"Even better, they pay a commission. The more business I do, the more money I make."

She was not totally convinced; I could tell by the wrinkle on her forehead.

"It's a first," I went on with all my enthusiasm, "there is no competition in the insurance business up here. The field is wide open. R.J. Bell has done it again."

"What do you plan to live on?" she demanded, "that business won't pay money overnight."

"Insurance is a profession," I went on, without answering, "it will raise our social status. When business gets good I can employ a clerk, and a secretary, maybe two or three."

"Richard Bell," she broke in severely, "you haven't answered my question. What are we going to live on?"

I stopped rambling, for I saw she was serious. It was a problem all right, I no longer had my Clerk's job, and though it had only paid $35 a year it was regular.

"I have several things in mind," I assured her.

"That's not enough for me to move on," she declared, "we can't live on social status."

"Harry Portas is looking for a book-keeper in the Mammoth Emporium," I mentioned, "it's a couple of days a week. But you have to look after the counter too."

"When you're a big business man, you can quit looking after the counter," she said with an edge in her voice, "in the meantime, go and get the job."

Next morning, first thing, I went back to town. I felt embarrassed, because store clerking was not my idea of social status. On the way I decided to add "accountant" to my occupations of land agent and insurance. Harry agreed to become my first client. That satisfied everybody. Some of my friends got together and helped me finish the house. Soon we moved in to Bracebridge. Goodbye, sinkhole.

How I enjoyed those first weeks in town! One social event followed another that January, and they were happy, welcoming affairs. First the Church of England had its concert in aid of the building fund. Amid the chattering crowd the warm, brightly lit hall literally glowed with friendliness. People went out of their way to make us welcome. Everyone of importance for miles around was there. The concert itself was brilliant, and we were all amazed at the talent in our little town. Dashing young Dr. Bridgland was a mimic, and kept everyone in stitches with his act. There were songs and recitations, piano solos and quartets. The warmth and closeness of our frontier community, the talent and the applause it brought, were all intoxicating. Anne, though uncomfortable in her approach to confinement, came out of her shell that night and became the girl I first met. We went home delighted with our new life.

A week later the Methodists held a social evening. I was asked to take part, and accepted at once. I sang for that crowd as I had never sung before; my tenor notes rung the rafters, followed by prolonged applause. It pleased me to be part of the community, not just a visitor from the country. Anne didn't come that night; said she didn't feel well. It disappointed me that she didn't see me perform. But being alone had its compensations. The ladies paid me a lot of attention, which was very flattering. And the men shook my hand and congratulated me on my voice. Many of them didn't even know I could sing. I'm sure it raised my stock among them; it was a sign of refinement.

The Winter Evening Amusement group presented a play; the Presbyterians had a bake sale and church supper. I faithfully attended all events, making my presence felt in the community. I particularly enjoyed the bake sale, where I was the only man present. Anne never understood the way I felt among the ladies. To me it was an exciting, sensual, experience. I loved to be fussed over, to exchange furtive glances with some, open smiles with others. I felt friendly, even desirous. I appreciated the femininity of a woman, without having to do anything about it. To Anne I was simply making a play for this one, or that; she saw something wicked in it. I could never explain my feelings to her. But there was a combination of business with pleasure at these events. I was being seen, and appreciated.

I wanted to be in town when opportunity knocked. And within a few weeks, it did.

In January, A.P. Cockburn announced that he was not running for re-election. The truth is, he was trapped. He had backed Sandfield Macdonald, but Sandfield's star had fallen; ill and performing badly the Premier was under constant attack in the Assembly and on the street. His great expansion plan for Ontario died down as the money ran out. The Macdonald alliance between Ottawa and Toronto had weakened, and in any case Sir John's own stock was down in Ontario. The Globe continually reported Sandfield on the point of death or insanity. The opposition, which Cockburn had abandoned, was finding its feet and seemed destined to win the next election.

136

Cockburn was too smart to run on Sandfield's ticket. Even if Sanfield won, which wasn't likely, George Brown was waiting for Cockburn like a loaded pistol. He couldn't survive another assault by the Globe, and that would come if he ran Tory. He couldn't run in Brown's Reform party, after all the fuss over the Nine Martyrs. And he couldn't even run independent. That would be a repudiation of Sandfield, who was still Premier, and Cockburn wanted the Port Carling lock and the Port Sandfield canal finished. So he followed the only course open.

"Business matters now require all my personal attention," he announced, "and therefore I will not be a candidate."

The Liberals thereupon nominated a man named Dalton Ullyot from Victoria County. The way was wide open for a Muskoka Conservative to carry the Riding. And I was right on hand.

Another item in my good fortune was completely unexpected. One day in February when I was at the Emporium, working on the books, a neighbour boy came running in.

"The doctor wants you right away," he gasped.

I grabbed my coat and ran all the way home. Dr. Bridgland was waiting.

"It was a near thing," he said, "but the crisis has passed; you are the father of twins."

"Twins!" I exclaimed, "are they all right?"

"Just fine," he assured me, "it's your wife you have to worry about."

"Is she in danger?"

"For a few days. Physically I think she'll recover, but . . . "

"But what?"

"She had a very hard time of it," he declared, "and her mental state seems unsettled. I don't know what to think."

Having twins overwhelmed me completely. There hadn't been twins in the whole district as far as I could remember. Two healthy boys, too. I had really wanted a boy this time, but two was unbelievable. What a boost to my image that was; not only a family man but the father of twins! Three children in two years was quite a record.

But Anne lay exhausted in her bed all day. When I came into the room she didn't seem to recognize me; just lay there staring as if she were alone. Next day it didn't change, nor the next. She finally got back on her feet, but I could see she was different. At best she ignored me, at worst she seemed to loathe me. If I had not been so fully involved in the election, it would have driven me to distraction.

With all the excitement, I overlooked something crucial. I should have declared my political intentions loud and clear. George Gow knew I had ambitions to run provincially, and I thought that was enough. But he got mixed up in some terrible wrangles as Reeve and neglected everything else. In February, council refused to reverse decisions made in his absence at the first meeting. He was so mad he resigned; but council refused to accept his resignation. When he insisted, they adjourned the meeting. Then he refused to sign the disputed by-laws; council met without him and appointed a councillor to sign the books. And all this on the verge of a provincial election.

Gow was even too busy to go to the insiders' meeting called to discuss a provincial candidate. Instead he sent John Teviotdale. And though Teviotdale knew I was a hardworking party man, he didn't realize I wanted the nomination. I was completely disgusted with George Gow; that was twice he let me down in as many months. The first I heard about the nomination was from Teviotdale at Lodge. He took me aside so as not to involve the others in politics.

"Suppose you'll work this election," he mumbled, breaking into the subject.

"Didn't know it was called," I replied.

"It isn't yet. Coming in a few days."

"When is the nomination?"

"Won't be one," he stated flatly, "we have our man already."

"And who is that?"

"Duncan McRae from Bolsover. Lumberman, lots of money, ready to go."

138

I looked at him speechless, and he must have seen the surprise in my eyes.

"Nobody after it up here," he explained, "they wanted a Victoria County man against Ullyot."

"I would have considered it," I said, declaring myself much too late.

"You, R.J.?" he asked, surprised, "yes, you might at that. But then, it's all settled you know."

"So I see."

"No use fighting it. They had it all settled before I got there."

"Who is they?" I asked, not a little annoyed.

"Oh, the others, you know. Word from up above. Not much discussion."

"Didn't Gow tell you I was interested?"

"He mentioned you - sort of. Just in passing. Funny I never thought of it."

He wrinkled his brow trying to remember.

"It wouldn't have mattered anyway," he said finally, "McRae was there with his manager. We worked on plans for the campaign."

"All cut and dried," I muttered.

"Sorry, R.J. Maybe next time. Let us know sooner, eh? Then we can put up a fight for you. McRae's coming up. Nice fellow, you'll like him."

He shuffled off to do something else, shaking his head and muttering. I went through the meeting with a lump in my stomach, and it didn't go away for two days. And that's how I lost my first election, without even getting started.

I was despondent for those two days. I went out to the farm, lit a fire in the house and put myself to work. Deep down I knew I'd come out of it and pitch in for McRae. But in the meantime I didn't want to see anybody. I took out my frustrations chopping up firewood. The harder I worked the better I felt, and finally I had it worked off and went back into town. That's the day McRae arrived.

He was a nice fellow, all right. A group of us met him at the

Dominion Hotel. I guess he heard how I was pushed aside, for he made a special effort.

"I hope you can work for me, Mr. Bell," he said, "though I know you'd rather be working for yourself."

"That's all right," I answered, not denying it, "I didn't move fast enough."

"Good man," he exclaimed, "your turn will come and you won't be forgotten."

I accepted that as a promise.

"Now, I'm pretty safe in Victoria," he went on, getting down to business, "if you fellows can carry me up here, we can win."

"We'll do it," declared George Gow, back on the scene now that things were moving, "just give me a free hand."

"You have it," said McRae, reaching into his pocket.

Well, we had money to work with, disinterested Grits and A.P. Cockburn out of the picture. Our party was still the government and we got all the breaks they could give us. In that election I saw George Gow at his best, or worst, whichever side you were on. He got names on the voters lists, he lined up carriages and drivers for voting day, he arranged time off for workers and paid them their lost salary and then some. He also had some doubtful and downright shocking tricks too; arm twisting, veiled threats, promises he couldn't carry out, appeals to prejudice, money on the side or a bottle of liquor. It depended on what your vote was worth.

When the 1871 election was over on March 21st, Duncan McRae had won, with 518 votes to Ullyot's 428. It was a clear victory. It made me sick to think that it could have been me. Of course, Gow had bought votes which I couldn't afford, but the swing was our way in the Riding. With Cockburn out of the picture in Muskoka, I could have got a lot of the votes that went to Ullyot.

Across the province, though, it was a different story. Sandfield Macdonald lost out to Edward Blake and his Liberals, but he didn't resign as Premier. He chose to carry on "until defeated in the Assembly". And he didn't call the Assembly.

140

The election was barely over when my brother Decimus and his wife Jane showed up to visit us. As I met them at the door they swept past me and embraced Anne with such tears and sympathy that I wondered what had happened.

"Oh you poor girl," Decimus oozed, "I know how you must feel."

"We came right away," Jane declared.

"What's happened?" I asked, bewildered, "why are you carrying on like this?"

All three of them stopped their weeping and wailing and stared at me.

"Look at that. He doesn't even understand what he's doing," exclaimed Decimus, "what a boor. How you must suffer!"

I understood one thing. I had been tried and convicted of something without being accused. I also knew something else. I disliked my brother more than ever before. When he was with men he was disgusting enough, looking like a gigolo with his slicked down hair, smooth face and impudent manner. But with women he was like one, simpering and whining. I don't know how we ever came from the same parents. In fact, I sometimes wondered if he'd been adopted.

"Would you please tell me what this is all about?" I pleaded.

"Plain and simple neglect," said Decimus, "it's a crying shame."

"Is there something specific?" I asked, trying to get an answer.

"Something specific!" he mimicked, "three years of cruelty and neglect, and you want something specific."

I began to piece it together. Anne had written them a letter in one of her bad moods, telling some terrible tale of woe. Jane was probably sympathetic. But Decimus saw the chance to humiliate me in my own home. How I hated him. Why didn't he stay home and mind his own business? A cold fury took hold of me.

"Now that you are both here," I announced quietly, "I can leave my poor wife in your hands. I have wood to cut."

I put on my coat and turned to go out. Fleetingly I saw a look of dismay on Anne's face. It wasn't going as she had expected. Well, she'd learn to tell our troubles to others! And they would learn something about interfering. If they thought it was all my fault, they hadn't been around the past few months.

I went out, locked up my office and put a notice on the door. Then I hired a horse, and went out to the farm again. As we crossed the sinkhole, the nag never wavered; straight ahead without faltering. That set me thinking. It's when you hesitate that you get into trouble. Worry about the dangers and you lose your judgement. Even a horse can lose its sense. I stayed at the farm for three days, until I figured my kinfolk would be sick of each other. The minute I got back to Bracebridge, Decimus and Jane left.

Maybe it wasn't a very smart thing to do. But I felt a lot better.

Oddly enough, the atmosphere around home improved. I felt sheepish about going off that way and Anne knew it. She never let me apologize, which kept me in line, so to speak. I knew she was embarrassed about writing to Decimus. She talked more openly about her fits of depression, and showed some sympathy for the disappointments I had.

Now I'm not a morose type of person; but that Spring I was really out of whack. The move into town had started off great, then thudded into personal failures. I'd been Clerk for three years, now I was out. I'd lost what seemed to be the real chance for nomination. County status was no further ahead, and there was no county clerk's job to work for. My home life wasn't the best, and business was slow.

Then a ray of light shone through the gloom. About the end of June, John Teviotdale came down to ask what I was doing Wednesday night.

"Nothing, I guess."

"Having a presentation," he mumbled, "like you to help out."

"You want me to sing?"

"Appreciate it."

"Who's being honoured?"

"Fellow you know. Keep it secret."

142

I practised up a couple of numbers, got all dressed up on Wednesday night, and went to the Orange Hall. To my surprise, Anne decided to come along.

"I really should get out more," she explained, and I was delighted.

It was a friendly crowd. We stood around talking and laughing, and a lot of our friends were there. I glowed with pleasure, for I like nothing better than a happy social occasion. Mr. Teviotdale finally went up on the stage and started the proceedings. He said a few words about the honoured guest, what a fine job he had done for the community and so on. "I'd like Richard Bell to come up here," he said when he had finished, and I suddenly suspected I wasn't there to sing. I walked up to the platform in sort of a red haze as everybody applauded and hurrahed. Mr. Teviotdale read out a formal address.

"The valuable services which you have rendered the municipality, your cordial assistance to the Agricultural Society, your deep interest in everything calculated to advance the interests of the district, call for this mark of appreciation and esteem."

It was signed on behalf of the ratepayers of the former united townships of Draper, Macaulay, Stephenson, Ryde and Oakley, which I had served as Clerk. He also handed me a package containing a keyless watch manufactured by Thomas Russell and Sons of Liverpool; a very valuable time-piece.

They gave me three hearty cheers and everyone stood around afterwards to shake my hand. I was deeply moved.

"What we're tryin' to say," George Gow explained over a cup of tea, "is that we like havin' you around. Don't let misfortune throw you off. Just keep drivin' straight ahead, and eventually you'll get where yer goin'."

"Straight through the ol' sinkhole," I said, picking up the rough tongue he'd lapsed into.

He looked blank.

"Oh never mind," I added, "I won't give up."

He understood that, and brightened up into a near smile. He knew I had the message.

CHAPTER 12
DIRTY TRICKS

Early in April of 1872 the main events of my political career had their beginning. First came the news that Muskoka would become a separate riding for the coming federal election. That raised my spirits immensely. Right here in our district we would run our own campaign; no more outsiders crowding in from Victoria County. Among us we would select our own candidates, name our election officials and control our own affairs. It seemed almost as if they had done it for me. I was well known in Muskoka, our party was in power at Ottawa and I worked closely with those who ran things locally. I was now township clerk of Macaulay. I had the feeling that my time had come.

But almost immediately my high hopes faltered. George Gow told me that someone named Boulton was proposed as the federal candidate in the new riding. He was an outsider, but "in" with the big wheels of the party. Gow told me that Boulton was probably picked by Sir John A. Macdonald himself. I was really crushed and it must have shown in my face, for Gow clapped me on the shoulder and even managed to look embarrassed.

"Don't feel bad about it," he sympathized, "you've still lots of time. Back the party and some day the party will back you."

"And when will that be?"

"Who knows," he shrugged, "it might be five years; it might be tomorrow. Boulton might even change his mind."

All the same, it seemed unfair that after getting our independence, so to speak, we immediately lost it to someone from outside. I debated with myself for several days, feeling angry and resentful. Didn't a man ever have the opportunity to test his popularity? It seemed not, for there wasn't even a suggestion of a nominating meeting.

"The demand for Boulton will overwhelm us, once they know he's interested," Gow explained but he avoided my questions about how the choice was made. I never did find out. The

144

Northern Light of Orillia, not even a Tory paper, jumped on the bandwagon for Boulton as soon as the news was leaked.

"Mr. Boulton is a Liberal-Conservative and would make a remarkably strong run. We doubt if any man could successfully oppose him," the editor wrote in his most enthusiastic comment on any Tory.

I was still wondering what was so special about Boulton when I walked into H.J. McDonald's little store that he built beside the Royal Hotel and found him all worked up.

"I've heard some danged wild rumours in my time," he burst out, "but this one is the wildest."

"What have you heard?" I asked.

"That Charlie Lount is talking in favour of D'Arcy Boulton."

"What's strange about that? Lount's a Sandfield Macdonald man and Boulton is running for Sir John."

"Did you ever hear of Col. Samuel Lount?" he asked curiously.

"Vaguely," I recalled, "wasn't he hanged as a rebel?"

"Exactly. Now people around here believe that Charlie Lount is one of his relatives. And the people that hanged Samuel Lount was the old Family Compact. And the Boultons were part of the Compact! Now why would a Lount have anything favourable to say about a Bouton?"

"Beats me," I agreed, "and I wonder why a judge would get mixed up in politics anyway."

"I can't figure it out."

I thought about this situation seriously. If there was something underhanded going on, I wanted to know about it. I figured I should go to Lount, because I knew him well; but he was a crusty character, capable of anything. I found an excuse to go up to the Registry Office one day and found him alone.

"They say you're supporting D'Arcy Boulton as our candidate," I began, "I didn't think judges got involved in politics."

"Hell, man, I'm no judge," he said, waving his hand to dismiss the thought, "I'm only a justice of the peace and I settle piddling disputes between settlers in the Division Court.

They call me a judge to make people think we have civilization up here."

"Some people," I went on cautiously, "think it strange that a Lount would be supporting a Boulton."

He looked at me angrily for a couple of minutes, and I began to regret my curiosity.

"How much do you know about it?" he asked finally.

"Not much," I admitted, "I wasn't born over here, and had my schooling in the old country. I just pick up things on my own."

"Well you might as well get the truth of the matter. You hear it seldom enough," he began, sitting down in his chair and putting his feet up, "so I'll tell you a few things. Old D'Arcy Boulton, this D'Arcy's grandfather, came to Upper Canada before the turn of the century. He was smart, that old man. He was made a barrister, then became Attorney General, the premier of the province. Later he was Chief Justice. He spawned a big brood of Boultons. His son Henry also went into politics and also became Attorney-General. But they're not a family to sit back and watch others being wronged. Mark that, because it's the reason for my feeling towards them. Right then the common people of Upper Canada were treated like chattels. Henry got up in the Assembly one day in 1833 and raked over the Colonial Office for the way they treated us. He was dismissed from office, for it was considered an attack on the Crown, almost treason. But Henry went over to England where the family has influence, and raised hell about it. They appointed him Chief Justice of Newfoundland to keep him quiet."

He paused for a moment to consider his words.

"Now, just four years later my uncle, Samuel Lount, also challenged the authorities on behalf of the people. He stood at the head of a group of farmers at Montgomery's Tavern, and they threatened violence if things weren't put to rights. He was deceived by a man named Rolph who came to him from the Lieutenant Governor and led him into a trap. My uncle was found guilty of treason and they had him executed. It led to

146

reforms and our present system of government. My uncle was a patriot, not a rebel. Everybody was against the hanging."

"I'm glad to know that," I said sincerely, and he seemed to warm to me.

"There were other Boultons, too," he went on, "George Boulton the old man's second son was high in the military. William his grandson was in the Assembly and was also Mayor of Toronto. And you have probably heard of Charles, his great grandson who served in the Red River Rebellion, was condemned to death and reprieved a couple of years ago. But the man who tried to put things right on my uncle's behalf was William Boulton. Fifteen years after Rolph deceived my uncle, William Boulton accused Rolph to his face in the House of Assembly at Quebec. There were words, but Boulton won his point; and the name of Samuel Lount was once again honoured. They're a fine family, the Boultons, and if any man named D'Arcy Boulton chooses to run in this Riding, I'll do anything I can for him; Family Compact or not. Yes, they were part of it, but they were among the first to right its wrongs."

"You seem very close to these events," I said, overwhelmed by the story so few people knew.

"How else could I be?" he asked, "ten years ago I helped take my uncle's body from the potter's field where they buried it to a place of honour in the Toronto Necropolis."

He got up suddenly and went over to fiddle with some books on a shelf. I knew he was emotional and wanted no one to see it.

"Thank you, I have to go," I called out and left the building. I understood Charles W. Lount a lot better after that. Never again did he seem the terrible despot that others called him. And I knew a lot more about D'Arcy Boulton.

But for all Boulton's family I still resented his intrusion into our territory. What gave him the right to come up here and present himself as one of us? We had people here who could carry the banner for Sir John, people who had travelled the roads, and settled the wilderness. I could believe myself one of these. I thought we had left privilege and pedigree in the old country. I tried to talk to Anne about it, for there was no use in talking to Gow or Lount. They were delighted about Boulton. And Anne just passed it off too.

"Who else is there around here?" she asked sarcastically, knowing very well who else there was. She had little sympathy for my ambitions; she only wanted me to stay home and be a husband. But the disdain in her voice really upset me. I left the house despondently and walked along the river to the edge of the falls; a place where the roar of the waters drowned out everything else and left a man at peace with his thoughts.

And when I came back, my mind was clear and settled. I would go out and work for D'Arcy Boulton with everything I had. The alternatives were so bleak they were not worth considering. If Sir John Macdonald and George Gow and Charles W. Lount were all for Boulton, what chance was there for me? I couldn't even get support at home. It was all or nothing, for nobody is neutral in politics. I chose all. When the faithful were recognized, R.J. Bell would be in the front ranks.

It was well that my mind was settled, for I had hardly come up from my place of decision before George Gow pounced on me.

"Boulton's coming up soon," he told me, "we have to hold some meetings before he gets here."

"I'm ready," said I, with firmness in my voice.

"Good man!" Gow exclaimed, "I knew you'd come round."

"I hardly faltered,"

We started right then to organize for Boulton. We set up a meeting at Rosseau to suggest a candidate for Sir John. Over 50 men turned out. When they got the word that D'Arcy Boulton was the choice they passed a resolution asking him to run, gave three cheers and then set to scheming against the Grits. I marvelled at how simple it was. George Gow merely mentioned Boulton's name and they all fell in behind. No questions, no doubts, no hesitation. Gow was the man with the word and they believed him. It crossed my mind that he could have named anyone.

Then we had another meeting at Utterson, in the school

house. Forty big men crowded into the small room. The bigwigs sat up at the front by the teacher's desk in their highbuttoned coats and hard hats. Down below husky settlers in their best suits squeezed into the children's desks or stood around awkwardly at the back. "Boulton's the man," the word went round, and they all signed a petition for him to run. Loyal speeches were made, Sir John praised for his wisdom and three cheers for the Queen. Then they went home, their duty done.

But Bracebridge was the climax. Nothing was left out when the local Tories addressed a crowd of 150 people at the Orange Hall.

"D'Arcy Boulton is the third generation of that illustrious name," declared the Chairman, John Teviotdale, "and we would be honoured to have him as our representative. His grandfather was known as the great Chief Justice. And his mother's brother was also Chief Justice, Sir John Beverly Robinson."

He paused as the meeting burst into applause.

"He was educated at Upper Canada College, called to the bar in 1847 and has made a name of his own as an advocate. Not only that, he is presently Grand Master of Ontario West."

This brought the whole crowd to its feet. No need to explain. To belong to the Orange Order, to be high in its councils, was the final achievement. Such a man would maintain the faith, stand firm against popish greed, and lead the protestants of Muskoka into their rightful place in the new order of things. A petition went round at the end of the meeting, and every man signed. Such a candidate must not escape! Now I could see the strategy. Boulton wasn't seeking the job; the people were seeking him. And I certainly knew he was ready.

The other side wasn't idle; far from it. Just a few days after our Bracebridge meeting, the Liberals held a nominating convention at the Dominion Hotel in Bracebridge. I went at George Gow's suggestion, on the surface as township clerk, but really as a spy to see how things went. Though Gow was Reeve he wouldn't be found dead at a Grit meeting.

As I walked down the main street the promise of summer was in the air. The trees were blanketed with fresh green foliage; the sun was shining fitfully, gathering strength for the hot days ahead. The water of the Muskoka River tumbled over the North Falls nearby in a torrent of sound and spray. And when I entered the hotel I found the same cheerfulness inside. The dining room was filled with laughter and gaiety; there was handshaking and backslapping. Shouts of recognition for old friends rang across the room and out into the hallway. "Well look who's here" was called out time and again as new arrivals were recognized. They seemed confident and excited. A man beside me poked me in the ribs and pointed out William Beatty from Parry Sound.

"He's the man who founded the place and practically owns the whole west side," he explained, "they call him 'the Governor' and his word is law over there. He's into everything, lumber, shipping, land development, storekeeping, road building, just everything."

"That's quite a record," I agreed, knowing it already.

"That's not all. He's been in politics too; a provincial Member down south and a federal candidate. What a man to have with us!"

All at once I saw A.P. Cockburn and that really surprised me. What was he doing here at a Grit gathering? But there he was, large as life and looking quite self-assured. There were others there too, that I was surprised to see; all Liberals of a sort, but men who were with us in the last provincial. It set me thinking as I stood unobtrusively in the shadows.

It seemed that I was witnessing a revival. It could be temporary, and I hoped it was. But I had a cold feeling that the Liberals were pulling themselves together to give us a battle. Sandfield Macdonald was dead. The man who drew so many Liberals into the Conservative fold of Sir John Macdonald had been defeated in the Assembly last December, and then faded away. A new crowd was in power in Ontario. Edward Blake was Premier and Alexander Mackenzie his Provincial Treasurer. Liberals all, they were sweeping away the memories

150

of a Conservative past. The political fence-sitters were easing back to the Liberal side. Grits, Reformers, Liberals, no matter what they called themselves, they now had a winner in the Ontario Assembly and they were showing their true colours.

I had seen it all too clearly in Muskoka. The Liberals had the provincial patronage and they were using it to the full. All the road contracts, public works, timber licenses and government jobs were going to Liberals or to those who would switch over. Conservatives were laid off in droves, and their ranks were filled with supporters of the new order. George Gow was going wild as he saw his best men pitched out. If you wanted a pick and shovel job on the road, you saw the Grit foreman. If you wanted to be foreman you had to prove your loyalty and commit your family to the Grits. If there was no job open, you found a Tory still working and had him fired.

And all the time Blake and Mackenzie were talking publicly about high-mindedness and principle in government, while buying support with every bit of influence and money they had. I found it revolting. Sir John Macdonald used patronage too, but he never put on a pious front about it.

And now, having cleaned up provincially, they were looking for the federal spoils. As the noisy, confident crowd flowed around me at Bracebridge on that 11th day of June 1872 I felt a touch of desperation. Things were not going well for Sir John in Ottawa. A lot of Orangemen were mighty displeased with him. He had allowed separate schools for the Catholics in the new province of Manitoba. He had failed to crack down on Louis Riel, who was causing a disturbance out west. Riel was a son of the church, and mollycoddling him was the same as bowing to the priests. And Sir John always seemed to be giving in to Quebec. Charges of corruption were floating around as usual, but this time they weren't going away. And there was a lot in the papers about the fisheries treaty with the United States. It was something I didn't understand, but some papers said he had botched things up.

And everyone knew that the ship of state sometimes drifted while Sir John drank in the wheelhouse.

151

Our former supporters, now strutting around this hive of Grits, were proof of the problems. They were deserting the old ship for a new one. How many more would we lose? It made me sick to think of it. As I stood there musing on the fickleness of men, and the rottenness of politics, the meeting was called to order.

When nominations for candidate were called, someone jumped up immediately and nominated William Beatty. What a tumult that raised! They had their man and they applauded with glee. Beatty went to the platform and started his speech. "I thank my mover and seconder for this expression of confidence," he began. And they all cheered.

"The presence of such a large and eminent group proves that the party is thriving and headed for great things."

"Hurrah! You bet. We're behind you!" they shouted.

"I am supporting this great party one hundred per cent in the coming months."

The glasses on the sideboard shook with the stamping and cheering.

"However," he concluded, "I am not a candidate."

The silence that followed was total. They looked at each other in disappointment. Not a candidate? It had sounded so good. As he left the platform they gave him a big ovation anyway. He was with them and that meant a lot.

Then they nominated Tom Myers of Bracebridge. That brought another round of applause; but Myers also declined. He would work, he said, but he couldn't run.

Then it was Dr. A.G. Stephens from Parry Sound. He was a great prospect, popular and until now politically neutral. In fact the Tories had made him census commissioner last year. But when he took the platform, he declined also.

The exuberance began to dampen off and confidence waned. Where was their man; had nobody been lined up? All they needed was a good man and they could put him in. When Dr. Stephens nominated A.P. Cockburn the applause was restrained. It began to look like they were jockeying around.

152

Cockburn was a good man, but he had left politics a year before. His business affairs, he said, occupied him full time. He was on bad terms with Brown and the Globe, and had supported Sandfield. Still, he was here at the meeting and that was the main thing.

"I want to thank Dr. Stephens for nominating me," he began and you could almost hear the groan. Beatty had begun his speech the same way. Cockburn began to explain himself, and that was obviously why he had been nominated.

"I have always been a Reformer from the beginning of my career," he declared, "I still am. Some of my actions have been misunderstood. It is difficult to act according to your conscience."

The crowd was silent. There is a certain thrill in hearing confessions, and they were hearing a big one.

"I want to make it clear that I completely support the present Ontario government and our cause in the federal field as well."

This raised some applause and Cockburn went doggedly on. The audience began to warm to him a bit; it takes a good man to stand up and admit his mistakes. Shortly he concluded. "After considerable thought," he announced, "I have decided to stand for nomination."

It was so unexpected that there was a brief silence. Then all hell broke loose. They stood up and cheered and stamped and shouted. The relief was complete. Beatty, Myers, everyone on the platform rushed over to shake his hand. People came up from the crowd to pat him on the back. The Chairman called for order.

"I move nominations close," someone shouted.

"I second the motion," came from all over the room.

Without even putting the motion, the Chairman considered it carried when everybody in the audience stood up and applauded.

"Mr. A.P. Cockburn is our candidate," he announced, and that was it.

A few people there must have known all along that Cockburn was standing. But that wasn't enough. The convention had to take him back with all sins forgiven. The local Liberals had to support him completely. And they had.

Our man wasted no time after Cockburn declared himself. Two days later a copy of a petition signed by 300 men was published. "Muskoka June 13, 1872. We ask you, D'Arcy Boulton to look after our interest in the Dominion Parliament. Your well known ability . . . high standing at the bar, . . . integrity and influence will be highly beneficial." What could Boulton do in the face of such pressure? He announced that he too would run.

Well, after Cockburn was nominated, everyone waited to see what the Globe would say. And George Brown swallowed himself whole.

"An excellent choice," he wrote of Cockburn, and praised him to the skies. Forgotten were the Nine Martyrs, and Cockburn's betrayal; dead in the files were those awful charges of corruption. It was enough that Cockburn was running as a Liberal.

They didn't all forget. The Orillia Packet came right out and exposed Brown's dishonesty.

"The Globe, with characteristic affrontery," wrote the editor savouring his words, "now comes out in favour of Mr. A.P. Cockburn, one of the Nine Martyrs, not long since denounced by it as a traitor, the most venal and corrupt of politicians."

And the letter-writers came to life. "If Cockburn and Beattie get in," warned the Stephenson correspondent of the Packet, "they will work a hand-in-hand game and swindle Bracebridge of its greatness in favour of Parry Sound and Gravenhurst."

And a Cockburn critic who signed himself "Incola" wrote to the Bracebridge paper: "We want a representative who will occasionally make a direct study of our grievances and will forget self interest and petty flunkeyism."

Cockburn even had some trouble with a leading Grit. Mr.

J.B. Browning, a Bracebridge lawyer, couldn't accept Cockburn as a true Grit or a friend of Bracebridge, and announced that he would run against him. But in some way or another, he was persuaded to withdraw. And another Grit, Fred Sims from Ullswater refused to support him, because he was not longer independent.

"Cockburn is now running as a mere party man, pledged to follow wherever the Globe leads," he wrote.

It wasn't all one sided. They said Boulton was a Barrie man, an outsider.

"Muskoka is so peculiarly situated," declared E.F. Stephenson who had just started up the Free Grant Gazette in Bracebridge, "that no outside candidate can gain a parliamentary seat for the county."

And Boulton didn't have the most popular worker in the world.

"I would advise Mr. Boulton," wrote 'Wolfe' from Watt township after a meeting there, "that the next time he comes up here, to leave the dominee at home and bring only gentlemen in his wake."

There were lots of people who didn't like George Gow.

Boulton, with his legal mind, answered the charge of being an outsider very well. He put it in his published statement. "I have no local preferences to warp my judgement," he said, "the country as a whole shall be my constant care; and my God, my country and my Queen my motto."

That was a good point, and the loyal settlers were quick to note his facility with the word.

As the battle raged the heavy artillery was brought up. Someone, probably Gow, started the rumour that Cockburn had been involved in last year's Muskoka land scandal. There, a number of surveyors had swindled the government by making false returns. The mess had been hushed up, and a lot of higher ups were suspected. Now it was said that Cockburn had retired from the Assembly to save his skin. The rumour was solid enough that the Gazette rushed to his defence in print.

"We believe these extra-ordinary rumours to be completely untrue," wrote the editor, "they have been circulated to injure Mr. Cockburn."

That, of course, was quite obvious. Whether they succeeded or not was the real question.

But A.P. Cockburn was not sitting around listening to rumours. He had the provincial patronage and he used it. First he reminded everybody that he was back in the good graces of the provincial Liberals. That he was federal candidate made no difference.

"I will bring the wants of the county before the government of Ontario," he said in his published statement. And then he began to prove it. All over the district settlers were calling for roads. The massive settlement that Sandfield undertook had run ahead of highways. Cockburn, with the connivance of the provincial government, did something about it.

There was a certain Mr. Reid in Parry Sound, a Conservative on Boulton's local committee. He dabbled in road construction, so Cockburn approached him about doing some work on the Rosseau Road. When Reid agreed, Cockburn arranged things in Toronto, and next thing we knew the work had been authorized. Reid was put in charge and given an immediate cash advance. He then announced that he was supporting Cockburn.

The Muskoka Road had gone as far as Huntsville and stopped. The Chaffey residents to the north had been agitating for at least two years to have it extended. The provincial government now authorized the extension and let Cockburn make the announcement. Our provincial Member, Duncan McRae, was furious; as a Tory, they totally ignored him. Cockburn then "appointed" George Hunt, the founder of the village, as contractor, and Hunt received an immediate advance. Next thing we knew he was supporting A.P. Cockburn in the federal election.

The Great North Road out of Parry Sound had been stalled for lack of funds. Cockburn put it into operation again, and the men went back to work. James Armstrong got the

156

necessary funds through Cockburn. John Bailey was put to work on the Macaulay Road and John Shannon at Lake Joseph. The provincial government let Cockburn act as if he were the provincial Member, and he made any deal he wanted. The authority and funds followed right along. Mr. McRae came up to put a halt to it, but it was hopeless. All the contractors, normally Tories, declared for Cockburn.

The best deal of all was reserved for Gilman Willson, our storekeeper. I heard about it direct from Willson himself. He had some timber limits out in McLean, but the road hadn't reached them. Along came Cockburn one day and told him he could build the road right out to his limits at government expense, and get paid for supervising it into the bargain. It was a hard offer to turn down.

"I want the road," Willson told Cockburn, "and I want the job. But it sounds like election bribery to me."

"It's a provincial contract," Cockburn assured him, "it has nothing to do with the federal election."

"Then how do you happen to be handing it out?"

"I'm afraid our Member lives a long piece away, and isn't too interested," Cockburn answered.

That got Willson annoyed for he had worked for McRae.

"Well, Mr. Cockburn," he decided, "I'll do the job after the election is over. But it won't change my vote. A Tory I am, and a Tory I remain."

Cockburn went away, and nothing more was heard about that job. But with all these Conservatives committed, Cockburn was able to announce that he was a candidate "at the earnest solicitation of nearly all the leading men of the county." We had a big fight ahead of us.

Right then a counter-attack against Cockburn was launched at a high level. The objective was to neutralize William Beatty on the west side of the riding. Mr. Ferguson M.P. of Barrie, who had us under his wing, wrote a letter to Sir John, pointing out that Beatty should really be supporting us. He got a lot from the federal government and was even now requesting more.

It was well known that the Beattys had profited under John A. Macdonald's governments, both before and after Confederation. For Macdonald they had built the Parry Sound Road; from Macdonald they had received their timber licences. The Beatty stage was carrying federal mail and John Beatty got his job as Crown Lands agent as a Conservative. And still they wanted more, shipping contracts and postal subsidies. They owed Sir John a lot. But it was easy to see their problem. The provincial patronage was Liberal now and the Beattys needed that for timber licenses and road work. They couldn't be sure that Sir John would hold the federal House in the coming election. But they knew his strength; time and again he had seemed to be down and out, but he always came back. They had to straddle the fence some way.

The heat was turned on, and a letter dispatched to Beatty for an explanation. A couple of weeks later Mr. Ferguson arrived in Bracebridge with a copy of a letter William Beatty had written to Sir John.

"Use this if it will help," he said, "there was no confidentiality attached. It can be quoted in whole or in part."

"We'll quote it in part," Gow declared after reading it over, "there are some good parts in there."

He handed it to me, and I found a masterpiece of double talk in my hands.

"I understood," Beatty wrote, explaining why he had given his support to Cockburn, "that both Mr. Boulton and Mr. Cockburn were friendly to your government. Certainly Mr. Cockburn was a supporter of the late Sandfield Macdonald."

The last part was true. Everyone knew about the Nine Martyrs.

"The contest here seems to be personal, not political. I supported Cockburn because I thought him more deserving than his opponent, and also because I thought he would be friendly to your government."

How he could have thought that was beyond me. Cockburn had pledged his support to the Liberals. Beatty seems to have questioned it himself, for he ended on a more positive note, seeming to tip the balance towards our party.

"You are quite right in believing that I am friendly to your government personally and also that I approve of your general policy, and I shall have pleasure in showing my friendship during the coming contest in several counties where I have some influence."

"There's the part we'll use," said Gow, pointing to the last paragraph, "Beatty can't deny writing it. The rest is hogwash."

"Did Sir John see this letter?" I asked Mr. Ferguson curiously.

"He did."

"And what did he say?"

"He wasn't fooled. He told me in Toronto that Beatty had sold us in Muskoka."

"And how does he view the riding?"

"He said Boulton would have a hard fight on his hands; and he was bitter about Cockburn. He always believed Cockburn to be one of us when he came over to Sandfield. Sir John promised me then and there that Cockburn would have his reward."

I was certainly willing to help him get it.

CHAPTER 13
RETURNING OFFICER

The morning of July 18th, 1872 was dull and overcast. I had trouble stirring myself to meet the day ahead. Anne was up half an hour doing her household duties before I managed to crawl out of bed. It looked like another routine day.

Things were a lot easier since we moved into town; no long trips up the road from Uffington, no back-breaking work on the farm. I was township clerk of Macaulay and George Gow was Reeve. The township office was in a side room at my house and I did my general agency and insurance there too. I went for the mail in the morning, stopped to chat on the way home, looked after my correspondence, wrote up the books and stepped in to the house for lunch. After noon I had a rest, worked in the garden or sat reading the paper. The tinkle of the bell on my office door summoned me when business called. The coming election provided interest, but made little difference in the routine. Polling had not been ordered and I had no official functions.

Most of my activity happened when George Gow was around. In many ways he was my boss; Reeve of the township of which I was Clerk, County Master of the Lodge in which I was involved, and the Tories' man in Muskoka, to whom I looked for direction. I hadn't seen him for several days then. He was off somewhere on business; lodge, political or personal, you never knew.

I headed up town for the mail that morning, stopping as I went to pass the time of day with the store clerks sweeping the sidewalk and the business men on their way to work. It was a pleasant duty, and I did it happily. I always got an appreciative response. I finally arrived at the post office, a little lean-to beside the store which Mr. Perry operated on the main street. No sooner had I opened the door than he called out to me, quite excited.

"Register for you, Mr. Bell. It looks important."

"Somebody complaining about the roads, I suppose."

160

"No, no, it's about your new job."

"New job?" I asked, "what new job? Have you been opening the mail again?"

"Certainly not," he said indignantly, "It's written right on the envelope. Here, come and get it."

After I signed for it, he shoved a bulky official-looking envelope through the wicket. It was postmarked Ottawa and was addressed to:

Richard James Bell, Esq.,
Returning Officer for the Electoral District of Muskoka,
Bracebridge, Ontario.

I turned the envelope over and there was a coat of arms, together with the words "Clerk of the Crown in Chancery". It was real, positively and undeniably. If the address was correct, I was the Returning Officer for Muskoka. Somehow I didn't want to show my surprise, so I thanked Mr. Perry, took the envelope and headed for home as fast as I could decently go. I was burning with excitement.

When I got inside my office I closed the door and opened the envelope with fumbling fingers. Inside there were two sheets of heavy parchment. I unfolded the first, and scanned it quickly. His Excellency, the Earl of Dufferin, Governor General of Canada, Cousin and Councillor of Her Majesty the Queen, Viscount and Baron Clandeboye of Clandeboye, Baronet, Knight Commander of the Order of St. Patrick, etc. having confidence in my loyalty, integrity and ability appointed me, Richard James Bell, to be Returning Officer for the Electoral District of the County of Muskoka. It was signed personally by the Governor General at the bottom of the page, impressed with the Royal Seal and had a big red ribbon streaming down the side. It was Recorded in the Office of the Secretary of State. I had never seen such a beautiful instrument.

I opened the second parchment, wondering what further honour could have been bestowed on me. This also bore a red ribbon, official seal and the signature of the Governor General. In this I was advised that His Excellency had some

161

great and weighty affairs of state to consider concerning the Dominion of Canada, and required some Common men to confer with. He commanded me to proclaim an election for Muskoka and to cause one Member or Representative to be freely chosen. Thereafter, he instructed me to make my Return to the Clerk of the Crown in Chancery and to send back the Writ. The signature "Dufferin" was written at the upper left hand corner, confirming the instructions of the Clerk of the Crown in Chancery who signed at the bottom. Both parchments were dated the 15th day of July, 1872. I set them down on my table, and sat back to contemplate this unexpected good fortune.

Returning Officer! The man who runs the election, makes the rules, decides on polling places and officials, counts the votes and declares the winner - the most important man in government. Everybody defers to him. There are no "higher-ups" during an election; they are all candidates, seeking any help you can give them. I had run municipal elections and knew that much. And this was the federal job - big. If I couldn't be a candidate, this was next best.

I knew what the new Muskoka riding was - everything from the Severn River north to the Nipissing, from Georgian Bay to the eastern reaches of Muskoka settlement. It was vast and I had travelled a lot of it on foot. But this time I would be Mr. R.J. Bell, Returning Officer, the man in charge of the election for the whole settled northland. How proud they would be of me in Uffington! Even Decimus would mention me to his friends.

I got down my Statutes to find out what they said about the Returning Officer. I had the Election Act of 1859 for the old Province of Canada, and believed they were still using it. The Returning Officer was the key figure all right. Clause after clause outlined his duties, privileges and discretions. Everything seemed to turn on his decision. Nothing happened without his approval.

I had to go in and tell Anne the news.

"You won't believe this," I burst out, "but I've just had a letter

162

from the Governor General, and he's made me Returning Officer."

She looked at me doubtfully.

"And what," she asked, "is a Returning Officer?"

"He's the man in charge, the central figure, the man who runs the elections."

"For the whole country?"

I thumped the table in exasperation.

"No. For all Muskoka and the north country."

"Oh."

"It's really important. I'm the political manager of the whole area, from north to south, from east to west."

"Well," she decided, "I suppose I'll have to hoe the garden again this summer."

It was useless trying to impress her. Politics simply drove her into a shell.

I went back to the office to consider where I should begin. I shook out the big envelope to see if there were any instructions, but it was empty. I wondered about a suitable date for polling, but realized I had no idea. Where should I hold the polls? Where did I get the forms? The Governor General had told me nothing; just appointed me and told me to get on with the election.

As I sat there feeling desperate the office door opened and in clomped George Gow.

"Just got back," he explained, "heard at the post office you got your appointment. I guess you'll need these."

He threw me a big envelope full of forms, instructions and dates. I wondered why His Excellency hadn't sent all this stuff to me, and Gow never told me where he got it. It was one of his secrets. However, it all seemed authentic, and Gow gave me a list of polling places from an old sheet he had turned up somewhere. So I took it all and went to work.

The first thing I had to do was take an oath of office. I went up to the Court House right away and saw Judge Lount.

"Humph," he said, reading it over, "you swear this to be true."

"I do."

"Well see that you do the job right," he growled, "there are forces around here trying to get their fingers in."

I wasn't sure exactly what he meant, but I knew it was McMurray and the Grits. I assured him everything was under control. He signed the form "Chas. W. Lount, J.P. for District Muskoka" and handed it back.

"If you need any help, come and see me," he said, "don't take any chances."

He turned away abruptly to do something else, but I felt better with the force of the law behind me.

The job wasn't a complete mystery, for I had conducted municipal elections. This was on a bigger scale, and the rules much more complicated. I found my statutes useful. First, I was to issue a proclamation setting the place and date for nominations. Then I would hold the nomination meeting in a public place, and if more than one person was nominated, I would hold an election. I had to set up polling places, appoint Deputy Returning Officers to run them, and finally receive the return from each poll. It was open voting, with the voter declaring his choice aloud. The candidate with the most votes was declared by me elected. On the surface, it was simple enough. But the very first day brought its problems.

I had to list organized and unorganized townships separately on my Proclamation, and I wasn't sure about some of them. I went to see George Gow, because he seemed to have the answers. I found him down by the wharf below the falls.

"These polling places have to be settled," I told him, "and there is one I'm not sure of."

"Give me a hand with this stuff," he answered," and we'll talk about it."

There he was, hotel owner, storekeeper, contractor, reeve, political organizer and general factotum hauling produce from the wharf to his store. He was carrying sacks and boxes and piling them on a one horse sledge. I took off my coat and helped him finish the loading.

"Giddap," he shouted at the horse, slapping the lines on its back.

We started up the hill toward the main street.

"Well what's your problem?" he asked as the sledge scraped along the dusty track "I gave you the list we want used."

"I know but you've shown Stephensen township as unorganized," I explained "I thought they were organized last year."

"I'm not too sure," he answered innocently "but show them as unorganized. It's better for us."

"How do you mean?"

He stopped the horse for a rest and stared at me.

"My God, for a man that's been around as long as you have ... " he began, and his voice trailed off in disgust.

"Don't beat around the bush," I asked him, "say it out."

"Well, when a township is organized, with a Reeve and Council, they have a municipal voters list; right?"

"Right," I agreed, "and that's the one we use for the federal."

"And when a township is not organized, they have no list."

"Of course not," I agreed, "nobody knows who's back in the bush."

"Nobody knows," he agreed, "so you have an open poll; no list and no check. That's when we pack it. With good organization you can vote a man twice at least, then move him on to another open poll. And we're well organized in Stephenson."

That made it clear enough. But I had just been appointed by the personal hand of the Governor General, who had confidence in my loyalty, integrity and ability.

"Do what you like," I said, "but I'd better check out Stephenson."

He turned on me so fiercely I though he would hit me.

"Check it out?" he shouted, "I'm telling you it's unorganized. Have you any idea what those damn Grits did to us when they had the chance? And anyway, why do you think you were appointed - to help Grits?"

"You don't have to shout," I shouted, "I can hear you."

"Give somebody a job," Gow declared, "and suddenly he thinks he's important."

"Did you give me this job?" I demanded sarcastically, "I

165

thought I saw the Governor General's name on my appointment.''

"And where do you think he heard about you? From Santa
Claus?''

I knew he was right.

"We shouldn't be quarrelling," I said, "we're both on the
same side. But don't tell me all the gory details.''

"You weren't so finicky before," he grumbled.

"Just tell me what you want and I'll do what I can, if it means
defeating Cockburn," I promised, "but I have my self-respect
and I intend to keep it.''

"Well, don't let it go to your head," he warned. Anyway, he
had made his point and I had made mine, so things were
understood. I went back to the office and entered Stephenson
as unorganized. And I set up an open poll there.

I jumped right into the job and loved it. The riding was large
and communications terrible. Settlements were scattered all
over the place, most of the area was unorganized, and I had to
find polling places and Deputy Returning Officers. But I knew
the area, had friends all around, and Gow's old list was a god-
send.

The job meant a lot of travelling and I enjoyed that too.
What a pleasure it was to drop in on Anthony Suffern, the
man I promised to remember, and tell him the poll was at his
house, and he would be the Deputy. It was influence for him
and a tidy sum of money into the bargain. And to go back
home to Uffington and appoint Matt Patterson to run the poll.
Memories flooded back to my first days there, when I was an
unknown newcomer. And then going to the Orange Lodges at
Bracebridge, Huntsville, Port Carling, Rosseau Junction and
McKellar Falls to tell my acquaintances there that we were using the Hall as a polling place. And all the places I had visited
on my long trek up the Parry Sound Road years before; I called on some to make appointments; at others I just got down
from my carriage, and made myself known. It was very
satisfying.

On these long jaunts into the country, I was required to give every qualified settler an opportunity to vote. At first I worried about making the right decisions, but Gow told me to stop fussing.

"You're the boss," he pointed out, "whatever you say goes. There's nobody above you."

That eventually became clear to me. I had expected trouble over the open poll in Stephenson as soon as the proclamation was posted up. But nobody said a word. When one of the Grits came in and suggested I set up a poll at Coates' mill on the Georgian Bay, I turned him down.

"It's not in this riding," I decided after looking over my papers, "we only take in surveyed townships and that area's not been surveyed."

Anyway, if a Grit wanted it, you could be sure they had some scheme to rig the poll. He grumbled a bit and went away.

I hadn't set up a poll in McLean township. There were only a few people out there, and we had no idea how they voted. When one of them came in and complained, I stood fast.

"The proclamation is already out," I ruled, "you can vote at the nearest poll."

I made decisions left and right, and soon began to enjoy my authority.

The nomination meeting was set for August 15th. That was the big event for me, but not everybody understood what was going on. William Kennedy, the shoemaker, told me what happened at his place, for example. His wife got the shock of her life that morning. She was giving Tommy and Billy their breakfast when she heard the sound of hammering outside. It seemed to come from the Orange Hall, just across the main street and she went to the side door to look out. Then she went running into the shop.

"William," she called out in terror, "they're building a gallows over there, right on the main street. Somebody's going to hang." Her husband got up from his last, and came to the door.

"Bless you," he said when he had a look, "it's not a gallows. It's the hustings."

"What's that?" she asked vaguely.

"It's where they make the election speeches," he explained, "it should be a rare lively do."

"When do they have them?"

"Likely around noon," he answered, "and we have front seats."

Across the road, that's exactly what I was doing. We built a rough wooden platform, right out on the street, where everybody could see. Two workmen put the final touches to the job by building the steps.

"We'll put up a flag and some bunting," I said when they were finished, "and then we're ready."

Things soon began to happen in Bracebridge. D'Arcy Boulton had come up from Barrie the night before and he took advantage of the morning to stroll around the village and talk to the natives.

I liked Mr. Boulton. He was a big, friendly man with broad, slightly stooping, shoulders, large hands and a good-natured countenance. He wore his well-tailored clothes easily; he wasn't dressed up for the occasion. He was always cheerful, with a funny story or a new joke. I had little experience with lawyers, but always imagined them small, prim, serious men. Boulton was the opposite, he didn't seem like a lawyer at all. He looked more like a working man. He carried his family and education naturally, and there were no airs about him. When you raised a subject, or gave an opinion, he considered your remarks seriously, and gave an answer. If there was anyone to whom I could give my confidence, it was D'Arcy Boulton. I realized that if there had to be an outside candidate, he was the best.

Alexander P. Cockburn was another type of man completely. He had money and influence, but it showed in everything he did and said. I began to think that he was aloof and cold so that no one would find him out. He didn't have the family background or breeding that Boulton had. As I compared the two men I began to understand the difference between true nobility and artificial. I knew I was in the right party, the party of solid background, but with true concern for the people. Cockburn arrived that morning as well, but he huddled with his Grit supporters and didn't even pay me a courtesy call. Men were arriving in Bracebridge from all over the district to see the nominations. There had been a lot of nasty talk, and it would all come out today. The Dominion Hotel, right next door to the hustings, had a busy morning as the travellers dropped in to "wash down the dust."

I was the centre of attention, the man in charge. Everyone came to me for information and advice. People I had met only once, and years before, recalled the occasion. "Yes, Mr. Bell" - "No, Mr. Bell" - "thank you Mr. Bell". It made me proud, though I tried not to puff up or gloat. Some of them hadn't been too friendly before, but I didn't mention it. Enough that they were friendly now.

At twelve noon I stepped onto the platform. First I read the writ of election from the Governor General. Then I read my appointment, with all its glowing references to my loyalty, integrity and ability, signed by the Governor General. Then my proclamation of an election for Muskoka. When it was finished I made my announcement.

"I am now open for nominations for a Member to represent Muskoka in the House of Commons."

Thomas Myers was standing right by the steps, and he rushed up to be first there.

"I nominate Mr. A.P. Cockburn as a fit and proper person to represent us in the House of Commons," he said, and made a speech.

"I second the motion," said Dr. Stephens from the crowd.

"I nominate Mr. D'Arcy Boulton as a fit and proper person to represent us in the House of Commons," said John Teviotdale, coming to the platform. He made his speech, and the nomination was seconded by Sam Greer.

It could have stopped there. Those were the only candidates. But there was the usual by-play; people with hurt feelings had to be soothed by a nomination, others wanted the opportunity to make a speech. One person with hurt feelings was Tom

169

McMurray. He had been publishing the Northern Advocate with liberal leanings for two years, all the while supporting A.P. Cockburn in a restrained sort of way. Now E.F. Stephenson had come to Bracebridge and started the Free Grant Gazette. He was supporting Cockburn too, and all out. Two newspapers can't print the same stuff in one place, and there was a danger McMurray would jump the fence.

"I nominate Mr. Thomas McMurray," said John P. Cockburn, a brother of A.P. He went to the platform and made a little speech about how much McMurray had done for Muskoka.

"I second that motion," announced Alex Cockburn in a loud voice.

Then George Gow nominated D'Arcy Boulton again.

"He's already been nominated, you damn old fool," somebody shouted from the crowd.

Gow paid no attention and went up to the platform and started making a speech. When loyalty to Boulton was involved, George Gow would not be found wanting. They heckled, booed and finally drowned him out.

"I hear the potato bug from Watt squeaking," shouted Gow above the din, turning on a persistent heckler.

The Colorado beetle had just arrived in Muskoka and was the scourge of the settlers.

"He'll strip your leaves," came a shout from the crowd.

Gow came right back and soon they were at it. The Grits in the crowd gave Gow a terrible time and Boulton's men took it for a while. Gow deserved a little razzing. But when it kept up, they started to intervene.

"Shut up and let the man talk," somebody shouted.

"Who's telling me to shut up?" asked the noisemaker from Watt, looking around.

"I am, and I'll shut your big mouth with my fist."

There was a scuffle as they headed for each other and their friends tried to hold them back. I stepped quickly to the front of the platform.

"Order, please, gentlemen," I called out, "we must have order."

170

In a minute, Gow started up again but it was hopeless. They just wouldn't let him speak. He finally raised his stick and shook it at his tormentors.

"I'll mark the lot of yez," he shouted; but he gave up and left the platform.

All the candidates withdrew except Cockburn and Boulton. Boulton spoke first, and a masterful bit of oratory it was, worthy of a man prepared to do his duty. Cockburn followed. Why he ever did it, I don't know. Maybe he was referring to all the dirty rumours that were floating around; maybe it was part of his prepared text; but he started off with a quote from Shakespeare's Henry IV.

"Lord, lord, how this world is given to lying," he began.

Boulton flushed an angry red and there was a hushed silence in the crowd. Cockburn realized he had made a mistake, so he added hastily:

"I'm not necessarily referring to anyone present."

It wasn't exactly a withdrawal but he went ahead with his remarks. When he had finished there was a fuss in the audience.

"He called D'Arcy Boulton a liar, the bastard," someone said out loud.

"No he didn't."

"Well I heard him. He can't get away with that when I'm around."

There was a movement in the crowd, as the angry man pushed his way toward the front. I thought it a propitious time to close the nomination meeting, and we all hustled from the platform.

Down below the arguments went on. They adjourned to the Dominion Hotel, the Royal, the Victoria and the new North American, where the hostilities continued. Up at the North American, there was a brawl over the secret ballot. I heard all about it the next morning.

"We need a secret ballot," one of the Liberals declared, "then there wouldn't be all this argument."

"What are you, a man or a mouse?" a Tory shouted, "are you ashamed to vote for that Cockburn?"

171

"I'd be ashamed to vote for a carpetbagger."

"You don't have the guts to stand up and be counted," the Tory accused him, "a secret vote is not only unmanly, it's un-British."

"We wouldn't have all this corruption with a secret ballot."

"You're crazy. There'd be worse corruption. A man could take your money and then vote the other way. Nobody would ever know. In fact, he could take money from both sides."

"Balls."

And so it went until the early hours of the morning. Words got louder, tempers higher, until somebody tried to prove his point with his fist. Then reason went to the winds, and a brawl started. The North American hotel lost all it profits in the damage.

Gow couldn't get over Cockburn's men actually drowning him out on the platform. He expected some razzing, but his vanity was really shaken. He was particularly annoyed at the loud-mouth from Watt, who pushed the thing beyond reason. Gow mentioned it several times when we talked the next day. I had some sympathy for him too. Those damn Grits were too confident and insolent; they swaggered around as if the election was already won. I didn't say anything, I was supposed to be neutral; but I sure thought plenty.

A couple of days after the nomination I was able to help Gow get even. Watt and Cardwell had been organized as a township the year before. So I set up the poll at Suffern's and treated it as a closed poll with a list as the law required. But the new township clerk failed to send me a list. Perhaps he didn't have one; perhaps he didn't know he should send it. In any case I had no list for my Deputy when the time came to send out the poll documents. At the last minute I declared Watt and Cardwell to be an open poll; no list, no limitation.

I dropped the word to George Gow and he was delighted. "Now we'll squash that Grit potato bug," he vowed gleefully, and went off to Watt township to get things organized.

172

CANADA

By His Excellency the Right Honorable Sir *Frederick Temple*, Earl of *Dufferin*, V
and Baron *Clandeboye* of *Clandeboye* in the County *Down*, in the Peerage
United Kingdom, Baron *Dufferin* and *Clandeboye* of *Ballyleidy* and *Killeleagh*
County *Down*, in the Peerage of *Ireland*, one of Her Majesty's Most Hon
Privy Council, and a Baronet, Knight of the most Illustrious Order of *Saint P*
and Knight Commander of the most Honorable Order of the Bath, Governor G
of *Canada*, and Governor and Commander in Chief in and over the Island of
Edward.

    To *Richard James Bell*, Esquire, and to all to whom these presents shall co

                                                              GREETI

(Endorsed) Commission
appointing Richard James
Bell, Esquire, Returning
Officer for the Elec-
trict of the Coun[ty]
Muskoka.

Recorded
Lib
(Si

WHEREAS The Interim Parliamentary Election
    amongst other things in effect enacted
    elections of Members to serve in the
    nor General shall cause Writs to be
    dressed to such Returning Office

    w ye, that having confidence in the l
    you, the said *Richard James Bell*,
    erick Temple, Earl of *Dufferin*, Go
    ested, have nominated and app
    the said *Richard James Bell*
    ict of the County of *Muskoka*,

    t, and office of Returning Officer
    es, authorities and emoluments
    long and appertain.

    ity of *Ottawa*, in our said Don
    rd, one thousand eight hundr
    esty's Reign.

        DUFFERIN.

    in Chancery

DOUARD J LAN IN,
    Cle the Cr Chanc
    anada.

ON.

Electoral Distric of the *Muskoka*, in the Province of *Ontario*, TO WIT
PUBLIC Notice is hereby the Electors of the Electoral District of the C
    of *Muskoka*, that obed to Her Majesty's writ to me directed, and b
date the 15th day of the month uly, 1872, I require the presence of the said El
at the Orange Hall, in the vill of *Bracebridge* in the said County of *Muskok*
the fifteenth day of the month of August, at twelve for the purp

CHAPTER 14
THE LOST POLL

Out to unknown hands in the farthest limits of settlement I sent the instruments of election; to McKellar Falls and Dodger's Mill, to Rosseau Junction and The Dam, to places with no names like "halfway to Magnetawan, W. Beasley's" and "North Road 8 miles above Falls at John Stevenson's". I sent off my packets blindly, hoping the mails would deliver them, or that news would travel in the manner of the backwoods.

To those distant outposts I sent a copy of my proclamation of the election for Muskoka, the list of polling places, my official appointment of the Deputy Returning Officer, forms for appointment of a poll clerk to assist him, oaths, instructions and most important of all, the poll book. That poll book had to be returned to me, for I must personally count up the votes in each book before making a final return. Some of my deputies didn't even know they were appointed until the papers arrived.

At the centres closer to Bracebridge my election clerk, Jake Dill, and I delivered the packets personally. We only had eight days after nomination to set things up for the voting, and it was no easy task. The riding that Sir John Macdonald had created on June 14th of that year included 42 named townships and villages "and all other surveyed townships lying north of Victoria and south of the Nipissing District". It was a vast and lonely land, and I knew well the wandering instinct which took some men past the bounds of civilization. But every man with his bit of land was entitled to a vote, and it was my job to see that he got it.

While I was getting ready at the official level the candidates and their agents were working at fever pitch. Meetings were held, arms twisted, promises of support extracted. An influential voter couldn't declare himself quietly; he had to do it publicly in advance so that all his relatives, employees and debtors would know how to vote. It was too late for word to get around after he arrived at the poll. Everything was public then;

no secret ballot or hiding behind a curtain. They stood before the deputy and spoke their vote aloud to all those assembled.

I was in something of an odd position. The Returning Officer was impartial in his duties, but never neutral in his feelings. He did little things to swing the vote towards his own party, to give them an inside break whenever possible. He did quiet political errands while on official business. It was common practise; the opposition complained loudly if they lost, and praised the Returning Officer for his honesty if they won. At least, that's the way I understood it.

A few days before the election Mr. Teviotdale, the Tory president, came to see me.

"We hear things are bad down in Morrison," he said, "have you been there yet?"

"Not yet," I answered, "I'm planning to take the papers down there tomorrow."

"Well see what you can find out," he asked, "and do what you can."

It was a reasonable request, and I agreed.

I had appointed Henry Anderson as Deputy Returning Officer there. He was one of the township's most respected pioneers; the first school teacher back in '63, before I even came up to Muskoka. I had been in his home and knew him well. He was the first clerk of the council when it was organized in '69 and census commissioner in '71. He was well read, farmed lot 13 on the West side of the Free Grant Road and knew everybody in the township. At age 51 he had a big family, ranging down to four year old Christina. His wife Helen was a cheerful little woman, full of old country expressions and deft with needle and thread. They were Scottish Presbyterians with conservative leanings. So when I needed a D.R.O. for Morrison, I naturally appointed Henry. And he had done the job before.

When I got to Anderson's place the next day, I found him ready, and expecting me. That was really the only way an election could be held in the backwoods; most everybody knew what to expect.

175

"Things are bad around here," he said. "Cockburns are buying timber from the settlers all over the township. Nobody dares to vote against A.P."

"There must be some loyal Tories around."

"They're mighty few right now," he declared, "I don't even know who I'll get for poll clerk."

"What about Charlie McKenzie?"

"I was thinking about him. Let's go down and talk to him."

"Certainly," I agreed, deciding that I could combine a local trip with my official duties.

Charlie was known as the Tories' man in Morrison, and had the hotel at Severn Bridge. We got into my rig and drove down.

When we got to Severn Bridge we found Charlie tending bar. He was very friendly and anxious to help the cause.

"Will you take poll clerk on election day, Charlie?" Anderson asked after the preliminaries.

"Nope."

"Why not?"

"I'd lose my vote. And from what I hear around, we'll need every one."

"Who do you suggest?" asked Anderson.

"Pick up one of the Grits", suggested Charlie, "I wouldn't mind seeing them lose a vote."

"We need one of our own men in the poll. You never know what Cockburn will do."

"I'd send Duke over, but he can't write," Charlie explained.

"What about making him scrutineer?"

"Duke could do that. He doesn't have a vote anyway and he's always looking for an extra buck."

Loud voices were coming from the bar. The man called Duke, big and red-faced, with a glass in his hand, was holding forth.

"Cockburn's just a rich schemer, filling his pockets with our money," he claimed, poking a finger into another man's stomach.

176

"He's done a lot for Muskoka" said the other defensively.

"Like what?"

"Well, he put the boats on the lake."

"His own boats," said Duke "he gets the profit."

"He got the Free Grants when he was provincial Member."

"And what a mess that is. Lumbermen come right onto a man's farm and cut timber. A guy told me about it last week."

"They're trying to straighten that out."

"Bah."

McKenzie broke in.

"Will you scrutineer for Boulton election day?" he asked Duke.

"Your damn right I will," answered Duke, "there'a a man worth working for. Him and Sir John."

"Macdonald's finished" the other man threw in, "washed up".

Duke gasped as if he had been slapped. He slammed down his glass and turned fiercely to face the culprit.

"What?"

"That's what I said. Finished."

Duke reached out and grabbed the other by his coat collar, pulled it tight around his throat and shook.

"You say that once more and I'll push your face right through that bar," he warned.

"Finished," gasped his victim. He reached under Duke's arms and landed a blow on the stomach. Duke took him by the shoulders and threw him to the floor. He started to punch.

"Here, stop it", shouted McKenzie, "I won't have fighting in here."

He went over and grabbed Duke around the waist and pulled him off.

"Don't get so excited, Duke," said McKenzie calmly, "the man's entitled to his opinions."

"Well he can't say a thing like that when I'm around."

The other man got up off the floor and headed across the room.

"He's finished," he shouted as he reached the door.

Duke made as if to follow, but McKenzie grabbed him by the arm.

"Here, have one on the house," he offered, and that settled it.

Duke sat down at the bar and waited for his free drink.

"You see what it's like," Anderson said as we left, "one of the few Tories around here and he has no vote and just wants to fight."

"Well, do what you can," I encouraged him, and went back to Bracebridge feeling I had done my duty. I put Morrison right out of my mind; I thought Anderson would manage.

There were other polls that worried me more. I had no way of knowing that all my Deputies were on the job. I couldn't check each one, so I just kept my fingers crossed. Looking back, it seems strange that my troubles came in the two oldest settlements in the riding, while the others managed against all odds to make their returns without problems. But that's what happened.

Election day, August 23rd, passed quietly. My job was done; the election was in the hands of the poll-masters and candidates. Out there the battle was waged. Deputies nearby called on me to settle a few disputes, but for the most part they were on their own. After the polls closed I had verbal results from the parties. The official count would come later, when I had all the poll books. Until then I relied on the results gathered up by the candidates through their own system of couriers.

Right from the beginning Cockburn was ahead; not much, but enough to make the result evident. Only a complete upset on the west side could change things in Boulton's favour, but that didn't seem likely. I closed the office about ten o'clock, and with Jake Dill, my election clerk, visited the committee rooms of the two candidates in Bracebridge.

Boulton's rooms were serious and subdued. Things didn't look good.

"You never know," Mr. Boulton said, looking much more

178

cheerful than I expected, "but it looks as if Cockburn has won."

"I'm sorry to hear that," I commented honestly, "you deserved to win."

"Well you did a good job anyway, Mr. Bell," he declared, "no complaint on that score. Only myself to blame."

"You're very generous."

That was the mark of the man. Cheerful in defeat; no casting around for a scape-goat. I felt really bad about the result. We went over to Cockburn's committee room and they were all standing around laughing and cheering. Cockburn was there himself, and when I came in he held up his hand.

"Here comes our Returning Officer," he shouted jovially, "how about three cheers for him too."

I couldn't tell if he was being sarcastic or not. But they all gathered around and cheered.

"You did a good job," he declared, adding as an afterthought, "so long as Jake Dill kept an eye on you."

That was like him; couldn't say a decent word about someone without reservation. Anyway, they all laughed, and I pretended to think it funny. All the same, it was happening as I had expected; so long as the opposition won, they could afford some words of praise. I went home to bed, feeling bitterly disappointed about the outcome. My only comfort was that nothing had gone wrong in the arrangements.

It was the following day that some inkling of trouble arrived with the results from Parry Sound. There had been a problem over a poll clerk, but it was apparently straightened out. The clear thing was that Cockburn had won. After that the closing operations remained; return of the poll books and my report on the result.

They came knocking on the door of our River Street house for several days after that; big men mostly, uncomfortable in their rough tweed suits, vests, stiff collars and lumpy ties, but conscious of their importance in the order of things. Each one carried with him the poll book which the law required him to

179

deliver to the Returning Officer. I invited in each of my Deputy Returning Officers, checked the oaths, signatures and totals in their books. When I was satisfied, we chatted a while about the election and the problems they had, and then I paid off the poll. I had never stood so high.

Henry Anderson arrived late the second afternoon and I thought he looked glum.

"Pretty one-sided," I commented, for Cockburn had cleaned up in Morrison.

"It was terrible," he groaned, "Cockburn had an agent there with pencil and paper, and he wrote down the name and vote of every person who came in. He let them know who he worked for. Not one of the settlers had the guts to vote against Cockburn. Some sell timber to the Cockburns, some work in the mill, and the rest owe him money at the store."

"And what about that fellow Duke?" I asked, "did he show up?"

"Better he had stayed at home. He argued all day with the voters, and ended up by challenging the German immigrants as not being British. Well, they were on my list, so I let them vote. They got even by voting against Boulton."

"Sounds like a disaster," I said.

"Total disaster; 34 votes for Cockburn, 3 for Boulton."

"Well leave me your book and I'll pay you off."

"I was going to mention that," he said hesitantly, "somebody stole it."

"Stole the poll book?" I exclaimed, "who on earth would want to steal a poll book? You must have mislaid it."

"I came to Bracebridge on the stage," he explained, "then I went out back to relieve myself. When I came back in, it was gone."

"I've got to have the book," I explained, "it says so in my instructions. If someone asks to see it, I have to produce it."

"Everybody knows how it turned out," he argued.

I looked through the statutes and showed him section 65 of the Election Act.

"The Returning Officer shall not proclaim any person

180

duly elected unless all the poll books have been returned to him by all his Deputy Returning Officers.''

"You see I've got to have the book," I insisted, "I'm sure it will turn up. Have a good look around. Maybe it's still at home.''

He got up wearily and went away. I was sure he'd find it. Yet ... Anderson was thorough, and I wondered what I would do if he didn't. Then somebody else arrived, and I turned my attention to him.

The next day I went over to Parry Sound to collect the poll books from the west side and to pay my Deputies. That's when I got details of the trouble there.

"I appointed this fellow Wilson to be my poll clerk," explained Mr. Gilchrist, the D.R.O. at Parry Sound, "and he got a bit tipsy waiting for voters to show up."

"Were they slow coming in?"

"Only two people came before Mr. William Beatty voted at noon. He kept a close mouth on his intentions until he walked into the poll. Copies of a letter he wrote floated around the area showing that he favoured the party of Sir John Macdonald. He never denied it, but most people thought he would vote for Cockburn.''

"And he did."

"Loud and clear," said the D.R.O. "Word got around and the vote poured in for Cockburn all afternoon."

"So what about your clerk? Did he insult Beatty?"

"Nothing like that, although I blame it all on Beatty," Gilchrist said, shaking his head, "as we sat around waiting he got talkative and said something about 'back home in the States'. Turned out he's an American. I had to let him go and pick up somebody else.''

"That was the right thing to do," I assured him.

"But the problem is, Wilson was already sworn in as poll clerk and had signed the poll book. There wasn't any place for the new man, Foley, to sign.''

"Did you have Foley sign the poll certificate when you closed up?"

181

"No. Wilson's name was already in the front of the book. It wouldn't do to have two different names, so I got Wilson to sign the poll certificate."

"But it was actually Foley who kept the book and made the entries?"

"All but two," agreed the Deputy.

I looked at the poll book. The first two entries were written in a terrible scrawl, and the rest were in a neat, completely different hand.

" I suppose you swore Foley in as clerk when he took over," I said.

"How could I? Wilson's name was already in the book."

"So the man who kept the book was never sworn, and didn't sign."

"That's about it. And the man who signed wasn't qualified, and didn't act."

"What a mess!"

It worried me. This was the second thing to go wrong, and I'd thought everything went so well. What to do? I decided there wasn't really any basic error, just an administrative oversight. And representatives of all the parties were there and nobody objected. I decided not to make an issue of it and quietly took the book. One problem was enough.

When Anthony Suffern came in with the Watt and Cardwell book, he threw it on my table with a laugh.

"Boulton's men sure did their job," he declared, "80 votes for Boulton, and not a man challenged. I didn't know half of them."

"What about Cockburn?"

"Only 57, and I didn't know half of them either."

"Was there anything illegal?"

"They all took the oath," he said, shrugging his shoulders.

I thanked him and paid him off. He was very pleased.

It was even better in the open polls in Stephenson. Boulton won by 4 votes in Utterson, and in spite of George Hunt's declaration for Cockburn, Boulton won by 15 in Huntsville. It was clear to me now what Gow meant about open polls.

182

However, Cockburn had his own tricks, and in South Muskoka he won most of the polls. With Beatty's support on the West side, Cockburn had an overall majority of 121.

But still there was our problem in Morrison. Henry Anderson came back to my office several days later, completely bewildered.

"I've looked everywhere," he exclaimed, "at home, in the hotel, at the stage office. It's all silly, because I know I had the book when I got to Bracebridge. It has simply been stolen."

I'd been doing some reading in the meantime, and had the answer.

"Those fellows who draft up our laws aren't completely stupid," I told him, "They have an escape clause to cover us." I read out section 68 to him.

> "In case any poll book is stolen . . . or has been lost . . . the Deputy Returning Officer and the Poll Clerk shall forthwith attend personally upon the Returning Officer. 2. The Returning Officer shall examine them upon oath as to the contents of the Poll Book: and the number of votes so determined . . . shall be included as if taken from the poll book."

Anderson sat there as if he didn't understand what I read.

"It's all right, you see," I explained, "I can take the sworn statement of yourself and the Poll Clerk."

Still he said nothing and I thought I didn't made it clear. I started to read the section again, but he held up his hand.

"I didn't have a poll clerk," he mumbled faintly.

"No poll clerk?"

"No. The fellow didn't show up, so I went ahead without one."

We sat there in silence for a while, numb with the disaster of the thing. Then I read through the statute to see if there was another escape clause, but I found nothing. We decided to go and see J.B. Browning. He was a Grit lawyer, but my instinct told me to consult him about this; I could never be accused of political skiniving. He read the statutes and all the up-to-date amendments, and shook his head.

"I don't see anything here to help you," he said, "the law is silent on such a situation."

"What do I do then?" I asked him.

He shook his head again.

"You'll have to use your own judgment," he decided, "there's nothing in the statutes."

We left his office and walked down the main street.

"I'm sorry," said Anderson, "I'm really sorry. I knew at the time I shouldn't have done it, but everybody there said to go ahead."

"It was one chance in a million," I assured him, "I'll just have to find someway out of it." I went to bed that night with a troubled heart.

At five the next morning I suddenly awoke. Some fleeting thought had crossed my mind and flitted away again. What was it? Some bit of logic so obvious that awake I couldn't grasp it. Cockburn; the lost poll book; the substitute poll clerk. It flashed again. Why was I trying so hard to save A.P. Cockburn's election?

I lay there trying not to get excited. Why was I fighting Cockburn's battle? Surely it was his loss if the election went foul. If the law said I couldn't return him as elected, why not accept it? My own pride was at stake. It was my election too. But it wasn't my fault that Henry Anderson had failed to appoint a poll clerk, then lost the poll book. It wasn't my fault that William Beatty had held up the vote in Parry Sound so long that the poll clerk gave himself away. If anybody was to blame for that it was Cockburn's own supporter. Instead of hushing these problems up, I should really be making them public. The marvellous idea of giving A.P. Cockburn his just reward was born that moment.

Nobody knew my change of plan. I moved off in the opposite direction completely unobserved. When I got up that morning I simply started to talk about my problem. I told Mr. McMurray at the Advocate and Mr. Stephenson at the Gazette. I just happened to drop in to say good morning. I told

Albert Spring, a Grit from Uffington whom I met on the street. I chatted about it in Willson's store, and knew it would be all over town by nightfall. I made it very clear that I was not allowed, indeed that I was forbidden by the Election Act, to declare anyone elected for the riding of Muskoka because of the lost poll book. I also said there was a foul-up in Parry Sound and the vote there was probably illegal. I blamed Mr. Beatty for it, but didn't go into detail. I mentioned that Mr. J.B. Browning had advised me and I asked for help in my dilemma. I was reasonably sure that nobody could. I made no move to file a return.

I did it all with fiendish delight. I never forgave Cockburn for that first time he made a fool of me, in the presence of my equally scornful brother. Nor the other times when he passed me by unnoticed, or brushed me off contemptuously. I knew that even when he was polite it was from necessity. He never thought I would amount to anything. Even in victory he couldn't compliment me without a nasty implication. Now I had the power to with-hold what he wanted most. And I had no remorse for doing so.

Two days later I was down at the Bracebridge wharf looking for a parcel I expected on the boat. I paid no particular attention to a group of men there until I saw one of them pointing my way. Suddenly A.P. Cockburn himself burst from the group and sailed toward me, his black topcoat flaring out, his hand beckoning me imperiously.

"I hear you have not returned me elected yet, Mr. Bell," he said in a loud voice, "how is that?"

"I have some technical problems," I answered, "I believe you know what they are."

"I won fair and square," he declared, "I do not intend to suffer for your incompetence."

That wasn't true, and it wasn't fair. But in a way I was responsible, for Anderson was my appointment. So I replied as reasonably as I could.

"I'm considering what to do," I explained.

I stood there uncertainly. The rest of his group had gathered round us, and I was at a disadvantage. He saw that and pressed on.

"If you want to avoid trouble," he warned me, "you will make that return immediately. I'm not going to stand for it, you know."

To this day, I don't know whether it was an accidental use of words, or whether they surged up from the subconscious.

"Now, Mr. Cockburn," I heard myself saying, "don't be such a martyr."

He stood there, his mouth agape, the blood drained from his face and all the hatred a man could muster showing on his countenance. There was a shocked silence in the group. It was only a few seconds, but it seemed much more. I saw his lips move and his voice came forth in a low snarl.

"I wonder," he said deliberately and contemptuously, "who in hell you think you are. Perhaps somebody important?"

"We shall see, Mr. Cockburn," was all I said, though I was trembling with anger. Nobody had ever spoken to me like that before.

The lingering resentment and suspicion that had always existed between us, sometimes suppressed, occasionally open, suddenly hardened into something intense. From that time on, we hated each other.

186

CHAPTER 15
THE SPECIAL RETURN

Late one night when I was ready for bed, Jake Dill came knocking on my door. Jake was my election clerk, an intelligent fellow, generally known as a Liberal. I had appointed him to lend some appearance of neutrality in my office, and we got along well together. George Gow had grumbled a bit; thought the job should go to a loyal Conservative.

"You're crazy if you think they'll appreciate it," he warned, "they'll just use him to find out what's going on."

However, he went along with the appointment and Jake did a good job.

The time of night and the look on Jake's face told me there was trouble brewing.

"Sorry to disturb you so late," he apologized, "but something important has come up."

"Come on in, Jake," I said, "you're always welcome."

He came in and sat down, twisting his cap in his hand.

"I had a visitor tonight," he finally explained, "a man we both know, but I'd rather not name him."

"That's up to you."

"Well this fellow came to me on instructions from Cockburn," he went on, "Cockburn has seen a lawyer in Toronto about the return. The lawyer told him that if Anderson acted as both D.R.O. and poll clerk, you can take his statement on the result. It doesn't say you have to interview two people."

"I'm not a lawyer," I said, "but I didn't read it that way."

"Well the fellow explained it like Charlie Lount," Jake went on, "if you needed the signatures of the Division Court Judge and the Registrar of Deeds on something, how many people would you see?"

"Just one," I admitted.

"Well that's it."

I thought about it for a while, and it sounded reasonable.

But it wasn't enough to bring Jake Dill to see me after bedtime.
"There's something else," he added.
"I thought so."
"This fellow was to tell me," Jake went on, "that if you didn't get Anderson's statement and file the return within a week, Cockburn was going to sue us both in the High Court."

It was a shock but I knew Cockburn would do it, and I felt my heart pounding.
"But why you?" I asked, "I'm the one responsible."
"I guess I'm to turn the pressure on," he admitted, "or else get out of it by giving evidence against you."
Gow was right, I thought. With Jake Dill the Grits have a pipeline right into my office. Jake saw what I was thinking.
"I consider myself your associate, R.J.," he assured me, "we're in this together. Whatever you decide, I'll go along with."
"Thanks Jake, I appreciate that," I said relieved, "I'll have to think about it."

I wobbled after that.

The more I thought about it the more possible it seemed that Cockburn's lawyer was right. But something nagged at me; Cockburn was awfully anxious to have it done with. He had gone out of his way to push me at the wharf and just three days later he had seen a lawyer in Toronto and was threatening a lawsuit. He knew about the lost poll book, he knew I had a problem on my hands. There was something fishy about it.

My mind must have worked on it all night, for early in the morning before I even got up, it came to me like a flash: Cockburn's oath of qualification. There had been something strange about it when he filed. Instead of simply coming in to my office as Boulton had done, Cockburn had the form drawn by J.B. Browning who came in with him at the last minute. I wondered about it at the time, just a fleeting thought, but since Browning was with him I figured everything must be all right. I was in a hurry then, with people in the office and problems to sort out. I had taken his oath, signed the form and set it to one side. Now I went and got it out, and looked at the date. He had filed late.

188

I had been reading about the election in West Peterborough and maybe that put it all in my mind. The Liberal there had the most votes, but the Returning Officer had returned the Conservative as elected. He found something wrong with the Liberal's papers and disqualified him. Maybe I could do the same thing to Cockburn. I might be able to declare Boulton elected.

That's when I wobbled again.

I decided I had better get a Toronto lawyer too, before I did anything so drastic. I couldn't disclose my idea to Browning, so I went to see Judge Lount. He recommended a Mr. Harrison, a well-known Tory lawyer, so I went off to Toronto to consult him about the whole affair. But Harrison wasn't too helpful.

"The law is vague on late filing," he said after reading up on it, "in any case you accepted the form and let the election go ahead. Even if he was late, you can't use your own mistake as an excuse."

"But he brought a lawyer with him," I protested, "they deceived me."

"Not in words," Harrison answered, "didn't the lawyer's presence warn you? No, if you raise this matter of a late filing now, you might suffer more than Cockburn. If he really was disqualified, you might have to pay the cost of an unnecessary election."

That was a chilling thought, and I cooled right off.

"Well, what about the Peterborough case?" I argued.

"I don't know all the facts there," he said, "I'm advising you on your own situation."

"Can I declare a fouled election on account of the lost poll book?" I asked, hoping to get Cockburn that way.

"No," he decided, "only the House of Commons can do that."

"Well, can I just sit on it indefinitely."

"I doubt it," he answered, "your instruction from the Governor General is clear enough."

"So you're saying I must make a return," I decided.

"That's the way it looks to me."

That's when I wobbled the other way. It seemed I had to declare Cockburn the winner. I came back home, ready to finish it off. It annoyed me, it burned me; but if I paid a laywer for advice I would be foolish not to take it. So I got Henry Anderson back to my office on September 3rd.

"Now Henry," I told him, "I have to make a return, but I should explain what happened. Would you say that you acted as both D.R.O. and poll clerk?"

"I suppose so," he answered, "I kept the poll book, and that's the poll clerk's job."

I asked him to explain what happened in his own words, and wrote it down in the form of an oath.

"I was appointed Deputy Returning Officer for Morrison during the late election. I took my oath of office and acted as Deputy Returning Officer and Poll Clerk myself on polling day. I had appointed a poll clerk but he did not come in time and I thought I could do the work myself . . . I came to Bracebridge on the 26th of August with the book, to return it to the Returning Officer. I think it was stolen from me that day . . . The whole number of votes polled were 37, whereof D'Arcy Boulton polled 3 votes and A.P. Cockburn polled 34."

I read it back to Anderson and he signed the sheet. I swore him and signed as Returning Officer.

I started then to make up my Return as the Governor General had ordered. I decided to explain everything fully and maybe they would disqualify Cockburn in Parliament. I certainly had to leave the way open. I was still working on it when George Gow came in.

"I hope you haven't sent in your Return yet," he said.

"No but I'm working on it."

"Well hold everything," he cautioned, "I've just had word from higher up. They think you should make a special Return."

"A special Return?" I asked, "I never heard of that."

"It's never been done before," he admitted, "but it will stop Cockburn in his tracks. You make a Return saying that nobody was properly elected.''

I wobbled again; back to ruining Cockburn. This idea was much better. Disqualifying Cockburn was too dangerous; and returning him elected was surrender. But simply pointing out the state of the law was innocence itself. It had vaguely crossed my mind, but I didn't know how to do it. Now the way had been made clear. The law said I couldn't return a Member elected without having all the poll books, but my orders were to make a Return. Well, they would have a Return. And Cockburn could hardly sue me for default in my duties. But I had to be sure.

"I want to get advice on this from Mr. Harrison," I told Gow, "we never discussed a Special Return."

"I'm going to Toronto tomorrow," he said "I'll get it for you in writing."

It put things in a new light and I began to kick myself for giving in so easily. I certainly didn't want to knuckle under to Cockburn with his insulting remarks and threats of a law suit. If Mr. Harrison agreed, I would do what they suggested. In a couple of days I got a telegram from Gow in Toronto.

"Harrison away. Seeing Read."

I had no idea who Read was, so I just had to wait. In a couple more days, Gow was back with a letter which he threw on my desk. "Read that," he said with a satisfied smirk, "and see how you like it."

It was dated September 7th, 1872 and was written on the legal letter paper of D.B. Read, Q.C. of Osgoode Hall, Barrister-at-law, Toronto. It looked very responsible.

"As regards the duty of a returning officer in a case where a poll book has been lost . . . and no poll clerk having been appointed, I think the returning officer should make a special return of the facts to the House."

He quoted the Election Act and then concluded with a question.

"Now, not having the means required by the statute, how can he sum up the votes?"

"Exactly," I agreed. I was surprised that a lawyer would read

191

the law so simply, exactly the way it was written. They always seemed to find something difficult.

That settled all my doubts. I launched the new system of Special Returns.

I had to do it well, since I was creating a new procedure. So I sent everything I could think of to prove the case. There was no form for a Special Return, so I made up my own, sensing that I was making history. I headed it up like the ordinary Return, mentioning my appointment and instructions and told how I carried out my duties.

I declared that the Return for the Township of Morrison had not been duly made to me and that I could not comply with the statute because there was no poll clerk to be sworn.

I told about the problems at the Parry Sound poll.

I concluded that on the state of the facts I was unable to return a Member in compliance with the law. I dated the return September 14th, 1872 and signed it. I called in Jake Dill and told him what I was doing and the advice I had received.

"As I already told you, I go along with whatever you decide," he assured me, "Cockburn lost my sympathy when he theatened to sue me."

"Didn't he demand a statement from Anderson, and a Return within a week?"

"Exactly."

"Well that's what he's getting. But I don't think he's going to like it."

"Put it right to him," said Jake enthusiastically, "I'm beginning to enjoy it."

I put the Special Return in a big envelope, together with my oath of office signed by Judge Lount, a copy of my Proclamation with polling places attached, Henry Anderson's oath of office and his sworn statement about the lost poll book and the lack of a poll clerk. I put in a copy of the Morrison voters list, a summary of the nomination meeting and the declarations of qualification by Boulton and Cockburn. I decided not to mention Cockburn's late qualification. That bit about me having to pay the cost of an unnecessary election really scared me. I checked it all over, then sealed it up to be mailed.

Anne hovered around as I chuckled about it all.

"I don't like these tricky ideas," she said, "they always bring trouble."

"It's not a tricky idea," I told her, "It was recommended by a lawyer. In fact, it may have come from a lot higher than that. Cockburn's getting exactly what he asked for - a Return."

"Just the way you say it worries me," she fretted, shaking her head.

"Stop fussing and leave men's business to me," I scolded her, "you just look after the house."

"Oh, I hate you," she cried out angrily, "you think you're a man, but you're just a little boy. I've had my fill of it."

I shouldn't have said what I did, but when I went out into the men's world, I found the approval I deserved. Judge Lount thought the Special Return a brilliant idea. John Teviotdale pumped my hand vigorously. George Gow was delighted. As soon as I told him the Special Return was in the mail, his face lit up.

"That will fix Cockburn," he crowed, "I have it right from the top that he'll not take his seat this session - if ever."

Mr. A.P. Cockburn, it seemed, was finally having his reward.

I found one dissenting male, though, unexpected and with views that disturbed me. I was surprised one day to find Jimmy Patterson in the bar at the Royal. I hadn't seen him in a long time. He was tall, grown-up and well dressed, and he seemed quite at ease.

"My goodness, Jimmy," I said, "are you old enough to be in here?"

"Certainly am, Mr. Bell, I guess you remember me as a youth."

"I never saw your father in here."

"No, but times are changing. I come in to listen to the talk, mainly."

"Have you been away?" I asked, "It seems ages since I saw

you last.''

''I was in the city for a couple of years. It really changed my outlook.''

I sat down with him, and Jim McDonald came over to join us. ''You've become quite famous since I first helped build your shanty, Mr. Bell,'' Jimmy said, ''I've followed your career right along. Makes me proud to have helped you start out.''

It pleased me to hear him say that. Really, that was the sort of compliment I had worked all those years for.

''Are you interested in politics?'' I asked, thinking I might give him some friendly advice.

''I follow things very close; just like my dad. I hear you're not returning Mr. Cockburn as elected.''

''That's true,'' I agreed, glad that he was interested in the inside story.

''I think that's wrong, Mr. Bell,'' he declared, ''Mr. Cockburn really won. You should find a way to give him his seat.''

It gave an awful shock to hear Jimmy talk to me like that. He was polite and straight-forward, but I sure didn't expect it.

''Politics is a hard business,'' I explained.

''I find it all quite dishonest. All that trickery and bribing at election time. Perhaps Sir John Macdonald will be forced to change things now that he doesn't have a majority.''

''Oh, but he has a majority,'' I informed Jimmy, ''at least 25.''

''Those are his figures. But he counts a lot of Liberals from the maritimes who only support him on Confederation. They won't follow him on moral matters. He'll have a hard time on those.''

Jimmy Patterson was beginning to annoy me. I felt like picking him up and shaking him. What nerve! What did he know about it?

''You're beginning to sound like a Reformer,'' I accused him, ''where did all this stuff come from?''

''I had friends in the city, and they tried to look at things realistically,'' Jimmy explained, ''I know why Sir John wants to keep Cockburn out, and those other two Liberals from

Renfrew and Peterborough. If they get in, the Liberals might control the House of Commons.''

I looked at H.J. McDonald to see his reaction to all this. He could see I was vexed and his amusement showed in his face.

''Your age is showing, R.J.'' he said, ''this is a new generation, born and raised in this country.''

''Thank you, Mr. McDonald,'' said Jimmy, ''I can see you understand.''

Well, I wasn't too impressed with this new generation. They seemed quite impertinent to me.

''And do you think it quite moral for Mr. Edward Blake and Mr. Alexander Mackenzie to hold seats in the House of Commons and still draw their salaries as Premier and Treasurer of the Province of Ontario?''

''I was reading about that just yesterday,'' Jimmy said, ''and I certainly think it's wrong. They are taking advantage of a technicality.''

''See?''

''I see they are wrong. That doesn't make the Tories right.''

My old friend H.J. Mcdonald got up from the table and went out the door. I knew the beggar was laughing, and it made me mad.

''Now Jimmy,'' I said, getting serious, ''Sir John Macdonald is our greatest statesman. He's had a long and distinguished career. His only concern is our country. He can't give good government if he doesn't have Parliament behind him. You know that.''

''I certainly do, Mr. Bell, I'm sure he'll keep out all the opposition Members he can. And I know how hard it is to keep a country like ours going in one direction. I guess that's why he gets drunk so often.''

I was glad McDonald had left. Was this boy all innocence, or was he baiting me? I couldn't believe he was Matt Patterson's son.

''Tell me, Jimmy - or maybe I should call you Mr. Patterson''

''Jimmy will be fine,'' he agreed seriously, ''you've always called me that.''

"Tell me Jimmy, what would you like? I've heard a lot of things you don't like."

"Well," he began, thinking deeply, "I would like to see the day when every man has a free vote. Not just men with property, but all men. And a man should be able to vote privately."

"The secret ballot," I prompted.

"Yes. The secret ballot. Bribery and tyranny would all pass away. Politicians wouldn't have to pay off big interests, either, like Sir John is doing now."

"What's that?" I demanded, suddenly annoyed, "Sir John paying off big interests? How can you say that?"

"Everybody knows it. He spent more than he had in the election this summer."

"What about Blake and Mackenzie? . . . "

"I know, I know," he agreed, "they bribed everybody in sight. I had my first vote this year and they tried to buy it; a job, money, anything. Cockburn's people thought I would jump the fence, just because I speak out. But I wouldn't hurt my dad like that."

"I'm glad you voted right," I said, much relieved.

"I'm not too sure I did," he replied doubtfully.

It was time for me to leave, so I got up and held out my hand to him. In spite of his odd ideas, he had resisted temptation, and there was something admirable about his boyish frankness.

"And how's Mrs. Bell?" he asked as we parted.

"Quite well, thank you."

"I'm glad to hear that. Some people wonder how she keeps her sanity."

His frankness suddenly lost its appeal. I took off before I had any more of it. My God, I thought, what's the world coming to? No respect. Wild ideas. It seems you can't count on anybody any more.

It took a couple of comfortable talks with George Gow and Charlie Lount before I recovered my complacency.

CHAPTER 16
SKULDUGGERY

My first press conference was a disaster. Some careless words I used caused me all sorts of trouble. Thomas McMurray came down to my office, ostensibly on a story for the Advocate, but really for A.P. Cockburn.

In spite of our long association, McMurray seemed preoccupied, almost nervous. His clear blue eyes, normally direct and piercing under bushy eyebrows, wandered around the office as if he hadn't seen it before. He cleared his throat, made some comments about the weather and then looked at his boots for a while. It gave him away. He was an honest man, and this bit of subterfuge about an interview made him uncomfortable. It seemed I had him at a disadvantage some way, and it made me careless. He finally leaned forward and started to ask questions.

"Now, R.J." he began, "what's this Special Return all about?"

It was my turn to fiddle. I looked at his pink lips, surrounded by the blackness of his pointed beard and heavy moustache. It reminded me vaguely of a trap. I thought carefully.

"It's really simple - in a way," I explained finally, "the Election Act says I can't return a Member elected, without having all the poll books. But the Governor General ordered me in his Writ to make a return. And Cockburn threatened me with a law suit if I didn't do something. So I made a return of the facts."

"And what precedent do you have?" McMurray asked, "I never heard of it before."

"Nobody else had either," I replied, "It's something new."

"You couldn't have done it all on you own," he said; and it was both a statement and a question.

"My lawyer advised me."

"That would be J.B. Browning," he guessed, and as I shook my head, he suddenly had a horrible suspicion.

"It was that old scoundrel Lount," he declared, "don't take

advice from him. He doesn't know any law.''

"No," I declared, "I went to see a lawyer in Toronto. This thing is too big for the local men.''

McMurray opened his eyes with sudden interest, and I knew I had used the wrong words.

"I see," he said slowly, "high-ups involved, eh?''

I tried to play it down.

"No, no. The local lawyers don't handle this kind of law," I explained, "I had to see a man with experience in election cases.''

"You call it an election case. Do you expect a law suit?''

"I certainly hope not.''

"But you might get into one?''

"Mr. Cockburn threatened that.''

"But you say this is really big. How far up the ladder does it go?''

I should have answered modestly, but my vanity took over.

"I'd rather not give names," I replied, inferring high connections.

"I suppose Sir John Macdonald would like the seat," he went on, supplying one.

"I'm sure he would, but . . . ''

"And he's told you to do Cockburn in.''

"No!" I exclaimed, "that's not it at all.''

"Then what is it?''

I was at a loss for words, having painted myself into a corner, so to speak.

"I'm afraid that's all I can tell you," I said, "I'm doing the best I can in the circumstances.''

"I hope so, R.J." he declared, and there was a warning in his voice, "But Mr. Cockburn really won, you know.''

"I realize he got the most votes," I agreed, "and at one point I would have declared him elected. But the law is the law, and I couldn't legally do it. It's against the election Act.''

To my relief, McMurray gave up, and after a few general questions, he left. But I knew that wasn't the end of it.

Immediately stories of a big plot against A.P. Cockburn

began to circulate. The Advocate wasn't unkind to me, on the surface anyway, but the words I told McMurray got around. The plot was well planned and directed from the top. The Morrison poll book had conveniently disappeared. Some sharp Tory lawyers were providing me with advice and direction. The events at Morrison and at Parry Sound were no accident. When William Beatty voted against us, we had fouled up the poll at Parry Sound on purpose. And I was the king pin in the whole affair.

Even my friends kept me off balance. George Gow worried me with a story about a mysterious stranger in town.

"Fellow I never saw before," he told me, "showed up yesterday asking a lot of questions. I advised him to talk to you, but he wanted to hear from somebody else. Sounded like some kind of an investigator."

"Any idea who he was?"

"He was no friend of yours. Could be working for the Grits."

"What did he ask?"

"Wanted to know if Sir John Macdonald had been up here, for one thing. He asked several people."

"Maybe he was just starting a rumour," I suggested, knowing how those things are done.

That visit started a new round of stories about the Premier's involvement in the plot.

"Sir John himself had a hand in it," they whispered around. It was said that he had driven up to Bracebridge to tell me what to do. Stories of a midnight ride up the Muskoka Road by the First Minister of Canada sent shivers of excitement through local spines. He had come by night, they said, so he would not be seen; and by road to avoid Cockburn's boats. It was obvious nonsense, but it had its believers.

The mysterious stranger was never seen again, but the big plot idea kept building up. Cockburn's agents at the polls suddenly remembered strange occurences, and told them around.

"I'm sure our poll book was stolen," recalled Cockburn's agent at Huntsville, "they were using an old scribbler. I wondered about it at the time.''

"Our poll book must have been switched,'' said the agent at Watt and Cardwell, "it looked different when we tallied up the vote.''

Cockburn helped spread the rumours himself.

"They tried to steal the election from me by purloining poll books,'' he wrote, "but the rascals only got away with one book.''

Cockburn took the opportunity to puff himself up. The plot was directed by Sir John Macdonald, he claimed, against one of the most feared opposition candidates. Macdonald would do anything to keep Cockburn away from Ottawa. The Returning Officer was jealous of Cockburn, and a willing accomplice. The Special Return was invented especially against A.P. Cockburn.

As the pressure on me began to build, I hoped for some sympathy at home. But I didn't get it.

"I told you not to send that Special Return thing,'' Anne reminded me when I complained of the mess I was in.

"What else could I do?'' I asked plaintively, "the law is the law. I got legal advice.''

"Some advice!''

"Just like a woman,'' I complained, "always objecting. Never suggesting.''

"If you want a suggestion,'' Anne declared, "you'd better find somebody to help you get out of this thing. And don't go running off to those political lawyers in Toronto.''

So I went up to the Court House to see Judge Lount. He was no High Court judge, but he had a lot of experience. He was a people's judge, and if Anne wanted an ordinary lawyer's opinion, I couldn't think of anyone better.

"Hmm,'' he pondered when I put the matter to him, "let's think about it this way. If you came before me charged with making a Special Return contrary to law, would you be guilty?''

"That puts it about right,'' I agreed.

"I'd throw the case out because there's no such charge.''

200

His reasoning surprised me, but the result suited me well enough.

"And what can I do about the rumours?" I asked, "they even have Sir John A. Macdonald coming to see me."

"What's wrong with that? I wish he'd come to see me."

"But it's not true," I complained.

"You can't stop rumours. You should hear some of the things they say about me."

That reminded me about all the positions he held.

"They say that Henry Anderson could have been D.R.O. and poll clerk at the same time. You were used as an example."

He thought about that for a while.

"There's a difference," he decided, "I could never be my own assistant. Anderson couldn't be his own poll clerk."

It seemed to make sense, but I wondered if he was only justifying himself. In any case he hadn't answered Anne's question.

"What can I do to get out of this mess?" I asked.

"Just hold tight and keep your mouth shut," he advised me, "eventually it will all blow over."

That was more or less what I wanted to hear, so I thanked him and left.

But it didn't blow over. It seemed to get worse. I heard that Cockburn had seen Edward Blake, the man everyone expected to lead the Opposition when the House of Commons opened in Ottawa. Blake was no longer Premier; both he and Alexander Mackenzie had finally resigned their provincial positions. But they still had offices in the Legislative Buildings in Toronto. Jake Dill told me about Cockburn's visit; he had heard Cockburn telling McMurray about it.

"Cockburn went down to complain to Blake," said Jake, "he wants them to get his seat in Parliament."

"What can they do?" I asked, alarmed.

"Blake promised him nothing," Jake answered, "and Sir John isn't calling parliament until next year."

"That must annoy them."

"They're angry as hornets, according to Cockburn," Jake

declared, "Blake and Mackenzie were forced to resign their Ontario ministries, and now the House of Commons isn't being called. They have no indemnity till the House sits, and no platform for their complaints. They are putting in time without income or occupation."

"Serves them right."

"The only thing is," Jake went on, "they have time to listen to people like Cockburn. Blake's legal mind snapped right on to the Special Return thing, and he's going to look at the law. He's a pretty smart lawyer."

My heart sank. Edward Blake in court was the most feared counsel in Ontario. His cross-examinations were said to be brilliant, cunning and ruthless.

"What do you suppose he'll do?" I asked.

"Nobody knows. He asked Cockburn a lot of questions, but gave him no answers."

That discussion added nothing to my composure. I felt I should get out and talk to people, justifying my actions, clearing up the false rumours, and denying Sir John's involvement. But I knew that Lount was right; I should keep my mouth shut. I'd said too much already. I fervently hoped I would never be cross-examined by Edward Blake.

At my lowest ebb, D'Arcy Boulton arrived in Bracebridge, and he came right down to see me. He was a ray of sunshine in the gloom. It lifted me right out of the dumps to talk to him; a man with a family background that even Blake would envy; a lawyer with no fear of Edward Blake or any other counsel; a man with confidence and good humour.

"I hear you're worried about things," he said, shaking my hand heartily, "what can I do to help?"

"I'm no longer sure about that Special Return," I explained, "I don't want to get into a lawsuit."

"Well don't worry about it. I can tell you this much; Sir John knows all about it, and you have him with you. What more does any man need? And as for me, my services are available, such as they are."

"That's great," I said, relieved already, "it's mostly the

rumours that get me down. Cockburn's making himself a martyr again. I'm accused of leading a plot to keep him from his seat. They even have Sir John coming up here to instruct me."

"Have you denied that?"

"In a way, but nobody ever accused me to my face. And every time I open my mouth I say the wrong thing. It's an honour to be tied in with the Premier; but it's a problem too."

"It will all blow over," Boulton declared, repeating Lount's words, "they'll find something else to chatter about."

"For a while there," I said feeling comradely towards him, "I was going to declare you elected."

"Me? How could you do that?"

"I thought I could disqualify Cockburn, but it didn't work out. Mr. Harrison advised against it."

"It was a nice thought, anyway," he said warmly.

"Well, I would do it if I could," I assured him, "even now. But everybody is watching my every move, and listening to false rumours. They are all blaming me."

"Why not create a diversion?" he suggested, "surely you have something on Cockburn."

"Something!" I exploded, "just about everything. He pressured, twisted and bribed all sorts of people. Provincial road contracts were the worst of all."

"I heard that, but can you prove it?"

"I know one, for sure. That was Gillman Willson. He told me himself that Cockburn tried to bribe him."

"The Mail would be very interested in that," Boulton declared, "all they need is a lead on it. Here, have someone get in touch with this man. He'll see that it's all made public."

He wrote a name and address on a piece of paper and handed it to me. Then with a hearty slap on the back he went his way.

The story of the big plot kept on growing. And A.P. Cockburn didn't just let things ride, either. He fed the flames with stories of the wrong done to him. He and his cronies kept people talking about it. With their "isn't it a shame?" and "poor Mr. Cockburn" and "that rascal Bell" they kept public opinion in his favour.

Cockburn let it be known that the great Mr. Blake, former Premier, and possible leader of the Opposition in the House of Commons, was behind him. Cockburn had seen him again, and passed out news of the interview."

"We're ready for Parliament," Blake had told him, "and we'll get you your seat."

"What will you do about the Returning Officer?" Cockburn had asked, to which Blake had replied: "we'll find a suitable reward for him."

Cockburn had to keep the pot boiling. He had no access to the federal government, no federal patronage and not even the title Member of Parliament. He had no seat in the House of Commons when it was called and no political influence in Ottawa. He couldn't even promise things, for he was in no position to deliver. The Ontario Grits gave him no more appointments to make; the election was over and they wanted credit to go to their provincial friends. All Cockburn had, thanks to me, was a claim to sympathy. And he had no intention of losing that.

But one day in October the tide turned. The attention of the whole district was suddenly diverted from my disrepute to Cockburn's.   An article in the Toronto Mail exposed Cockburn's election bribery.

The Mail pulled no punches. It said plainly that Cockburn had engaged in corrupt practices with the connivance of the Liberal government of Ontario. He had gone to the Provincial government in Toronto during the election campaign to see what they could do for him. They did plenty. Among other things they allowed him to appoint several Muskoka and Parry Sound men as road contractors.

"These parties had all voted the Tory ticket in previous elections," the editorial claimed, "and to the astonishment of their political friends, they suddenly changed front and became rabid supporters of Mr. Cockburn."

The Mail talked money too.

"A few days before the election, the mountebanks received

204

$1000 each from the Ontario government, . . . only about half of which has been honestly and legitimately used."

Journalism in Toronto then was the bitter enmity between the Grit Globe and the Tory Mail. No political story was worth printing unless it struck a mortal blow at the other side. And this story filled the bill to perfection. The Globe was caught between its vicious charges against Cockburn at the time of the Nine Martyrs and its present support of him. So the Mail called on Brown of the Globe to defend Cockburn, the man he had accused of "selling his vote" and "open and unblushing corruption". It challenged the Globe to explain government bribery, if, as the Globe claimed, the Liberals were incapable of fraud.

"In view of the shockingly bad character given him by Mr. Brown, we are anxious to know Mr. Cockburn's connection with the road arrangement," the Mail taunted, "and we surmise the Ontario government aided the corruptionist 'with fox-like face and eye' in swindling the country in order to bribe its electors."

Well that issue of the Mail got passed from hand to hand, quoted, disputed and argued over throughout the whole of Muskoka. Since it mentioned the names of local men in all parts of Parry Sound and Muskoka, and accused them of accepting bribes, the news spread like wildfire. Cockburn rushed off to Toronto to see Brown and get the damage patched up. Everybody waited to see what the Globe would say. And when the answer came the following Tuesday, October 22nd, the defence was lame and weak. It looked almost as if Brown were damning Cockburn with faint praise, still holding his old grudge.

"None of the persons named are contractors," Brown claimed, "they are simply overseers or foremen."
He denied any political intervention - sort of.
"Only two of them were appointed on the application of Mr. Cockburn, the remaining five being appointed without knowledge of their political leanings."
He denied they received $1000.

205

"The said persons each received only $200 before the election, not $1000 as claimed."

The Globe waved it all away as the usual Mail trash. "It is one of those mean and miserable attempts at vilification from the same quarter, each one as contemptible and false as the predecessor."

That gave both sides locally their cases to argue. The wise and perceptive writings of the two great Toronto papers were gospel for their readers. Our side quoted the truth of the Mail's statements and the weakness of the Globe's reply. Along those lines we used a comment made by our local judge to good effect.

"Brown and Cockburn were caught like a pair of dolts," he said to a group of citizens gathered one day in the Land Office to look at Crown lists, "if a man charged with stealing seven sheep comes into court all indignant swearing he only stole two, he's still guilty. That's Cockburn. He only corrupted two foremen, not seven contractors; he only bribed five people with $200, not seven with $1000. But he's still guilty."

And so it went. Now Cockburn, instead of making himself visible all over the district and complaining about injustice, found things to do in Montreal. He was away a long time, presumably involved in important business deals about his boats. It was a relief not to have him around.

It worked out very well for me, though. The nasty rumours about the lost poll book and the Special Return died off, and people were arguing about the bribery. They began to discuss Cockburn's honesty, not mine.

Nobody ever knew who sent all that information to the Mail. I imagine that Cockburn suspected one of those jolly fellows who just two years earlier had voted unanimously at the Dominion Hotel in Bracebridge. "That we have the fullest confidence in Mr. Cockburn as our representative."

It wasn't true any more.

206

CHAPTER 17
A CASE OF JEALOUSY

Troubles never come singly, they say, and I was no exception. In the midst of my struggle in the hostile world of politics, my wife turned on me at home.

Now I'm the first to admit I was hard to live with. If I hadn't recognized it myself, others took the trouble to point it out. Right from the beginning of our marriage I spent more time away from our home than in it. While other husbands came home promptly for meals, did all the heavy chores and took the wife out occasionally, I was off in Bracebridge at a council meeting, or a Lodge meeting, or a political gathering, or what not. Often I didn't come home at night and there was no way of letting Anne know. I simply didn't arrive. She would lie awake half the night waiting, then drop off to sleep for a few hours until the children woke her for a new day. When she got tired of complaining about my habits, I assumed she understood my problems. That made me even more careless. It didn't improve much after we moved into town; there were simply different irritations.

I justified myself in my own mind. A man who would get ahead must make sacrifices. An ordinary settler like myself had to exert himself more and pamper himself less, in order to raise his standing. That went for his wife and family too, and I assumed they accepted that simple fact. But I was wrong. Anne knew how I felt, for I told her at least once a week, but she never accepted it. She wanted the benefits without the sacrifice.

After the twins came, Anne's irritation turned into gloomy despair; she withdrew into herself and hardly spoke to me. I would have preferred a good tongue-lashing. For a while I thought it was the hard birth, weariness and extra work. I tried to help out more around the house, come home promptly for meals and make life as easy as I could for her. I asked Dr. Bridgland to watch her carefully, and he was very faithful. But it wasn't enough.

"I'll hire a girl to help out part time," I offered after one of her worst days.

"I can manage," she answered shortly.

"Is something wrong?"

"No."

She didn't convince me, but I could see no reason for her to be unhappy. We had a good home in town, a wonderful family and social standing. Anne managed to dress herself and the children well, and though we were not rolling in money we were at least comfortable.

After we moved into Bracebridge I became a better husband around the house. My bachelor days on the farm had trained me into doing a lot of chores that women did in other households. I made up in some ways for my neglect on the farm. I looked after the garden. In the early Spring I planted tomato and cabbage plants in little boxes inside, and let them grow by the window. I transplanted them late to prevent damage by any unexpected frost, and I had the knack of timing it well. We always had a long crop of tomatoes for fresh use, and Anne made chili sauce and preserves from the last growth. The garden itself I dug, manured, planted and weeded, and our table was well provided. I made a root mound at the back of the garden to keep the hardy vegetables until Spring, and I kept indoors in soft earth and a dark place, our needs for the winter. There were few homes where the men did all this.

I also looked after the animals and poultry. We had a stable at the back of the lot where I kept a cow, and sometimes a calf as well, and my good flock of chickens. I got in enough hay for winter feeding the animals and some grain as a supplement for the chickens. I no longer kept a horse; my days of long journeys into town were over. But we had fresh milk and eggs most of the year and Anne sold a few of the eggs for pin money.

The house was Anne's charge. She looked after the children, the meals, the clothing and the purchases. I thought we had a fair division of the duties and I was proud of my own contribution.

We generally went walking on Sunday afternoons. It was a thrill to be in town, and now we could show off the twins as well. On our walks Anne was usually delightful and showed little sign of her discontent. One such day in December of 1872 we got all bundled up for our stroll. A light snow had fallen that morning, and little white fringes hung on the long pine branches. The sun came out at noon and cast smoky shadows on the snow. As I opened the door and stepped out, the world seemed a beautiful place. The river babbled along peacefully across the road, as it made for the Falls half a mile below. A blue jay called across the quiet landscape and a woodpecker knocked away at a fencepost nearby. Otherwise, there was a peaceful silence. I filled my lungs with the clean fresh air, and felt its stimulation. Our little frame house looked good; the sash and trim were painted green and the rest of it was white. A few cedars I had planted along the road were thriving.

Little Maggie came out the back door, looking pleased in her Sunday best. She wore a broad-brimmed felt hat, with pretty red ribbons hanging down behind. She smoothed down her long coat and pulled on a pair of white woolen gloves.

Then Anne appeared, fussing with Freddy, while Tommy tottered along behind. I went and got Tommy and put him in the little double wagon I had rigged up for the twins. Anne set Freddy in, and pulled their woollen bonnets around their ears and tied the strings. She was a real picture herself. Above her long black coat she wore a fancy hat, all flowers and bows, with a ribbon tied below her chin. It made me proud and happy, I can tell you. I fastened the top button of my coat, straightened my bowler hat and took hold of the wagon. We proceeded up River Street towards town, past George Gow's warehouse and the fair grounds to Thomas Street. We took the long hill up to main street in easy stages, and then turned South towards the bridge.

In some places there was a board walk where the wagon

wheels thumped across the boards. In other places it was gravel and the wheels dragged heavily among the stones. We made a game of it, jerking and pulling, and the twins laughed out loud as they held onto the sides. Cooper's carpentry shop near the corner gave off its fresh pine smell, and we stopped to look in the window. Then we went on past the little post office, the big frame Perry and Myers store, the Dominion Hotel, the Orange Hall, and jogged left towards the bridge. Mr. Simington's sash and blind factory, Frank Cheney's grocery store and the little plant where they made ginger beer came and went as we travelled. Then we were at the river again.

It was exciting for the children to go up onto the bridge, which soared on its high pillars like a rainbow. The planks rattled as I pulled the wagon across them. Anne held Maggie firmly by the hand and we stopped in the middle to peer into the water below.

"The falls always give me a thrill," I said, "like the first time we walked along them together."

"Do you still walk along the path?" Anne asked, for she seldom came with me any more.

"Quite often."

"Alone?"

"Of course," I exclaimed, "what a silly question."

When I looked at her, I saw that her face had turned sullen and dark. Her lips were compressed and her jaw set. She stared in a strange, blank way. This happened more often now, and she could change suddenly, like a shadow passing. I wondered vaguely about her sanity, but couldn't bring myself to think seriously about it. Dr. Bridgland must have suspected it too, for he came often, and her problems weren't always physical.

We turned now and went back up the other side of Manitoba Street stopping to look in the windows: Mr. Kennedy's shoe shop, Clerihue's store, Dill's shop and Daniels' tinsmith. Anne didn't speak to me; acted as if I weren't there. We met a few people out walking and they stopped to admire the twins and make a fuss over Maggie. Anne would brighten up briefly, then lapse into her sullen silence.

210

Eventually we reached the Agricultural Hall, the name Mr. Teviotdale gave to his exciting new store. That store was proof of the rapid strides our community was making. It had two giant windows facing onto the street, filled with all kinds of merchandise. Inside it was 30 feet wide, and 60 feet long, and you could hardly see the other end from the street. In addition to the displays there were two closed-in offices and a fireproof vault. The second floor was a large hall, used for banquets, agricultural gatherings and social events. And on the roof was an observatory, from which you could see away down the river.

"This is quite a place," I gushed enthusiastically.

"So I hear," answered Anne, and her voice was harsh and bitter, the brief words stressed in some strange way. It was too nice a day to argue, so I picked up the wagon handle, and we finished our walk.

Monday morning I went up town as usual to get the mail, talk to the citizens and generally to see that the place was in order. I turned in to the Agricultural Hall, and as I put my hand towards the door, it all hit me like a ton of brick. Anne was jealous.

It had never entered my head before. But there was a certain young lady working in the store whom I saw every day. Something had more or less developed between us over the last few months. I always dropped in to say hello to Mr. Teviotdale, jolly the staff and pass the time of day. On the way out I stopped to talk to her by the south counter, where she sold yard goods. There was something different about her, and I guess I stopped there a little longer and talked a little more. One day I walked home with her to carry some parcels; just a pleasant civic duty as a gentleman and municipal clerk. You wouldn't think anyone could take something wrong from that. But that's where I was mistaken; people notice and talk and add things together.

There was the time, though, when they had the grand opening of the store and there was a celebration upstairs. The public was invited and the staff served refreshments from the kitchen. The party became quite jolly. I was there alone, for

Anne didn't feel like taking the children out after supper, and really didn't want to go anyway. The kitchen was at the back of the second floor, and they had put up a screen inside so the women could work unobserved. For some reason I can't remember, I wandered out into the kitchen and peered behind the screen. She was there alone, with one foot on a chair, her dress up to her knees, making some adjustments. I had a quick flash of a well-shaped leg, white underwear and a red petticoat. It was an interesting sight.

At that moment she noticed that someone was there, and straightened up, gasping. I was embarrassed, but when she saw who it was, she relaxed.

"Oh, it's only you," she said casually.

There was something in the way she said it, sort of intimate. I never knew she felt that way. Anyway, I took her by the arm to apologize or something and suddenly we were kissing. It must have been the drink. I'm pretty sure nobody saw it, but you can never tell. After that, things were different between us.

I could never understand what that young lady saw in a portly, middle-aged married man with three children. It could hardly have been the prospect of marriage. But perhaps that was the attraction of the thing; a flirtation without having to make a decision. Then again, perhaps she didn't like Anne for some reason and wanted to feel superior; or it could have been my growing notoriety in the district. I fairly well ruled out physical attraction, although I do admit to a genial disposition, not bad looking features and . . . well, I'm starting to disprove my modesty. Frankly, I don't understand women at all. The fact is that she made a play for my attention, and as things became more strained at home, I began to enjoy it.

Well anyway, there I was on that Monday morning with my hand on the latch of the Agricultural Hall, and my brain suddenly functioning. All Anne's little comments had gone right over my head, but now they added up. Someone had been talking, that was for sure, and what had been said I couldn't tell. All at once I decided not to go into the Agricultural Hall right then, and I turned up main street to spread my good will somewhere else.

I had no idea how to get out of the fix I was in. There was nothing really improper in my new relationship; it was just a sort of special understanding, little looks and glances, suggestive words that thrilled us with their rashness. That's what made it all the more difficult; there was nothing to either confess or deny. If Anne would only have asked me, or accused me, I could have answered. But she didn't do that, she just kept tantalizing me with nasty little comments. I tried to think up some kind of an opener, but everything sounded silly. "You know that affair you think I'm having," I could say, "well there's nothing in it."
And I knew exactly what she would answer.
"What affair is this? It sounds interesting."
No, I was on the hook, and there was no way off.

There were times when I looked at my wife and tried to recapture the image I had carried with me over the lonely years. And it wouldn't come. She seemed like another person now - somehow remote and distant from me. She seldom looked at me, except with a hard or skeptical glance as if wondering how I would hurt her next. There seemed nothing I could do to bring her to me, to get over the wall or through the fence that separated us. It was there, invisible to me, though I had built it myself, I suppose, with acts of carelessness and neglect.

I was torn over what to do. If it was all over between Anne and I - the love and affection and tender care we once had - I had another love waiting. But did I? Perhaps she was just flirting and would run at the first sign of persistence on my part. Then at times I thought I should avoid my new friend completely, so that our troubles would fade away. But I knew that was impossible as well; it would make things the more obvious. So I went along blindly, doing nothing and saying nothing. I put it down as the price I had to pay for being a public figure. For that's what I had become.

I was more than township clerk, and county Returning Officer now; there was talk that I might be the next candidate for the provincial or federal seat. I was credited by the Conservatives with spiking Cockburn's wheel, and nobody had done that before. Up until the summer of '72 there had been little feeling against him; he was Muskoka's man and an independent. But now he had shown his true Grit colours. That put him on the other side for at least half the people, though some voted for him anyway. An outsider would still have a tough time against him, but a local man could defeat him. And an early election for Muskoka was quite possible. My Special Return could result in another vote.

Once people spoke of me in political terms, though, the Grits turned against me. They tried to discredit me in the eyes of the public to prevent me being a candidate. It made me feel important, in one sense, but also made life difficult for me. I was one of the prime targets in November, 1872 when the Grits started a movement for a new council in Macaulay township. "It's the same old Tory bunch running things," someone wrote to the Advocate, "it's time for a change."

Now that letter might have been made up by Thomas McMurray himself, for we often suspected that these open letters to the editor were made up right in his office. Be that as it may, it was easy for them to find converts. The council had very little money and they spent it sparingly. Every road unrepaired, every license refused, left another unhappy citizen. George Gow was Reeve and he did nothing to please people. He quarrelled constantly with publisher Thomas McMurray. In October they had a row over a printing account, and the council thereafter sent its minutes to the Northern Light in Orillia. That riled both the Advocate and the Gazette. The Reeve, the four councillors and the clerk were all Conservatives and it was easy enough to stir up the partisans. Both local newspapers lined up against the councillors, and harped away at them for a month. The voters only got one side of the story, but the press proved its power. When the elections were over in December the campaign had succeeded; three of the four new councillors were Grits, and Gow was out. I was next in line for the chop by the new council.

214

It wasn't much of a Christmas that year. My job was up in the air until the January council meeting. Anne kept her sullen silence except to scold me. I was waiting for the axe to fall.

When council met on January 20th, the lone Conservative councillor took the bull by the horns and moved that I be reappointed Clerk at a salary of $40 per annum. There was silence as they looked at each other for a seconder. I felt my time had come. I was on the point of picking up my papers and departing when William Kirk spoke up.

"I'll second that motion, if nobody else will," he said.

I was elated. Though we had been friendly I never knew how he felt about me. He was a young man in his twenties, not disposed to words and playing very close to the chest. Now I knew he respected me and that was very important.

If they had voted right then, I would have been reappointed, for the Reeve was in my favour. But the other two councillors were ready for this situation.

"I move in amendment that James Boyer be appointed Clerk at a salary of $35 per year," said councillor Moore, and Tookey seconded it. It was quite a manoeuvre. By knocking $5 off the salary, a vote for me was a vote for extravagance. That was the one thing Kirk had pledged himself against. Kirk was annoyed, but he held his ground, and the vote was 2-2. It felt strange to me sitting there and recording the judgment of council on myself. There were no explanations, just the motions and the votes; like a game of checkers between two silent players.

The Reeve had to break the tie.

"My vote is against the amendment," he announced, "and therefore for the motion."

I was Clerk of the Township of Macaulay for another year.

But it was an uneasy victory and the council began its term at odds. I went into the new year far from happy; unsettled at home, uncertain at council and under criticism as Returning Officer. I began to turn sour. There were few places I could turn for solace, for the odd slap on the back, "you're doing a good job" bit.

I stopped trying to please Anne; it seemed hopeless after nearly a year. I snapped at the children, stayed out late after meetings and took to hanging around the Royal Hotel.

It was after one of those late nights at the Royal that I found Anne waiting up for me.

"I think we should have a talk," she began.

"I can't think of anything to talk about," I answered peevishly, though it came to me clearly that she was about to surrender.

"I haven't been too easy to get along with recently," she admitted.

"That's right." It was mean, but there was no point in going soft at this stage. I had nothing to lose.

She sat there silently for a while, not knowing what else to say. It was something new for me to be firm after a confession like that. Usually I found excuses for her, but not this time.

"I was jealous," she said finally. It was the opening I had been waiting for, and I knew what to say.

"There is nothing to be jealous of," I declared firmly.

"I know," she admitted.

She leaned toward me and opened her mouth as if to say something more, but as I looked at her expectantly she changed her mind. Perhaps my thoughts showed in my face.

I knew I had won. She must realize how unfair she has been to me; jealous without reason; resentful while I sacrificed; critical when I was in trouble. And now that I am driven to drink she is shocked into reality. For my part, I am willing to forgive and forget. I know it was hard for her too; the children a handful, the house a burden. But just for now she sees me as I really am. She understands that all my efforts are for her and the children, to provide them a better home, give them better social standing, bring them the good things of life. We both know it's slow coming, but together we are approaching our goal. I suppose I look tired and discouraged tonight; her affection for me has revived; just for this short time we are together once more.

I waited for her to explain it all so that I could tell her I understood. But nothing came. So I forgave her anyway.

"It's hard for you to say these things in explanation," I said, "but I understand."

"Do you?" she asked softly, and the moment passed.

Things went better after that. I applied myself to improving relations in our divided council, and patching things up with my former friends. I came home promptly for meals and loosened up a bit with the money. Anne's disposition was a lot better and life seemed almost back to normal.

One afternoon when council broke up early I decided to go home instead of doing up the books. It was much more pleasant around the house now; not exactly sentimental, but at least friendly. When I turned onto River Street I saw Dr. Bridgland's buggy in front of the house. He was in the habit of calling regularly, but it worried me all the same. I hurried home, and went in the back door quietly, just in case. As I opened the door I heard Anne laughing. It was a vibrant, girlish laugh, the sort of giggle I hadn't heard since we were first married. It pleased me that she was feeling so well.

I looked into the living room and they were sitting together on the sofa with their backs to me. They were half facing each other, talking excitedly, and I suddenly realized there was something more there than a medical call. I came right down to earth with a crash. There was nothing improper that I could see, but they had a depth of understanding that Anne and I never achieved.

I turned and went out quietly.

How blind I had been! She hadn't come crawling to me that other night, she had been dealing from strength - the strength of another friendship. Perhaps she had wanted understanding, but it was another kind, and I didn't have it in my eyes. When I with-held my understanding, she lost her guilt. And her sulky moods of the past were not directed against me, but against herself. And her friendship with Dr. Bridgland was probably nothing more than the other friendship I had. I went back up town and into the Royal Hotel, where I should have gone in the first place.

That night as we sat in the kitchen, I opened up the subject. "When we were talking the other night," I began, "I intended to explain why I have been so difficult recently."

"I understand," she replied.

"And I intended to ask your forgiveness."

"I forgive you."

I settled back to read the paper, satisfied that I had it all figured out. Of course, I was just as wrong as I'd been the first time.

CHAPTER 18
CALLED TO JUDGEMENT

The blow fell without warning. We had just finished lunch in our River Street home in Bracebridge when a knock came at the side door. I opened it, and a boy was standing there. "Telegram for Mr. Bell," he said, holding out a slip of paper for me to sign. When I obliged he handed me a sealed envelope and went his way.

I held it in my hand for a moment, trying to imagine who would be sending me a telegram. It was a rare event around Bracebridge, the line was just new, and it generally meant bad news. Nothing came to mind. I had no close relatives overseas who might have died, and my own family was here with me. I opened the envelope and looked at the signature: "Alfred Patrick, Clerk of the House of Commons". It meant nothing, so I looked at the date and heading. It was from Ottawa, March 10th, 1873; that very day. Then I read the message: "You are required to attend before the bar of the House of Commons on Monday the 24th instant. Letter following."

I was still dense. I looked at the address to see if it was for someone else. But it was my name, Richard James Bell, Bracebridge, Ontario. Then, with all hope of a mistake ruled out, a feeling of doom flooded through me. I tried to hold off panic, to remain very calm, to think it was all very normal. I read it once more, letting the words run over the surface of my mind, without sinking in. Maybe the letter would clear things up, explaining that it was an experiment of some sort, a test of public opinion. But deep down I knew better. A lump began to form in my stomach. I felt as if my name had just been called on judgement day.

"Is something wrong?" Anne's voice came from behind me, as if from another world. I was standing there in the open doorway, the winter wind blowing past me into the house. I went in and shut the door and handed her the telegram. After she read it, she opened her mouth to say something, then closed it again. I knew she was about to remind me of her warnings. I didn't need that, and she knew it.

"Is it something to do with the Return?" she asked finally.

"It looks that way."

I sat down at the kitchen table and Anne went on cleaning up in silence. I just sat there. After a while she broke the stillness a bit impatiently.

"Well, there's no use in just sitting there," she said, "why don't you go and talk to somebody about it."

I got up, put on my coat and hat and went out. I started up town without any idea of where I was going, but I finally thought of Charlie Lount and went to the Court House. Fortunately he was there, and I handed him the telegram without any explanation.

"By God, I never saw anything like this before," he exclaimed after he read it, "What are you going to do?"

"I don't know," I answered, "That's why I came to you."

"Well, you'll have to go, that's one thing sure," he said.

"But I haven't done anything wrong," I argued, "I just did what the lawyer told me."

"The ways of the politicians are strange," he said, "they'll let the worst kind of corruption go on right under their noses and never take any notice; then they'll pick on some little thing like this to make a fuss over."

"How can I afford to travel to Ottawa?" I asked him, looking for an excuse, "I don't have that kind of money."

"Write and ask for the fare," he advised, "even in Division Court they have to pay a witness fee. And this is the highest court in the land."

"What happens to people they call before Parliament?" I asked, looking for some kind of assurance.

He shrugged his shoulders, took down an old leather-bound book from the shelf and blew off the dust.

He looked in the index, thumbed through it and finally found a page which he mumbled away at for a while.

"This is English stuff and probably out of date." he explained finally, "I don't know what they do here, but in England people called before the bar of Parliament are kept in the Tower of London.''

"The Tower of London!'' I exclaimed, really frightened. It sent shivers through my spine.

"Well, we don't have a Tower of London here,'' he assured me, "so you needn't worry about that.''

He couldn't find anything else, and I left his office feeling worse than when I went in. I decided to go home again, and wait for the letter from Ottawa.

Next day I went for the mail and there was no letter. I decided to see George Gow.

"That's bad luck,'' he said after he read the telegram, "I heard something about it this morning.''

"What do you suppose happened?'' I asked.

"Well I had a letter from a certain source,'' he said in that mysterious tone he used about his dealings with the unseen powers, "it seems that they had to give Cockburn his seat to satisfy the Grits. But that wasn't enough and Blake pushed right on to have you summoned.''

"Couldn't they stop it?''

"It seems John A. was in a bind and had to agree.''

There was still something bothering me, so I mentioned it. Gow seemed to have the right connections.

"Who's going to pay my fare?'' I asked, "have you got funds?''

His attitude changed immediately.

"Sorry,'' he said "the money's all gone. In fact I'm away in the hole after that last election. I've put up a lot of my own money already.''

"I thought maybe somebody would back me up,'' I suggested tentatively.

"When you get your fingers caught in this game,'' he declared, "you're on your own. Maybe they will send you the fare.''

He turned to do something else. It was sickening for he had suggested the special Return himself. But that was my friend George Gow all over.

I got up and left his office. I didn't seem to have a friend in the world, now that I was in trouble. I wandered down to the river, and the splash of water at the edge of the frozen falls sounded welcome. I crossed the bridge and took my favourite walk along the edge of the rapids. It was treacherous walking, and the path was covered with snow and little runs of ice. Normally I would have turned back. But now I didn't care and the exertion of the climb down somehow relieved the pressure. At the bottom by the falls I found a bare rock and sat down to rest. From here, everything seemed normal; the river, the forest, the falls, the silent little village covered with snow. Nothing had changed, it was timeless. I finally climbed back up the steep slope feeling much better.

The letter came next morning. I opened it carefully, almost afraid of what I would find inside, yet hopeful of a miracle. There was no miracle, instead there was a copy of resolution passed by the House of Commons, that awesome temple of power so far away. It sent another chill through my nervous system.

"On motion of Mr. Blake, seconded by Hon. Mr. Holton, ORDERED that Mr. Speaker do issue his Warrant summoning Richard James Bell Esquire the Returning Officer at the last election for the Electoral District of Muskoka to the Bar of this House on Monday the 24th day of March, 1873 to answer for his return to the Writ of Election for the said District."

I couldn't believe it was happening; R.J. Bell charged with some kind of high treason. I had to wake up; the dream was too real. But I was awake-terribly awake. There was no money in the envelope, so I took the advice of Judge Lount and George Gow and wrote a letter asking for the fare.

"To answer for his return." Those words kept running through my mind. It sounded as though I had already been found guilty.

I knew that parliament had been called into session the previous Monday. In fact, I had read the accounts of the formal opening in the Toronto papers. The main figure in the proceedings was more than a name to me now; he was the Earl of Dufferin, Governor General of Canada, Cousin and Councillor of Her majesty, Viscount and Baron Clandeboye, etc. who had appointed me Returning Officer by his own hand, and had sent me the Writ of Election. I read all the details of the magnificent opening ceremonies, the Governor General arriving on Parliament Hill in his carriage, the glittering parade through the halls of Parliament, and the Speech from the Throne read in the Senate.

Another name in that event took my attention: James Cockburn, who was elected Speaker of the House of Commons. I wasn't too clear on what the Speaker did, but the Mail attached a lot of importance to his appointment. It was his name that struck me; I wondered it he was any relative of A.P. Cockburn. If so, he might be favourable to him. I was more conscious of these things than ever before.

Back I went to talk to George Gow. I was drawn to him like a moth to a flame; dangerous, but a source of enlightenment. "Not him," he said of James Cockburn, "he's no Grit. He's one of John A.'s men. Even if he was related he'd do nothing to put A.P. Cockburn into Parliament."

"But the Toronto Mail particularly mentioned his impartiality," I insisted, "doesn't that mean something?"

"That's not what the Globe says," Gow replied, "George Brown hates James Cockburn. He does everything short of using libellous language. You don't insult the Speaker, because he's above criticism, even by the Members. But Brown gets at him in his own sneaky way. I don't know the whole story, but that Cockburn is certainly no Grit. He was Speaker in the last Parliament too."

How little I knew about Parliament! It made me nervous. What had happened down there in Ottawa? Why was I called? The telegram and letter explained nothing. Elections I understood, but the procedures in Ottawa were another world; remote and unknown. George Gow was little help; he knew a lot of people, he had been around politics for quite a while. But he was really a rural man too, tied up in local quarrels and bickering, fast with election tricks, knowing who were friends and who enemies. But Parliament concerned him very little.

"Who can I talk to?" I asked him, "isn't there someone who knows the ins and outs down there, and heard what happened? I have to be there in ten days and I know practically nothing."

"They all know more that I do," he replied, "you'll have to talk to one of them. Nobody from around here went but Cockburn."

"Who do you mean by 'them'?"

"Oh, Boulton, T.R. Ferguson, that crowd. If they can wangle an invitation to the opening they go. Their wives buy a lot of new clothes and parade themselves in front of the Governor General. Then they hang around Ottawa for a couple of weeks and go to all the parties. It's real high society."

"What about Mr. Ferguson? He was a Member once."

"He probably went. Why not ask him? Should be home by now."

I took the stage for Barrie on Saturday, the 15th, without even enquiring. If Mr. Ferguson wasn't home I intended to find Mr. Boulton or someone who could help. But luck was with me. Ferguson had just arrived back from Ottawa.

"Yep. They gave Cockburn his seat," he informed me right away, "I dropped a line about it to County Master Gow."

So that's where Gow got his information. Orange Order and politics and T.R. Ferguson, M.P.P. That son-of-a-gun Gow didn't even admit Ferguson was in Ottawa. Just tells me what he wants to.

"And what happened?" I asked eagerly.

"Well Blake surprised everybody the first day of the session. He didn't even have the courtesy to wait for debate on Her Majesty's speech. He got up on a question of privilege and said there were gentlemen occupying seats in the House to which they were not entitled, and one seat was vacant that should be occupied."

"That would be the Muskoka seat," I suggested.

"Right. And the other two are the Conservatives from Renfrew South and Peterborough West. The Grits are all worked up about them as well. Claim the Liberal in

224

Peterborough shouldn't have been disqualified."

"I know about that one," I said, "I considered the same thing for Muskoka."

"Blake went on to demand that the election returns for all three Ridings be brought before the House. Sir John didn't oppose it, and the Clerk of the Crown in Chancery produced all the papers. Next day Blake pushed in again with another question of privilege. Now a question of privilege comes before anything else, and Blake's point was that the membership of the House was a matter of privilege. Sir John didn't argue about that either. He doesn't engage in skirmishes he might lose; he waits for the main battle. And this was an important battle, for if the three seats went Grit it could finish him."

Ferguson got up and walked around with some agitation. I could see that he was totally immersed in the events and needed no prodding; so I waited.

"On Friday Blake brought a motion that the House declare the Peterborough Grit properly elected. It was the strongest case for the opposition. The Liberal clearly had the most votes and the Returning Officer disqualified him after the election was over. That was too late."

"I was told that," I said, "good thing I didn't try it."

"Well it didn't matter here anyway because the Premier planted his flag and did battle. He didn't argue the merits of the case. He simply said that if the House of Commons could vote one Member out and another in by a majority vote, there was no safety for the minority. The whole principle of parliamentary institutions would be endangered. He preferred that the matter be sent to a committee where it could be carefully examined. He made a good case, and even some of the Liberals backed him. He won the vote easily, 95 to 75. The Ottawa papers agreed. So that Riding goes to committee and into limbo. They'll keep it there for months. And Sir John said he would deal with the other election cases the same way."

"Then what happened to ours?" I demanded, "how did Cockburn get seated?"

I was eager for news, but Ferguson took his own time.

225

"Well that was last Friday," he replied, "and over that week-end a whole bunch of Maritime Members blew into Ottawa with the winter wind. They'd been stalled on the train for a couple of days, and knew little of what went on Friday. They figured it was all a lot of Upper Canadian skulduggery. 'Give the man his seat' they said for Cockburn."

"Couldn't Sir John convince them? Weren't they his supporters?

"You have to understand about those Maritimers," Ferguson explained, "down there the 1872 election was fought on the issue of Confederation. Sir John publicly counts those who declared for Confederation as his supporters. But he knows most of them are Liberals. They're as apt to vote against him as for him. That's why it's all so shaky."

"So he gave in?" I asked and there was some vexation in my voice.

"Sir John Macdonald occasionally loses a battle, but never loses the war."

"I'm sorry," I added hastily, "I wasn't being critical of him."

"Hillyard Cameron, who was put in charge of the election cases, apparently advised the Premier that we would lose the vote on Cockburn. It seemed true, because the Grits were strutting around on Monday morning as if they were in government already. Defeat of the government on a vote means it has to resign. Then the Grits would take over. We couldn't chance it for one seat."

"I can understand that."

"Our people didn't lie down and die, though," he went on, "Blake made his motion on Monday to seat Cockburn, and he said you should have reported who had a majority; but since you didn't, the House should take note of it and seat him. He wasn't too critical. Then Hillyard Cameron replied, saying you had done the right thing. But he went on to say that if the matter went to a committee, and if the facts were as Blake stated them, he might have to vote to seat Cockburn."

"And what about Sir John? Did he say anything?"

"Indeed he did. I don't recall his exact words, but he said you did your best and acted on advice. However, he said that Blake had made a strong case, and he wouldn't oppose the motion."

"So Cockburn was seated?"

"Right away. He was sitting there in the gallery hoping for something like that to happen. Anyway he was sworn in at the Clerk's Table and escorted to the Speaker's Chair by Mr. Alexander Mackenzie, Leader of the Opposition, and A.A. Dorion. Then he took his seat."

"What about me? Why was I summoned?" I asked, "it doesn't sound like anybody blamed me."

"No, but the Grits were hot on the trail for a vote over this thing. They had the floaters with them. So they hatched up this outrageous thing about calling you before the House. Hillyard Cameron and Sir John had both defended you. So Blake figured they wouldn't reverse themselves and allow you to be summoned. But he was wrong. They couldn't risk a vote, so they agreed."

"My God," I exclaimed, "I nearly brought down the government with my Special Return."

"Twice," he agreed, "but the Grits would have tried it with something else. And they'll keep on trying. Election cases are great for the opposition; they can always find something wrong."

"That was very helpful, Mr. Ferguson," I said, "now can you tell me what to do in Ottawa?"

"I haven't any idea. I never saw it happen. All I can suggest is that you go to Ottawa early and have a look around. Talk to someone in our party and you'll probably get some help. Be sure and take all your papers with you, so you can answer any question, no matter now stupid. And don't worry about it. Our fellows are just as smart as theirs."

"But am I?"

"That remains to be seen. Just be modest and straightforward, and don't pretend to be something you're not. You don't want to outshine some of the dolts there. Then they will go after you."

"I'm grateful to you once again, Mr. Ferguson," I said as I

took my leave, "I feel much better about the whole thing."

I went back to Bracebridge and spent the next few days sorting out my papers. On Thursday I received a bank draft from the House of Commons for my travelling expenses. I was ready to meet my fate.

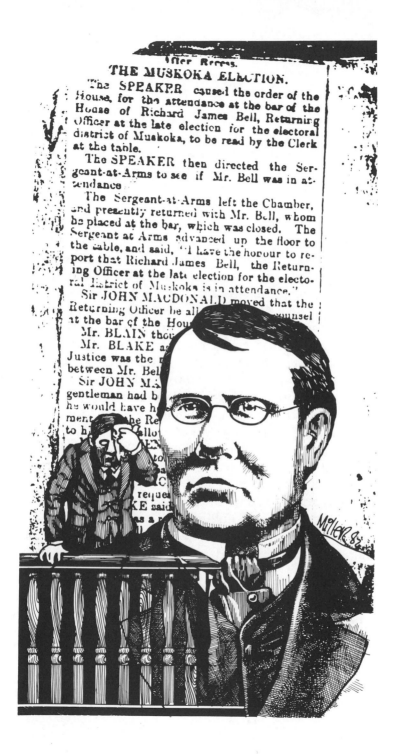

After Recess.

THE MUSKOKA ELECTION.

The SPEAKER caused the order of the House, for the attendance at the bar of the House of Richard James Bell, Returning Officer at the late election for the electoral district of Muskoka, to be read by the Clerk at the table.

The SPEAKER then directed the Sergeant-at-Arms to see if Mr. Bell was in attendance.

The Sergeant-at-Arms left the Chamber, and presently returned with Mr. Bell, whom he placed at the bar, which was closed. The Sergeant at Arms advanced up the floor to the table, and said, "I have the honour to report that Richard James Bell, the Returning Officer at the late election for the electoral District of Muskoka is in attendance."

Sir JOHN MACDONALD moved that the Returning Officer be all   counsel at the bar of the Hou

Mr. BLAIN thou

Mr. BLAKE as
Justice was the
between Mr. Bel

Sir JOHN MA
gentleman had b
he would have h
ment   the Re
to h   allo
            to
            re
            requ
KE said
            as a

CHAPTER 19
OTTAWA

On Friday morning, March 21st, I took up my valise, bade farewell to my family, and headed out to meet my fate. I walked through the snow along River Street beside the frozen Muskoka River, up the slippery hill on Thomas Street and turned left along main street towards the Dominion Hotel. The feeling persisted that I was saying farewell to all this; that I was taking some sort of a final journey. I don't know why I felt that way; nobody had suggested it. Yet my fingers tingled and I felt slightly disembodied, as if I weren't really there; just a body moving along. It was a strange feeling, and as I pressed along I hoped that God would keep me from harm and bring me safely home again. I held tight to my valise, with all my papers enclosed, as if it were my passport to safety.

It was snowing heavily for the third day in a row, keeping us firmly in the grip of winter. It almost seemed an omen that our earlier expectation of Spring was snatched away, like my hopes for an early release from my troubles. The walking was hard and I wondered if the stage would leave in this weather. But there were passengers waiting in the hotel lobby and the sound of bells came from the stable. Shortly, the heavy cutter came to the door and we climbed aboard.

I found myself sitting beside a stranger, and though he smiled pleasantly, I said nothing.

"Name's Johnston, George Johnston," he said finally "commercial traveller; hardware and such. Awful weather to be on the road."

"My name is Bell," I answered, not feeling like talking.

"Not R.J. Bell, the Returning Officer?"

I nodded.

"Well, isn't that interesting. I've been reading about you. On your way to Ottawa, eh?"

"That's right," I admitted.

"I've been hearing a lot about you the last few days," he went on.

"All bad probably," I muttered pulling the buffalo robe over my lap.

"Oh not at all," he assured me, "I'm a John A. man myself. Can't stand those sour old Grits, Mackenzie, Brown and Company. They're awful."

He was trying to start a conversation, and I had the feeling he was drawing me out. But he obviously got around and heard things and I was interested in knowing what he heard. I opened up a bit, beginning to feel important.

"They are after me, that's certain," I admitted.

"They'll never catch you," he said, "not with Sir John protecting you. Did he really come up and tell you what to do? Most people think he did,"

"I'd rather not talk about that," I said; and he winked at me.

"I understand," he replied, "I can't tell all my secrets either."

We settled back to endure the cold ride to Orillia. The snow was so heavy and the road so bad that we had to change horses at Gravenhurst and again at Washago. The icy wind whipped in our faces and cut across the eyes; the horses tugged and snorted through the heavy drifts. The cutter heaved dangerously, first one way, then the other as we hit concealed rocks and logs, and it seemed ready to tip over more than once. I gripped the seat, the side, anywhere that was solid. The country was barren and deserted, the hardwood trees stark and lifeless, and tips of dark rock jutted up here and there through the snow. After the first few miles we didn't talk much as the chill set in; a chill that no robes or coat, woollen socks or heavy underwear could hold out. At the stops we got out and stamped around to start the circulation again. The dreary hotel lobbies seemed wonderfully warm and we hated to go out again. But each stop brought us closer to journey's end and finally we arrived at the new Orillia Railway Station. The train was sitting there, steaming away in a comforting warmth, and we got aboard the coach for the trip to Toronto.

My traveller friend took a seat beside me, and we talked now and then as the engine chugged along towards Toronto. My mind kept coming back to my problems.

231

"To answer for his return," it said. Why had they really summoned me?

"Why?" I muttered aloud.

"What's that?" he asked.

"I'm sorry. I just can't figure out why they summoned me."

"It's not you they're after," he said with a shake of his head, "it's Sir John."

"Sir John?"

"Sure. It's an open secret. The Grits hope you'll spill the beans, then they'll have him for fraud or something."

It was startling to hear it said that way. Something like that had crossed my mind, but I couldn't believe I was that important. My position was crucial.

"And you think his future is riding on me?" I asked.

"That's the way I see it."

The weight of the world seemed suddenly on my shoulders.

I arrived in Ottawa late Saturday. Nobody was on hand to meet me and there were no messages at the station. I took a small hotel in centre town, changed my clothes and then went to see the sights. I asked my way to Parliament Hill and walked along Sparks Street and up Metcalfe. As I reached the corner of Wellington I stopped and caught my breath at the sight of the magnificent Parliament Buildings before me.

There were three great buildings forming three sides of a square, and the other side was open snow-covered field. The tall tower of the centre building stretched skyward, swelling at the top into a huge crown. The bell in the tower boomed out as I stood there, and I could see the clock face high up near the top. On all corners of that building were towers, and arches made up the entire face; the main door, the windows and the smaller doors all curved upward. It was three storeys high and the tower must have been 200 feet.

The centre building was flanked by the East and West blocks. They were built in the same style, towers, spires and arches. Up the centre was a broad walk to the main building, guarded near the entrance by two huge cannon. A great iron fence along Wellington Street protected the whole hill.

232

Everything was quiet; blanketed with snow. There was hardly anyone around. In the midst of my admiration I felt a sudden chill pass through me. Was it the wind, or something inside me? I couldn't tell. Those sombre buildings standing in their cold landscape suddenly frightened me. Somewhere inside, surrounded by all the magnificence, was the hidden chamber where I would have to answer; where I would meet my fate. It took away the beauty of the place and filled me with apprehension. I turned back to my hotel.

On Monday morning I made a big decision. I was determined to go and see the great man himself. If his fate was really riding on me, he would surely want to talk to me. I walked up to the door of the East Block, where his office was, and said I had business with the Premier. They directed me to his office, and I was amazed how easy it was. An attendent there asked me to wait and then disappeared. As I sat down I realized how presumptious I was to come here. With so many affairs of state the Premier could hardly have time for a backwoodsman from Muskoka.

Without warning a door opened and there he was - Sir John A. Macdonald. He was so real that I started; the hair standing out to frame his face, the large nose, the heavy lidded eyes. I had seen them so often in cartoons and engravings that I was surprised to see they were real. And for me, Richard James Bell, he had a big smile and an outstretched hand. "Come in, Bell, come in," he said heartily and waved me in to his office.

The interview was brief and most of the time I just sat there, scarcely believing where I was.

"It's unfortunate the way things happened," he was saying from behind his big desk, "but it goes that way some times." I nodded, hardly knowing what to say.

"It's quite all right," I mumbled. He could have been explaining why I was being executed, and I would have agreed.

"Someone will explain the procedures to you," he said, "you just have to keep your head."

"Will I be standing there alone?" I asked. Somehow that worried me more than anything.

"We will try to have counsel with you," he assured me, "Blake will probably object, but they can hardly deny you a lawyer."

"Can I see the lawyer first?"

"Indeed you may," he said, "we have already spoken to Robert Lyon, a reliable Ottawa barrister. He knows his way around Parliament."

As I got up to go, I remembered that Sir John's whole future was in jeopardy and I wondered how he could be so casual about it. He hadn't even asked what I was going to say.

"I suppose this happens all the time," I remarked lightly at the door.

"No," he answered, shaking his head, "you're the first."

"The first person to be called before the House of Commons?" I asked, surprised.

"The very first in the Canadian House," he agreed, "it should be quite interesting."

To me, somehow, that wasn't the right word.

I decided to see Robert Lyon at once. His Chambers were just two blocks from the hill, and he was in when I called. He kept me waiting only a minute while he hustled another client out. I clearly had priority. He approached me briskly and introduced himself.

"I'm Robert Lyon; and I believe you are R.J. Bell. Come into my office."

He walked quickly down the corridor and into his office. I had to move to keep the door from slamming in my face. He was a red-faced, impatient man, shorter than average and attired in light clothes that seemed a bit flashy for a lawyer. He stood on no ceremony and waved me to a chair.

"Now, we have work to do," he began, "you've never been to Parliament before?"

"Never."

"That's a great start," he declared sarcastically, "we've no way to go but up. Do you know who the Speaker is?"

"James Cockburn," I answered, pleased that I knew.

234

"No, no. This isn't a school contest. Do you know what he does?"

"I believe he is Chairman of the House."

"Correct. He's in full charge up there. You always address him no matter who asks you a question. Call him Mr. Speaker. If he stands up, you stop talking. Is that clear?"

"That's clear."

"Now they'll be asking you questions about the election, and God knows what else. You have to know the answers yourself. I can't help you with that. All I can do is point out the pitfalls."

"I understand," I declared.

"Now whatever you do, don't come up with that old chestnut, 'I don't remember.' It's the mark of a liar. If you really can't remember express it in some other way 'I'll have to refer to my papers' or 'it's a detail I cannot recall at the moment'. Do you know what I mean?"

"Yes, I do," I agreed, "I've heard people do it before council, and the same thing struck me."

"Try to answer questions promptly. If you hesitate too long, they think you're inventing a story. If I'm with you, you can consult me to kill time, or give me a signal and I'll make some objection. But I can't answer questions."

"What kind of questions can I expect?" I wondered.

"God knows. I don't even know why you're here, let alone what they want from you. I really think they're trying to pull Sir John in on it. They'd really like to get something on him. But it's enough to catch you. It reflects on his leadership."

Half an hour later I reeled from his office, full of advice which I hoped I could remember. But even before I got out of the building he called me back.

"I'm told they're putting it off until Wednesday," he said, "you can sit in the gallery and watch what goes on."

I went up to the House of Commons that night to observe the proceedings. I got a seat in the gallery at the end of the Chamber, so I could see everything. I looked down for the first time on the Chamber of the House. It seemed to me like a

battlefield and I studied it that way. Nobody had told me how
my affair would proceed, but one thing was clear; when I got
in there I was on my own. The questions were unknown, and
the answers were for me alone.

"Keep your head," was all Sir John could advise me.

"I can't answer questions," was what Lyon had warned.

The Chamber was almost square, divided in the middle by a
narrow aisle, at one end of which the Speaker sat in his elegant
throne. There were seven rows of double desks rising steeply
away from the aisle on each side.

Sir John Macdonald occupied a front row desk near the
middle on the Speaker's right. He slouched carelessly in his seat,
his feet extending out into the aisle. He didn't seem to be
listening to what went on; but once he interrupted a Member
to put him straight, and I realized that nothing escaped him.

Directly across the aisle sat Mr. Alexander Mackenzie,
Leader of the Opposition. I had thought that Mr. Blake held
that position, for I heard of him much more than Mr.
Mackenzie. But apparently Blake had turned the job down. I
saw Mr. Mackenzie for the first time, and his severity surprised
me. His thin lips were closed tight, his countenance was severe
and his whole appearance was forbidding. He had a full beard
and heavy moustache. He reminded me of a Presbyterian
preacher who once frightened me with a description of hell,
and declared I would go there. Mr. Mackenzie said nothing
whatever; he sat there silently listening and watching. I had the
feeling, though, that nothing escaped him either.

Beside Mr. Mackenzie sat Edward Blake. I recognized him
easily, but I was surprised at the size of the man. He had heavy
shoulders, a full clean-shaven face and large hands like those
of a labouring man. But something gave him a scholarly,
youthful appearance and I finally realized it was his spectacles.
They were small, silver rimmed and set close to his eyeballs.
They seemed almost ridiculous, framed against his large face
like a practical joke. But he wasn't funny. He was intense and
nervous, moving around constantly and interrupting proceedings in an abrupt way.

236

There was a man on the other side of Mr. Mackenzie whom I didn't know, but he seemed important. He was heavy-set, dressed in a dark, striped suit and quite self possessed. Other Members seemed to consult him from time to time, and I learned later that he was A.A. Dorion, an eminent Quebec lawyer.

The government supporters sat in the rows behind the Premier, Sir John Macdonald. I decided that if two Members fired questions at me at the same time, I would answer the one who sat behind Sir John. He would be more friendly to me than the one behind Mr. Mackenzie.

I noticed also that the acoustics were bad. I could hardly hear what some of the Members said, and they seemed to have the same problem on the floor of the House. Often a Member asked that something be repeated. That brought my second decision. If I were stuck for a quick answer, I would ask that the question be repeated, while I figured out my reply.

I looked particularly at the Speaker, for I feared him most. He seemed like the judge in this big Court, seated magnificently on his throne, quiet and confident. He was a small man with keen eyes. He seemed to take in the whole Chamber at a glance, calling on Members in the farthest rows. His mouth turned down at the corners, giving him a sceptical look, though it was not unpleasant. His sanctity and virtue impressed me greatly; the Members gave deference to his every move and his word was never questioned. I had the feeling that he would never approve some of the terrible things that went on at elections, including some of the things I had done. I decided to keep an eye on him all the time I was in the Chamber. I noticed also that he seldom intervened in the arguments; he let them say what they pleased. I could expect no help from him.

In front of the Speaker was a Table at which the Clerk and his two assistants were sitting. The Clerk was Mr. Alfred Patrick, the man who had sent me the telegram; a big man with a broad heavy face and a white moustache. I didn't know what part the clerks would play in my affair, but I learned to recognize them. There was a calendar on the Table with the day of the month -24- in big letters on four sides; and a clock ticked away on each wall. I could see the time and date in case my mind went blank.

I couldn't see A.P. Cockburn. He must have had a back seat under the gallery. But I knew he was there and made up my mind that if he asked me a question, I would be especially polite. The Members would know that my feelings towards him were quite impersonal.

I went again Tuesday, and when the House rose that night, I had studied the battle ground and was ready to take my place. I felt like David facing Goliath. One thing still worried me. Somewhere in that great building, while I sat unaware in the gallery, some unknown person was figuring out the question I couldn't answer.

CHAPTER 20
FIRST DAY FIZZLE

The night of my crisis found me strangely calm. I suppose my nervous system was reacting to the shocks it had received; the fearful summons, the trip to Ottawa, the unknown buildings, the ominous advice about my trial. Now I had recovered my stability, conscious of the dangers about me, but not battered by them. I was ready for whatever might happen.

At 7:45 p.m. on Wednesday I reported to Lt. Col. Donald W. Macdonnell, the Sergeant-at-Arms, in his office in the Parliament Buildings. I felt like a fugitive surrendering into custody, and his appearance didn't help any. Col. Macdonnell was a military man, erect of carriage, determined of visage; a sword dangling at his side, his medals and chain of office sparkling on his chest. His parade-ground dress was softened a bit by a high buttoned civilian jacket and a white bow tie. He took me around to the main door of the Chamber and told me to wait there until he came for me. He showed me where I would stand within the Chamber, and said he would try to have a chair available. That sounded encouraging - a little less formal. He advised me not to speak unless I was spoken to, and to enunciate clearly. Then he left to prepare for the opening of the evening session.

In a few minutes Robert Lyon appeared. He bustled through the Members milling towards the Chamber and came directly to me. He wasted no time in preliminaries.

"There's a new Grit Member here by the name of David Blain," he said, "he's a lawyer and specializes in cross-examination. They're going to let him do the questioning."

"My God," I moaned, "I'll be crucified."

"He'll try, that's for certain."

"Why are they doing this to me?" I lamented, "I'm just a simple man trying to do a job."

"You may think that," he admitted, "But the Grits don't. They see you as a scheming Tory henchman, trying to do them out of a seat in the House."

"Don't I have any protection from Blain?"

"I hope to sit with you as counsel," Lyon assured me.

"That's a relief," I sighed, wiping my forehead with the back of my hand, "I know the facts, but not the tricks they play here."

"They're about the same everywhere," he assured me, "and you seem to be pretty well up on them. Anyway, Sir John has a few of his own."

"I'm sure he has. But do you think he'll really fight for me. He's the Premier, you know."

"Oh, they're after him too, and he knows it. I heard a couple of Grits talking as I came in. They didn't know who I was or they would have shut up. But they obviously think he's going to be caught in this thing, and it will happen tonight. They're all excited about it."

"I won't let him down," I promised; but inside I wasn't all that confident.

The bell began to ring for the evening session. Members looked at us curiously as they went into the Chamber. When the bell stopped ringing we could hear voices faintly from inside, but had no idea what was happening. As time went by I began to wonder why I wasn't called. Lyon was agitated and paced nervously back and forth in the corridor. At last the big door swung open and Col. Macdonnell beckoned me in; but when Lyon made to follow, Macdonnell waved him back. I was alone after all.

As we entered the Chamber the aisle was barred by a metal railing which extended completely across the room. The bar was several feet inside the door and left a comfortable space in which to stand. Col. Macdonnell pushed back a moveable section of the railing and passed through. He snapped it shut behind him and left me standing outside. I was now at the bar of the House.

"I have the honour to report," he announced, "that Richard James Bell, the Returning Officer at the late election for the electoral district of Muskoka is in attendance."

Sir John Macdonald was immediately on his feet.

240

"I move," he said, "that the Returning Officer be allowed to have counsel at the bar of the House."

His request brought immediate reaction.

"That's not usual," protested a Member who was already on his feet, and whom I took to be Blain. Sir John just looked at him, and said nothing.

Then Blake jumped up.

"Is the Minister of Justice (Mr. Macdonald) the medium of communication between Mr. Bell and the House?" he asked in a sarcastic voice.

Sir John was quite unruffled.

"I mentioned on Monday that the Returning Officer wanted counsel," he said reprovingly, as if none of them had been listening.

"That's not the way I understood it," protested Mr. Mackenzie.

"Well, it's a reasonable request," Sir John declared, waving his hand in Mackenzie's direction.

"It's not a request at all," argued Blake, "the Returning Officer hasn't made any request."

They were flailing around so the Premier went on the offensive.

"Am I to take it then," he asked, "that the honourable gentlemen would deprive this man of counsel?"

Blake stood there blinking for a minute. It was a basic principle that no accused man should be deprived of counsel. And that's what Sir John was accusing one of Ontario's leading lawyers of doing.

"That's not a fair statement," Blake complained, "the Returning Officer should himself apply to the House."

I was jubilant. Here were three of my principal accusers all snarled up by one man, and he was on my side. Sir John didn't press his advantage right then; he sat down as if satisfied. I knew instinctively what I had to do; I could see the game. It was just like working with George Gow at a council meeting. He set them up and I followed through. Blake was set up now for me to request counsel. When I did, he could hardly refuse.

I had to wait for the right moment, and it was not now. My turn to speak had not yet arrived.

Then the third member of the Grits' big three jumped up. I could see that they were on the defensive, struggling to find an excuse for refusing me assistance.

"Mr. Bell is only a witness," claimed A.A. Dorion, the Quebec legal light, "it's not usual for a witness to have counsel."

I expected Speaker James Cockburn to get up then and make a ruling. But he surprised me by staying impassively in the Chair. I had been studying up on him the past couple of days, reading biographies, taking to Lyon and making casual enquiries of people in the know. I was sure he must be favourable. Like the others in the House, he was an elected Member of Parliament, a politician who went through the bitter campaigning. He must know the devious means that many of the Members use to get there, and the schemes which leave others on the outside.

I had learned that he became a member almost by accident in 1861 when the Reformers in West Northumberland lost their candidate, and turned to him. They got him out of bed one night, and read him a petition signed by 350 residents of the riding. He must, in the name of conscience, accept their call to run for the House of Commons. Cockburn was then a well-known lawyer in Cobourg, and conservative in his views; but right then he was favourable to the Grit call for "rep by pop", a move to give Upper Canada more seats than Lower Canada in the House of Assembly. So he ran as a Grit.

When riding nominations were held on June 20th, 1861, John A. Macdonald himself had arrived to speak in favour of Cockburn's opponent, Sidney Smith. But it was not a painful experience for James Cockburn. With his usual courtesy for the opposition, John A. spoke against him good naturedly.

"I have never met Mr. Cockburn before," said the Tory leader, "and I am impressed by the high esteem in which he is held here. However, I am grieved that he has made such a political mistake."

242

John A. Macdonald never closed the door on one who might later see his error.

It was a hard-fought battle in that riding, but James Cockburn won. He learned the tricks of the trade quickly, and someone complained about his methods. "A protest has been entered against the return of Mr. Cockburn," announced the Returning Officer when declaring him elected, "the grounds are bribery and other unlawful means."

But James Cockburn took his seat; and after three years he repented of his "political mistake." On March 30th, 1864 he accepted an offer by John A. Macdonald to switch over and took the position of Solicitor-General for Upper Canada. On accepting this office from the Crown, he had to stand for re-election. Then he discovered how miserable George Brown could be.

The election was bitter. George Brown and the Grit party were vicious. It was later reported:

"Every effort that human foresight could devise, or human cunning put into motion was expended to carry that riding for the Grits and to defeat James Cockburn."

But he had the confidence of his people, and he won. In October of that very year James Cockburn was a delegate from Upper Canada to the Quebec Conference and became one of the Fathers of Confederation. When the first Parliament met, Sir John selected him as Speaker of the House. He was no political novice, that mild man in the big Chair. I knew that now. He knew what went on at elections. And he knew who his friends were.

He was not, so far as I ever learned, a relative of Alexander P. Cockburn. But he did have an interesting connection. Away back in 1846, when James Cockburn was a rising young graduate in Cobourg, he went into partnership with another young lawyer. That man's name was D'Arcy Boulton.

Now, watching the proceedings, Speaker Cockburn could see that David Blain was on his feet again, straining to get into action, anxious to start the ruthless grilling that would expose Conservative corruption. Blain turned towards me with his papers in his hand.

"Mr. Bell," he began in accusing tones; but Speaker Cockburn rose to his feet and Blain had to sit down.

"Order," said the Speaker mildly, "the witness is not within the bar. Therefore he can not be questioned directly, nor can he reply directly." Then he resumed his seat. Blain got up again but couldn't think of anything to say, and stood there looking foolish. Blake, Mackenzie and Dorion looked at each other in surprise, but didn't move.

The Speaker rose again.

"Questions must be in writing and delivered to the Chair," he ruled, "they will be read aloud from the Chair so that everyone can hear them. Each question will then be delivered to the witness who will reply. However, as the witness cannot address the House, his answer will be dictated to the assistant clerk, who will write it down for the record and then read it aloud."

They sat there stunned.

They had planned to hit me with a series of rapid-fire questions, drawing inferences, making accusations, getting me confused. That was Blain's specialty. The Speaker's procedure made the whole thing hopeless. I would know the question well before it was delivered to me; I could take my time dictating the answer; and there would be a long delay between questions. The examination would have all the punch of a feather pillow.

Dorion was the first to recover. He rose in his place to make some objection, but no words came. It was a new procedure and he knew there had to be rules. There was nothing illogical about the ruling, yet everything was wrong with it.

I saw him look across at Sir John, sitting easily in his place; then up at Speaker Cockburn seated impassively in the chair. There was no flicker of the eyes or twitch of the face to indicate that those two even knew each other. Dorion knew better; they understood each other without even speaking. But there was absolutely nothing he could say about it. So he leaned over and scribbled out the first question while Blain was recovering his senses.

244

"What is your name, residence and occupation?" Speaker Cockburn read out when he had received the question. He handed the paper to Bourinot, one of the assistant clerks, v) brought it down the length of the Chamber and gave it to me. "My name is Richard James Bell, my residence is Bracebridge and my occupation clerk," I said in a low voice to the clerk who had set up a small table across the bar from me. He wrote it down and then stood up and read my answer aloud. Somewhere, up in the ranks behind Sir John, somebody let out a raucous laugh. I could see Mr. Mackenzie's lips tighten angrily and Blake turned red as he sat looking straight ahead.

Blain had now adjusted to the procedure and sent up his question. He wanted to know if I was indeed the Returning Officer at the late election for Muskoka. The answer, as everyone knew, was a simple yes. So they watched curiously as the clerk scribbled away at the reply. Then he stood up and read:

"I respectfully ask this Honourable House to allow me to be assisted by counsel."

I watched Sir John as the reply was being read. He brightened right up and I thought he would laugh out loud. He looked over in my direction and the expression on his face said it as clearly as words:

"By Jove, you're bright enough after all. We should have some fun with this."

Speaker Cockburn got right to his feet.

"Does the House agree to grant the witness counsel?" he enquired.

Now Mr. Mackenzie was no fool. He could see how easily things were going for me, and he didn't like it. He thought the Speaker was being entirely too helpful, and he got up to object.

"There is no motion before the House," he said primly, "your Honour has no proposal to deal with."

That problem was overcome quickly enough. Sir John moved at once that I be allowed the assistance of counsel. Blake was boxed in his corner; for he had only insisted that I make the

245

request myself and I had just done that. So he never moved off his big fat behind. Dorion repeated his objection that I was only a witness, but he sounded half-hearted about it. A few remarks were thrown at him from the back benches like, "That's Quebec's great lawyer" and "no defence for the poor." He backed off.

"Well, there's no very great objection to him having counsel," he admitted, "except that it is creating a precedent which is very inconvenient."

There were howls of laughter from the government side and Dorion looked annoyed. It was inconvenient, all right. That was the idea. He sat down and nobody else got up. So the Speaker put the motion and they let it pass without further comment. Almost immediately the Sergeant-at-Arms admitted Robert Lyon and you could hear a groan in the opposition ranks. If there was anybody in Ottawa the Grits disliked, it was Lyon. He was a partisan Tory, had little respect for Members in general and none at all for Grits. The Sergeant-at-Arms placed a chair for Lyon beside me.

For the third time, now almost in desperation, Blain started his questioning.

"When were you first informed that you had been appointed Returning Officer?" his question read.

Since I now had a lawyer, I decided to use him. I didn't think Gow's casual visit to my house was "being informed". So I whispered in Lyon's ear. Immediately a Member who I learned was A.J. Smith, former Premier of New Brunswick, jumped to his feet.

"The witness should not consult counsel as to his answers," he complained.

"Quite right," agreed Sir John solemnly "counsel is there to object to irregular questions."

Blake apparently felt he should say something too.

"Objection should be taken before the House allows the question," he claimed righteously, "as we are adopting a new principle, we should make it consistent with common sense and decency."

246

"Hurrah," somebody shouted and there was laughter again. They enjoyed seeing the opposition squirm. It was their trap, and now they were caught in it. The Speaker advised Mr. Lyon that he should not help the witness answer, then sat down to enjoy the event. Blain got up wearily to begin again. Almost an hour had passed, and he hadn't succeeded in having a single question answered without interruption, most of it from his own colleagues.

From my new position in the House, I could now see A.P. Cockburn in his seat away up in the seventh row of the opposition. He wasn't sitting there quietly. From time to time I could see him leaning forward, trying to say something to Blain. He was complaining to the Members around him, and I could see him pounding his desk and shaking his head. His face showed red above his heavy beard, and you could tell he was angry. He wasn't happy at the way things were going. Apparently he had asked Blain to do the questioning, for he had seen him in Court somewhere tearing witnesses apart. Now Blain was completely impotent; while great lawyers like Blake and Dorion were all tangled up in Sir John Macdonald's red tape. The government Members were laughing and jibing, and even some of his own colleagues thought it was funny at times.

Blain was still struggling away, and some of his questions were tough. I was glad I had time to think of the answers. Had I taken part in any meetings on Mr. Boulton's behalf? Not after I received my appointment, I replied. Who did I consult about polling places and the like? George Gow who was Reeve of the township of which I was Clerk.

The name Gow seemed to strike a chord with Blain. "Was Mr. Gow a supporter of Mr. Boulton or Mr. Cockburn?" he asked, "and did he take an active part in the campaign for either of them?"

I didn't know just how to answer that, so I signalled Lyon. He got up right away and objected to the question. He said it was not relevant to my duties as Returning Officer.

"Put it to a vote," said a voice from the back row, and I saw that it was A.P. Cockburn. He was standing there, waving and angry and the Members were curious. So they voted for me to answer the question.

"I believe Mr. Gow was a supporter of Mr. Boulton," I replied carefully, "but he was absent a good part of the time."

"Was he not an agent of Mr. Boulton?" Blain insisted. I was beginning to sweat, but I answered:

"Not that I know of."

I was skating on thin ice there, but Blain hadn't said what he meant by an agent. I saw A.P. Cockburn moving around again. He knew very well I was playing innocent and he was waving and calling to Blain. But Blain couldn't see him, and if he heard, he ignored it. He accepted my answer and went on to something else; and I saw A.P. Cockburn hammer his desk again with his fist. He got up and went forward to where Blain was working, and I could see him say something about "open polls." Blain nodded and in a moment came to the part that got me into trouble.

One thing had been obvious from the returns. Cockburn won every poll with a list, while Boulton only won in open polls. This looked like foul play on the surface, but I could hardly be blamed for it, except where open polls had been improperly set up. That's what they tried to prove next. First it was Watt and Cardwell.

"Did you change the polling in those polls?" Blain asked.

"It was an organized township," I replied, "but the Clerk sent me no list. I took advice and threw it open as an unorganized poll."

"Who did you consult?" was the next question the Speaker read.

"Yes, who did you consult?" Cockburn echoed out loud, and everybody looked at him. He was sure it must have been some high Tory lawyer. The House waited expectantly for the answer, though they could hardly have thought I would name Sir John A. Macdonald.

"James B. Browning of Bracebridge," read Mr. Piche.

They looked at Cockburn to see his reaction; the name meant

248

nothing to anyone else. But Cockburn just sat there with his face frozen in grim annoyance; what could he say about a Grit lawyer who had withdrawn to let him run?

That was a dead end, so Blain started on Stephenson. "Did you instruct the Deputy Returning Officer for Stephenson to receive votes as an unorganized territory?"

"It was part of the unorganized territory," I replied.

"It was not," Cockburn said clearly.

Blain looked around helplessly. He could only ask questions and those in writing. Cockburn came up to him again.

"Were you not aware," asked Blain "that the electors of Stephenson township voted in 1871 on a list?"

I nudged Lyon to let him know I was having trouble and he jumped up to raise an objection. My mind went back to that conversation about Stephenson with George Gow so many months ago. I never imagined then the possibility of being in this place, answering this question. My own caution had warned me, and I had let him wave it away. I tried to remember what he had said to put me off the track, it might help me now; something about not being too sure. But I couldn't admit I had made no enquiries at all.

Lyon's objection got nowhere. The Members were a little impatient about these legal arguments over what was relevant and what was irrelevant. The Speaker took the sense of the House and directed me to answer. By now, I was ready. Did I not know Stephenson township had voted on a list in 1871? "They may have," I dictated, "but I found no municipal organization."

It wasn't good enough. Gow had convinced a willing listener, but he didn't have the sceptics I had in that House. Dorion saw that I was having trouble, and pressed the advantage. He couldn't harangue me, but he could draw attention to the weakness of my answer; and he did.

"Mr. Speaker," he complained aloud "the question has not been answered. That is no answer."

I tried again.

"I heard they had done so, but I did not know they had lists."

Dorion shook his head in disgust and I knew very well he was right. I waited for an onslaught from Dorion or Blain but it didn't come. I realized then how tight a yoke Speaker Cockburn had fastened on them. They couldn't cross-examine me verbally nor question my reply.

Something else came to my rescue; it was getting late and the promised spectacle had died away in technical arguments. The significance of the question was lost on the other Members; they didn't know the vote pattern or how the open polls affected it. They began to see a confused Returning Officer barging around in the backwoods trying to find his voters.

"Get on with it," someone called out impatiently, and Blain went on to another subject.

I could see he was on the last sheet of questions and I began to breathe easier. He wanted to know about my legal adviser and I told him it was Mr. Browning during the election and Mr. Read afterwards. I told him about applying to Mr. Harrison for an opinion about my return and getting one from Mr. Read. It seemed to satisfy him.

He had one more subject, and I sat ready for the blow. If I could just hold out a little longer, it would be over. His next question was really two, and I realized that he originally planned to ask them separately, in court room style. That's when I kew he was defeated.

"Did you decide to give a vote to the people at Houston and Coates Mill on Georgian Bay; and then refuse to grant them a polling place?"

The answer to that was easy; I threw it right back onto Parliament, for that's where the problem lay.

"I decided it was not in my electoral district," I explained, "it was not a surveyed township as defined in the Act of Parliament forming the electoral county of Muskoka."

That stopped him cold. They couldn't blame me for that Maybe the Speaker will just read out the opinion."

and they had spent the whole evening chasing me around Muskoka and getting no where. I'm sure the Members suspected I had helped out the government man. But how

250

could I set up a poll in every little clearing where a few settlers decided to squat? Blain felt the rumblings, in fact he could hear them. He was finished. "I have no more questions, Mr. Speaker," he said, and sat down.

Speaker Cockburn told me I could retire, and I did. Col. Macdonnell came out in a couple of minutes and told me to return the next day, in case there was anything else.

It was my day. Cockburn and Blain and all the big Grits in parliament had fizzled out.

CHAPTER 21
NOT GUILTY

Next morning found me in Robert Lyon's office, summoned for a conference. He was out when I arrived, so I sat and waited. After a long time the sound of running footsteps clattered up the hall, and everybody sprang into motion. The secretary pushed her novel into a drawer, the office boy shoved his half-finished apple into his pocket and the clerk got back to scratching his quill on parchment. The door flew open and Robert Lyon appeared.

"Get the Bell file," he called out to his secretary; "bring me a coffee" he said to the office boy; "come in to my office," he commanded me. The place began to move like a puppet show. It was day number two of my hearing, Thursday, March 27th, 1873.

I hurried into Lyon's private office, feeling almost as if I should run. He threw his hat and coat onto a chair and motioned me to sit down.

"You're not finished yet," he announced, "Cockburn has convinced them you can still be caught. They are going at you again today."

I was crushed, but curious.

"Where do you get all this information?" I asked.

"Not sitting on my ass in my office, if that's what you're thinking," he declared, "and by the way, where in hell have you been?" He always reacted offensively.

"Sitting on my ass in your office," I replied, taking out my keyless Russell watch, "I've been here for one hour and twenty-five minutes."

"Hmph" he grunted. It was neither a reply nor an apology. He seemed surprised that I possessed a watch. He stared at it for a moment, fascinated. Then he went around behind his desk and sat down.

"You told them last night you were advised to make a Special Return," he said finally "I hope you have it in writing."

"I certainly have," I answered, feeling pleased that I kept

everything in place, "I have it right here in my papers. I'm sure it will prove me right."

"Listen," he exclaimed like an impatient school teacher, "they don't give a damn whether you're right or wrong. Some of them are so stupid they'll argue black is white. All they want is to get something on us."

I handed him the letter of advice. He took one look at it.

"For Christ's sake," he shouted, "It's addressed to D'Arcy Boulton. How did you get it?"

"It's a little mixed up," I admitted, "Mr. Gow went to Toronto to get a letter of advice from my lawyer Mr. Harrison, but he was away. So Gow asked Mr. Boulton, who has an office in Toronto, who else he could see. Boulton introduced him to Read and Read addressed the letter to Boulton."

Lyon stared at me in disbelief.

"Don't say it again," he warned, "just let me figure it out in my own way."

It didn't take him long.

"So you ended up with the letter that Read wrote Boulton?"

"That's right."

"Very smart!" he exclaimed, "very smart indeed. That's what happens when a lawyer like Boulton gets into politics. And I suppose that's all you have!"

"Yes," I said, "I never thought I'd have to use it."

"Never thought he'd have to use it!" Lyon repeated, "did it ever occur to you, even after all the trouble started, that this letter does about as much harm as good?"

"It crossed my mind," I admitted, "but it was all I had."

It was hard to explain to him, in his big office at the centre of things, how helpless you are in those isolated and distant places. You accept what you get, and are thankful. There are lots of things wrong, but you don't send back letters to have the address corrected.

"It's proof that you were in league with Boulton," he went on accusingly, "how do you propose to get around that?".

"I know. I know." I said helplessly, "but I didn't get it from Boulton. I got it from Gow."

253

"Is that any better?" he asked.

I didn't answer. There was no answer.

He sat there thinking for a moment, then picked up the letter and read it through.

"Truth is stranger than fiction," he said finally, "the only thing you can do is tell the truth. Some of those feeble minds up there might even believe you. If not, you'll have them so confused they don't know what to believe."

"I've tried to be honest," I said, speaking relatively.

"That's obvious to me," he answered, "I hope they see it that way. There's always a chance they won't notice the address. Maybe the Speaker will just read out the opinion."

He dropped the letter into my hand, as if it would burn his fingers.

"Tell me about that poll book" he asked suddenly, "was it really stolen or did it just conveniently disappear?".

"I don't know," I answered, "I never saw it. At first I was glad of the excuse to keep Cockburn out. But later, when things got hot, I really tried to find it. I went down to see the D.R.O. again; I went over the hotel inch by inch with the owner, in the shed, the stable, everywhere. It absolutely disappeared."

"I just wondered," he mused, "I don't want any more surprises today."

He said nothing for a moment; then sprang up suddenly, as if he had been rewinding. He called his secretary.

"That's all," he said to me abruptly. I turned to go. It bothered me that he spent so little time in serious thought. Yet he had spotted that flaw in my letter immediately. There was one thing I wanted to know. Nobody had ever told me.

"What can they do to me if they think I'm guilty?"

He laughed in a nasty way.

"Anything," he said, "any damn thing. They can fine you, gaol you or hang you. They have no limits. Our job is to see that they discharge you."

Over in his apartment, as I later learned, Speaker James Cockburn had a late lunch with congenial friends. They talked, philosophized and discussed the affairs of the day; the terrible situation in Ireland and the continuing riots in Belfast; the late winter storms and whether a new ice age was approaching. At 3:00 o'clock an attendant appeared and whispered in his ear. He nodded, but made no move to end the discussion. He was a sociable man, enjoying his friends and well aware of his position. The world could wait until he was ready. After another 15 minutes, when there was a lull in the conversation, he got up and bade his guests adieu. He put on his gown and three-cornered hat and went out to open the day's sitting of the House of Commons, twenty minutes late.

I waited by the main door of the Chamber, nervous today, the numb calm of the night before gone. Lyon certainly had no bedside manner, he did nothing to reassure me. Still, I had heard that the best lawyers, like doctors, tell you the straight truth. I couldn't think of anything but that letter, and how stupid I had been about it. I didn't know what they would think in the House. It was possible nobody would see the original, or notice who it was addressed to. As the time for opening the House passed, I began to worry. In a vague way, I feared the delay was dangerous for me.

When the bell started to ring, I actually felt relieved. I was anxious to get it over with. The Speaker's parade came down the corridor towards me and I saw it for the first time. Col. Macdonnell walked ahead, tall and erect, with the mace over his shoulder. Then came Speaker Cockburn walking easily as befitted the man in charge. He gave a faint nod of recognition as he passed and it reassured me. The Clerk and his assistants followed the Speaker through the big doors, which closed slowly on their heavy hinges. Lyon arrived right behind the parade and I marvelled that he knew exactly when to come. But he said nothing and paced around impatiently as time went by; an hour, an hour and a half. The afternoon was passing and nobody told us anything. I could only suspect the worst. At last, the big door opened a couple of feet and Col. Macdonnell waved us in. We took chairs side by side before the bar, and waited. Speaker Cockburn rose with a sheet of paper in his hand, and it turned out to be a question.

255

"Can you produce Mr. Read's opinion which you referred to yesterday," he read, "and if so produce it."

"I can," I replied, "and I produce it herewith."

I handed the letter to Bourinot who carried it towards the Speaker's Chair. But as he passed Mr. Mackenzie, the Leader of the Opposition held out his hand for it. Lyon jumped right up.

"I think the opinion ought to be submitted to you, Mr. Speaker," he declared, "before it is shown to any member of the Opposition." That was Lyon; right to the point without any delay. Mr. Mackenzie's head jerked sideways to look at Lyon. He complained to the Speaker.

"The language of counsel at the bar is extraordinary," he said angrily, "I consider it most disrespectful to the House." I thought so too, and it was also a bit obvious. However, I had to admire Lyon for his guts.

Mr. Bourinot was new in his job. He didn't want to insult the Leader of the Opposition but he apparently felt that Lyon was right. He paused while the point of order was made, and then proceeded up the aisle to the Chair. When Mr. Mackenzie sat down a Member behind him called out:

"Don't take it seriously. The counsel is not at present responsible for his actions."

It was an insult to Lyon: a suggestion that he was drunk. And Lyon, whose face was normally red anyway, turned the colour of a beet. I thought for a moment he would do or say something rash, but the Speaker began reading aloud Read's letter. When he came to the part advising the Returning Officer to make a special return, I saw some heads nodding in agreement. The letter made it clear that I had done the right thing.

When he finished reading, the Speaker sent the letter back to the Leader of the Opposition. Mr. Mackenzie read it through carefully and then handed it to Blake. They had a discussion. I saw a nodding of heads and Mackenzie wrote a question. I held my breath. "How did you become possessed of the opinion just read?" The worst had happened. They had seen whose name was on it. Well, Lyon had told me honesty was the best policy.

"It was brought by Mr. Gow to me as the opinion of Mr. Read, which he got at the time he was down for Mr. Harrison's opinion," I explained, "Mr. Harrison being absent he got Mr. Read's opinion."

As the clerk read my answer I glanced quickly around to see how it was taken. Lyon was right, the Members were confused. Who was Harrison? Who was Gow? You had to follow the case closely to keep the characters straight, and many of them didn't. But Mackenzie wasn't confused.

"Was this letter, addressed to Mr. Boulton, one of the candidates, the only legal opinion before you?" he asked.

"It was," I replied.

"Did you obtain any explanation as to how Mr. Read's letter came to be addressed to Mr. Boulton?"

"Mr. Gow explained to me that Mr. Boulton had introduced him to Mr. Read."

There was something in the way he wrote the next question that alarmed me. Grim satisfaction, I guess you could call it. I could see it in his face, and Blake sat there smirking. When the question was read, I knew why.

"Was it you or Mr. Boulton who paid Mr. Read's fee for his legal opinion?"

It was impossible to answer.

If Boulton had paid, it was sure proof of collusion. If I had paid, it would have to show in my accounts, and I knew it didn't. If Read hadn't charged, he must be involved and his opinion useless.

The House was silent as the question was handed to me. I didn't need to look around to know what was happening. They were waiting to see if the fish would take the hook. My mind worked feverishly and the words were there for several seconds as I searched for flaws. I could see none.

"I have not paid for the legal advice I had during the election yet," I finally dictated.

I could see Mackenzie's big stonemason's fist come down

heavily on his desk. I had slipped through his net. He picked up his pen and started to write furiously. I knew there was trouble coming and braced for the next question. But before he finished writing, I was rescued.

"It being six o'clock, I do now leave the Chair," announced Speaker Cockburn and he disappeared from the Chamber. The sitting was suspended.

The Leader of the Opposition dropped his pen and sat back disgustedly.

"Our Speaker is prompt when he wants to be," he said in a voice that could be heard all over the Chamber.

I can't even remember eating that night. I know Lyon took me somewhere for dinner and we talked a bit. But I was far away. How would I answer the questions that were sure to come? Why hadn't I paid my bills, seven months after the election was over? Had Read submitted an account, and if so, produce it? If not, why not? It was certain they could push me into a corner. I couldn't see a way out

The House sat again at 8:00, and I braced for the assault. To my utter amazement, they dropped the subject and went on to something else. I could never figure out why.

"Did you obtain any legal advice as to the polling in Parry Sound?"

I was weak on this point. There had been irregularities, but nothing really fatal. Lots of worse things had happened, but I had thrown it in to strengthen my case. I decided to admit my weakness.

"I obtained no legal advice," I answered, "I only mentioned it as an irregularity that had occurred."

That seemed to satisfy them; it narrowed the issue to one point. I breathed with relief, for they were now charging around in the dark. I had avoided the pitfalls this far.

They asked me then if I had discussed the whole affair with Mr. Boulton after the election. I told them I had not and there was no argument.

It was the lawyers that had me in trouble all the same. The party was full of them; the parliament was full of them. It was

258

hard for an ordinary working man like myself. They spent their time arguing how the laws should be written, and now they couldn't agree on what they, or their predecessors, had meant. That's the mess I was in now, trying to interpret the laws they had passed. At election time I was prepared to declare Cockburn elected; not happy, but prepared. He had the most votes no matter how you looked at it. Forget the Morrison poll and the Parry Sound poll, he still had won.

Then I fell in with the lawyers, willingly I must admit, eagerly grasping at the retribution they offered against A.P. Cockburn. It was my choice, it was my game, and I was in it up to my neck. But underneath was the question a layman found hard to answer; how can you say Cockburn didn't win when he got the most votes? It was a question I didn't like to be asked.

And that was the question they asked me next. "Was there a majority for Mr. Cockburn, exclusive of Morrison and Parry Sound," Speaker Cockburn read, "and did your evidence indicate he had a majority at each of these polls?"
I knew all along it would come, and I knew it would be difficult. But I was stuck with the legal game. So I answered like a lawyer.
"It appeared that Mr. Cockburn had a majority at Morrison and Parry Sound, and exclusive of these he may have had a majority; but not having summed up the polls I am unable to state the numbers."
I assumed that the lawyers there, including Blake and Dorion, knew what I meant. Summing up was the formal and final act of the Returning Officer. Section 68 said I could not sum up until all the returns were properly received. Since I didn't receive all the returns, I could not sum up.

But all at once the Grit lawyers, among the country's greatest, turned into politicians. They wouldn't understand the difference between summing up and adding up. They acted surprised. Didn't even add up the figures? What a lie! The next question was almost an accusation; an expression of disbelief. "Did you not sum up the votes taken at the polls, exclusive of Parry Sound and Morrison?"

It was an impossible question; how could I sum up part of a return? They were changing from law to politics, but they wouldn't make me change. I had taken my stand.

"The Morrison poll book being lost, and being advised to make a special return of the fact to the House," I insisted, "I thought it unnecessary."

It was wrong to say unnecessary, I should simply have repeated that I could not sum up. But they were beginning to confuse me. Lyon had been right about the lawyers in politics, they couldn't be both at the same time so they switched back and forth. And that's what Mr. Edward Blake, brilliant lawyer, proceeded to do. He took off his lawyer's hat and put on his political one.

"That's not an answer, Mr. Speaker," he complained, "the question has not been fully answered."

How could any honest lawyer say that?

Speaker Cockburn saw what they were doing to me and he dealt with it in his own way. He rose from the Chair and looked directly at me. Contrary to his own rules, he addressed me aloud.

"Did you or did you not sum up the votes?" he asked.

He was the judge, asking if I were guilty or not guilty. But his words allowed me to reply on my own terms. The House fell silent, as if they too were waiting for my plea. If I summed up, apparently, I should have declared Cockburn elected. If not, I was in the clear. It was illogical, it was crazy; and I was deciding my own fate.

"I did not do so," I replied firmly and clearly in my own voice. They were the only words I spoke aloud in that House. And they were the final words.

The Speaker sat down, as if the matter had been settled. To my great surprise, nobody else moved or spoke. "You may withdraw, Mr. Bell," came the voice from the Chair. The final act in my trial had been the plea of not guilty. The questioning was over.

260

CHAPTER 22
HERO AGAIN

We raced for the gallery as soon as the main door closed, begrudging every second that passed. The time for a verdict had come, and the House was down there considering my fate. For better or worse, I had to hear it.

I reached the gallery door, puffing from the exertion of the stairs, with Lyon right behind. The guard recognized us and opened the door immediately. We found front seats overlooking the centre of the Chamber, and I peered down to see what was happening. The House was quiet; they were all listening intently. I could see that A.A. Dorion was speaking. He seemed to be a senior Member of the Opposition, and perhaps was speaking on its behalf. There was an echo in the Chamber, and with Dorion's accent and quite a bit of coughing it was hard to hear. I held my breath to cut down interference, and could hear better, though I felt like an idiot doing it.

"A Returning Officer has no right to form an opinion," I heard Dorion saying, "he must return the candidate having the most votes."

That seemed critical of me, though nobody heckled him from the other side.

"On the other hand," he added, seeming to balance things off, "the Returning Officer acted upon legal advice."

There was some nodding of heads in agreement and apparently the House felt his remarks were reasonable. Dorion then started on the subject of what they should do with me. I took a deep breath and sat very still so that I could hear. I felt my heart pounding in suspense.

"I do not think the Returning Officer should be visited with any punishment, or even reprimanded," he began. I looked at Lyon elated, and he raised an eyebrow and cocked his head to show he had heard. It was the best news of the day for me. After all that had happened, they found me blameless; the very people who had summoned me here. But again Dorion added a rider, as if to balance things off.

"However, he acted illegally in making a special return, and the House should warn Returning Officers in future cases against obtaining legal advice through one of the candidates."

He paused to take a sip of water and look at his notes. I wondered then why so many Upper Canadians were critical of our French population. Here was one who seemed to be doing his duty in a fair and considerate way. As he began again, his words strengthened that feeling.

"I will admit that the position of a Returning Officer in the back country is frequently a difficult one," he acknowledged, "and I can not say that this Returning Officer did not act to the best of his knowledge."

Either from his legal way of speaking, or to avoid being too obvious, he had backed into it; but there it was, the admission that I had done my best. When I looked at Lyon again, he had his thumb and forefinger together in a signal of satisfaction. Things were going well.

These constant references to "the back country" and "the best of his knowledge" upset me a bit. Dorion wasn't the only one; even some of the government supporters had called me a "backwoods returning officer". It made me out as something of a country bumpkin, of whom too much could not be expected. I suppose those who backed me considered it part of my defence, like a plea of insanity. And if that was the price I had to pay for getting off, I was prepared to pay it. But it made me wince all the same.

Dorion wound up his remarks by moving a complicated resolution which seemed to cover the points he had made, and when Speaker Cockburn read it from the Chair, it didn't sound too bad.

"That R.J. Bell, Returning Officer, acted illegally in making a special return instead of returning as elected A.P. Cockburn; but that as the said R.J. Bell has acted under legal advice he be discharged; although this House cannot approve the mode of obtaining the said advice through one of the candidates."

Lyon was nodding his head slowly, a bit uncertain, but he

seemed satisfied. It was beyond me.

I watched anxiously to see who would speak next. If he was speaking for the Opposition, Dorion's views and his motion seemed reasonable. But it had been Blake, among the front benchers, who had carried the case and he seemed much more hostile. That was one aspect of parliament I didn't quite understand. All the Members seemed to express their own personal views when they felt like it. Yet I knew there were times when they were speaking for their party. I suppose the other Members knew when someone was speaking officially, but I certainly didn't. Perhaps somebody else was going after me. Had they just delegated Dorion to lend soft words to a hard motion? Before I could think that out, Sir John Macdonald himself took the floor and the House lapsed once again into silence. I could hear him more distinctly as he was directly across from us and there was less echo to contend with. "I quite appreciate the view taken by my honourable friend," he acknowledged generously, seeming to approve what Dorion had said, "but I would ask to allow the matter to stand over until tomorrow."

I wished they would get it over with. That motion didn't sound too bad and I wondered why Sir John was stalling. "Old tomorrow" they called him, and now I could see why. The resolution Dorion proposed would let me out with my hide, and Sir John had not been mentioned at all. But he held back. "I would not say at once that I accept the motion in its entirety," he explained.

I resigned myself to his tactics, and sat back to hear him say some thing nice about me. That's when I came to reality with a jolt. Sir John proceeded to shock me to the core by agreeing with the most damaging part of the charge against me. I could hardly believe my ears.

"It should be recorded in the Journals," he agreed, "that the House does not approve of legal advice being taken by Returning Officers through the intervention of candidates." I looked over at Lyon in agony, and he was sitting there looking grim. But he held up a cautioning finger and nodded towards

Sir John, who was still speaking. "I want to read the evidence," he was explaining, "I understood that Mr. Gow saw Mr. Boulton, one of the candidates, and obtained the legal opinion through him; *but not at the request of the Returning Officer,* who sent for an opinion direct from Mr. Harrison" He agreed with the principle, but it didn't apply to me!

There are great moments in every life when a person "sees the light." Often it's a religious experience, but it was there in the gallery of the House of Commons that the light struck me. Canada's greatest leader, in my time of trouble, was using his quick mind and long experience to protect me. Through the welter of words, he had seen the way out. He was not being hasty, but was giving notice of his views, letting them think about it, reading the evidence. I recalled mentioning to Lyon that it was Gow who got the opinion, not me, but he had brushed it off. I hadn't really thought about that angle myself when I heard the motion read. But Sir John A. Macdonald did, and he seized on it. Tears came to my eyes when I recalled doubting him just a few moments past.

Down below us the case was being put over until the next day. Lyon got up to leave the gallery and I followed him out into the corridor.

"You looked worried," he twitted me when we were out of hearing.

"I was."

"Well don't sell the old man short," he advised me, "the opposition is stuck with its motion, and now Sir John will pull the barb out of it."

I didn't need convincing.

***

The veering and shifting around that place nearly drove me to distraction. Just when things seemed aimed in one direction they took off in another. I wasn't surprised, in a way, to find Lyon on a new course when I arrived at his office late next morning.

"Your friend, Mr. A.P. Cockburn is on the warpath," he opened up as soon as he saw me, "he's not going to let them do it."

"Do what?"

"Let you off. He's very unhappy at seeing you slip through their fingers unpunished. He's been stirring things up ever since the House rose last night."

"What's he been doing?"

"He confronted Dorion right in the lobby last night. Objected to the stupid admission that maybe you did your best. He complained to everybody around that the procedures were a farce and the examinations bungled. He claimed that Mackenzie and Blake had been outmanoeuvred and wondered what kind of a party he'd got into. It's been some time since the sparks flew like that around here."

"How can a new Member like Cockburn get away with it?"

"I don't think he will," Lyon said, "they say he went to both Mackenzie and Blake this morning. He wants your evidence contradicted. He demands that the plot against him be exposed and that you be punished. 'No whitewash' was his slogan. Mr Mackenzie was not amused."

"What next!" I exclaimed in anguish, "I thought I was through. Maybe Sir John should have accepted Dorion's motion after all."

"The waters run deep around here," Lyon explained, "there's more in this than meets the eye. Cockburn and you are both pawns in a sense, or at least they're willing to make you pawns. Right now, I think it's Cockburn's turn. The Grits wanted to end this yesterday and get on with something else. They're making a deal right now, and I don't think Cockburn can prevent it."

"What kind of a deal?"

"They've agreed to amend Dorion's motion to suit Sir John; but all the time clucking their sympathy to Cockburn."

"Serves him right!" I exclaimed gleefully; and then I began to wonder if my own people had done it to me a few weeks ago, "is that how they do things around here?"

"Often as not," Lyon agreed, "right now there's something else in the wind; it's very big. Sir John has his suspicions and that's one reason he didn't grab at Dorion's offer too fast. It was too easy."

"And I thought it was on my account."

"Oh it was, mainly. He wants to get you off. But he always looks a gift horse in the mouth and generally finds something rotten."

"As far as I'm concerned," I declared firmly, "I just want to get it over with and go home."

When I went to the House for the opening that day, Col. Macdonnell told me I could sit in the gallery until he called me. "But come right down if I send for you," he warned, and I readily agreed.

It was the third day, Friday March 28th.

When my case was called, A.A. Dorion was still in charge. Mr. Mackenzie seemed to have taken my fate right out of the hands of the Ontario Members. And Lyon was right as usual. When Dorion's motion was called, he made a statement.

"It has been suggested," he told the Members, without saying by whom, "that my motion be divided into two, and put to the House separately."

Nobody asked any questions or made any objection. So Dorion first proposed a resolution that I had acted illegally in making a special return, but as I had acted under legal advice, I be discharged. The Speaker promptly presented the motion and it was agreed to without any discussion.

Dorion then moved "that the practise of obtaining legal information by the returning officers through the intervention of a candidate is improper and cannot be countenanced in the future."

I saw what had happened. When the motion was divided, the second part became a generality. It didn't refer to me at all; it simply left the impression that everybody was doing it and the House had to stop it. Sir John had won his point. I was not guilty of conniving with Boulton.

"Carried," several Members called out, and I thought it was over.

But up in the far ranks of the House, under the gallery on the Speaker's left, a voice called out.

"Mr. Speaker." It was the voice of Alexander P. Cockburn, requesting leave to speak.

"The honourable Member for Muskoka," Speaker Cockburn responded, giving him the floor.

I braced myself for the worst. A.P. Cockburn would tell the House his own version of the things that happened so far away, so long ago. He would bring to them the story of a humming sawmill on the blue waters of Georgian Bay where William Beatty had all the votes tied up but I refused to grant a poll; the stumpy pathetic gaps in the forest of McLean township from which no one went to vote; the little log shanty of Anthony Suffern among the tall pines on the Parry Sound Road where the Tories brought in voters his agent didn't recognize; the unpainted frame house at the eastern narrows of Lake Vernon where George Hunt's promised majority somehow faded away. I could see it all in my mind. Then he would tell them about the plot, directed from Tory towers in Toronto, to steal the poll books and deprive him of his victory. He wouldn't tell them, but he would remember, the angry words between us at Bracebridge wharf; the rough stubbled face of George Gow hatching up plots to defeat him. The whole panorama of a Muskoka snatched from his grasp by scoundrels, of whom I was the worst, would float past him.

"Mr. Speaker," he began, "I had not intended to offer any remarks on this occasion. But in justice to my constituents I cannot remain silent."

Yes, it would all come out. I could hear it in his voice, the terrible injustice done him and the pathetic failure of his colleagues to put things right.

"I cannot help saying that the manner of eliciting information from the Returning Officer was a mere FARCE."

There was shocked silence, then shouts of "order." It was a

slap in the face to the Speaker, who had himself laid down the procedure.

"The honourable gentleman is not in order," Speaker Cockburn advised him from the Chair, quite mildly under the circumstances. "I withdraw the expression," A.P. said grimly, and went right ahead to use it again, "I intended to say the system was a farce."

Again the protests echoed through the Chamber. This was worse; he was casting reflections on the parliamentary system itself. Speaker Cockburn admonished him again.

"What I mean," A.P. Cockburn tried to explain, "is that the facts were not elicited because the officer was not sworn." What's wrong with the man! You could hear it all over the Chamber. He was now accusing me of lying, and blaming the Speaker for it. He had accepted the procedure, he should have complained before. In the buzz of protest he finally admitted his error and said simply:

"I think I should tell what I know of the circumstances."

That's what it came down to; A.P. Cockburn against R.J. Bell. I had said my piece, now it was his turn. There were only the two of us there; the others drifted into the background as spectators. I knew what he was reaching for; I saw the same images but they looked different from my side. And it seemed grossly unfair. I hadn't been able to tell a story. I could only answer the questions put to me by a critical opposition. Speaker Cockburn saw it that way too.

"There is a rule requiring a Member's absence when his seat is under discussion," he pointed out, "I do not believe the Member for Muskoka should continue."

That was when the pack instinct took hold of the Grits. A.P. Cockburn's colleagues were embarrassed by his blunders, and his leaders wanted a quick end to the whole affair. But a vital and more urgent concern took over; the struggle for self-preservation. A Member embarrassed by the other side is a party embarrassed. A Member silenced is a party silenced. The line between casual concern and party interest had been crossed. They wouldn't let their man go down without a fight.

"His seat is in no way affected, Mr. Speaker," argued Luther Holton, a front-bench Liberal, "he has already been seated. He has every right to speak."

"I agree entirely," added Edward Blake, "the rule has no application in this case. The seat is no longer in question."

Sir John Macdonald got into the argument right away.

"Whatever the rule may be," he declared, "no good end can be obtained by continuing the discussion. It would be most unseemly if the Member for Muskoka disputes statements made at the bar."

It was easy to see what the Premier was concerned about. If A.P. Cockburn undertook to differ sharply with my statements, the arrangement made with the opposition could fall apart. The Grit leaders would have to back up Cockburn if he made an issue of it. Worse, Cockburn in his angry mood could easily make some wild charges about Sir John's involvement. He might repeat some of the nasty rumours already hinted at in the House. They could be denied, of course, but the Premier had no intention of being diverted into a quarrel with small game like A.P. Cockburn. He had much bigger targets.

Cockburn got to his feet anyway, and seemed ready to challenge the House. Sir John had a big club, and he used it then.

"If the Member for Muskoka persists," he declared, "The whole matter may have to go before an Election Committee."

Cockburn did not want that. The Election Committee was a strong one; no shaky government supporters were found there. If the Committee dug into some of Cockburn's election tricks, and reported them back to the House, he could easily lose his seat again. Hardly a man there could survive an enquiry into his election. As A.P. Cockburn wavered, the Leader of the Opposition came to his rescue.

"The Member for Muskoka has a perfect right to address the House on a subject in which he is deeply interested," Mackenzie declared firmly. Actually, he was perfectly happy to see Cockburn take on Sir John Macdonald; it was like

269

setting a dog on him. If Cockburn lost, it was no great loss. But if he scored, the Premier could suffer. Sir John saw that clearly.

"If the Member for Muskoka addresses the House now," he warned, "he will greatly err, and will probably do something he will regret for the rest of his life."

Alexander P. Cockburn was a stubborn man. He had set out to balance things up, to denounce me and to let House know how badly he had been treated. If his leader felt he should speak, no Tory would deter him. So he took the floor and began his speech. He wasted little time in getting to the attack. "The Returning Officer is a partisan of the deepest dye," he declared angrily, "I can show that parts of the riding were excluded from voting because they were favourable to me."

"Hear, hear," said voices around him.

"Careful," warned the Members across the aisle.

He plunged on.

"The Returning Officer would have excluded me, if he could, from this House," he charged, "and so deprived the people of their right."

He was annoyed at A.A. Dorion over that soft speech, and now he let it be known.

"He spoke with commiseration for the Returning Officer," Cockburn declared almost contemptuously, as if Dorion had been taken in, "but in fact the whole thing was premeditated." He was working himself into a fury. He raised his arm above his head and banged his fist down angrily on his desk.

"It was a gross outrage," he shouted "the law was trampled upon in the most outrageous way."

The Members opposite began to mimic him and his colleagues sat in silence. Sir John was smiling, for Cockburn was making a fool of himself, just as he had predicted. And having let his anger get the best of him, Cockburn suddenly realized the spectacle he was making of himself, and the danger he was running. He hadn't missed Sir John's warning about a committee and he had no desire to reopen the affair at the risk of his seat. Up to this point he was safe; he had not

270

contradicted any of my statements, nor made any specific charges. There was nothing yet to send to a committee; the Premier needn't think he was that stupid.

"The leader of the government pronounced judgment before I spoke," he scoffed, pointing at the Premier, "the wicked flee when no man pursueth."

Then he abruptly sat down.

There was laughter in the Chamber, for it was not clear who was wicked and who was pursuing.

"I think the honourable gentleman has justified my statement," Sir John remarked, without getting up.

I felt no sympathy whatever for Cockburn as he covered himself with confusion. I gloated over his failure, rejoiced inwardly to see him forced down by warnings and ridicule. When his temper flared and disgraced him, I was glad to see the fire go out. I only saw him as an enemy, clawing at me, trying to destroy me.

Just once, for a fleeting moment, did I have any feeling for him at all. When Lyon told me that Cockburn's leaders were dropping him, I wondered if something similar had happened to me earlier. Were we both pawns in a bigger game? But the idea vanished quickly; I didn't want to think about it.

As Cockburn gave up then, his party colleagues came to the rescue. They could see he had been damaged and that Sir John's threat had worked, for Cockburn had cut his speech to nothing. They took up the fight against me where he left off. First, Mr. Joly, a prominent opposition Member jumped in. "I don't wonder at the feelings displayed by the Member for Muskoka," he granted sympathetically, "the Returning Officer obtained his opinion under false pretenses. He deserves the most severe censure."

That brought Hillyard Cameron to his feet.

"That's a terrible statement," he charged. The Members behind him agreed loudly. "It is utterly unfair and unjust, after the House has discharged the Returning Officer without one word of censure."

"Shame," they cried at Joly.

"The Returning Officer dared not strike off the votes of the two townships," Cameron declared "The House could do it, but not the Returning Officer."

He glared around the Chamber at his fellow Members.

"I challenge any legal gentleman in the House to say that he could."

He paused, but nobody spoke. Cameron was, after all, the senior legal gentleman in the House; Treasurer and Head of the Law Society of Upper Canada. He was not to be lightly contradicted. So he went on.

"An unlettered man, living in the backwoods, but showing so much intelligence as this Returning Officer, had taken a legal opinion," he began, and I shuddered, feeling like a trained monkey, "how can this House have a thought of censuring him?"

Edward Blake got into it then. He didn't take up the quarrel with Cameron, but made excuses for Cockburn.

"It ill becomes Members opposite to object to the Member for Muskoka speaking," he complained, "the House has twice declared that the Returning Officer should have taken another course."

The direction of the debate worried me. The Members were flailing about and anything could happen when tempers were high. It got worse when that aristocratic stinker, Edward Blake, undertook to humiliate me publicly.

"He couldn't even pay his own expenses from Muskoka to Ottawa," he claimed contemptuously "there's no social standing in such officials."

He went on to charge that I was guided and led by George Gow during the whole election. He made me out a real dupe. The dying embers of Cockburn's bitterness were being fanned into a destructive flame. Sir John must have felt it, for he got up to defend me when Blake finished.

"His appointment was no discredit to the government," Sir John affirmed quietly, "I would ask gentlemen on both sides of the House whether the officer did not show himself, as far as intellect and capacity are concerned, well fitted for the performance of his duties."

272

He paused, but nobody took up the challenge.

"He proved amply at the bar his good faith and good conduct. He has vindicated his conduct strongly. There was no dereliction of duty."

When he said that, I didn't care what any of them thought. His opinion was enough for me. Then the Premier turned on my tormentor, A.P. Cockburn.

"He spoke of the injustice to the constituency by his absence," Sir John said sarcastically, raising his hand in mock horror, "but it remains to be seen whether the constituency is more wronged by his presence."

It was a hard clean blow. Then he came back to me.

"The Returning Officer is open to no censure," he repeated, "he could have done nothing more than he did."

As I listened tensely a messenger suddenly arrived from Col. Macdonnell asking me to return to the main door. I left with reluctance, for the Premier's words pleased me; and I was eager to know what would happen. But I had no choice, so I followed the messenger down to my seat in the corridor. I was cut off once again from events in the Chamber. I waited, and waited. When Col. Macdonnell finally came out from the Chamber, I jumped up but he shook his head.

"I just came out to make sure you were here," he explained.

"What's happening?" I asked.

"They're still talking. It's not getting any better."

Obviously things had taken a turn for the worse. I had seen how suddenly the mood could change, and Sir John Macdonald for all his strength and oratory had no firm support in the House. I had learned that to my sorrow.

When the summons finally came, Col. Macdonnell led me to the bar and stood beside me. He hadn't done that before and it worried me. He seemed ready to take me in charge. Speaker Cockburn rose and I felt the hush of doom; judgment was upon me.

"Mr. Bell," he said, his voice coming as from a far distance, "the House has passed two motions of concern to you. The Clerk will read them."

Mr. Patrick stood and read the first motion from the Clerk's

273

Table. I had heard it passed while in the gallery, so it was no surprise to me. It was the second one that had me worried. But as he read, it was the one Dorion had proposed. When the Clerk had finished he looked uncertainly at the Speaker. My heart was in my mouth; there was something more! James Cockburn rose and spoke to me aloud.

"You may retire, Mr. Bell," he directed with finality, "your presence is no longer required."

It was over. I had won. Cockburn's last ditch stand had accomplished nothing.

As I left the Chamber, my thoughts turned suddenly to home and family. How good it would be to sit peacefully in my own house again with my wife and children. I could walk the streets of Bracebridge now, with my head high. I was vindicated. I had been to Ottawa, the seat of government, I had rubbed shoulders with the great, and matched wits with the best the Grits could put up. What stories I would have to tell!

A Member I didn't know followed me out of the Chamber and invited me to come to his office when the House rose. I hesitated. "It's all right," he assured me, "a few of the government supporters would like to meet you."

I really wanted to go. It was a great honour to be accepted into the inner confines of the Hill. I went, and it was a big success. The Members gathered round me, offered me a drink, and pumped my arm.

"You did well, Mr. Bell," one of them said, "you stood up to the test."

It made me proud. Not one word had clouded the record of my Premier or the party. After a while, Sir John himself dropped in, shook my hand and left.

"A toast to the Returning Officer," someone called out, and they all drank to it.

I left Parliament Hill like a hero.

CHAPTER 23
DISASTER

I could hardly wait to get home. Visions of that snug little village in the forest, with its rushing falls and down-to-earth people flashed constantly across my mind. I could feel the warm embraces, the cheers and laughter as they welcomed back their own celebrity; back from his struggle with giants who had failed to subdue him.

The miles dragged by as I sat next day in the swaying, clacking coach on the train to Toronto. I would stop and see Decimus, lord it over him gently, let him introduce me to his friends at the office. News travelled fast then, what with the telegraph and a vigilant press, and I had no doubt that every word spoken in Parliament was reported. When I got into Toronto I went immediately to Gundy and Langley on Victoria Street, where Deciumus worked.

As soon as he saw me, Decimus left his drafting board and came over to see me. But there was no joy in his expression; his doleful, spiteful face seemed angry, somehow, and he was nervous.

"Here, come into this office," he directed roughly, steering me into a vacant cubicle, "what do you want?"

"To say hello to my brother."

"I'd just as soon you didn't come here," he said.

"Why not? Don't you want them to see your famous brother?"

"Infamous is more like it."

"What do you mean?"

"It's been in all the papers," he whispered, "you being dragged before Parliament to make an example of, and then found guilty of an unlawful act."

"Illegal," I corrected him, "that's entirely different. It meant than my return wasn't authorized by the Election Act. Unlawful means against the law. I did nothing wrong; I was discharged."

"Illegal, unlawful, you're splitting hairs. I've been mortified.

The honest name of Bell has been disgraced."

His look was hard, cold, unforgiving. All that old, sickening hostility was in his face and my revulsion of him flooded back. I couldn't stand him another minute, and decided to leave.

"You're sick, Decimus," I spat out, "I never want to see you again."

"That suits me," he declared angrily.

I went out and shut the door on my brother once and for all.

It shook me, though. Somehow I had believed that Decimus would give me that one word of praise I had spent my life working for. But he wouldn't. And his explanation of the Ottawa result left me desolate. I caught the next train north.

I took the stage at Orillia, and when it stopped at Severn Bridge I felt I had arrived home. I hurried in to the hotel and Charlie Mackenzie was there. He didn't disappoint me, and gave me the grand welcome I had been expecting.

"Well, here comes our hero," he exclaimed, patting me on the back, "matched wits with the biggest Grits in the country and got the best of them."

"It came out rather well," I admitted modestly, "but it was an awful struggle."

"We were just reading about it in the paper. They never caught you at all. Just made Cockburn look a fool."

"I had to watch every word," I declared, "the Grits just wanted me to make one slip, and boom - I was for it; and Sir John with me."

"They had you over a barrel, all right," admitted Charlie, "could have thrown you in jail quicker than wink."

"They should have," said a sour voice at the bar.

I looked to see who it was, and recognized the man who had quarrelled with Duke at election time.

"Don't pay no attention to him," advised Charlie, "he's just a mean Grit. Wouldn't even drink here if there was another decent place around."

"I'm not sure I want to associate with thieves and crooks anyway," declared the Grit heatedly.

"Shut up, " said Charlie.

"Don't like to hear about it, do you?" he went on, "I know about Duke stealing that poll book. This guy here put him up to it."

"I did nothing of the kind," I shouted, very loud and very angry, "Take that back or I'll sue you for slander."

"Well I can't prove it, so I'll take it back," the customer said, drawing in his horns, "but I know Duke stole the book."

"How do you know that?" I demanded.

"He told me so himself."

"All right, that's enough," Charlie broke in, "knock it off."

"No, I want to hear this," I said, "I don't know anything about it."

"Duke's gone now, so it doesn't matter."

"It matters to me. I'm accused of putting him up to it."

"I took that back, mister," said the Grit, "I talked too fast. But I know Duke went up to Bracebridge and stole the book at the hotel. He was mad over the result. Threw it in the river. Told me one night when he was drunk."

"Stage is leaving," the driver shouted in the door, and I went out and got aboard. The warm glow of my arrival had turned to ice.

As Severn Bridge passed behind us, I began to build my expectations once again for Bracebridge. I should really have foreseen jealousy from Decimus, and nothing more from a partisan Grit in Severn Bridge. Bracebridge would be different; it was home, the people there respected me as a citizen and township clerk.

I was terribly wrong. My arrival in the bosom of my home town was like a splash of cold water. The place was still divided and bitter. The smiling faces and admiring handclasps I had so eagerly awaited were few and far between. To the Conservatives and my true friends I was the hero I had been when I left Parliament Hill. But to the Grits I was a bum. They passed me on the street in the most punctilious way, sometimes without speaking. Even at Lodge Cockburn's admirers talked among themselves and divided us into two groups, which was very much against the spirit of our brotherhood.

My first council meeting was a disaster. The councillors acted as if I wasn't even there, and that some machine was taking the minutes. Of course, they were mostly all Grits, but that didn't justify them acting that way. The Reeve explained afterwards that they were simply being polite, and didn't want to embarrass me by asking questions or making comments. I went home feeling like a stranger in my own township.

"What's wrong with me?" I asked Jim Mcdonald who heard everything.

"Nothing, but they've been told by Cockburn that you were found guilty of improper conduct," he explained, "the House said you acted illegally."

"But that's not true," I protested, "they agreed it was a common practice, and they had to clear things up for the future. Anyway, that shouldn't make them resent me."

"No," he agreed, "it's really the stories about what you did to A.P. Cockburn."

"What kind of stories?"

"Oh, that you told lies to get him into trouble," Jim explained, "the Grits have to blame Cockburn's failure on somebody. After all that fuss in calling you to Ottawa, they can't admit it flopped."

I had been riding so high that it took a lot to bring me down. But one by one those barbed arrows found their mark. My friends did their best to revive my spirits. They explained to people that I had got off scot free; that A.P. Cockburn had lost his temper because he couldn't prove his nasty charges against me. They cut out favourable articles from the press.

"Look at this," said John Teviotdale the Wednesday after I came back "the Toronto Mail says Cockburn used unparliamentary language and was called to order three times. He really lost his head. He must have been furious."

"He was," I agreed "he took it very hard."

"They say you did real well."

"Thanks."

There was one pleasant surprise in all the gloom - Jimmy Patterson. I passed him on the street one day, and almost hoped he wouldn't see me. I was in no mood to hear the opinions of the new generation. But he saw me and turned back.

"Hello, Mr. Bell," he called out, "I'm glad to see you back."

"It's nice to be back, Jimmy," I said, exaggerating a bit.

"I've been studying up on your case," he went on, "I found it very interesting."

"No doubt."

"Now I find the people around here very narrow-minded. They don't understand the significance of your actions."

"Is that so?" I asked, beginning to listen.

"What you did was a real sign of progress. You tried to make the laws work - to find a meaning in the jumble of words. You stepped out and took a new course when you made your Special Return. It was quite surprising, for a man your age."

"I'm not that old."

"That's what my dad says, but he really is. Anyway, you could expect the old fogies in Ottawa to follow the letter of the law. I'm not surprised they took you to task."

"Actually," I explained, "they let me off completely."

"I'm glad to hear that. Some people around here don't think so."

"Just the old fogies," I explained.

"Right," he agreed, "that's exactly right. Just what I was thinking."

He took off up the street, leaving me a bit more cheerful.

But on Friday the Orillia Times arrived. It was a Grit paper of course, but it practically called me a liar. "Mr. Bell has earned notoriety by his evidence," one of the columns read, "many were surprised that he was not acquainted with the political proclivities of his *intimate aquaintance* and dear friend, Mr. G.F. Gow."

The same day the Free Grant Gazette came out in Bracebridge. Cockburn's friend, E.F. Stephenson, hit me again. "Until now we attached no serious blame to Mr. Bell," he began, preparing his readers for the assault, "but when it comes to light that his advice came indirectly through Mr.

279

Boulton, we cannot refrain from saying that the Returning Officer is open to some censure."

How could he say that? It was all thrashed out in Parliament, and I was discharged with no censure. But it was useless to reply.

Some people believed I made a lot of money out of the whole thing. I couldn't have gone down there to protect the party without being well rewarded. They heard my trip to Ottawa had been paid, and assumed I had padded the account well. One day in May for example, Anne and I were in Mr. Twidle's jewellery store, looking at a bracelet for Margaret. He showed us a very fine piece.

"I don't know," I said, hestitating "it's quite a lot of money."

"Oh you don't have to worry about that surely," he said with a broad wink. It made me so mad I walked right out of the store.

My peaceful life was gone. The Orange Hall was no longer a haven, the council no longer a refuge. I had hoped for greater things, power, fame and social standing, but I had lost what I wanted most, respect. I had been to the heights and I wanted to enjoy the experience. A few accolades from my fellow man, admiration and respect was all I asked, but I didn't get it. It was such a short time ago that I enjoyed my quiet competence as municipal clerk, the success of a Fall Fair banquet, the gathering of friends at church and lodge. I appreciated a pat on the back when I sang well, summarized a difficult situation, had my books in order. But this new life was hateful.

It was no better for Anne. When men didn't talk to me, their wives didn't talk to her. She had once admitted to a friend in a fit of frustration how hard it was to live with me. Now it became a good tid-bit to add to the conversation at teas. Word got around that we had quarreled and were on the verge of breaking up. In my impatience I scolded her, and she took it badly.

I began to realize how hard it is for people to know what really happens in Parliament. The partisans didn't care about the truth at all; they only wanted to tell one side of it. And nobody else really knew what went on. I was sure Mr. McMurray wouldn't let me down. We had been friends since the first day I arrived, and never had a serious disagreement. An intelligent man like him would see the truth of the matter and tell it that way in the Northern Advocate. But that was the cruelest blow of all.

One of the friends who came to my defence was Judge Charles W. Lount. One day when he had a captive audience, he took advantage of the occasion to talk about me.

"We have a hero in this town," he declared "a man who isn't afraid to do his duty. But do you suppose any of the idiots who run the newspapers around here will recognize it? Not very likely; they can't see past their ink-smudged noses."

Feelings ran high right then, because Lount had started a High Court law suit against McMurray and the Advocate for libel. That feud was at its peak and I was caught in the middle. When Lount's words got around, I was finished with McMurray. He never tried to defend me. Instead, The Northern Advocate treated me as an embarrassment to Bracebridge. I felt as if I had lost my last friend.

I had to talk to somebody and Jim McDonald was always a good listener. I took to dropping in more and more at the Royal. He tried to encourage me with worldly wisdom.

"Don't let it worry you so much," he admonished me, "we've all had our troubles. Anyway, big men make good targets."

"But I've lost half my friends," I lamented.

"They aren't really friends if they let you down now," he consoled me, "find some new ones."

"But Anne is upset," I added, hardly listening to what he was saying, "she can't understand the way these people are acting. Not only that, she says it was my own foolishness that caused it all."

"I'm sorry about that," he said sincerely, for he always liked her from the first day they met on the train, "you'll just have to sit it out. Time is a healer. Something else will turn up to attract their attention and your little affair will be forgotten."

He was right, in a way. Something else did turn up to attract attention. Things were happening in Ottawa. It's an old story now, told and retold so often, in so many ways, that other events of the time were forgotten. It was just beginning then, unfolding bit by bit like a serial story on the front page of a newspaper.

They called it the Pacific Railway Scandal. Even when I was in Ottawa there were whispers of something big in the wind. Robert Lyon heard them, but couldn't pinpoint the particulars. The Wednesday after I left, April 2nd, the rumours began to take shape and form. A Liberal Member named Huntington charged in the House that Sir Hugh Allan had donated large sums of money to the Conservatives in the 1872 election. In return he was to receive the contract for construction of the Pacific Railway.

But Huntington was vague and offered no proof of his allegations. He used weasel words to protect himself.

"I am credibly informed and believe that I can establish by satisfactory evidence," was the way he introduced his complaint. The Members turned down his request for an enquiry by an overwhelming vote of 107 to 76. Until the man was serious enough to put his seat on the line, he needn't expect the House of Commons to waste its time.

There was another quarter, though, where his words were picked up immediately. The smell of scandal was delicious to the Globe, and George Brown began printing all the rumours, accusations, suspicions and conjectures he could dream up. Right until the whole Pacific Scandal came to its terrible conclusion the Globe kept the matter alive.

These reports of scandal in Sir John's government swung back to Muskoka and hit me squarely between the eyes. It was strange. In every other part of the country my three days in the limelight were forgotten in the excitement of this new event. But in Muskoka it worked the other way. The local Grits tied me in with it, whispering around that all the election fraud, bribery and corruption had been uncovered while I was in Ottawa. Instead of dying away, the accusations became worse.

282

They made me the local agent of the national scandal.

And A.P. Cockburn himself helped their cause along. After making such a fusss about getting his seat in Parliament he didn't spend much time in it. He came back to Muskoka to justify himself to his constituents, and to run me down.

"Cockburn was in to see me a couple of days ago," the Reeve told me one day early in May.

"What about?" I asked, "if it was council business, I should know."

"It was nothing in particular," he recalled, "but I remember him talking about your experience in Ottawa."

"And what is he saying?"

"Well, he sure tells a different story than you do," said the Reeve, as if he half believed it. That really upset me. I kept hearing about Cockburn's travels in the district, and wished he would stay in Ottawa where he belonged.

As if that weren't enough, the effects of Black Friday hit us in Muskoka in late May of 1873. It had started in New York the previous fall; a Friday when business failures and a stock market crash shocked the world. In Muskoka we didn't know what it all meant until the black rot of it began to seep across the border and up into the bush country. Then lumber began to pile up in the mills and unsold logs clogged the waterways. They began to lay men off in mill and forest. A.P. Cockburn decided to get something out of the disaster, if not money, and persuaded Cockburn and Company to sent out a circular blaming the government.

"We do not expect to purchase any logs this coming season," they concluded.

The other mills, not realizing the politics involved, followed suit, and panic hit the district. The local settlers were left to wonder how they would survive the coming winter. But they didn't have to guess at the cause.

"Bad management of the country's affairs," word went around, "it's John A. Macdonald and all the bribe money that's drained the coffers dry."

Suddenly the early warnings turned into a catastrophe.

Construction fell off to nothing in the States and a new American tariff halted the export of lumber from Ontario. Lumbering in Muskoka came to a stop and the great depression of the seventies began. The mills closed and the workers were laid off. Hard times struck us. A few men worked at clearing up the silent mill yards, doing a boy's work piling slabs at a few cents a cord. The others hunted rabbits or partridge for food and the women gathered greens from the roadside and fence corners. The same soup bone stayed in the pot for days. The talk was bitter. Ignorant of the real causes, the men blamed Sir John A. Macdonald, and the Tories, and the scandal. But worst of all they blamed me. One day late in May I came home to find Anne in one of her black moods.

"I hate this town," she announced as soon as I came in the door.

"So do I," I agreed.

"And sometimes I hate you," she added, running suddenly to the bedroom.

I decided right then we had to leave.

An hour later I was sitting on a rock at the foot of North Falls where the rushing waters end in a deep pool. I liked it there; it was proof to me that the wildest turmoil eventually ends in calm waters.

"Now Mr. Spirit-of-the falls," I muttered aloud, "if you're here to help, give me some thoughts."

I laughed at myself for talking to the Indian spirit there, but it was an easy thing to do. This was a place where you felt the presence of some unknown power. And it wasn't long before I thought of the very man who could help me. I wouldn't ask anyone in Bracebridge, or any of the politicians like Mr. Boulton. That part of my life was ended; those debts were cancelled off. I wanted to forget them. But there was a man I had almost forgotten, influential in Lodge and government and that was Mr. T.R. Ferguson of Barrie. I hurried back up the hill to write him a letter, convinced there really was a spirit in those falls.

In two weeks I had an answer.

"I hear there is an opening at Inland Revenue in Toronto," he wrote, "I suggest you go and apply in person. You need only mention your municipal experience and my name."

I went to Toronto right away and applied. The officer seemed favourable to me, but told me there were a lot of people looking for one position. But my references were good. I went home and waited. In the middle of June I was accepted, to start in July. I went back to the city again, and found a couple of rooms we could stay in. Then we started packing.

It was a terrible time to dispose of things, what with all the unemployment and hardship. I practically gave away my prize flock of chickens, for nobody wanted to buy them. The garden wasn't ready and we had to leave everything in the ground. I found a tenant for the house but barely got enough rent to pay taxes and interest. We had to leave our heavy furniture, for these was little enough space in Toronto. We packed bedding, clothing and small items.

"I wish we had a bigger place," Anne complained for the tenth time, at least, "two rooms aren't enough for five people. I simply don't feel like moving in."

"I know," I agreed, "but it won't be for long. We can look around for a house when we get there."

"I hate leaving my furniture for somebody else to use," she said, and I agreed again.

"There's one thing about it though," she went on, "we're also leaving behind some of your so-called friends that did you no good, male and female."

"Oh let's not start that again," I pleaded, "there's never been anyone but you."

"I'd like to think that," she answered sharply, "you talk in your sleep, you know. It's not always my name you mumble away at. It must be that other one."

"I couldn't be saying her name," I argued without thinking, "I don't even know her name."

I could have bitten off my tongue, for I knew she had sucked me in. But the words were out. Sometimes I did think of that friendly woman in Orillia when things got tough at home.

"Whose name?" she snapped right back, "the one you brawled over in Orillia?"

I was at a loss for words. If I said yes, I was admitting something; if no, there must be others. How on earth did she know?

"What do you mean?" I asked innocently.

"You thought I didn't know," she taunted me, "well I know a lot more than you think."

"So do I."

She coloured a bit.

"You don't know anything," she declared haughtily; but the discussion went no further.

I sent my resignation as Clerk to the Reeve, and he read it to council on July 3rd. I didn't go myself because there was bad feeling among them. If they wanted to thank me for my years of service, they could pass a resolution or write a letter. But my resignation was accepted without any comment whatever. I realize now that I should have gone; a coward generally gets his reward, and I got mine. Those cussed councillors didn't even let me go in peace. When the council meeting was just about over, one of them raised a question about my returning to council some money. He heard that I had collected statute labour funds and wanted to be sure the township got it back. "I think the Clerk should write to Mr. R.J. Bell, our late Township Clerk," he proposed spitefully, "and ask that the three dollars of statute labour money he collected from Joe Cartwright be turned over to the Reeve."

Then he made a formal motion to that effect. It was really a mean thing to do. The new Clerk, Mr. James Boyer, wrote it down for posterity. My former friend Mr. William Kirk seconded the motion, and it was passed. After four and a half years of careful and faithful work for council, that was all the thanks I got. The last entry about R.J. Bell on the township books questioned my honesty.

The morning of our departure, when the flurry was over, I suddenly felt remorse. I was leaving behind all my struggles for success. Eight years of hard work, successful farming, service to the community and gradual rise to prominence were shattered. I had to start again, like a bankrupt. I remembered our first night in Bracebridge after Anne and I were married, our happy walk along the falls, and our friendly reception in Uffington.

"I think I'll go for a walk," I said to Anne when everything was ready, "would you like to come along."

"No thanks," she answered briefly. So I went alone.

I crossed the road to the path along the river bank. In front of our house the water ran deep and still. As I dawdled down stream the river moved faster and the sound of the falls became louder. From across the wide river the sound of an axe rang out, cutting deep into timber, and shortly a tree came crashing to the ground. The village, my village, was growing, but the thought no longer brought joy. It was mine no more, its future belonged to others.

When I came to the bridge I crossed over and went down the steep path beside the falls. It was noisy there, the water splashed and whirled, and the spray flew into my face cooling it with a pleasant freshness. I climbed down to the very bottom and sat on my rock in the sun. No change disturbed my haven, all seemed peaceful in the village. I tried to recover my perspective, my sense of security, but it wouldn't come. Behind those walls, on those dusty streets, were former friends who shunned me. I knew I couldn't live like that. My life here was over; and all because of one stolen book.

I started back up the steep slope, convinced at least that my decision was right, and ready to go. As I neared the bridge I stopped for a rest beside the rapids there.

"I'll come back," I promised myself aloud, "I'll come back with honour and influence."

I didn't doubt that with my experience and knowledge I would advance quickly. I could see myself returning in a few years as Chief of the Excise Division. I would meet my former friends and enemies and treat them kindly. Perhaps they were doing me a favour now, getting me out of the backwoods and into the centre of things.

I stepped up onto the roadway and saw a lady crossing the bridge towards me. As she came closer I saw it was my friend from the store. I didn't see her often any more, choosing to avoid any problems or gossip. But I was glad to see her, and she hurried to meet me. She held out her hand and I took it, holding without letting go.

"I hear you are leaving," she said.

"Yes, tomorrow morning."

"I'll miss you; the village won't be the same without you."

"I'll miss you too. I have so many happy memories."

We talked for a while about the party where we met; the time we became good friends; the other times and places we remembered. My day was brightened, for this was someone who liked me without restraint, who had no strings on her affections. She cared not whether I had been to Ottawa or what I ever did. She liked me as I was and I returned it the same way.

But the time came for us to move on, and I was still holding her hand. I thought a little kiss on the cheek would be acceptable, and she complied willingly. She went on up the hill, and I turned to go back up town, a smile still on my face.

I took one step up the rise of the bridge, and found myself staring into Anne's bitter face. She turned and marched back to our house, with me tagging along, sometimes beside her, sometimes behind. She took no more notice of me than if I wasn't there. And I truly wished I wasn't.

288

Free Grant Gazette,

FRIDAY, APRIL 4, 1873.

The Muskoka Election Case.

As will be seen in another column,
Mr. R. J. Bell, Returning Officer for
Muskoka, during the late parliamentary
election, has received the mildest possible form of censure for not returning
A. P. Cockburn, Esq., instead of mak-
~~~~~~~~ return. Until now we
~~~~~~~~ clined to attach any
~~~~~~~~ r. Bell for the course
~~~~~~~~ g him to be under
~~~~~~~~ cc of his duty, and
~~~~~~~~ as acting under
~~~~~~~~ n it comes to light
~~~~~~~~ s obtained (indirect
~~~~~~~~ lton, one of the
~~~~~~~~ ot refrain from say
~~~~~~~~ fficer is open to som
~~~~~~~~ ll had sought advic
~~~~~~~~ rn, he would hav
~~~~~~~~ lame, though

CHAPTER 24
THE FINAL REWARD

The move to Toronto started off well for both of us. Anne liked the city life. She took the children out of our cramped rooms as often as she could, and walked with them on the streets and in the park. People didn't point her out or even notice her; she was just another person in the crowd. She liked that, and she hated attention, and I realized how much the situation in Bracebridge had upset her. We were two different people, for I loved to be in the limelight and she only wanted to be left alone. I hoped that our new life would make her feel better.

For me it was a new world. I had only been in Toronto to pass through. Lindsay and Muskoka had been my homes in Canada, and I was accustomed to the easy life of a small town. The sounds and sights of the city dazzled me. Elegant people strolling casually on the streets, clerks bustling along with important papers, big stores with their abundant merchandise, they all fascinated me. It thrilled me to stand on the corner of Bay and Front Streets, near where I worked, and take in the world of tall buildings, prancing horses, police whistles and beautiful women. My work was not difficult, checking and stamping papers at the big front desk of the Revenue offices on Front Street. The day was long and to some it was boring. But the relief from the devastation of jealous and hateful people was wonderful, for my customers here found it prudent to be nice to me. My old jovial nature returned, and that eased things a bit at home too.

As the weeks passed the bad memories went with them. An October event, in fact, turned those memories into something of a victory. It happened as I was out on my noon-day stroll, and I chanced upon a door with a big brass plate, "Boulton & Gordon, Barristers, etc." I was sure that was D'Arcy Boulton's firm, and on impulse I decided to accept his frequent invitation to call on him. I opened the door and went in. Everything was quiet and elegant inside. Two clerks were sitting on high stools near the window, engrossing title deeds. I could hear the scratch of their pens on parchment. At the end of the corridor I could see shelves of law books through an open door and I heard muffled voices. The secretary at the desk was breath-taking, crisp and cool in a high-collared blouse with lace at the cuffs and collar, and with her hair piled high on her head. She wore long sparkly ear-rings and she smelled of lavender. I stood gaping.

"Can I help you?" she asked as I stood there awkwardly.

"I'd like to see Mr. Boulton, please," I answered.

"Have you an appointment?"

"No," I admitted, "but I'm sure he'll see me."

"He's busy right now," she said, "he has someone important with him."

"That's all right, I'll wait," I said, "would you tell him that Richard Bell is here."

She seemed surprised at my nerve, and made no move, perhaps hoping I would go away. But I stood my ground and after a while she went to the back office. She came right out again.

"He'll see you in a minute," she said, much more agreeably. She showed me a chair and I sat down, feeling quite smug. It seemed only a moment before D'Arcy Boulton himself bounced out.

"Well, well," he exclaimed heartily, "it's the Returning Officer from Muskoka. I wondered if that's who it was."

The clerks looked up from their work, and the secretary actually smiled at me. It was good to be recognized at last.

"Come right into my office," Mr. Boulton said, "I have someone here who knows you."

I followed him down the corridor and into his office. The man waiting there looked very distinguished in a morning coat and striped trousers. He seemed familiar.

"This is the honourable Hillyard Cameron," Boulton said, "I believe you two met in Ottawa."

"We did indeed," said Cameron, coming over to greet me,

"it's a pleasure to meet you again, Mr. Bell."

"It's an honour to meet you personally," I replied and it really was.

"We were just talking about you," said Boulton, "what's happening in Muskoka these days."

"I'm in Toronto now."

"Is that so? When did you leave Bracebridge,"

"This summer after I returned from Ottawa," I explained, "it got too unpleasant for us up there."

"Over that election thing?" he asked, and I nodded.

"The local Grits had me a real scoundrel. My wife couldn't stand it, nor could I."

Boulton paced the floor a while, obviously upset.

"People like you who break new ground often suffer for it," he reflected, "sometimes they even become . . . "

"Don't say martyrs," I broke in, "one is enough for Muskoka."

They both laughed, and it flattered me to share an inside joke with such eminent people.

"You know what I mean," Boulton declared.

"I'm afraid I didn't accomplish much; just a martyr without a cause."

"Not at all! You made law, Bell, new law," he exclaimed, "you went to the highest Court in the land and got a decision. Most lawyers spend their lives trying for that. You settled the question of Special Returns forever."

"Is that so?"

"There's another thing," Cameron added, "you have raised the status of Returning Officers."

"I'm glad to hear that," I said ruefully, "I thought I had lowered it."

"No. When the House declared that you should have made a decision on the law, it gave the Returning Officer the power of judges. From now on they have real authority."

"I certainly didn't understand that," I declared.

"Well it's true. That's the word around Osgoode Hall. We have talked about it quite a lot."

My self-importance began to return. I remembered reading about some new election laws and wondered if they had anything to do with my case; so I asked.

"They most certainly did," Cameron assured me, "Parliament made a lot of changes in the election laws after you were in Ottawa. The Grits admitted you were right in excluding that poll on the Georgian Bay. It was in unsurveyed area, as you said. So we passed the Muskoka Division bill, defining your riding properly for the future. The drafting there had been sloppy, and we won't make the same mistake again. We actually had to amend the constitution to put that right. Then we changed the Election Act to clear up some of the bad situations you outlined. And we made special provisions for taking the vote in northern districts like yours."

"That's good," I declared, "we're different from the settled counties."

"We also passed a new law about controverted elections," Cameron went on, "they've been taken out of Parliament and put into the hand of the Courts. You'll remember that Sir John mentioned this during your appearance."

"I remember it well."

"We also introduced a bill to vote by ballot," Cameron explained, "though personally I'm not in favour of the ballot. It's too easy for people to avoid their responsibility, and it makes bribery hard to detect. It didn't become law this session, but it's being considered. Oh, and something else. The problem you had over disappearing poll books will never happen again. We're giving the Returning Officer the right to make his own decision if a book is lost. He'll have the last word on how to sum up the vote."

Cameron stopped for a breath after his long dissertation, and I sat there dumbfounded. I never knew all that was going on. I had seen little bits and pieces in the papers about the election bills, but nobody had ever explained it to me that way. It was an eye-opener; and I wished the people in Muskoka knew about it.

"And it was all on my account!" I exclaimed.

"Well, between you and D'Arcy here; and a few others," he agreed, "these problems have been building up for years, but last year's election brought them to a head. Sir John doesn't like these dirty elections any more than anyone else; but he plays to win by the rules that exist."

"And my Special Return caused it all," I repeated, almost to myself.

"It was a catalyst," he agreed.

I felt big when he put it that way, though I wasn't sure of the meaning.

"I really appreciated your support, Mr. Cameron," I said, "If you hadn't defended me so well in the House I'm sure things would have gone much worse."

"You deserved to be protected," he declared, "If any man was a martyr there, it was you."

"And it was a privilege to work with you, Mr. Boulton," I went on, "if you hadn't been such a fine gentleman I might never have made that Special Return. But I just couldn't see Cockburn getting away with what he did."

I felt I had intruded long enough, and my lunch hour was well over. As I left we shook hands warmly, and I realized I was one of them. I had served my country too, in my own way. I had sacrificed myself for a cause. And I had glimpsed briefly the corridors of power where the destiny of our country developed, where new directions are taken. I had taken my stand, and caused parliament to open up new directions. They had called A.P. Cockburn a martyr, but he hadn't really done much except write letters. I knew that I was the real martyr. And soon my country would recognize it. I smiled a faint smile and walked proudly from the office.

That was the beginning of better things. Shortly after my visit with Mr. Boulton, my standing at the office began to improve. My supervisor opened the door of his private office one morning and came out to the main reception.

"How are you this morning, Mr. Bell," he asked graciously, strolling along behind the big desk and looking at everything.

"Very well, sir," I answered politely.

"I'd like to see you in my office for a moment," he said, and I left my desk a bit reluctantly. I thought he approved of my work, but nobody likes to be called in. The supervisor was a funny little fellow, very self-important and always seeming to have some little scheme going.

"Don't worry, I'm quite happy with your work," he began, as I stood waiting for a lecture, "you seem to understand the job and get along well with the public."

"I've had experience with people," I told him, "I was a municipal clerk for some years."

He came over to me and lowered his voice.

"This is confidential," he began, "but my assistant is retiring at the end of the year, and there will be promotions."

"Do I have a chance?" I asked hopefully.

"You certainly do," he said, "I like your work, and that's important. But you also came highly recommended by the right people."

I thanked him, and as he had no more to say, I went back to my post.

That gave the day a real lift. A promotion was just what I needed to relieve things at home. My salary of $26.30 a month was hardly enough to keep us alive in the city. We had no garden, no cow and no chickens, and had to buy everything. I had been out looking for a house, but it seemed hopeless. There was nothing we could afford. A promotion and better salary could make it possible.

When I got home that night I announced the good news to Anne.

"I'm up for promotion already," I said proudly, "we'll soon have our own place."

"I certainly hope so," she answered grimly, "I can't stand it here much longer."

I was quite shocked, and thought it a poor way to receive the good news.

"Oh, it's not that bad," I said, trying to pacify her.

"How would you know?" she snapped, "you're not around here all day."

"Well it's better than Bracebridge," I maintained. That generally ended the discussion, but not this time.

"You think so?" she disagreed, curling her lips.

Well I hadn't changed my mind. Everything up there seemed so small and petty now; the judge fighting with the newspaper editor; the nasty little tricks in council; the small-town gossips; the dirty politics. Yes, I thought, I'm glad to be away from it. Anne isn't satisfied with anything. Never was. Almost getting back to her bad times of two years ago. Surely she knows I'm trying to get started again. The least she could do is help.

That night after supper as I read the news from Ottawa, I knew I was right. Things would still be bad for us in Bracebridge. The news on the Scandal was worse, Sir John and his government were in deep trouble. A thief the Grits had hired early in the summer had stolen documents in a law office which implicated Sir John himself. He had sent a telegram during the election requesting ten thousand dollars from Sir Hugh Allan, who wanted to build the Pacific Railway. The documents were printed in the Globe and other Grit papers. After that, public opinion turned against the grand old leader. Now the news headlined once again events in the House of Commons. The opposition had moved non-confidence, and it looked as if Sir John would be defeated. All those floating Members had deserted. Even some committed ones had gone. But I was sure he would survive when he spoke to the House. I remembered my own troubles there, how things had looked hopeless, and then he arranged everything, used his skill with people, and . . .

"Wake up and come to bed," Anne called, shaking me. I had dozed off in my chair. I got up and followed her, half awake.

"Things would be worse in Bracebridge, all right," I declared obstinately. She didn't answer.

The next few days were tense. Everyone grabbed the papers as soon as they appeared on the street, to get the latest news from Ottawa. I said little at the office and kept out of the discussions. They didn't know about my past, and I was willing to leave it that way. Then on Monday evening,

November 3rd, 1873 Sir John defended himself in the House. Even in the dull print of the newspapers, his speech sounded dramatic. He explained his actions, holding back nothing. Everything he did, he did for the Confederation. He made no apology, except for being misunderstood.

"I throw myself upon this House; I throw myself upon posterity," he ended, "and I believe, and I know, that notwithstanding the many failings of my life I shall have the voice of this country and this House rallying around me. I leave it to this House with every confidence. I am equal to either fortune. I can see past the decision of this House, either for me or against me."

But it was too late. The deserters were gone beyond recall. Life-long Conservatives could neither understand, nor explain to their constituents, the begging of money from a man who wanted government favours. They forgot all the times John A. Macdonald had helped them get elected, or saved them from defeat. But with the foresight his speech revealed, he looked beyond the day, and saw that a vote on his conduct would split friend from friend, and divide the party for years. So on Wednesday November 5th, without waiting for a vote, without dividing the House or his party, Sir John and his ministers resigned.

And after seeing the Governor General, he announced that Mr. Alexander Mackenzie would be the new Premier. The Liberals then formed a government.

Such outpourings of righteousness emerged from that new government! Mr. Mackenzie's one promise to the country was honesty and fairness. It seemed possible he might give it. I remembered him sitting there in the House, his thin lips pressed tight together in outrage as charges of favouritism and corruption were made. When the new ministry was announced, it strengthened my belief. Mr. Dorion became Minister of Justice, and he was the one Grit in that place I believed honest. When Blake was given no portfolio I thought that Mackenzie was separating himself from the pork-barrel politics of Liberal Ontario.

A new day in politics was promised.

"In the midst of venality and corruption," George Brown wrote, "Mr. Mackenzie's hands have never been defiled."

The new Premier made it clear himself.

"We shall strive," he said, "to conduct public affairs upon principles of which honest men can approve, and by practises which will bear the light of day."

Brave words! They began to call him the Stainless Statesman.

Our crowded home life showed no signs of strain until ten days before Christmas. I merely walked a young neighbour lady to her door, just being friendly. She invited me in for a cup of tea, and I went. Anne was furious.

"I won't stay here another minute," she cried, "I'm leaving."

"Over one cup of tea?"

"That's the last straw," she declared, "you don't care about us anyway. Keeping us in a hovel like this."

"Wait just a little longer," I pleaded, "my promotion is on its way. Then we can get a house."

"I'm going right now."

"Right now?" I asked, "where would you go? Don't I have something to say about it?"

"The children and I will stay with Jane and Decimus. They've agreed."

"My brother?" I cried, "my brother who hates me. How could you?"

"He treats me decently."

"And don't I?"

"No."

She was firm and cold. Her eyes looked at me without feeling, as if I were an object. It almost made me hate her.

"Go, then," I said, "but I'll get a house, and then you'll have to come back."

"If you get a house, which I doubt, and stop your philandering, which I doubt even more, we can talk about it."

We were both hovering near the edge of final words, but didn't use them. What we said was too much anyway. The next day, when I came home from work, she was gone. I gave up our

298

place and went to a rooming house. It was lonesome and bleak there, but it was a place to wait until my promotion came through. Then things would start to move again.

It was on the Monday night before Christmas, when I was out walking, that I saw a hand-written sign on a house: For Rent, Enquire Within. It was just a small frame house, but it seemed plumb and solid, and had an upstairs. An elderly lady answered my knock.

"How much is the rent on this place?" I asked.

"Seven dollars a month."

"When is it available?"

"The first of January," she answered, "and I want a month in advance now."

Down in the bottom of my wallet was a five dollar bill, tucked away for Christmas presents. With the change in my pocket, it was just enough. But it was all I had in the world. I went through the living room and kitchen, upstairs to see the bedrooms and out back to look at the shed and yard. It was just right. When my promotion came through I could manage the extra rent. So I paid the seven dollars and took a receipt. Then I left all excited and went back to my room. The house would bring us together again. I would have no little gifts for my family this Christmas; just one big one.

I was still basking in the glow of my good fortune next morning when my supervisor called me in.

"Well, how are things going?" he asked cheerfully.

"Just wonderful," I answered, anxious to tell him the good news, "last night I . . "

But he didn't seem interested and broke in.

"Do you know people in Ottawa?" he asked.

"Yes, I do," I answered, "I know quite a few people of importance there."

I had never talked to him about my broad acquaintance among the Members of Parliament, and this seemed to be a good time to tell him. But he gave me no chance.

"Were you ever involved in politics?" he asked.

"In a way, yes."

"Were you the Returning Officer for Muskoka?"

"Yes I was," I answered right away.

"In that case," he said, "you've just been fired."

It hit me like a ton of brick. I thought we were talking about my promotion. I stood there speechless.

"I never saw anything like this before," he said, to cover my confusion, "right from the new Minister's office in Ottawa." He handed me a letter.

"Reference Richard J. Bell, Toronto office. If this is the same Richard James Bell who was Returning Officer for Muskoka, relieve him of his duties."

"Doesn't leave me much choice, does it?"

"No," I agreed, "not much choice."

"I might have waited until after Christmas," he explained, "but I thought it better to tell you before you spent all your money."

"It's a little late. I've already spent it."

I knew exactly who to blame. They were vicious; they were vindicative.

"Stainless Statesman!" I muttered sarcastically.

"What?"

"Father of Boats!"

It came out like an oath.

The supervisor looked at me strangely and took a sheaf of papers from his drawer.

"I really shouldn't show you this," he said, "but you seem to know what happened. We were asked to sent a list of all our employees to Ottawa, and it came back with that letter about you. Who knows, I may be next."

I picked up the list and shuffled through it until I found my name. Beside it, in a hand I recognized as Cockburn's three words were written. I handed it back, thanked the supervisor for his courtesy and left his office. I got my few belongings at the main desk and went out. When I got to the street I just stood there. Where to go? No use going shopping; my money was gone. No thrill to look at the house, I would lose it, and the deposit too. A man walking past slowed down and glared

at me angrily, and I realized I was talking. He seemed ready to start an argument, but after a moment went on, assuming I was crazy. I remembered what I had said, for fresh on my lips were those three words I had read opposite my name:
"One of them."

I stepped onto the sidewalk and began the long walk back. Numb, head down, shoulders bent, I dragged my way north along Yonge Street, through the crowds of merry shoppers, into the quiet streets beyond. When I got to Grosvenor Avenue I turned onto it and walked towards house number 93. I stood in front of it for a while, then went to the door and knocked. My brother's wife, Jane, came to the door. She didn't say a word when she saw me, just turned and went back in. Then Anne came.

"What do you want?" she demanded, and when I didn't answer she looked at me, "are you sick?"

"No. I lost my job."

"Lost your job," she exclaimed, "how did you do that?"

"Politics."

"Again? Well how do you propose to keep your family?"

"I don't know."

I raised my eyes to look at her, and saw my brother Decimus hovering in the background. His pasty, supercilious face was more disgusting than ever. The hooked hose, arched over his sneering mouth, his black hair pasted down in a false wave, his eyebrows arched suspiciously, made him look like the villain in a play. But he was real, much too real. I remembered the day in our childhood when he tattled on me, and then watched maliciously while I got whipped. He had the same look on his face now.

"Let him in," he said to Anne, as if I were a dog, "he can sleep on the couch."

I went in, for there was nothing else to do.